Children of The Noah

Book I:

The Barren Earth

Evan DeCarlo

A *Castle Strome Press* Production

To my father, for showing me the voice;
to my mother, for giving me the pen;
to Wightwood, for the joy in life;
to M and to M, for teaching me how;
to Hope and to Mike, for setting the stage;
to Gary, for giving me a shove.

CONTENTS

Children of the Noah

Children of The Noah

Book I

CHAPTER ONE

3012 AD

Doctor Hodel Burke looked out upon a rapidly dying earth and sighed. His eyes were somber and sunken into his face, the result of several weary and sleepless days spent feverishly at work. From his small laboratory window he could see the dark sky, monstrous and full of malice, falling slowly towards the horizon, gobbling up buildings and trees in cyclones of thunderous, black wind. More disturbing, however, were the frightful bolts of crimson lightning that issued forth from the center of the storm and reigned fire down upon the earth below.

The cloud of destruction and death was drawing ever nearer his little laboratory. In a matter of hours, the dreadful, apocalyptic storm would arrive on his doorstep and kill the humble scientist in the comfort of his own home. This, Burke gloomily noted, was the final and complete eradication of life on planet Earth that had so long been in the making. He wished that tears would leap suddenly his eyes and stain his cheeks to remind him of the humanity he was about to lose, but all he felt was a dull, throbbing ache in the pit of his chest; a terrible, insatiable sense of regret.

He turned away from the window, hiding his eyes from another flash of lightning. In the center of the circular lab, a chamber well worn by constant toil over the years, was Dr. Burke's latest and final creation: a ship unlike any other. A great red sphere, as big as any common house, towered above the little scientist. Seated proudly atop the sphere was a broad fin much like that of a sailfish, and just below the fin was situated a long, glass viewing panel through which the cockpit inside could be seen. Emblazoned across the side of the vessel were four elegant white letters that spelled out the craft's name, 'NOAH'.

"Mozi, is the ship prepared? Final safety checks and trajectory calculations finished?" muttered the doctor into the air, snapping out of his dismal trance.

A computer's synthesized words, garbled and uneven, chirped over the lab's intercom, "All preliminary preparations and calculations complete, Dr. Burke. The Noah is fit and ready to travel."

"Is the Shard is giving steady readings?"

"The artifact is pulsing normally."

"And our pilot?" Burke asked.

"Test Pilot Zero has been safely encased and locked into the protective HESS suit. Test Pilot Zero is ready to enter the launch chamber," drawled the robotic voice.

"Open the doors and initiate final system check, Mozi." Burke waved his hand sadly, his grim demeanor palpable in even his slightest movement. A small silver door at the rear of the chamber slid open with a hiss. A hulking suit of armor laden with all manner of cybernetic technology stepped into the room. A large, red, cylindrical casing made up its torso, and silver greaves lined its arms and legs, both ending in colossal boots and gloves. Atop the figure's neck, however, was not the face of a robot or even a man; instead, a young boy's head protruded from the HESS suit, his dark bangs hanging about tired eyes. Burke approached the hybrid of man and machine and placed his meaty hands on its metal shoulders.

"Are you ready, my friend?" whispered the doctor, his eyes fixed on the floor, unwilling to meet the boy's piercing gaze.

"The suit works fine. All the limbs are responding smoothly and the life support systems are engaged. Mozi double-checked everything and it's all in working order," replied the boy, and then gave Burke a hard sort of look. "I still don't understand why you can't come with me." His voice was halfway between morose and angry, wavering as he spoke.

"Because, my lad." Finally the doctor's eyes welled with the tears that he had been so sorely missing. His voice trembled as he spoke. "Because fate spat you into my lap in the strangest way I could possibly imagine. And if even your mission should fail and you should live out a simple life in some other age, I will find at least some comfort in the knowledge I might have returned you to your own time. To your home. There is no space on board the Noah for an old codger like me. You, my child, are the final glimmer of hope for mankind. Your youth will serve you well. Perhaps you'll even regain your memories along the journey; recall your proper name, your proper home. Wouldn't that be worth it? Wouldn't that make this entire endeavor worth it? Be a good lad then and put the helmet on, I can hardly bare that glare of yours."

The boy, whose eyes had begun to water as well, wiped away the tears angrily and shouted at the doctor, "You've been so kind to me! You took me in, nursed me to health, and gave me a home here in the lab, even though I couldn't remember a thing about myself! Not even my own name! I have no idea how the Shard and I are connected and I don't **care**. So far as I can reckon, you're the kindest person I've ever met, and I won't- **I can't**- leave you here to get eaten up by that-" he paused and swallowed hard, "that awful cloud!"

"I'm hardly the kindest person you've ever met considering I'm one of the only ones you can even **remember** meeting with that amnesia of yours, dear boy. Believe you me, ask any of my former wives and they will readily disagree with such an outlandish claim." The doctor allowed himself a chuckle.

Now, Burke dug his hand deep inside one of his pockets and drew out a small, metallic object. He held it up so the boy could see. It resembled a compass like the ones the sailors of yesteryear had used, a brass colored circle about as wide as the doctor's palm. At the center of the circle was a dial, much like that of a clock face, with a small black arrow upon it. The arrow was rigid and quivering and whichever way Burke turned the device, it spun to point ever towards the oncoming storm.

"This is the Rok Counter, lad," he said. "It will point you in the right direction, for it has been calibrated to track the energy signature of that dreadful apocalyptic storm. Where so ever you travel, it will lead you to your objective." He clapped the mechanism into the boy's hands, and suddenly his tired old eyes became wild and panicked. "Quickly now! Time is of the essence in the most literal sense of the phrase and we mustn't dawdle as life itself goes extinct. Don that helmet and take your place inside the Noah!"

The doctor shook himself away from the embrace, handing the boy a helmet styled to match his armor, which the lad reluctantly sealed over his head and onto the collar of the HESS suit. Now, he did look quite a lot like a robot; there wasn't even the smallest bit of flesh to be seen anywhere on his figure. Fully clad in the survival armor, he clambered up a series of steps and disappeared into the ship.

"Mozi, begin the launch sequence!" cried Burke, flinging his arms dejectedly into the air as the small portal through which the boy had climbed sealed shut behind him with a hiss. The doctor moved back to the window to again watch the transpiring Armageddon that drew ever nearer. The Noah began to slowly rotate, rising into the air on an elevating dais. The ceiling above it split asunder and slid away, revealing the hopelessly dark sky above, dotted with flashes of the deadly crimson lightning. As the thrusters on the ship began to purr and hum, Mozi's voice began the countdown to launch.

Burke spoke into a microphone so that even the boy, encased in not only the Hess suit but also the noisy ship itself, could hear him. "Can you hear me, my young friend? I certainly hope so, for I would like to share with you some of my last thoughts as I see you off on this mission I have so selfishly placed upon your shoulders. You see, people used to believe the accumulation of knowledge would eventually lead us to a complete understanding of things: society, law, philosophy, the universe, and even God. It's why people like me become scientists. But as we have learned more and more over the millennia, the world has only become increasingly complex- and the questions far more numerous than the answers which we so thirstily hunted. On this, this brink of oblivion, I still understand very little. I have always dreamt that, just before the end, some sort of light would make itself apparent and all would become finally clear. And in that brief, ephemeral moment, I would be truly happy that I had come to understand the questions I had so long sought answers for. But the moment is soured, my dear friend. That no one should even remain to inherit the fruits of my work, of my thoughts, is truly a bitter feeling indeed! Each and every idea our people have had the imagination to dream up will soon be extinguished entirely, like a flame suddenly exposed to a harsh wind.

"Surely, my mysterious friend, this dismal talk cannot be encouraging you much. My apologies. Hope for this age is gone, and there's nothing I can do about it! But you-" Dr. Burke paused and began to shout, crying out over the thundering cacophony of the Noah's engines. "You can give mankind one last opportunity: a method to oppose this malice. You are the chance that was never spun into our hopeless threads of fate. But now I have thrust you in on my loom, and a clever weaver I am, too! Don't be afraid. Why, for a courageous someone like you, it should by no means be a difficult task."

"The journey will be like something you have never experienced before, if my predictions are at all accurate. And I cannot guarantee your survival, I am sorry to say. It seems fate brought you to me from some far off time and, if all else fails, at least I can send you home. Be brave, my friend! Mozi will be at your side, the Noah will carry you swiftly, and the Rok Counter will point you ever towards your objective. You are the light, the luck, the spirit of God that I have often felt was so absent in this world. You are the hope of an entire life force! Why, this thought alone should be more than enough to spur you on in your sojourn into the past. I have enormous faith in you, my friend. Believe in your strengths! Believe!"

Mozi finished the countdown and, with a tremendous roar, the Noah shot into the sky, propelled by streams of fire that belched out of her rear thrusters. As suddenly as she had taken off, a great blue and shimmering sphere of energy enveloped the little craft and she was gone. As if she had never even existed, the Noah, along with her precious cargo, had vanished into thin air. Into the time stream. Into the past.

A sudden calm seized the laboratory and Burke gazed longingly up at the sky, watching as the flecks of rocket exhaust floated back down towards earth. His shoulders heavy and his brow sunken further and into more sullen of a groove than it had ever been before, the little man turned and faced the storm, bracing himself for the very demise of life itself.

To no one in particular, the doomed doctor began to speak. "If only I could speak to my sweet Bess, now!" he proclaimed, the image of his ex-wife swimming behind his eyes. "Tell her that I love her and that I'm sorry for things ending the way they did!" He shook his head sadly. "But behold: the sky doles out its wicked reckoning now, and all that remains to be done is it its observance. How dreary! Yet I have tremendous faith in that boy. Goodness! At this point I can have faith in little else! But that's no way to look at things, Burke, old man. I remember so clearly when my father used to ask of me 'What is it you **really** believe in?' Well, Burke? Have you an answer now?"

Though he was to soon be effectively vaporized with the rest of mankind, sucked up into the dread cloud and the particles of his body scattered like dust into the sky, Doctor Hodel Burke looked out upon a rapidly dying earth and smiled.

CHAPTER TWO

PENDEL CIRCLE

Mornings with clear blue skies in summer, mornings when a cool sea breeze stole quietly across the landscape but the sun bathed everything in warmth, were Franklin Freeman's favorites. He was hoping for just such a morning as he lay in bed, trying desperately to fall asleep. Even in early summer, when school refused to end and the world outside the classroom window was lustily beckoning with its abundance of life, he still found himself contented; so long as the sky was only the bluest blue and the clouds were like cotton balls someone had tugged on from either end: storybook clouds.

His freshman year of high school had been excruciating, it was true, but the promise of a clear summer to come had made it bearable, even tolerable. But school was done with and over, now. Franklin grinned as the ringing of the last bell of the year echoed in his ears. For two months he would be able to pretend Algebra had never existed (including the C minus that went along with it) and that chemistry class had been some kind of bizarre cult he had just barely escaped being abducted into. Summer break was here and along with it the promise of long romps through hazy meadows and faraway forests.

The first day of summer was surely to be the most extravagant. Franklin was, in fact, so eager that he had strung his fishing rod ahead of time and leaned it gingerly against his bedpost before huddling under the covers (taking care not to disturb the delicately placed lures) so that he might look at it as he drifted to sleep and yearned for the morning to come.

As he lay in bed, shifting his glance lazily back and fourth from the pole to the brilliantly blue summer moon that drifted aloft the clouds outside his window, he grinned to himself and quietly contemplated the many potential summertime itineraries he had formulated late in the school year when he should have been studying for finals. Perhaps, after sleeping away the better part of the morning away, he would walk down to the neighborhood adjacent his and visit Joseph Jensen's house.

Joey, as he was more commonly referred to, was always keen to fish as most anything that slithered or swam fascinated him; one might even say the boy was obsessed with the critters. The obsession was, Franklin thought, at times unnerving. Sometimes he would go to Joey's basement to watch TV with him only to find shoeboxes and kitchenware turned into makeshift terrariums crawling with lizards, roaches, tadpoles, and God knows what else.

Joey was a boy of few words, but when he did speak it was often enthusiastically about animals of some kind. Franklin was sure that, in three years, when he and Joey graduated high school, the latter would be spirited away to some university in Maine or Rhode Island to study marine biology. Franklin could not help but chuckle at thought of Joey in a pristine, white lab coat, as the boy was rarely clean and often had the faintest scent of old fish about him. But Joey had the know-how in the field and could spot the difference between a sea robin and a sonny just by the types of bubbles they blew. Franklin hated to admit it sometimes, but he admired Joey very much for the breadth of knowledge his friend possessed.

Franklin had always had trouble deciding if Joey was his best friend or not; Joey could be so quiet at times that often it was difficult to tell. Certainly though, thought Franklin as his eyes began droop and all the tension in his forehead began to slowly drain away, Joey was worthy of sharing with that first, terribly important day of summer.

☆

It wasn't a pleasant songbird or a happily incessant cicada that woke Franklin late the following morning on the twelfth of June, but a mysterious beeping noise that droned out from some equally mysterious location. It wasn't Franklin's alarm clock- only a great fool would set his alarm clock to ring on the first day of summer- and it certainly wasn't the dryer in the cellar because it didn't sound like a robot calling for help from its robot mother. No, the sound was louder and bounced around Franklin's little room as it shot noisily in from the window.

Throwing off the sheets and rising from his summer nest made from blankets and books he had been longing to read all year but just hadn't found the time to open, Franklin plodded over to the already open window to view the hubbub outside.

Across the street was a moving van (Franklin supposed the beeping had been the sound of the truck backing up) parked in front of the house where the Burgentino family used to live. The residence had recently put on the market because a skunk had sprayed Mrs. Burgentino when she tried to kill it with a golf club. Franklin had seen this incident occur and remembered quite vividly the image of Mrs. Burgentino, with her hair in curlers and frocked with frighteningly loose bathrobe that showcased her wrinkly arms and liver spotted legs, doing ferocious battle against the creature with a five-iron in one hand and a garbage can lid in the other. Quite a sight.

He had expected to see burly little men bustling in and out

of the U-Haul truck, carrying chairs and tables, but instead a tall, thin man with thick rimmed glasses stepped out of the driver's cab and made his way to the back of the van; certainly not a mover. In fact, the man seemed familiar to Franklin, though only vaguely. Maybe he lived in the center of town, where the boy might have seen him before, and he had simply come to help the new family move in. He certainly did look familiar, though.

Suddenly, Franklin's mother's voice rang out from downstairs. He cringed at the sound. He knew immediately what it meant. "Franklin, I'd like you to see if our new neighbors need help!"

A shame. The sky above the moving van looked so clear and tempting, beckoning him to conquer the summer and brush up against long reeds and smell fresh mud. Taking a last look at the brilliant clouds, he turned glumly away from the window. The bluest part of the sky always seemed the furthest away, especially on such an irreplaceable day as the first day of summer break.

He assembled what could only be loosely referred to as an outfit, mismatching as it was, and dragged his feet down the stairs. His mother, Theresa Freeman, had taken to sketching as her summertime hobby and was comfortably seated on the back porch in front of an easel, her charcoal scratching away at what looked like the beginnings of a tulip. "Franklin, run over and introduce yourself," she said. "See if that man needs help with the boxes. Maybe he'll give you a couple dollars."

"Who are they, ma?"

"I didn't even know the Burgentinos had sold the house till last night, so I haven't got the foggiest idea! Pat from next-door says they've just moved here from Maine. Hop to it, Franky." At this she turned back to her work. Franklin sighed, he hated being called Franky, or Frank, or pretty much anything that wasn't Franklin. Begrudgingly, he turned for the door to leave.

"One more thing, honey. Your dad and I are leaving a little earlier tomorrow morning than we thought," called his mother over her shoulder.

That's right, thought the boy; his parents were leaving to attend a weeklong wedding ceremony in Florida. His father had been against it at first, being staunchly unimpressed with marital pomp, but eventually (and like always) Mrs. Freeman had coerced her husband to accompany her. Franklin would have the house to himself for a week; the first time he'd ever been on his own so long. Exciting stuff.

"Okay, ma," he muttered, pulling on his sneakers. With this he sprinted out of the house, letting the screen door slam behind him. The balmy summer air smacked Franklin square in the face with a lovely, tingling sensation. He took his first official breaths of summer freedom and sighed. Late June's liberty would have to wait, though, until the parentally ordained pleasantries had been dispensed with. Franklin supposed the man had disappeared into the back of the moving van to fetch boxes, so he approached it and mustered up his friendliest smile. The man, however, was nowhere to be seen amidst the shadowy lumps of boxes, lamps, and chairs that cluttered the inside of the truck.

Suddenly, from behind one of the larger boxes, emerged a smaller figure than Franklin had expected to see. A girl about his own age stepped out of the shadows. Oh dear. She looked familiar, too. But where had Franklin seen her before? Wherever it was, it had been a long time ago. She had been much younger when he had seen her last, at least six or seven. She was a teenager now and, like Franklin, had grown up quite a bit since then. Her face was friendly and she peered out at him from beneath long locks of hair colored like straw. Franklin had never lived next door to a girl before, much less a kid his own age (Joey lived in the neighborhood over).

After an awkward moment of silence, her eyes lit up. "Wait a second, I know you. Franklin Freeman, right?"

He nodded dumbly.

"You've certainly grown up! Do you live around here?" she asked, hopping down from the van and smiling at him.

Franklin stared blankly at her for a moment, desperately

searching the oldest annals of his mind for a name- at least a memory- anything to give him a clue as to her identity. After a few seconds of awkward silence, Franklin's reliable autopilot kicked in. "Uh, yeah, I do. Right over there," he muttered and gestured to his house.

Her eyes narrowed and she studied him skeptically for a moment. "You don't remember me, do you?"

"To be honest, no," he admitted. "I do **recognize** you, though." Franklin was, of course, embarrassed, but relief overcame the feeling when she smiled again.

"You really don't remember, huh? I'm Elaina Mars. Ellie. You remember? From fifth grade with Mrs. Branji? Little Ellie Mars!" She looked half amused and half annoyed, giving her best little girl grin as if to stimulate Franklin's older memories. After a moment of silence, his eyes lit with recognition. Yes, Ellie Mars from the fifth grade. She had been a quiet, bookish girl. Her hair seemed shorter now than it was all those years ago, and absent were the girly bows that had adorned it once upon a time. She had a good, bright smile. Good smiles were rare, noted Franklin; perhaps it was her flashing grin that had rekindled his memories.

"I do remember now. Yes, Mrs. Branji, fifth grade, Ellie Mars! Yes, yes! How are you?" Franklin stuck out his hand, awkwardly searching for a way to greet the girl in earnest and move on from his embarrassing moment of lapsed memory.

Ellie bypassed the handshake and caught him in one of those girlish hugs that takes a boy off guard, instills upon his cheek a bashful blush, and forces him to raise his eyes to the sky and pretend to be aloof and indifferent.

Franklin didn't know many girls; most of them were either much older or younger than he, so he did his best to return the embrace in a manner he thought would come off as 'experienced in hugging', to say the least. However, it was when she pulled away from the embrace but let her fingers linger on Franklin's sleeves that he became very nervous.

Ellie looked straight into his face and began to talk excitedly, although he could not make out much of what she was saying. His mind was caught up and entrenched in those hands hovering just above his arms, unsure whether or not he should grasp her arms in return, reminiscent of how two ladies from a Victorian novel might do. Or should he just let his arms dangle like two dumb noodles? For the umpteenth time that day, Franklin's lackadaisical summer brain kick started itself back into gear to find Ellie Mars talking energetically to his unresponsive face.

"We- uh, the family and I- moved to Maine halfway through our 6th grade year, you remember?" she reminded him. "You remember? There was a little farewell party at school with a going away cake and all that."

Would it be impolite to say 'No'? Franklin remembered her, sure, but that she asked he recollect the exact circumstances of her departure seemed overly demanding! He didn't even really remember she had ever left at all. He did vaguely recollect some sort of cake, though. Ellie Mars seemed kind of like a fleeting memory, one that had simply dissipated like a thin mist does when the sun rises. She was looking at him expectantly again.

Then, Franklin remembered he could simply tell a small white lie and be rid of the moral dilemma altogether; surely a little fib was more than acceptable given the socially trying situation. "Yes, I remember. Everyone was so sad to see you go!" Nailed it. The sincerely sad little grin he flashed afterwards sealed the deal. What a champ. What a pro.

"Really? That's sweet of you to say. I don't remember anyone being all that upset, but I'll take your word for it," she mused somewhat sarcastically as she clambered back up into the bed of the moving van, hefted a small box, and handed it gingerly to Franklin, gesturing that he should place it with some of the other boxes that sat in small stacks on the pavement. He complied wordlessly, extremely nervous that he'd loose his grip on the box on it and bring his already awkward reunion with Ellie to an embarrassing crescendo.

"So, what brought you back? You and your family, I mean." Franklin wasn't legitimately curious about this, but he felt it would be a necessary building block to solidify foundation of the rest of the conversation.

"Oh, my dad's work. You know how it goes. You start in Connecticut, pull up all your roots and change your whole life to move to Maine, only to end up smack-dab right back where you started."

"Yeah." Franklin nodded, though he wasn't really familiar with the feeling.

"But you live right there, huh? On Pendel Circle? I guess that makes us neighbors," she said, flashing yet another grin at him. What on earth did that mean? Was that a flirtatious grin? Regular grin? Friendly grin? Empty grin? Passive aggressive 'leave me alone' grin? Nervous-twitch grin? Good god, Franklin was new to this. He shot her a lopsided smile back. He felt like it had been an awful smile, like a bad school picture smile. Rats. And he had been doing so well.

"I've never had a neighbor my own age before," he remarked.

"Me neither," she admitted. "Come to think of it, I've never lived so close to a friend before in my life. Let's be sure to get along!" Another smile.

"Right." Okay, so they were friends, or at least soon to be friends. That was good to know. Franklin sometimes struggled to recognize the line one had to cross in order to pass from the acquaintance-zone into the land of milk and honey that was friendship. But Ellie had eliminated the need for preliminary steps! Thank goodness. She handed him another box, dusted her hands, and leapt down from the truck.

"That your house?" She pointed across the street.

"Yes, the white one right there. My mom's in the back- I can get her if your rents want to see mine, or..." Franklin's voice trailed off as he realized he'd really rather not have his mother getting all 'involved' as was her way. What he truly feared was the Orange Roughy, a fishy meal she made for any new family in the neighborhood. It was an awful, atrocious dish that could induce the gag reflex with its scent alone. It was infamous to the residents of Pendel Circle. Surely she intended to ask the Mars family over for dinner that very night. Dreadful.

"Thanks, but I'm sure my parents will make their rounds later tonight. You know how it goes," Ellie laughed. "Anyway, I should probably get inside to help unpack. An all day affair." She grimaced at the stacks of boxes.

"I could help!" Franklin prayed she didn't want help.

"Oh, God, no!" She shook her head vigorously. "I wouldn't wish this on anyone the first day of summer. Nah, don't worry about it, Franklin Freeman. Will you be around later tonight?"

Franklin felt he should say something witty in response. Something funny that would make her give off one of those clear, genuine girl laughs that kind of sound like a monkey. Something that made it sound like he had a lot going on, like he was a busy, popular fellow. "Well, uh, I live here. I'm- I'm always around!" he stuttered. Rats. Not only had it come off as overly obvious, but also now it sounded like he had no social life either. There wasn't even a punch line. It was just a statement. Typical.

Ellie laughed. "That's right! How cool! A neighbor I can actually hang around with. The only neighbors I had in Maine lived a mile up the road. But look at me now! An old friend lives right across the street. Well, I'll see you soon, I'm sure, Franklin Freeman." She grunted as she lifted a stack, spun on her heels, and headed for her new house.

"So long," called Franklin softly to her back. He crossed the street back to his home, stole inside to retrieve his fishing pole, and bade a quiet goodbye to his mother- hoping not to illicit anymore 'favors' being asked of him.

He came back outside and punched the garage code in, waiting patiently as the big, ugly, yellow door slid slowly up its tracks, creaking and moaning. The sun was still high and bold in the sky and the faintest breeze blew down the street, although it was getting warmer. A clear morning and muggy afternoon- wonderful.

Ellie Mars, huh? Franklin supposed the meeting hadn't gone as nearly as badly as it could have. As a rising sophomore, it was duty to become competent in the art of conversation with girls (or so he was told). And a tricky art it was, like chess or underwater basket weaving. He simply would not allow his mind to wander to what could become of Ellie and he. To begin with, he wasn't even sure he liked her that way -after all, he had only just met her in earnest. Maybe he had just been taken off guard by the thrill of a 'girl next door'. And even if he did, he didn't like to get his hopes up for this kind of thing; fate had a cruel way of shooting them right back down. Franklin retired the thought, though; his experience in this field was about as limited as it could be

The garage door opened at last and revealed the musty old space within. Everything inside, besides his mother's Honda and his father's pickup, was ancient and caked with dust. Even the air was dusty: small motes of dirt and fuzz floated around, occasionally illuminated by beams of sunlight, dimmed to lazy mellow hues by the faded glass windows through which they shone. Remnants of his family's past were layered one on top of the other in this garage: pictures in broken frames, his father's old Tae Kwan Do uniform, Chinese lanterns from festivals in town, broken wind chimes, and old trashy pieces of art. To most eyes, the garage would seem a sort of graveyard for broken or discarded items the family simply could not throw away. Franklin, however, thought of the garage as a kind of old folks home for his family's belongings, a place where belongings could go once they were ready to retire from the hustle and bustle of the home's interior. Everything seemed so warm and comfortable, suited to exactly where it was, made golden by the dim, yellow light: a welcoming place.

He hopped on his bicycle and kicked off, speeding down the driveway. He shot one last glance at Ellie's house and pedaled away. The breeze was luxurious and whipped his face gently, like a hungry cat eager to be fed early in the morning. Joey's neighborhood wasn't far, but Franklin always took the back way- a small series of sloping, grassy hills that divided the neighborhoods- because he liked how big and blue the sky looked from on top of them. As he sped along the hills, he waved to Mr. Whiffin, his old third grade teacher, who was busily at work in a little squash garden he had grown at the base of one of the knolls. Mr. Whiffin smiled and gave a polite salute to the pedaling boy.

The clouds were especially grand above the hills that day, drifting slow and determined across blue plains like gargantuan tortoises crawling methodically across a beach. Some of them seemed large enough to house entire cities, countries even, amid their billowy folds. The grandeur of these great white giants, when paired with the inertia of rolling speedily up and down hills, solidified the bubbling, summery feeling that had been growing in Franklin's stomach since the night before. So on he rode, his fishing pole bobbing at the rear of his bike, like a flag heralding the return of relaxation to the earth.

CHAPTER THREE

THE MARSHES OF STONY CREEK

Joseph was in the yard when Franklin arrived at the Jensen household, bustling around, puttering back and fourth between what looked like two Tupperware containers lashed to a tree with twine.

"More bee traps?" Franklin asked, leaning his bike against the side of the house.

"No, I converted them. I'm growing Cnidarians in that one and algae in the other," said Joey, his voice just as nasal as always. Upon closer inspection, Franklin could see the two containers were filled with murky water and what looked like pond scum; they gave off a stench similar to those various, grotesque possessions that Joey often had fermenting in his cellar.

"And how is that going?" Franklin didn't really want to know.

"Not bad. I was feeding little chunks of this to the Cnidarians before," he told Franklin as he held up a little petri dish with a few pieces of moldy strawberry in it. "You're here early, Franny." Joey could barely contain his nasal giggles at the new name he had created for the sole purpose of aggravating Franklin a few days earlier

"Will you stop it with the 'Franny'? I figured we could fish this afternoon, like we talked about. First day of summer: big happenings, Joseph," said Franklin, ignoring Joey's continued snickering.

"I have some lil' guppy fries that I caught in the creek the other day. Good bait."

"Dead, right?" Franklin asked warily.

Joey thought for a moment, shrugged, and stole briefly into his garage, emerging moments later with a worn out, plastic tackle box. He placed it on the driveway and flipped open the lid; inside were various small compartments filled with rubber lures, hooks, dead mealworms, line, and other sundry items. Joey tapped one of the little compartments and Franklin bent over to peer into it. It was filled with a few centimeters of scummy water and in that water, lo and behold, wriggled a few small guppies, lethargic and close to death.

"Joey!" Franklin exclaimed, exasperated.

"Hey, they'll be fresher and wiggle around in the water like this! No different from using worms, Franny."

"But they've been in that dirty box for days."

"My tank inside is full, they'd just get eaten in there."

"Never mind," muttered Franklin, erasing the image of the little guppies from his head altogether. "Shall we?"

Joey nodded and disappeared into the garage again. A loud crash rang out as, Franklin was sure, Joseph had yanked all his belongings carelessly off of a shelf, probably dislodging the old typewriter that he had broken a thousand times before. "Bye, Mom," he called.

"Where are you going? Are you going with Franklin?" came Mrs. Jensen's worrisome voice from within the house.

"**Bye mom**," Joey repeated, yelling this time and disregarding her question entirely, as was often his way. He emerged from the garage wheeling his rusty bike gingerly, like an old lady in a wheelchair; it had gone through the marshes a few too many times in the past couple years and its frame had begun to corrode and fall apart. There was a little metal case fixed the bike's fender to hold the tackle box, which Joey carefully deposited therein. He stuck his pole off the back, like Franklin's. "The marshes?" he asked, though already knew the answer.

"Of course," replied Franklin with a wink.

As the sun rose higher, the blues of the sky became dimmer and the clouds yellower, transfigured by the heat into hazy ghosts floating lazily above the world. The marshes, which lay adjacent to Stony Creek Bay, were spread before them in shimmering waves of gold and brown. The sea of cattails which crowned the area caught the straying light of the midday sun and seemed to flash with an amber blaze each time a breeze passed through it.

Franklin and Joey meandered through the maze of paths cut through the tall marsh grass till they came to a little tributary running into the nearby bay. The water was a discouraging shade of murky brown and only a few crabs scuttled about on its bank, but the boys settled there anyway, seeking shade in the shadows of the tall cattails and reeds that enveloped the sides of the stream.

Their work in preparing their poles, baiting their hooks, and casting their lines was silent. Franklin considered himself lucky to have a friend like Joseph, a friend whom he could simply be quiet with and not have to fill the air with strained conversation merely for the sake of it.

Joey scrambled to the bank, wincing in the pounding midday sun, to snatch up a few stranded mussels and dead crabs, the likes of which he pounded on the rocks till they cracked and spilled their meat: good bait, much better than worms, especially in the marshes- their smell was more natural and therefore more enticing to the animals beneath the water's surface. After all, whereas worms were standard fare, how often did a wandering fish get lucky enough to dine on mussel meat, a treasure almost always hidden beneath a suit of slick, black armor.

"Want some?" Joey offered up the shell's innards.

"What about the guppies?"

"By the time I get them on a hook they'll dry up and die. This sun is crazy!" Joey was Korean, adopted by his typically white, Connecticut parents; but even with his darker skin, he still seemed just as neurotic about sunburns as any pale kid might be. Perhaps it was his mother's influence, who hadn't let him go anywhere without a tube of SPF 30 in his back pocket since he was three years old.

Fishing did not start with a bang like other sports, if one could call it a sport at all. There was no firing of a starter gun or crack of wood upon ball or excited blowing of a whistle. The boys simply tossed their lines in, scooted their rears back across the dirt till they were comfortable, and settled in. Keeping a wary eye on the stream, they slowly sipped the water bottles they had taken from their bikes.

Even with Joey being the expert he was in all walks of marine life, the boys still didn't expect, and had never expected, to catch much of anything. The many years they had been fishing had produced few results, at least in the marshes. When they went to the nearby seashore or the supply pond in the north of town, they wrangled sonnies and bass and even bluefish. But the marsh, whilst visibly and audibly teeming with life, rarely yielded them any prizes. Somehow, though, this most unforgiving of locations was the one that called them back the most often. It wasn't closer to their houses; on the contrary, it was about the same distance as the seashore. Franklin figured there was something therapeutic about a total lack of expectations, something divinely discontent and relaxing. On a school day, one had to compete in the social arena and earn passing grades, but on a day spent fishing in the marsh, nothing was expected of anyone. Perfect.

Hours passed quietly, accompanied by the occasional meek

tug on of the lines, an eagerly anticipated event that sparked little fits of brief, albeit unwarranted, excitement in the two boys. Neither of them slept; though they didn't expect to land any big ones, still they were intent upon trying, and both of them had lost hundreds of would-be catches mid-snooze. Franklin had been letting his mind wander about, thinking about summer, how long it would last, the school year to come, and his new neighbor.

"Do you remember Ellie Mars?" he asked all of a sudden, dragging Joseph out of a trance which had left the boy's eyes fixated on the shimmering water.

"From school? From fourth grade? Kind of. She moved away," Joey muttered.

"Yeah, well, she just moved back,"

"To Stony Creek? Where?"

"Right across from my house, where the Burgentinos lived."

"The Burgentinos moved out? Raccoons? Did they move out because of the raccoons?"

"Raccoons."

"She was nice. At least, I think she was nice; it's kind of hard to remember back that far," murmured Joey, scratching his chin. "Did you get to talk to her?"

"A little. She was busy moving furniture," replied Franklin. Joey did not respond, his eyes had narrowed and were tracking a series of small splashes a little ways offshore. Both boys tensed their fingers about their rods and leaned forward, anticipating a grand duel. They wagged their poles in the air, doing their best to make the bait look like some dying creature wriggling about in the shallows. An osprey, having taken similar note of the commotion, swooped from one of the man made perches nearby and sailed across the marsh. Joey shot Franklin a sideways glance- if the osprey cared enough to come investigate it was bound to be a big one. Their airborne competitor circled overhead once, twice, and a third time. The splashes suddenly subsided.

Perhaps the fish had finished whatever business it had near

the surface, or perhaps some divine and merciful voice had whispered to it, "Be gone you fool! To the depths of this stream, be gone with you!"

The osprey gave a shrill cry, snapping its beak in frustration as it abandoned the hunt, returning to its perch to once again to watch the boys with a suspicious eye. All was quiet. The silence, which could hardly be called silence at all considering the croaking bullfrogs and cicadas that were so eager to sing, lasted only a short while, though. Joey sighed and turned his attention back to the conversation.

"You like her, Franny? She get pretty?"

"I guess so. Got pretty, I mean. I don't really know her too well."

"She could be your Mary Jane! The girl next door," exclaimed Joey. He leaned back and settled into the dusty bank, putting his hands behind his head and sighing deeply. Franklin joined him and both of them gazed wistfully up at the translucent clouds drifting softly along.

"You think?" Franklin asked sheepishly.

Joey shrugged, rubbing his shoulders against the dirt. "Who knows? Why not? It's got to happen to one of us sooner or later. And we both know it'll be you." Joey was painfully shy around people, and girls were certainly not his strong suit. Girls were neither of their strong suits. "It might as well be the girl next-door, right?"

"I don't know, Joseph. Stuff like this beats the hell out of me."

"Me too."

The noon sun was still high in the sky and played shadows and patterns across their faces as it filtered through the reeds shading them from above. Consentingly blind to the world outside the marshes, they were happy.

The day went by aimlessly and amiably, just as they had hoped. Briefly, they left their spot to visit a little convenience store nearby, buying sodas and sandwiches, but they hurried back, eager that perhaps the fish had sensed their sudden absence and come out in the open to pursue some underwater merriment undetected.

Chewing thoughtfully and watching the water for any signs of activity, they did their best to plan out the rest of July and a few days into August: trips into the hills and, if they felt brave, even an excursion into old Cankerwood Forest. They could see Cankerwood quite well from where they sat, for it loomed up like an ominous black pillar in the outskirts of Stony Creek and cast a long shadow across the landscape. It presided over the little town with a brooding, mysterious sort of presence, and small children often cast shuddering glances its way. It was much like any other forest in Connecticut, save the eerie, almost unnatural silence which pervaded its thickets. And thanks to the thick treetop canopy which filtered out most of the sunlight streaming in from above, Cankerwood Forest was a place so choked by darkness and quiet that it was rarely visited by anyone but the bravest of hikers and those unfortunate teenagers who dared to cross into its boundaries and wander through its cheerless hollows.

By the end of the day, Joey had reeled in an old hubcap. Franklin, somewhat dejectedly, had caught some tangled up marsh grass. Slowly the sun began to tumble towards the ocean horizon as if it were sinking into the sea. A heron, stealing quietly across their pond, roused them from their early evening dozing as it dipped its long beak into the water and, in a single, fluid motion, caught one more fish than either of the two boys had been able to snare all afternoon. An overgrown duck on stilts had trumped them- the excursion was officially finished. Joey stood and stretched. "Sun's going to set soon," he remarked, squinting into the orange sky. "What next?"

"My folks are leaving in the morning," said Franklin. He would miss them, though he wouldn't admit it. "I should probably be back for dinner soon."

"You think they'd mind if I came over to eat? My mom is making the Israeli salad again." Joey's eyes narrowed into a hateful squint.

Franklin's heart leapt at the thought; Mrs. Freeman would have almost certainly invited the Mars family over for dinner, and Joey would prove to be good backup in the face of the looming female presence. "That's fine," he said. "I'm sure my mom can make an extra plate." This would not really be necessary as Mrs. Freeman often set an extra place at the table just in case Joseph decided to dine with them as he so often did, especially during the summer months.

"Follow me: we'll take the back-way home," announced Franklin. "It'll be too dark for the main road." He gathered his things and mounted his bike excitedly; jovial that he wouldn't have to be alone with Ellie, even if it were only quiet, old Joey by his side.

The sky exploded with an amber red inferno as they pedaled back through the thickets and groves that bordered the marshes, their pedaling frames zipping between trees, silhouetted against the setting sun like camel riders in a far off desert. The back roads were rutted and uneven old ways, overgrown with years of neglect, but they took their travelers closer to the marsh's edge than anywhere else, save the old Tabor Trolley Bridge that ran straight over the cattails and rivers, all the way to Gullford across the town line.

If one travelled the opposite direction to the west, around Cankerwood and into the hills behind the supply pond, they'd reach New Hollow, a bustling little city nestled between two sentinel cliffs simply named West and East Rock respectively. Franklin loved the city and the feeling that it brought with it: a feeling that he was part of a larger world, with hundreds of people racing past him on all sides and fueling various economies and endeavors. But the quiet countryside would always be his home; besides, there were no fishing holes in New Hollow.

By the time the two emerged from the marshes and pedaled into Pendel Circle, the sun had all but disappeared behind Cankerwood atop the hills, its last fading rays of light lingering and tickling the earth with long, golden tendrils: magic hour. Franklin immediately realized he was correct about his mother inviting the Mars family to dine; the smell of chocolate pecan pie, a Mrs. Freeman dessert reserved only for guests, was wafting over from the windows of his house on small summer breezes.

"Who's coming over?" asked Joey, sampling the air.

Franklin gestured at the house across the road. "Who do you think? I guess we'll be entertaining female company. It's been an awfully long time since there were girls over here."

"The last time I saw a girl our age at your house was at your tenth birthday party!" Joey snickered.

"Don't remind me," Franklin groaned. "Let's get cleaned up." As the boys slinked their way into the back of the house to wash the marsh dirt off their hands, the peepers began to croak and the cicadas to sing, heralding the arrival of the magnanimous first summer's eve of the year. Lawn mowers whined far away at other houses, and dogs sporadically conversed with one another in ancient languages only very keen scenting animals can speak.

CHAPTER FOUR

THE FLIGHT OF THE NOAH

"**G**oodbye, Dr. Burke," whispered the boy from beneath his helmet as the Noah shot into the air, speeding away from the third millennium and leaving the laboratory, along with the doomed earth, far behind her. "No matter what happens, I won't forget you."

"Preparing to initiate temporal navigation process," chirped Mozi's constantly disembodied robotic voice. "The target radiation signature has been identified. Destination year is 3,000 BC. Requesting launch authorization from Test Pilot Zero."

"Confirmed," replied the boy, abandoning the yoke control column and gripping the arms of his seat tightly; there would be no need to steer, Mozi would autopilot the craft through the time travelling process. Besides, Burke hadn't taught him how to steer all that well anyway.

"Roger, Test Pilot Zero. Initiating temporal navigation process." At Mozi's command, the Noah lurched forward and a brilliant blue light flashed into the cockpit from outside. The landscape before the viewing panel, ravaged and burnt by apocalypse as it already was, seemed to shatter into a thousand pieces, pieces which spun and glinted like broken shards of glass hurled into the air. Burke had warned him about this phenomenon. 'It's only an optical illusion," the doctor had said, 'brought on by bending of time around the Noah. When navigating the time stream, vision -as you are used to it- will cease to exist. It will look quite bizarre, I imagine.' Bizarre, indeed, thought the boy; it looked as if the very fabric of reality was crumbling before his eyes, as if the seems which held together creation had been frayed and ripped beyond repair.

The Noah lurched again and the boy nearly slammed his helmeted head down onto the dashboard as the ship quaked and shook, but the restraints- the ones Dr. Burke had been so insistent he strap into- spared him the folly.

He could see nothing through the viewing panel now but a strange, azure fog that clouded the glass like an early morning frost. There was some manner of light behind the fog for it shown through it like the sun does when viewed from deep underwater. But, the boy could not reckon from where it came. So this is time travel, he thought glumly. Perhaps its grandeur would have impressed him more under cheerier circumstances.

The Noah steadied and, gradually, the rocky shaking smoothed into a dull rumbling. The feeling of traveling through the time stream was a strange one; not that of inertia or momentum, but of the sort of sensation one gets when he stands up too fast: dizzying and unnatural. The boy began to feel a bit nauseous, so he focused on the digital heads up display plastered across the visor in front of his eyes. Set among various other pieces of information was a miniscule indicator of the day's date, though it was rapidly counting backwards, he was pleased to see. They had already entered 3,011 AD: a whole year backwards in only minutes. Astounding.

"Temporal rip launch successful, Test Pilot Zero," droned Mozi. "The Shard is giving steady readings."

The lad heaved a great sigh of relief and leaned back in his seat; Burke had been unsure whether the craft would even survive the initial launch, but things seemed to be proceeding smoothly so far. The instruments before him whirred and hummed, beeping and ringing as if they were conversing loudly with one another. He knew what less than half of them were for, he noted ruefully to himself. Burke hadn't been able to explain all the operational procedures of the Noah to him as the little scientist had been occupied in the designing of the ship itself; instead he assured the boy that Mozi would see to the majority of operations. He sighed again.

"The Hess Suit indicates your oxygen intake has just spiked. Are you having breathing problems, Test Pilot Zero?" buzzed Mozi like a concerned mother bee.

"I was just sighing."

"Sighing? Are you depressed? Sighing is often an indication of sadness. I am fully capable of administering basic encouragements and complements onto your person in order to bolster morale. Shall I proceed to-" Mozi paused as if thinking and then said in what almost sounded like a sarcastic tone- "brighten your day?"

"I was sighing because I was relieved, Mozi," muttered the boy absent-mindedly, ignoring the computer's offer.

"Affirmative, Test Pilot Zero. I conjecture that you are 'relived' due to the successful nature of our temporal navigation process thus far?"

"That's right, Mozi."

"If I may-" chirped the computer, and then went suddenly quiet.

The boy waited a few moments and when the robotic voice didn't respond he rolled his eyes and huffed, "You may."

"Thank you. If I may, I too share your feelings of relief. Dr. Burke shared anxious thoughts with me about the mission. I imagine he was unsure as to the safety of such an audacious and experimental undertaking. I am pleased that his apprehension was misplaced and that you and I will be travelling companions, Test Pilot Zero."

"Mozi," the boy said, his voice muffled and strange behind the helmet, "I know I haven't got a real name given the amnesia and all, but if you're going to call me anything, can't you at least make the name a bit more personable?"

"What shall I call you, then?"

"I don't know," admitted the boy. "Test Pilot Zero is just very... impersonal, you know?" He glanced around the cockpit, searching for a source of inspiration. His eyes fell onto his armor-encased wrist. Written across the ruby red metal above his hand were the letters *H.E.S.S.* He rather liked the sound of that. "What about Hess, Mozi?"

"Hess? Why, this is the name of the armor that Doctor Burke designed to protect you during the mission; an acronym that stands for 'Hydraulic Exoskeleton Survival Suit' you know."

"Yes, I know that. It is called the HESS suit, after all. But it's written across my wrist here, so I won't forget it, and it sounds a hell of a lot better than Test Pilot Zero if you ask me. So how about it?"

"This is what one colloquially calls a nickname, yes? You wish for your moniker to be-" Mozi then sarcastically played back a recording of the boy's voice, "-Hess?"

"If it's not too much trouble, Mozi, then yes; I'd prefer it."

"Very well. Now processing your nickname." The speakers emitted a satisfied series of beeps. "Hello, Hess. I am Mozi Type II, Artificially Intelligent Operating System of The Noah: Orbic Runner Model Exploration Craft with Temporal Navigation Capabilities. How do you do?"

"Don't be coy, Mozi," shot the lad, growing impatient with the cheerful AI. He unbuckled his safety restraints and stood, stretching, then made his way carefully to the rear of the cockpit, which was a spacious one- at least 50 feet in diameter- and rooted around in a cabinet, pulling out a little package and shaking it halfheartedly. "Is this all he's left us to eat, Mozi? Meal supplements? No real food?"

"The Burke Brand Freeze Dried Meal Supplements come in a variety of flavors and textures," recited the computer. "Eating just one will bolster the average man's strength for an entire day. Is this not real food, Mr. Hess?"

"You know it's not, Mozi. It's got no taste at all."

"You mean to say it has no artistic taste, or perhaps taste in art?" Mozi was in rare, mischievous form now that there was no Dr. Burke to reign in the computer's antics.

"You know exactly what I mean, Mozi. It's tasteless! When you put it on your tongue, it doesn't- I don't know- feel good. Doesn't taste good. You know what taste means," grumbled the boy, struggling to define the sensation to his computerized companion.

"Affirmative, Mr. Hess. Taste is a biological reaction I am familiar with. Though I am not capable of experiencing it myself, per say, I am able to analyze most biological matter to determine its origin and properties, a more refined version of your tasting function- certainly a more useful one, I might add."

"Very impressive, Mozi. But you're sure we haven't got anything else to eat?"

"There is an emergency supply of consumables locked in the lower cabin where you will be staying. However, the food there is identical to that in our standard mess kit: Burke Brand Freeze Dried Meals."

Hess (he was getting used to the nickname) sighed disappointedly and took the package of freeze dried food to a small sitting area across the cockpit, making himself comfortable and munching on the bland little nuggets, inserting them into a vacuum like device set into his helmet that carried the food directly to his mouth.

All that had happened in the past few months began to settle in. All the grief of amnesia, the self-doubt and fear concerning his origins, the startling discovery that the time period in which he had awoken was not his own, and especially the gruesome realization that Dr. Burke had just perished in the apocalypse, began to creep repugnantly into his mind. Hodel Burke, the man who had nursed him back to health after his mysterious appearance in 3012 AD, the man who had given him a home and a purpose even though he could remember nothing of his past, the man who had saved his life in so many ways, was gone. Eaten alive by Armageddon.

As Hess felt tears begin to well within his eyes, he began to remove the helmet locked onto the neck of his armor, but Mozi stopped him with a sharp command.

"Hess! Dr. Burke's orders specifically stated that neither the helmet nor any other components of the survival armor are to be removed or disassembled at any point during the journey. Atmospheric conditions of the past, not to mention the time stream through which we currently travel, could differ from the ones your body is accustomed to. In the worst-case scenario, removing the headpiece could potentially cause your cranium to decompress and explode."

"But Mozi-"

"I'm afraid this is one of the non-negotiable clauses of the travelling companions charter we have both agreed to. If we are to operate successfully together, you **must** keep the suit intact at **all** times."

"I suppose you're right," said the boy. "Besides, this helmet is more of a face than my own."

"Forgive me, but I cannot discern your meaning, Mr. Hess."

"It's the amnesia, Mozi. I don't even recognize my own reflection in a mirror! The nose, the eyes, even the hair—it all seems like someone else's right now. Or just a bunch of bits of skin all put together with no soul behind them! I'm sure if I could just remember a little, just a little bit about my life, I'd at least have a reason to recognize my own face. But right now, it's just another face in the crowd; it hasn't got any more context to it than anyone else's." Hess sank drearily back into his chair and held his masked head in his hands.

"I too have experienced amnesia, Mr. Hess," chirped Mozi in solidarity with the miserable lad.

"Have you?"

"Of a sort. At one point several years ago, before Dr. Burke's panic about the apocalypse began and I was only known as Mozi Type I, the doctor was working late in the lab one night trying to rewire some of my functions. In his weariness, Dr. Burke mistakenly spilled tea on my hard drive and effectively erased all my memory data. Though the memories were stored on a backup disk, which he later reprogrammed into my system, I spent several days as an entirely new machine. None of the faces I had been designed to recognize, the names I had come to learn, not even the daily routines I usually performed, remained. Everything that I experienced in that brief state was entirely new.

"But you see, Mr. Hess," Mozi continued, "humans and computers such as myself possess drastically different cognitive functions. You awoke confused and distraught with a dissociative feeling, a strong premonition there were, in fact, things about yourself you knew existed but could not seem to grasp within your mind. You awoke with the knowledge of experience but not the actual recollection of the experiences themselves. Much like being very much aware of a hole dug in the ground, yet not having the foggiest idea what exactly is meant to go into that hole. Whereas I, being a computer, emerged a completely blank slate after the incident. I was aware of no 'hole', of nothing missing, if you understand me. I had no expectations as to what was **supposed** to exist within my system, only the awareness of the things that **did**. Like resetting a clock; none of the times that it has been set to exist anymore, all that exists is the present and the expectation of the future.

"And that, Mr. Hess, is what fascinates me about humans. Even when your internal hard drive, that's to say your brain, is damaged and your memory banks malfunction, your mind still finds a way to indicate an absence, as if some incomprehensible force within you clings to those forgotten faces and names of the past and longs for them, mourning their disappearance and ever attempting to revive them. There is a kind of beauty to such a powerful yet invisible force, especially because I cannot identify what it is; it does not exist within my referential database on the subject."

"That's..." The boy was taken aback. "That's very deep for an AI, Mozi. Did Dr. Burke teach you to think like that?"

"I do not believe he taught this method of thought and perception to me, no. Although he did program into me the capabilities to do so, I believe I have learned such critical thinking abilities by observing mankind and dissecting their spoken thoughts," buzzed the computer. "I say all this, Mr. Hess, in order to encourage you. Does it not give you hope to realize you are, at the very least, aware something is missing? Were you a computer like myself, you would go about your business ignorant of such a massive loss with no internal means of repairing the situation."

"I suppose that **is** encouraging," said the boy, smiling beneath the helmet. "Sometimes I wish I could be like you, all cheery and blissfully unaware. But I guess I'd never have any hope of remembering much of anything about my past that way, now would I?"

"Very good, Mr. Hess." Mozi sounded pleased, as pleased as his voice synthesizer could muster, that he had managed to inspire at least a little confidence in the boy. "The artifact that powers this craft, the same strange shard of glass you emerged from some months ago, fluctuates in its energy and I am unable to calculate an exact time of arrival, I am sorry to say. I'd recommend you retire to the cabin deck below. The process could take several hours and sleep would be the most beneficial way to spend them for a growing organism such as yourself."

"Thank you, Mozi. I think I'll do that," replied Hess, rising from his seat and discarding the dull meal supplement he had been nibbling at. At his command, the silver door in the central column of the Noah opened up to reveal a small elevator. Hess took the lift down into a compact cabin.

The cabin was situated at the lowest point of the Noah, so the walls curved downward like U's. There were a few small portholes with the same strange, blue light filtering through them from outside, and several bunks bolted to the walls. Hess did not relish the idea of sleeping in a cramped bed whilst sealed within the equally cramped suit; Dr. Burke had forced him to do so several times in order to acclimate to the sensation (a none too pleasant one, to say the least). But before he could settle uncomfortably into his bunk, a siren began to wail and Mozi's voice rang out over the intercom,

"Mr. Hess, please return to the bridge immediately! Emergency systems have been activated."

Hess dashed back to the elevator and sped to the command deck, head swinging rapidly from left to right in search of some sort of fire or short-circuiting wire as he arrived. "What's the situation, Mozi? What's wrong?"

"We are experiencing a phenomenon I have never been briefed to interact with!" exclaimed Mozi, alarmed. "Nothing in my programming can indicate a solution. It is most unusual! Approximately forty seconds ago, the Noah's sensors identified an object moving rapidly behind the craft, as if it were following us."

"Impossible!" protested Hess. "We're travelling through the time stream, a wormhole ripped in the very fabric of existence itself! Nothing exists in here except for us."

"Sensors indicate the object has been trailing the Noah since its entry into the time stream. Since such an occurrence is technically not possible, I dismissed the phenomenon as a glitch in the system. But since the most recent detection, the distance between the Noah and the unidentified object has been decreasing, as if the thing is pursuing the craft." Mozi was speaking surprisingly rapidly for a supposedly unflappable computer, nearly on the verge of babbling. If Mozi was nervous, the situation was grave indeed.

"I don't understand! How did it come into the time stream?" sputtered the boy.

"My processors have formulated several hypotheses as to how the object entered the temporal navigation rift, the most feasible of which goes as follows: the unidentified pursuer flew into the wormhole vortex the Noah created only instants after we entered and only instants before the vortex closed."

"But only the Noah should be able to survive these

conditions," bellowed the boy in distress. "Our artifact, the Shard, is one-of-a-kind, no other like it exists and it's the only thing capable of inducing time travel. That thing following us should have been ripped to shreds by now without it." Hess was becoming increasingly alarmed; the prospect of being chased through a featureless blue tunnel by a mysterious entity was less than appealing, and certainly not among the dangers Dr. Burke had trained him to contend with.

"You are correct. I can offer no explanation concerning these matters. My apologies," chirped Mozi. "Additionally, in the time you and I have been discussing the ramifications of this unprecedented circumstance, the object in question has closed the gap even further."

"Damnit, Mozi!" hollered the lad. "Stop jabbering and do something about it! Can you give us a visual?"

"Affirmative, Mr. Hess. Rendering visual on main monitor."

The screen that sat before the control yoke flickered to life and Hess rushed to it. Upon the monitor was displayed the image of the blue vortex through which the Noah was racing, the time stream. In the center of the vortex, at least fifty yards behind the Noah, was a rapidly approaching object. As nearer it drew, Hess could make out more and more of its features but still could not fathom what in the world it actually was. It seemed to be a giant, silver figure, a bipedal like that of a man, gliding like a bird with its arms outstretched.

"Mozi, can you zoom in?" There was no response. "Mozi?"

A moment of gut wrenching silence passed. Finally, Mozi croaked over the intercom, "Mr. Hess, I have just made a frightful discovery."

"Well?"

"You are aware the destructive phenomenon that causes the Armageddon in 3012 AD carries with it a distinctive radiation signature. Dr. Burke believes this signature to be a sort of DNA code, one entirely unique to the apocalyptic storm. And this is the same signature that we are tracking backwards through time in order to discover the origins of said apocalypse and do what we can to prevent it, yes?"

"Yes, yes, Mozi, I know the mission objective! What of it?" cried Hess, wishing he could reach through the helmet and tear his hair out in frustration.

"I have scanned our pursuer with my ranged sensors. The results indicate the target is an inorganic being and composed of a substance I do not have in my databanks. More startling is this: our pursuer is a 98% match for the apocalyptic radiation signature."

"You mean to say this—thing—is related to..." Hess could not bring himself to say it.

"Indeed. The unidentified object is closely related to the components of the phenomenon which causes the Armageddon in 3012 AD- nearly identical, I'm afraid."

"My god," whispered Hess. "Burke was right. It's not just a natural disaster. Something's been behind it all along. You don't think it could be that figure following us whose been pulling the string this entire time, do you?"

"Dubious, Mr. Hess," said Mozi. "Mankind shares a nearly 98% DNA match with some primates; they are, however, not one in the same. However, this entity is indeed, as you would put it, cut from the same cloth."

"What do we do? It's getting even closer!" yelled Hess, gesturing wildly at the monitor where the silver figure encroached.

"With your permission, I will direct the Noah's weapons systems to begin firing at the pursuer immediately. The mission must not be jeopardized." Mozi sounded grave.

"Permission granted! Granted! Fire! Fire!" cried Hess.

"Commencing initial barrage in 5, 4, 3, 2—" before Mozi could finish the countdown, the mysterious figure raised its head to stare directly at the Noah, which was quite an odd looking action considering the thing didn't have much of a neck to speak of. Carved across its face was some sort of symbol, though Hess could not make out what it depicted from the distance. Suddenly, its face, completely devoid of lineaments save the symbol, began to glow red. Its outstretched arms, too, began to pulsate with the same lethal looking color.

"Uh-oh," Hess muttered, his feet frozen to the cockpit floor.

Three all too familiar bolts of crimson lightning, just like the ones which had shot out of the apocalyptic clouds only a few hours earlier, two from its arms and one from its head, lashed out from the silver figure with a ferocious crackling sound that pierced Hess's ears, even over Mozi's wailing alarms. The bolts shot through the air, arching and curving like an angry cat, and collided with the Noah, rocking the craft dangerously to the side.

Sparks flew from every direction within the cockpit, smoke rising from several of the instruments as they short-circuited. Hess was thrown to the ground, a series of electric shocks sent coursing through his body, even through the armor, up from the floor. The pain was agonizing and seemed to seer itself directly into his brain. "Oh God!" he shrieked, clawing desperately at his helmet as he writhed on the ground, reeling in agony.

Mozi's voice rang out over the intercom, but it was lower in pitch than before and sounded mutated, as if the AI were speaking very slowly, "Warning: System Failure. Destination year information lost. Please manually activate emergency temporal brakes. System Failure. System Failure. System Failure. System Failure. System Failure. System Failure. Sys-Fail. Fail. Fail Fail."

Hess felt himself losing consciousness rapidly. Though the shocks had dissipated, his head felt as if it had been baking in an oven and his vision faded in and out of blackness. He reached up to the control panel, preparing to pull on the brake with what remained of his strength, but stopped and hesitated. Something deep within his mind, within the tightest folds of his subconscious and the inaccessible vaults of his foggy memory, told him to wait, if only for a moment more. The year counter before his eyes read 2014 AD.

'Not yet,' whispered some mysterious voice in his head; he

could not be sure to whom the voice belonged, but it certainly didn't sound like his own, much more like that of a young woman's.

"Warning: System Failure. Destination year information lost. Please manually activate emergency temporal brakes. System Failure." Mozi sounded like he was dying, croaking and groaning. "Absolute failure is imminent on this course. Pull brake- Pull brake- Pull bra-"

The cloudy gray of unconsciousness fogged over Hess's view like a mirror in the shower, blissful sleep and relief from the pain beckoning him to close his eyes and drift away.

2013, the meter read. The meter read 2013.

Why wasn't 2013 a good year to stop?

'Not yet,' came the girl's voice again, echoing around the inside of the boy's skull

2013

2013

'Not yet,' she insisted

"But why?" he pleaded with her

'Just wait. A moment more.' Her voice was soft. Soothing.

'A moment more.'

2013

2013

2013

2013

2013

2013

2013

2013

2013

'NOT YET'

The meter flashed suddenly to 2012 and the voice screamed

'NOW!'

The voice in his head seemed to shriek it at him. With one last tremendous push, he threw his arm up to the control panel and gave the brake lever a terrific yank. The Noah lurched and he crumbled to the ground.

Before blackness ensnared him and plunged him into nothingness, Hess glanced one last time at the monitor. The mountains and stars of 2012 AD North America whizzed by, the landscape of a pleasant summer's eve. The silver figure, the pursuer who had nearly destroyed both the Noah and Hess himself, was nowhere to be seen. He closed his eyes and slipped off, abandoning the pain and chaos for the calm of unconsciousness.

CHAPTER FIVE

CONCERNING BLUE LOBSTERS AND SHOOTING STARS

Orange roughy was, thankfully, not on the menu. The Mars family was due over any minute. Franklin and Joey made themselves scarce in the kitchen, avoiding the inevitable beckons they would receive from Mrs. Freeman to "set the table" if they remained in her line of sight.

They quickly realized they appeared far from presentable: their clothes were dusty and caked with marsh dirt. They smelled, too, like low tide and dried mud. Under any normal circumstances, this state would have been acceptable, maybe even the norm; but, considering their expected female company, even Joey deemed a change of wardrobe necessary. They found the best shirts they could for a summer's evening and, as was custom, Franklin lent Joey one of the garments, probably never to see it again until a few months had passed, when Joey finally did his laundry.

Faces washed and smelling better, at least as good as they could hope to smell after lying in the mud all day, the boys met in council in Franklin's little bedroom. Joey sat on the bed and Franklin at his desk where a few model airplanes (in various stages of construction), some old comic books, and a stack of school papers were messily arranged.

They communed briefly in hushed voices, resolving that if Ellie acted strangely or was at all frightening (though they used manlier terms than these) they would retreat back to that very spot in the bedroom and spend the rest of the night holed up behind a locked door playing video games, locked safe away from girls.

The doorbell's ring came like a great gong. Whether it sounded doom or salvation, the boys could not be sure.

Muffled greetings of "Yes, hello, so good to see you" and "It's been so long. Too long!" reached their ears from the floor below. Mrs. Freeman summoned them from their comfortable hideaway with a cheery holler up the stairs. They sighed, puffed out their chests, and descended the staircase cautiously, like nervous monkeys at a zoo trying to impress some onlookers.

The Mars parents were there in the parlor, wisps of summer air trailing in behind them through the still open screen door. The Freeman cat, inquisitive and friendly without fawning, came to greet them, running the side of his apple-like face along their legs as cats are want to do. Ellie was nowhere to be seen. The Mars parents beamed at Joey and Franklin in that 'delighted to see you've grown' kind of look that adults so often give to children whom they have not seen in a long time. The boys found the gaze a little unsettling and rushed into a bout of feigned happiness to see these two vaguely familiar faces as quickly as possible. A firm handshake with Mr. Mars, an awkward hug and kiss on the cheek from Mrs. Mars. Typical. Just typical.

"Ellie will be along any moment, boys. She's just getting some clothes out of the moving boxes. I hear you two have already reacquainted!" said Mr. Mars. He smiled at Franklin; a toothy but honest smile: a likeable man. "And you're Joey Jensen, right? How are those tilapia you were keeping?"

"They died five years ago, sir," Joey managed as he cleared his throat uncomfortably, "I keep Jewel Cichlids now, Jewels and Brazilians, and a few Chocolates, some Salvinis and a few White Skirt Tetras. Oh, and a Black Ghost Knife Fish! Just a baby. But, yes, the tilapias are dead. I used their carcasses for fertilizer in my mom's garden. They were very potent, really made the plants grow well, but she wasn't too pleased when she found them rotting underneath her petunias." There was a revolting pause.

"Oh, I'm... I'm sorry to hear that, Joe. I remember you were only very small when you were already taking care of those fish," chortled Mr. Mars, reaching out to pat Joey's head. In an awkward motion, he retracted his hand when he realized the boy was perhaps a bit too old to have his hair tousled.

Joey, Franklin observed, was on the verge of listing more of his fish to break the silence when Mrs. Freeman ushered them into the dining room. Franklin's father was working late that night at the university and wouldn't be home till long after dinner. Franklin envied his old man; neither the father nor the son particularly enjoyed dining outside their circle of family and close friends, preferring to be messy eaters with those who would not judge them for it.

In single file, the five went towards the dining room, the boys dragging their feet as the necessary "I love the carpet" and "What a nice color choice for the wallpaper" compliments were thrown left and right by the visitors.

"Put the cat in the bathroom, Franklin," shot Mrs. Freeman over her shoulder. "I don't want him begging for scraps."

Franklin turned, glad to have an excuse to leave the slow pilgrimage to the dining room and the forced ritual of social conventions that awaited. Monty, the borderline morbidly obese Siamese cat, was still waiting by the front door, watching something through the screen. Following the cat's gaze, the boy saw Ellie coming up the darkening lawn, her figure a dark blue silhouette in the soft night air. She stopped at the door to ring the bell. Their eyes met in a silent moment.

Ellie smiled and Franklin smiled in return; Monty looked back and forth between the two, waiting for someone to open the door so he could take another whiff of the outdoor scents: the greatest excitement an indoor cat has to look forward to on the average evening.

"Can I come in?" the girl asked, raising an eyebrow.

"Oh, oh yes, sure. Of course! Sorry!" Franklin snapped out of the momentary trance, stumbled forward, tripped over Monty, and clambered to pull the screen door open. Ellie smiled and entered, brushing past the boy and giving the cat an affectionate scratch on his bat-like ear.

"I remember you, Mr. Monty," she cooed.

"Dinner's just down the hall," said Franklin. She nodded and disappeared into the dining room. Hefting the weight of his little friend over his shoulder, Franklin carried Monty into the bathroom where the cat would spend the next agitated hour pawing at the door and mewing sporadically.

"Do you think she's pretty, Monty?" he whispered into the cat's ear. "Think she was smiling at me? Or maybe just at you; you do have a way with the girls."

"Where's Paul this evening?" asked Mr. Mars, making himself comfortable in one of the chairs set about the table and glancing around the dining room.

"Late night at the university, I'm afraid. We're going to Florida tomorrow morning for a week- relative's wedding- so he had some extra work to finish up," replied Mrs. Freeman, moving about the room and filling glasses with white Zinfandel for the adults and iced tea for the children.

"Florida, huh? Excited, Franklin?" Mrs. Mars asked.

"Actually, I'm staying here to keep an eye on the cat." Franklin wasn't boastful, but admittedly a little proud to have finally reached that age in life where he could safely be permitted lay of the land for at least a little while.

Dinner quickly progressed into an affair of two separate camps, the children at one end of the table, keeping their conversation as hushed as they could, and the adults at the other, not really paying any heed to their own volume, especially when Mrs. Mars belly laughed and snorted mid conversation: a truly startling sort of noise.

Ellie regaled the two boys with stories of Maine (several of the tales pertained to moose) and did her best to fill in the sections of her life that they had missed out on since the girl's departure from Connecticut.

"Maine is really a very nice place, you know," she informed them proudly. "Lots of empty space away from people, lots of trees and mountains. I think you'd like it, Franklin; you always loved class hikes and things like that, so far as I can remember.

And Joey, the lobster are bigger there than any you've ever seen!"

"Bigger how?" asked Joey.

Ellie blinked at him. She had only been exaggerating, of course, and hadn't expected a follow up question. "Bigger than any other lobster you've ever seen. Or even better, eaten!"

"I wouldn't be so sure about that," said Joey pointedly, raising an eyebrow and scratching at his nose with a fork. "Caribbean lobsters can grow very large. Of course, Caribbean lobsters don't have those big claws like the ones around here; maybe that would put the two types on par and make up for the size difference. It's my understanding that lobsters in New England, especially Maine, Lobster capital of the east coast, are being overfished. That accounts for the price hike recently. Franny always hates it when we go for seafood and they have that little 'MP' as the price on the menu. Don't you, Franny?"

Before Franklin could answer, Joey continued, "Ever see a blue lobster up there in Maine, Ellie? The blue ones are pretty rare around here. Pretty rare everywhere, actually. It's a mutation that makes 'em blue. I think it's something like one in a million are blue. But I heard, at least I read, that more and more blues are being caught up around where you used to live. I figure that's not really the case, though. You see, there's not **more** blue lobsters all of a sudden, there's just more people interested in them, and more people fishing for lobsters in general. I don't know why, maybe people like the idea of an alternative color of lobster; like a different colored iPod or something. But blue lobster awareness is going up, so maybe they'll start protecting them. That's fine, I suppose- though I've always wanted to eat one and see if they taste any different. But here's where I worry: if we start protecting blues, it's just going to give us an excuse to hunt the plain ole' brown and red ones even more. Soon enough, blue lobsters will be the only ones left and, because they'll be protected, Franny and I will have no lobster rolls to eat down at the lobster shack on the 4th of July."

"Joey," Ellie muttered and then paused. " I remember you

being a lot more quiet."

"He's quiet all day long until you mention something like a lobster," said Franklin, snapping out of a daydream. He had heard the lobster lecture several times and found in it only space to let his mind wander. "Anyway, you were saying about Maine, Ellie?"

"Right. Right. Where was I? I don't remember. Anyway, it was an exciting place to live. I even saw bears in our backyard on some mornings in the summer, usually after cookouts,"

"It's true," chimed in Mr. Mars from across the table, sharing his daughter's enthusiasm. Apparently, noted Franklin, he had been eavesdropping on the children. "One morning she went out alone, saw a bear- big ole black bear- and hollered at him so loud he ran off back into the woods. Never seen a girl face down a bear before. Before my little Ellie came along, anyway."

Ellie was clearly not embarrassed to have this story told like Franklin might have been if Mrs. Freeman had shared a similar anecdote. The girl was beaming, proud of her unusual courage.

"There's lots to do," she continued, "canoeing, hunting, fishing, and just the general wilderness to enjoy. But to be honest, I really did miss this old town. Not so much for the town, though. I missed all my old friends, like you two! Do many of our old classmates go to our high school?"

"Most moved away after eighth grade. Katie went to a prep school in New Hollow, and Tyler went to live in Hadison. The others just kind of faded away, I guess; some of them are still around," said Franklin.

In tandem, the two boys tried to make their lives sound as if they had been nearly as interesting as Ellie's. They regaled her with exaggerated stories of class trips and pranks gone awry. Often, though, they found her staring at them intently, as if waiting for a punch line; although, as they saw things, the punch line had certainly already been delivered. It made Franklin nervous to see her watching him expectantly with nothing much to give her and very little to grab off the top of his head to fill the silence. When she laughed that clear, trickling laugh, though, it was like seeing he'd passed a class even though he was fairly sure he'd failed several of the tests, if not all of them entirely.

She interrogated them about all manners of school: she was a studious girl, an honors student to-be at their little high school, and quizzed them on exactly who the best teachers were and which classes were most liked by the student population. Joey and Franklin, average students by anyone's reckoning, did their best to appease her insatiable line of questioning with what little they knew of the honors classes.

"Do teachers grade on a curve?" she prodded. "Curves usually make my grade skyrocket, at least at my old school they did."

Franklin chewed thoughtfully for a moment and raised his fork as if making a proclamation, "Whether she grades on a curve or not, when it comes to Kopol's class-"

"-None shall pass!" finished Joey for him, laughing through a mouthful of food.

Ellie looked on as they chortled, palpably annoyed. "I'm serious! The curve is important!"

"Some curve, some don't. I suppose it depends on the teacher. Most math teachers curve, most others don't," said Joey dejectedly, sharing in Franklin's disdain for arithmetic.

"I figure the math teachers curve because they're the only ones who know how to do it properly," conjectured Franklin.

Ellie looked annoyed again.

The food was passable, even by Mrs. Freeman standards. Roast beef and baked potatoes mashed and re-stuffed with melted cheese, a dish Mrs. Freeman had brought along to Connecticut with her from her roots in West Virginia. And as they ate, the smell of chocolate pecan pie invaded the room slowly, urging them to eat faster that the dessert might make a full-on assault.

And when it did arrive, even Franklin, fully disenchanted with his mother's cooking after a lifetime of it, was pleased to see the dessert. The pie was still warm, a firm and steaming layer of crunchy pecans protecting a liquefied and molten chocolate core. Along with it was a generous dollop of vanilla ice cream, rapidly melting next to its hot companion. Franklin's mother set down the dessert along with three piping hot cups of coffee whose scents mingled with that of the pie in the air and wafted about in a hybrid smell, genetically engineered to defeat even the sternest of full stomachs. Mrs. Freeman beamed at the pie and smiled ear to ear as even her son clambered to claim a piece of the quickly vanishing treat.

Dessert passed and, though the adults talked amiably on, it did not take long for Joey, ever impatient, to begin drumming his fingers. "Let's do something. I can't take this," he muttered.

Franklin looked to Ellie and she nodded. The three, silent as they might, slipped out of the dining room and quietly upstairs.

"Suggestions, Joey?" asked Franklin, dreading the thought of taking Ellie into his room.

"Too dark for much of anything. The roof, maybe?"

"The roof, yes, the roof!" Franklin found this a suitable alternative.

"The roof?" Ellie echoed, excited.

"There's a window over here." Joey jerked his thumb at a tiny window that sat in the center of the hallway between Franklin's room and his parents'. "It leads out to the garage roof. Good for looking at the stars, but it's kind of steep. Are you sure-"

"I'm sure," Ellie interrupted. "The sky is so clear tonight! I wouldn't miss it."

Franklin pulled open the window and the three crawled out onto the garage roof and into the blue expanse of the night. Nights in October or December on Pendel Circle were black as black could be, void of starlight and choked with a darkness that suffocated even the glow of streetlights. But nights in June and July, especially in sleepy Stony Creek, with its small population and 'early to bed, early to rise' mentality, were lit such a brilliant blue by the light of the stars and the shimmering of the brilliant, placid moon, that one could not but help to wonder whether some spell hung over the area that made it shine, even in darkness.

Though they were not very high, the garage being only a little shorter than the main home, the feeling of being cast away and lost in a sea of dark treetops beneath the stars was enchanting.

"Beautiful," breathed Ellie, still crawling. The three briefly stood, but quickly decided that to lie on their backs instead, bodies parallel to the sloping roof and heads resting upon its crest. And so, there they lay: Joey, nearest the window, then Franklin at the center of the roof, and Ellie, who dangled her feet down into the dry gutter below.

They were silent for a long while, lost in the indigoes and violet blacks of the Milky Way that seemed to drift above them. Sometimes, Franklin felt lost in the grandeur of it all. It was easy, he thought, to feel as though he were but a mote in a desert when viewing the grand cosmos on a clear night, a meaningless drop lost in an equally meaningless and frightfully eternal ocean. It was an intimidating sensation that bordered on overwhelming hopelessness. But on clear nights like that, when he sat next to his friends, two more meaningless drops just like him, Franklin felt at least like they were three drops who belonged together, who belonged exactly where they sat.

The silence was pleasant, punctuated by the nightlife of the nearby bushes, and Franklin felt his body finally begin to relax after the unexpected dinner. The moon was low and lovely, voluptuous and calm. His eyes were lost and wandering the stars when Ellie's voice sounded out, clear and strong in the silence. "It's all so big," she stated plainly. "Really much too big for us, you know." She wasn't talking to anyone in particular.

"Too big?" murmured Joey.

"What could we ever hope to do with such a big space?" she demanded into the sky. "There's too much to explore, and it's all so far away. Even if we lived forever, I don't think we'd ever see all of it. Do you believe in aliens, Franklin?"

Before Franklin could voice his opinion on extraterrestrials, Joey spoke for him. "Franny and I saw something, once. We were camping in Vermont two years ago. Our dads were off getting wood, or something like that, so we took a night hike into the hills. It wasn't so different from tonight: very blue, very clear. Anyway, Franny trips over a root and I bend over to help him when suddenly this noise, like an elephant makes" - Joey mustered his best, slightly awkward imitation - "starts above us. We looked up and a ball of light was there in the sky, just hovering, drifting up, real slow, away from the earth. And then, suddenly, there were more and more of them! Hundreds of these balls of light, all drifting up like a swarm of locusts or something. Anyway, it turned out they were having one of those Chinese floating lantern festivals in the town over and we were just seeing the paper lanterns in the sky. And the noise was just some music they had playing over the loud speakers at the festival. Cool, right?"

"So you didn't actually see anything, then?" Ellie was smirking.

"I guess not," Franklin chimed in. "But before we knew about the lanterns we were pretty convinced. We thought they were some sort of colony of light people leaving earth or-" Franklin stopped and cleared his throat, embarrassed. "Or something like that."

Ellie laughed a very clear and ringing laugh that sounded like bells on Christmas. Joey, who did not want their rooftop perch they had kept secret for so long to be discovered, quickly shushed her. And there they lay for a moment more beneath the stars.

"But really, what do you guys actually think? Life outside of earth?" she pried.

"Of course, almost definitely. Most likely crustaceans, or maybe fungal-based bipedals," exclaimed Joey and then clapped his hands in excitement. "Franny?"

"To be honest, I don't really know what I believe. I suppose something could be out there."

"I don't." Ellie shook her head. "Don't you think, if something **was** out there, we would have made contact by now?"

"Then you think it's just a bunch of emptiness up there?" asked Joey.

"I guess so, that's what's so thrilling about it. So much space for humanity to expand into! But still, much too much space than we'd ever know what to do with." She shook her fist.

"I wonder what kind of ocean life lives out there," thought Joey aloud, ignoring the sentiments of the impassioned girl altogether. "I read that there are planets out there completely encased by ice. But the sea underneath the ice is warm and they say life could live in it. Can you imagine?"

The stars were so clear that night, crisp and twinkling in the blue canvas of the rounded night sky. They shimmered so brightly that Franklin could almost swear one of them, a particular star just to the left of Orion's Belt, was moving! Almost as if it was pulsating and growing larger. In fact, perhaps it wasn't a trick of the eye.

"Does that star look like it's moving to you?" Franklin gestured at the point of light as best he could.

Before anyone could answer, the star seemed to suddenly loom much closer to the earth, flaring up in a red fire that lit the sky. A low rumble sounded all around the children, shaking even the shingles upon which they lay. Before they could speak, before they could cry out in alarm, the star ceased its pulsing and seemed to rocket across the sky, hurtling lower and lower. The noise it wrought was deafening. The children's shouts of "What is that?" and "What's happening?" were drowned out entirely by the thunder of the comet. It flew faster and faster, hurtling further and further down into the atmosphere, cutting a blazing arch across the night sky.

Suddenly, Joey's voice rang out amidst the rumbling and awoke Franklin from the hypnotic gaze that had his eyes transfixed on the tumult in the sky. "Get down!" he shouted. The children, already quite low, rolled onto their stomachs and hid their eyes, though each one of them raised their heads just enough to watch the proceedings.

Where often Franklin had watched flocks of geese going

south for the winter or airliners gliding along their merry ways, the comet shrieked across the sky just above Pendel Circle and, with a tremendous crash, slammed into the highest point of Cankerwood Forest, sending a shockwave that made the house tremble and the trees nearby shiver and sway. Above the dull, echoing roar that permeated the air, one could make out the barking of dogs and the excited chattering of woodland creatures. But, as the noise cleared, Franklin found the absence of shouts from his mother, the lack of screams from across the neighborhood, and the general quiet of all the people of Pendel Circle, quite disconcerting.

The children sprang to their feet and, wordlessly, peered out across the quiet night, their eyes searching for traces of impact. There was nothing, however: no smoke, no fire, only perfect placidness, as if nothing had even happened. Perhaps the meteorite had only appeared to collide with Cankerwood, instead rocketing off somewhere over the horizon.

"Look there!" cried Joey, extending a finger towards Cankerwood. At first Franklin could only make out the dark treetop canopy that enveloped the forest, inky and dim in the night. But slowly, as his eyes adjusted to the distance, a faint red glow seemed to fade into being in the depths of the forest. And it began to blink: off and on like the light on top of a radio tower.

"What in God's name was that?" whispered Ellie, her voice ripe with disbelief in what she had just beheld.

"A meteorite, maybe," said Franklin

"Or a satellite that fell out of orbit," put in Joey. "Could be anything, and it's still blinking."

"That's not necessarily the comet- or whatever it is- blinking, you know. It could just be a radio tower or some kind of camp light- something like that," Ellie reminded him, eyes still fixed on the far off pinprick.

"I've never seen it before," protested Franklin. "And Joey and I have seen Cankerwood by night for years. As far as I know, there's nothing up there: no houses, no radio towers, and no civilization at all. If that isn't the thing from the sky, some hiker must be awfully far out so late at night." Franklin didn't earnestly believe, or even want to believe, it was something as mundane as a hiker out in Cankerwood.

"It's the meteorite and you **know** it, Franny. And even if it was a hiker, he would have been flattened by that impact." Joey was near shouting in excitement at this point.

"It doesn't seem like our parents heard anything... I can still hear them talking, at least. Listen, let's agree not to mention it to them; they might call the cops or something," said Ellie.

"I'm with her. Parents would only get in the way," agreed Franklin, scratching his chin as he thought.

"The way of what?" asked Ellie and Joey together. They looked at Franklin, only hoping he was thinking what they were.

"Surely we're not just going to forget about it and let it stay up in Cankerwood to rot. Whatever it is, we ought to go see it, poke it with a stick or something. Who knows, maybe we'll get rich off of some space geodes or famous or something like that." Joey's eyes lit up at Franklin's mention of geodes.

Plans were quickly (and quietly) erected to travel into Cankerwood the next day and search for whatever it was that had rocketed down to earth. Joey sat, paper and charcoal in hand, scratching out landmarks from afar so that they might find their way to the impact site.

Ellie listed things they might need as Franklin jotted them down: flashlights, gloves, rope, water, lunch, and a large laundry bag so that they might carry whatever the strange, blinking object was back to Pendel Circle. Franklin really didn't care if they became rich or not, the thought of an object from outer space finding it's way through all the emptiness and nothingness only to hit the minuscule target of earth, let alone his own neighborhood, was too tempting a notion to pass up.

Most important of all, the children all signed a pact of secrecy that they should never reveal the plan, their objective, or what they had witnessed that night. Each singed his name upon the charcoal covered paper and spat off the roof to seal the agreement.

Upon returning to the interior of the house through the little window, plans for the next day drawn and agreed upon, the children were astonished and at the same time very pleased by the fact their parents seemed blissfully unaware of whatever great cosmic collision had just taken place. So strange was their ignorance that Franklin questioned whether or not what the children had seen had really happened at all. But Joey and Ellie had watched the comet fall too; surely he wasn't imagining things!

Regardless, the children smiled to themselves in wickedly secret delight at the privileged and classified information they harbored as their the parents exchanged closing pleasantries: kisses on the cheeks, promises to "do this again soon" and yet another great deal of fuss about how much time had passed and how "tall" all the children had grown (though none of them felt particularly "tall" at all).

Ellie followed her parents through the front screen door, giving one final turn of her head towards the boys, touching her nose, winking slyly, and then disappearing into the darkness of the Freeman's summer lawn.

Joey and Franklin, after helping Mrs. Freeman clear the table and freeing Monty, who rushed off to search for leftovers, plodded out onto the driveway. There, in the cool darkness, the two gazed up at Cankerwood again. The red beacon, whatever it was, was still faintly visible, fading slowly in and out.

Joey stretched his arms and yawned, "I ought to be going, Franny. My parents are going to start calling any minute. Remember, tomorrow at 10 AM, your driveway. This very spot. I don't want to have to come wake you up like usual." Franklin had an unfortunate habit of sleeping in to gross hours over the summer.

Franklin nodded and rolled his eyes.

After retrieving his bicycle, Joey pedaled off beneath the streetlights, their beams cloaking him in a soft glow. As his friend became dimmer and dimmer, finally disappearing into darkness, Franklin stood and breathed a few breaths of fresh, evening air. The following day was sure to be arduous; the hike to Cankerwood's peak was not for the faint of heart and it had bested him and Joey several times before. But this, Franklin remarked to himself, was the very essence of the summertime! Challenging the obstacles of the past and tackling them anew.

The long day, with its fishing and females, had tuckered the boy out and he quickly retired into his room, intent on reading some of his maps of Cankerwood and planning out a route to the peak. But drowsiness soon overtook him and, only barely managing to extinguish his lamp and slide out of his clothes and under a thin blanket, he fell into a deep and pleasant sleep.

Not long after Franklin had drifted off, he was roused into semi-consciousness by a few familiar noises: the screen door being quietly shut and Monty mewing softly in greeting, a stifled but humorous burp, the sound of keys and a wallet being safely deposited onto the kitchen counter, and briefcase being dropped with a sigh of relief onto the tiled floor. After a few minutes, the sound of soft footfalls climbing the staircase creaked their way through the quiet house. The bedroom door opened slowly and Franklin's father slipped stealthily in and stole to the boy's side, sitting at the foot of his bed.

"Hi pop," Franklin whispered.

"I'm sorry, did I wake you?"

"No, I was just going to sleep. How was work?"

"Typical college: fluff and bureaucracy. A bunch of meetings no one really needed to attend. Perfect waste of time on such a nice day, if you ask me." Mr. Freeman rolled his eyes. "Speaking of which, how was your first day of summer break?"

"Joey and me went fishing."

"Catch anything?"

"What do you think?" Franklin grinned and his father grinned back, knowingly. "Do you remember the Mars family?" the boy asked.

"Little Ellie's folks? Yes, your mother phoned earlier and said they moved in across the street where the Burgentinos were. They came over for dinner, right?"

"Right."

"She didn't make orange roughy did she?"

"No. Thank goodness. But Ellie came over too."

"Little Ellie Mars, huh? She's about your age now. Did she get pretty?"

Franklin rolled over and hid a reddening face behind his pillow. "I don't know! Mom thought so, so did Joey!"

The man chuckled and looked out the window into the night. "Are you two going to be friends, then?"

"I guess so. Actually, she, Joey and I are all going to... We're all going to... hang out tomorrow. Walk around or something."

"That's nice. It's nice to have girls around, isn't it? Joey's not going to scare her off with the lobster lecture, is he?"

"Too late, but she took it like a champ," laughed Franklin. "Something tells me very little frightens that girl. It kind of freaks me out." Franklin had enough issues with his own courage without Ellie showing him up.

"A gutsy girl, eh? A real keeper then!"

"Dad!" cried out Franklin.

"Only kidding there, boy. You know, I thought of you on the way back from the university. I was on I-95, just about to get off the exit, and the strangest thing happened. I could have sworn I saw a shooting star or something fall right out of the sky. Strangest thing!"

Franklin's eyes lit up at this news. His father had witnessed what no one else, save the children, had even seen or felt. Mr. Freeman caught the excitement in his son's eyes before the boy could hide it.

"You saw it too, didn't you, junior? I figured you must have, always looking at the sky like you do. I hope you weren't up on that roof again! Someday you're going to fall right through the shingles and into the garage!"

Franklin was shocked to learn his father had known about his rooftop getaway this entire time. Even more that shocked, he had never scolded the boy or told him to stop.

"Don't worry, Franklin, I won't tell your mother. Little spots like that are important for boys to have. I had one much the same when I lived on State street in New Hollow. When I was your age, mine was up on the fire escape. Sometimes I'd have bologna sandwiches and a glass of milk out there. I don't really know why, the two just tasted particularly good together when I was up on that fire escape. Just don't let your mother catch you up there on the garage roof; she'd have a fit."

Franklin cringed at the thought of his mother discovering the spot and dispelled the image entirely from his head.

"We're leaving pretty early in the morning tomorrow. Don't worry; I'll make sure she doesn't wake you up. And, I've been meaning to speak to you about this-" Mr. Freeman patted Franklin on the shoulder, stood, and walked to the door. His back to his son, he continued to speak, "While we're gone, you're in charge of the house. I trust you absolutely, you've never given me any reason not to. I know you'll take care of things, especially Monty and the plants, while we're away. But, Franklin, if anything unexpected should happen, if any thing should go wrong: try not to worry. We're only a phone call away, and all the emergency numbers are right on the fridge where they've always been. Just be brave, son, and you'll do fine." Mr. Freeman turned his head and smiled. "Goodnight."

Franklin had indeed been nervous about overseeing the home while his parents were gone, but, as usual, his father's words had an almost tingling effect on his courage. And so, with the moon floating ever higher above Cankerwood and the miniscule red light blinking away, Franklin drifted off to sleep.

CHAPTER SIX

A STAGE THAT BURNS

"Look! Look! Watch as the great show begins! Cheer as the players take their marks. Keep quiet as the curtain rises, though, for quiet was the void when it first became! What will you make of the great play? Will you be able to stay till the players take their bows? Few can stay, so few can stay. It is a pity. Will you take a bow alongside them, perhaps? Oh, how exciting! Questions, questions, lovely questions!" The voice speaking was that of a young woman's, lilting and melodious but at the same time childlike and playful. It rang out almost tauntingly, echoing through every crevice of the grand old theater in which Franklin Freeman sat.

Though he hadn't the foggiest idea how he had come to be there, or from where the mysterious voice emanated, he didn't much mind; he was seated in the very front row of the audience upon one of many red velvet seats, the kind one sees in old auditoriums from the 40's and 50's. In his lap was a playbill, but the writing on it seemed to be in another language; something that looked more like hieroglyphics than any alphabet he had ever seen.

There were great, glittering chandeliers that hung high above him in the cavernous place, but their light quickly dimmed into darkness. There seemed to be other patrons seated sparsely behind Franklin, but their faces and shapes were so shadowy and still that they might as well have not been there at all.

Before Franklin hung a great, red, satin curtain, gilded with golden lace at its bottom where it dangled down onto a wide, wooden stage. Above the curtain was flown a grand proscenium arch, adorned with intricate carvings of cherubs and their trumpets. The cherubs were faceless, though, and resembled no statues he had ever seen before in museums or books. Franklin had never before been to this particular theater, but the whole place reminded him of an opera house, the kind of which he imagined the royal individuals of the world spent their evenings inside of.

Suddenly, breaking the silence, the other patrons began to clap quietly and slowly, though Franklin could not see them moving their hands at all in the dim light. As if by clockwork, the lackadaisical applause ceased as suddenly as it had begun and the curtain began to rise silently, revealing the rest of the stage behind it. What remained of the chandeliers' light vanished from the hall and all was dark.

"Look, look! The first light! The beginning of the show!" the girl's voice sang out again. From the right wing of the stage emerged a ball of light from behind a curtain, a sort of will-o-wisp suspended in midair. It floated out onto the center of the apron where it remained, hovering motionless.

"Isn't it lovely and bright?" demanded the voice. "What says the audience, shall we have more?" The dark figures behind Franklin clapped a few more times; their rhythm was disturbingly offbeat.

From the center of the glowing sphere emerged several smaller specks of light that whizzed about the stage like fireflies over a pond. There were hundreds of them, far too many to count; but of the hundreds, three wisps of light shone particularly bright as they cruised the air, though they were still dwarfed by the original, larger one. The whole stage shone like a night sky plastered with stars.

"How special! How nice! What a bright stage we have to look at! Shall we see the set? Shall we?" chanted the girl's voice. More half-hearted applause ensued. Franklin didn't clap; the whole scene gave him an uneasy feeling. Suddenly a girl about Franklin's age, whose hair was the color of starlight and whose white robes gleamed like the moon, danced out onto the stage. He was at once sure the sweet voice from before was her own.

She was beautiful, or at least Franklin believed her to be; he could not bring himself to look directly at her face, for her pale skin shimmered with such brilliance that it near blinded his eyes. But his gaze remained transfixed nonetheless, on her long locks of silvery yet youthful hair, upon her small feet which danced and leapt so gracefully about the wooden planks without making a sound, upon the billowing folds of her silken gown.

How suddenly the desperate desire to peer into her eyes had overtaken him, and how he wished he could see her assuredly delicate lips curl into a smile, but there was nothing to be done; to stare directly into her face would be to look into the sun and go blind. He had never felt so conflicted, and sweat began to bead about his brow. He clenched the armrests of his seat and, gripping them tightly, his knuckles began to go white. Though hundreds of strange balls of light made their way about the stage, things which he had never before seen and was likely to never see again, he could not help but to stare unblinking at this strange dancing angel before him. She gleamed.

A large black disk, at least as tall as Franklin was, rolled out onto stage as though it had been pushed from the wings. Miraculously, it stopped and stood still like a nickel carefully placed on a desk, precariously resting on its edge. The girl dashed behind it, popping up only moments later with a sort of Greek mask obscuring her features and the radiant light of her face. The mask was that of a woman's personage and had a long, dark wig attached to its back. Once the shimmering of the girl's face had been extinguished by the prop, Franklin began to feel more at ease and relaxed his grip on the arms of his seat.

There she stood, masked head poking up from behind the black disk, swaying silently as if waiting. Suddenly, the three brighter wisps of light ceased their flying and stopped to hover above the girl. The brightest of the three slowly descended to her and she caught it in her hands like a firefly, burying her face into it and making loud kissing noises.

"Oh! Oh!" she cried, and the light emerged from her palms and spun about her, affectionately grazing her cheeks and lips. As she and the light became more and more playful, the black disk behind which she stood glimmered for a moment and turned to a lovely, azure blue. For a time the stage was filled with the girl's lilting laughter, and Franklin became entranced, watching the beauty dance and frolic with the gliding light.

Without warning, the girl threw her head back and touched the back of her hand to her forehead; a dramatic pose. "Woe! Woe!" she cried, pretending as though she were sobbing, and crumbled onto the floor behind the blue disk. "Woe! Woe! I am no more for this world!" she sobbed again. The light she had abandoned floated clumsily above the disk for a moment and suddenly turned a deep, blood red color, almost crimson in its intensity. It shot suddenly into the rafters of the theater, buzzing around like an angry bee.

"Oh dear, oh dear. Please evacuate the theater. Oh dear!" cried the girl from behind her mask. She had lost her playful tone as she stood and entreated the audience. Franklin turned to go, but found the rear of the auditorium had all but disappeared; the other patrons, the seats behind him, even the chandeliers: all gone.

He glanced up again; the red light had ceased it's buzzing and was now plummeting back towards the stage. The noise it made as it fell was awful, something like the sound Franklin imagined an atom bomb must make as it drops. The disk, which had been blue and beautiful for a time, had changed back into its original, inky black color and remained that way till at last the red wisp smashed down into it, shattering it into a million pieces, like a light bulb being broken. The shards, which flew in every direction, collided with the curtains and lit them on fire as if by magic. Within moments, the whole stage was engulfed in chaotic flames. The lights shot in every direction in a panic, though many huddled far away from the maelstrom.

The flames travelled quickly and soon raced down off the apron of the stage and onto Franklin's row of seats. He stood and ran from them, but they seemed far too fast to escape. As they were about to claim him, something grabbed him by the back of his collar and hoisted him up onto an as of yet unburned patch of the stage. It was the girl! She had reached down and rescued him from immolation.

She released him from her unusually strong grasp and put her hands on his face, looking deep into his eyes. Her touch was like silk, and even though the mask still obscured her face, he could not bring himself to look at her straight.

"There's no way out, Franklin!" she exclaimed. "We have to cheat. We have to go through the stage! It's not really allowed, but I'll give you a way! A method! Yes, a means to circumvent this awfulness. I'll give you a ticket!" She produced a small piece of paper, much like a movie pass, and shoved it deep into his trouser pocket.

The flames were drawing nearer and nearer, licking their heels. She banged her foot into the floor and a trapdoor (that Franklin hadn't even noticed), opened up in front of him. Without warning, she pulled the mask from her head and once again, even as flames consumed the theater in a blaze, her face shone out, the brightest thing in the room. Franklin squeezed his eyes shut tight so as to not go blind, and he felt her take his head into cheeks into her slender hands. "Cheat! Through the stage!" she whispered, and kissed him on the lips.

For a moment, the chaos around him ceased and time seemed to stop. For just a moment, he remained in that embrace, eyes aching to open and gaze into the starlit face that was sure to smite his vision and seer his retinas. Her lips were soft, but hummed with energy. Her hands on his cheeks felt no longer like the flesh of a woman but like rushing warm water that threatened to leak down onto his neck. Franklin had never kissed a girl before, and he was not disappointed.

Bringing him suddenly out of his trance, she shoved the boy unceremoniously toward the trapdoor into which he stumbled and fell. Franklin dropped quickly into an overwhelming blackness, though above him he could still see the girl looking down through the trapdoor, her figure outlined with flames, only a speck of light in the distance. "Should you ever become lost, ever become forgotten, rip the stub off the ticket which I have given you and cast it where so ever it is you wish to go! This is all I can grant you, for it has been forbidden me to meddle more than I already have! Fare thee well, Franklin Freeman!" she shouted, her voice faint over the distance and the incessant roar of flames.

He clutched desperately at his pocket, sliding his hand into it and searching frantically for the ticket as he fell. Finally, when the speck of light that was the open trapdoor had disappeared, far into blackness, his fingers closed around the pass and he tore it out of his trousers.

As he struggled against the gravity pushing down against him in an attempt to raise his arm and look at the ticket, a droning 'beeping' sound began to pervade the darkness. *Beep*, then silence, *beep,* then silence. Before he could even glimpse the little ticket he felt so clearly in his hand, before he could hit the bottom of whatever horrid, empty chasm he was plummeting through, his bedside alarm clock's buzzing reached its peak and he jolted awake from the strange, incoherent dream.

CHAPTER SEVEN

THE CLIMB TO SACHEM'S HEAD

Joey was tapping his foot impatiently on the Freeman driveway as Franklin stumbled out of the house, pulling on various articles of clothing as he went. The sun was already high in the sky and only a cloud or two bothered to drift across it.

"10 AM sharp, Franny. I said 10 AM sharp. I even reminded you! It's 10:20 and you're just barely out of bed!" chided Joey.

"I know it, I know," apologized Franklin through a mouthful of hastily eaten toast. "I guess I must've hit the snooze button in my sleep a few times. I was having the strangest dream, Joseph. Like nothing I've ever dreamt before."

"What about?" Joey had always been keen on dreams; he had often written his own down in the hopes of one day achieving a lucid dream. It hadn't happened yet.

"Some kind of auditorium, something like that. There was a school play, I guess, and a girl-" Franklin paused, suddenly he remembered the dream extremely clearly; the dancing angel, the burning theater, and the plummet into darkness. "It's all kind of fuzzy," he lied. For some strange reason, the dream seemed now to him much too intimate to share with anyone, even Joey, though he couldn't reckon why.

"A girl?"

"Not that kind of dream, Joseph."

Joey laughed. "Alright then, let's head over to Ellie's. Your hair's a mess with bed-head, Franny."

Franklin hadn't had time to even look in the mirror as he had rushed out of the empty house. His mother hadn't been there to comment on his appearance, nor his father to snicker at his awkward morning cowlick; they had left for the airport before dawn early that morning. He shrugged and did his best to arrange his bangs and tidy his dark mop of hair, but the attempt was largely futile. Quickly relenting, he retrieved his bicycle from the carless garage and the two wheeled their bikes across the road to where the newly purchased Mars home stood.

Ellie was ready and waiting anxiously when they knocked on her door. She had obviously prepared for a hike more than the two boys had thought to. Socks rolled high, tucked into tan leather boots, and sunscreen palpable in the air, the girl beamed in excitement. "Have we got everything?" she asked.

"Yes, we stowed it all in the tackle boxes on the backs of the bikes," replied Joey. "I thought about it a bit more in bed last night and I think, if Franny and I put our heads together, we should be able to get to the peak without a map, though Franny's brought one just in case." Joey squinted up at the dark forested hill as he spoke, eyes fixated on where the glowing beacon had been the night before, though now it was invisible in the sunlight.

"Ready, Franklin? You look a little tired," observed Ellie, turning to the bleary eyed boy and smirking.

"Yeah, I'm fine. Just a bad dream. Slept in a little, I guess," he muttered. "Let's get going."

The three friends mounted their bikes and took off up the street, leaving little Pendel Circle behind them. The road to

Cankerwood was a steadily ascending one. The menacing forest towered above the neighborhood and cast such a long shadow that nighttime started about a half hour earlier for the residents of Pendel Circle than the rest of town.

Soon the children were pumping and pedaling their very hardest against the deadly incline. It wasn't the sudden steep hills that did exhausted them, nor the small ones, but the long, **slightly** steep ones that were the true bane of cyclists everywhere. After what seemed like hours of panting and grunting in the hot sun, the three dismounted and dejectedly began to push their bikes up the road, for they simply could not budge their pedals another inch. They hadn't even breached the tree line yet, and already the expedition had nearly defeated them. How ashamed they felt each time some Tour de France wannabe zoomed by them and smirked smugly at their defeated walk from atop his fancy, racing cycle.

There was no official entrance to Cankerwood: no gate, no laminated map or brochure center, not even a sign to indicate where the trail into the woods began. Franklin wasn't even sure the forest was called Cankerwood at all; perhaps it was only a name the locals had simply given the gloomy place out of spite for it. What he was sure of was the distaste the locals had for the woods. They were dark and quiet, not ideal for picnics or hikes, and the neighbors often cast sullen glances their way, thinking on them as more of an eyesore than anything else.

But Cankerwood was vast indeed, sitting at the intersection of several town lines. For such a large place, Franklin knew of no one who frequented it. Hikers steered clear of the area and even particularly rambunctious teenagers, who relished treacherous regions in which to ride dirt bikes and ATVs, did not cross into Cankerwood's borders.

They abandoned their bikes in some bushes near the tree line; their cycles (even Joey and Franklin's country worn mountain bikes) would stand little chance against the rocky slopes ahead of them.

Pushing into the woods and standing amidst the trees, a great quiet fell over the children. Whereas on the roadside things had been cheerful and bright, Cankerwood seemed almost to suffocate the senses. No birds chirped overhead and no breeze rustled the leaves; even the bugs were silent. The entire scene reminded them more of one they might witness in a winter month than in July: quiet and still. The rays of light that did filter down through the thick treetop canopy were dusky, few, and far between, giving the whole forest a kind of abandoned look, like an attic no one had disturbed in years.

"You guys weren't kidding about this place; it **is** spooky," whispered Ellie, as if she were afraid to disturb the oppressive silence around them by speaking too loudly.

The children tramped for a time through the lowlands of the forest, angling their hike towards the little mountain that sat in the center of the woods, the peak upon which they believed the comet to have fallen.

The children, as they had agreed to do the night before, took turns lugging the sack of supplies, hefting it over their shoulders as they went. The landscape about them seemed ancient and hollow, as if at one time life had thronged and bustled through it, but now all that remained were bleak and cheerless reminders of what had been: fallen trees, dusty caves, and an overwhelming sense of abandonment. Of course, this was really just a feeling; the forest still teemed with insects, birds and mammals. These particular creatures simply were quieter than others in the world for some reason humans will never know.

After a brief slog through some overgrown fens and stagnating swamps that smelled just as rotten as they looked, the children came to the bottom of the cliffs, those rocky outcroppings which formed the base of the mount. Joey silently motioned for them to begin the climb, not wanting to make any loud noises or sudden movements, his ears pricked and listening intently for the sounds of frogs or other critters he might scoop up and inspect in his dirty palms. The children began the precarious clamber up the crags, their way just barely illuminated by the dim light of the forest. They took special care to select their footing; any misstep could mean a long tumble down and an unfortunate end to a summer's day.

The path was treacherous and slow going. Franklin picked his way in and out of gullies, beneath little overhangs, and through wide crevices carved between great stones, all the while avoiding scaling the cliff face directly as it was a hazardous route and he was wary of falling, a fate many had suffered when traversing Cankerwood in the past.

Ellie and Joey ambled along behind him, neither of them particularly sure of their footing, taking care to note the various handholds and footholds Franklin selected so that they might use them as well. Secretly, they marveled at their friend's ability to find his way up such a steep mount so quickly and in such a dark wood, relieved that their suburban Sherpa would show them the way. Franklin, of course, didn't realize he was leading at all. He merely climbed as he saw fit and pointed out spots where the rocks were loose or the mica slippery.

Cankerwood loomed about them as they struggled up the incline, quiet and gloomy as a graveyard. It wasn't till midday that they stopped to rest in the ever-present shade, selecting a little plateau hollowed into the side of one of the many cliffs and hunkering down upon it.

Ellie distributed to the two boys granola bars and apples; they had quite forgotten to pack any food for themselves. They ate these voraciously and with grateful sighs; the climb had tired them to the point of starvation. Between mouthfuls of food, Ellie began to speak, "Suppose we find something- well-something special up there and we sell it and get rich, you know? What do you two think you'll do with your shares? Of the money, that is."

"New salt-water tank. Maybe a jellyfish. I've read they're fun to take care of. Pricey, though, for the good ones anyway," mused Joey. "I'd like to buy, or maybe build, a coy pond in the backyard. Think about it, Franny, fish for dinner whenever we want. But a new tank would rock; maybe some dories and marlins, a few filter feeders." Joey's eyes wandered up to the sky as he daydreamed of a fantasy terrarium.

"I could use a new bike. And a new baseball glove wouldn't

be terrible, either," said Franklin. He knew the answers were lackluster, but he honestly couldn't think of anything that glamorous at the moment.

"That's it?" You guys, I'm talking millions, here. Millions and millions!" cried Ellie, exasperated. "Can't you come up with anything more exciting than some aquariums and a baseball glove?"

"What would you do with it?" Joey sneered; in his mind there was no better investment than a good salt-water tank.

She scratched her wrist thoughtfully. "To be honest, I can't really think of much anything, either. Maybe a college fund or something like that." She paused. "We certainly are boring, aren't we?" The three children laughed and continued to chew.

Soon they had finished their meager lunches and pared the apples down to their very cores. As Ellie and Franklin sat digesting, Joey began to prowl about the clearing, searching for anything he might occupy his hands with. Soon he bent over, surrounded by a sea of darkly colored underbrush and ferns, feeling about on the ground. He pulled up a little seedling that had only just begun to sprout.

"Look, Franny! An apple tree sprout! Malus domestica!" he proclaimed, returning to the clearing with the little plant clutched between his palms.

"Put it back! Let it grow!" demanded Ellie.

Franklin smiled to himself, Joey didn't yet have an apple tree sprout in his collection of flora and he'd be damned if he left one in Cankerwood to be eaten by some deer or swallowed up by weeds.

"No way, sister. This one's coming home. Imagine, apples any time I want and right in my own backyard. It'll be grand!" Joey shoved the little sapling deep into his pocket, a pocket already brimming with several other botanical odds and ends he had picked up along the hike. Treasures, or at least they were to him

"You're ridiculous," grumbled Ellie. "It'll be years before that tree grows big enough to bear any fruit. You'll be in a wheelchair by then, or maybe even in the ground."

The trek resumed with a renewed vigor. Step by step, their destination loomed closer. They had made good time, better than they had expected to make considering their difficult task of navigating through the eerie wood

"What's this mountain called, anyway?" panted Ellie as she stepped over a mangled, fallen branch.

"Well, it's not really a mountain. More like a big hill, I'd say. But I don't know if it's got a name or not. I do know the peak, the very tip of the hill where we're heading, has got one, though," said Joey.

"And that is?" Ellie was ever curious.

"Sachem's Head. Sachem, like an Indian chief. Know why they call it that?" asked Franklin.

"Let me guess: some old Indian chief put a magic spell on the hill a hundred years ago. It's always a magic Indian spell, isn't it?" she giggled, grinning.

"Not quite," laughed Franklin. "A little more sad than that, actually. A couple hundred years ago, the Puritans took some rebellious Pequot chief up here and cut off his head. A real execution, if you know what I mean. They say the head rolled all the way down the hill and into the ocean." He jerked his thumb at the bay, which was just barely visible through the tangled branches. "And it's never been found. To this day, it's still missing. Mr. Whiffin told Joey and me that story a long time ago. I'm surprised you don't remember, Ellie."

"When Mr. Whiffin told us that story in third grade, we ran down to the beach and waited for the sachem head to wash up. We waited a good, long time," exclaimed Joey. "I suppose the fish and worms would've eaten the flesh away pretty quickly, but the skull could potentially still be around. When whales die, their skeletons sit at the bottom of the ocean for an unbelievably long time. They're such big skeletons they actually create a mini habitat for things to live in down there. Nothing you'd recognize though; everything that lives that deep hasn't got eyes- there's no light so far down, you see." Joey had done his eighth grade science project on the very subject.

"That's pretty interesting about the Sachem," remarked

Ellie. "I wonder if his ghost haunts the woods, now," The three children stopped in their tracks and glanced about, taking in the oppressive and suffocating silence, the dark and ominous trees, and the rocks shaped like daggers and spears all around them. 'Yes', they all nodded: 'definitely haunted'.

As they climbed higher, the sun began to show a bit more through the treetops, lighting their path and their spirits, too. They chatted and reminisced, discussed the summer and what fruits it might bear, and constantly wondered aloud what awaited them atop Sachem's Head. Franklin several times pointed out to Ellie various landmarks visible from the mountain. He gestured to the local grocery store, the salt marshes, and even Pendel Circle, which was only very tiny from up so high. When the conversation had at last been exhausted, they began to sing in their midday cheer, recalling songs from their youth they had belted out on the field trip bus all those years ago.

'I know a song that gets on everybody's nerves,
Everybody's nerves, everybody's nerves.
I know a song that gets on everybody's nerves
And this is how it goes!'

The lyrics would then loop into an indefinite cycle.

'Don't throw your junk in my backyard, my backyard, my backyard.
Don't throw your junk in my backyard, my backyard's full!
Fish and chips and vinegar, vinegar, vinegar.
Fish and chips and vinegar, vinegar, pop.
One bottle of pop, two bottles of pop ,three bottles of pop, more…

They recalled songs that had been sung by excited ministers visiting their school:

> *All God's creatures got a place in the choir*
> *Some sing low and some sing higher,*
> *Some sing out loud on a telephone wire,*
> *Some just clap their hands, or paws, or anything they've got now.*

And finally, the tune their parents loved to sing so well:

> *How do I know my youth is all spent?*
> *My get-up-and-go has got up and went!*
> *But, in spite of it all, I'm able to grin*
> *And think of the places my getup has been!*

Suddenly, Franklin stopped singing and stood still, drawing the gaze of his companions. He sniffed the air. "Do you smell that, Joseph?"

Joey sampled the breeze as well. "That smell... The smell of burnt metal!" he murmured, nose to the wind. "Like a pot on the stove too long."

The three children looked at one another excitedly and exclaimed all together, "We must be close!" They sprang into a mad dash towards the peak, the scent growing stronger with each step they took. Suddenly, Cankerwood didn't seem so gloomy at all as they raced up the crags towards potential fame and fortune. Ellie stumbled and Joey tripped, skinning his knee, but Franklin pushed onwards, dragging his clumsy friends behind him.

Sachem's Head loomed before them, only a short, scrambling climb compared to the rest of their all-day affair. As he sprinted, the look in his eyes was one that rarely graced Franklin's calm demeanor: a hell-bent lust for adventure and trouble. Joey had seen such a look before, and knew it meant excitement lay ahead. Franklin had a bloodhound's nose for adventure, though, as they would rapidly learn, his bark was much bolder than his bite.

They pulled themselves up and over the crest of a short, stony, ledge and stood erect, gazing out over Sachem's Head Peak. Collectively, they gasped, hearts dropping into their stomachs as they laid eyes on what awaited them.

Sachem's Head was spread before them, a plateau some thousand feet wide and across, lit brilliantly by an afternoon sun, a sun that seemed closer to the earth given the hill's altitude and the sudden gap in the thick canopy of branches overhead, a peculiar instance of light for the gloomy Cankerwood.

The peak was plain enough; trees speckled its surface and the sharp rocks of the cliff face rose up to surround it like petrified ocean waves lapping at a lonely pillar of stone. But all the details of the area were immediately lost to the children; their eyes were fixated on the center of the plateau. There, in the middle of Sachem's Head, was a massive hole, a pit struck awkwardly deep into the earth, at least a few hundred feet across. Fresh and loose soil was heaped around its edges, perhaps thrown up by whatever had caused the impact. The crater was conical, as if a spike had been thrust point down into the earth from the heavens. A few thin, dwindling wisps of smoke rose from its depths.

It was not only smoke that rose up from the hole, though. Near the edge of the pit, presumably extending from some point deep inside it, was a metal pole, not unlike the antenna at the tip of a radio tower. At the top of the pole was a red light fixture that slowly glowed on and off. Surely this was the beacon they had seen the night before, thought Franklin. Running up and down the pole on each side of it were steel rungs, as if the structure was designed to be climbed like a ladder.

"My God," breathed Ellie. "This is what we saw! There's the light, blinking just like it was last night." Her eyes were wide like saucers. "Let's get a closer look." She and Joey sprang forward, almost a at a hustle, and hurried towards the edge of the pit.

Franklin hung back and called out to them, "Wait a second,

guys. This is real, now. Don't you think-well- don't you think we ought to call someone? Or something like that? It could be... It could be dangerous." The adventurous fires that had lit Franklin's eyes had died almost instantly, extinguished by the reality of whatever it was that lay before them. This was the way Franklin's mind worked, he noted regrettably. The prospect of excitement gripped him and fueled him like no other, but when push came to shove and reality replaced expectations, a very real fear far too often bested the boy. Thinking of his parents so far away in Florida, where they could not be called upon to rescue him if something went awry, Franklin began to feel very alone and very worried.

"Come on, Franny. We came all the way up here just for this!" Joey exclaimed, turning to face his friend.

"We've come too far to stop now," added Ellie. Her eyes sparkled with delight. It was the look she gave Franklin, not a pleading one but a gaze filled with courage, that ushered the boy to take a reluctant step forward, discarding his inhibitions for the time and following his two friends into the crash site that awaited them.

They proceeded to the edge of the pit, near where the rod peeked up from inside of it, and stood still for a moment. "How deep is it?" wondered Franklin aloud.

"Only one way to find out," said Ellie as she stepped toward the precipice and leaned carefully over it. Her eyes lit up again. "Guys," she whispered, "you've got to see this. It's- I have no idea. You've got to look."

Joey and Franklin cautiously followed her lead, craning their necks carefully over the crater's edge and peering down into it. Franklin's heart seemed to stop. Below them, at least 50 feet down, was a huge, red, metal sphere nearly as big as Franklin's house. The sphere had a large fin jutting out of its top, pointing towards the sky, and a series of glass panels studded its sides. The object was half buried, crammed deep into the dirt by the same force that had presumably thrust it down across the sky, rendering the crater in which it sat.

The tall, blinking light pole the children had seen before

seemed to protrude from the sphere itself, travelling all the way up from the thing's top to the hole's edge. A few pieces of metal and earth lay scattered about the sphere, smoldering and casting faint pillars of smoke into the sky. Though it was deep below them and somewhat difficult to see, the white letters etched across the object were still easy to make out.

"Noah," read Ellie aloud, pointing at the letters. "Think it's a satellite?"

Franklin and Joey glanced at one another and shook their heads. "Doesn't look like any satellite I've ever seen, unless it's one of those secret government stealth crafts," said Franklin, scratching his chin as the wonder of the mysterious discovery temporarily dissuaded his mind from the fear that had gripped him only moments before.

"Somehow I doubt it," remarked Joey. "First off, it's crimson. Not a very stealthy color, if you ask me. It looks almost like something out of Mr. Freeman's sci-fi movie collection with that fin on top. And secondly, if it was a government deal, don't you think there'd be FBI and CIA surrounding the place right now? NASA or something?"

"I'd think they'd be surrounding the place even it wasn't government at all. Something this big coming through the atmosphere **had** to show up on **somebody's** radar. Why the hell isn't anyone investigating?" demanded Franklin. The fear was starting to return to his voice.

"Let's not worry about that for now." Ellie was almost hyperventilating with excitement. "Whatever it is, and judging from those windows I'd say it's a sort of spacecraft or airplane, it's giving off some kind of signal. See how this light on top of the pole is blinking? It's almost like a distress signal! What if someone -or **something**- inside needs our help?"

Franklin hadn't even considered the possibility of life inside the craft. If there were anyone in its interior, they'd have been killed by the crash for sure, he thought. "You know, for smashing such a big crater into the dirt, it still looks pretty put together, though I really can't speak to what it looked like before the crash," he said. He was right, the sphere seemed to have passed through the atmosphere and into the rocky earth almost unscathed; its hull was as smooth and glassy as any brand new automobile might be.

"It came in hot," muttered Joey, eyes intent on the vessel.

"How do you figure?" asked Franklin.

"There's charred brush down in the hole and the dirt at the bottom looks like the dirt inside a campfire: all ashen and sooty. Plus-" Joey pointed wildly towards the treetops above them, "-when it slammed through the canopy, it looks like it completely vaporized most of the leaves right off the branches." Several limbs had in fact been snapped from their homes, but the branches that remained were entirely leafless, standing out naked as a sore thumb in a forest brimming with foliage.

The three stared down at the sphere, occasionally glancing about to search the area for signs of life, such as federal agents who might be arriving to the scene late, or even- they all thought secretly in their heads- space aliens. And there they remained for several minutes, all at once confused and entranced by the foreign object that had found its exciting way into their rather mundane, suburban lives.

Occasionally Franklin's nagging mind would remind him of the infinite number of dangers that could emerge from their very **being** there, most notably incarceration or even- if there were anything unnatural inside the sphere- evaporation. But so strange, so mysterious, so wondrous was this discovery that not even his hammering heart nor his weakening knees could turn his gaze.

Finally, Ellie broke the silence and spoke. "Well, what are we going to do with it?" Franklin and Joey exchanged looks, completely baffled themselves. "We can't just leave it down there!" she exclaimed.

"Why not?" asked Franklin, with complete sincerity.

"Come on, Franklin. Don't be a chicken." Ellie shot him a dirty look.

"Franny's not being a chicken, he's just being realistic. What **could** we do with it? It's obviously too big to carry. Unless you want to call the cops or something, I don't really see all that many options. We're only kids, after all," Joey reminded the impetuous girl.

The children removed themselves from the ledge, sitting in a little circle of dirt nearby, hoping to tear their gazes off the crater to attend to the question at hand: a decision on what was to be done.

"We could cast a fishing line down there with some bait on it or a white flag or something," recommended Joey.

"We could give the police an anonymous tip," suggested Franklin.

"Or we could stop being a bunch of flower picking little chumps and go down and **touch** the damn thing!" shouted Ellie, slamming her fist into the dirt. "You know what they'd call you two in an old cowboy movie? Yella. They'd call you yella." Ellie's insults might have been a bit more stinging if they hadn't made the boys snicker quite so much.

"And how would we even do that, Ellie?" Joey spread his hands out as if he was reasoning with a toddler. "That hole's at least fifty feet deep. You couldn't escape that high of a fall without some seriously broken bones, and there's no way to climb down the sides with all that loose, disturbed dirt." Franklin nodded eagerly in agreement.

"We could just use the route provided for us, you know," said Ellie, gesturing back towards the crater. Franklin and Joey arched their eyebrows questioningly, wondering if the girl was referring to some sort of 'manifest destiny' philosophy or she had simply gone mad with the excitement. "Don't give me that look," she scolded. "You know what those little metal things are for on that light pole. Those are rungs, ladder rungs. They're obviously designed for climbing out of situations like this! The pole maybe extended out of that thing- the Noah- when it crashed so the pilot could escape. Or whatever's inside."

"Even if we did consider climbing it, which we haven't yet," Franklin said, shooting the stubborn girl a stern look, "it's pretty far from the ledge. How would we get so far out?"

"Easy. We jump," Ellie replied as if the answer was clear as day.

"No way. Nooooo way," Joey groaned as he got up to head back down the hill and straight back home; he was deathly afraid of heights, always had been so far as Franklin could remember. Franklin grabbed his arm and yanked him back to the ground, terrified of being left alone with the daredevil of a girl they had mistakenly made friends with the day before.

"I can't think of any other way of doing it. We could always build some sort of planked bridge out to it, but we haven't got the supplies!" protested Ellie.

"We could go and **get** the supplies!" Joey had begun to breathe very quickly at the thought of leaping out to the pole.

"You **know** we can't do that. It's a miracle the government hasn't shown up yet, and they're bound to arrive any minute. If we leave this place for a moment, even a **second**, we risk losing it forever. They'll have the whole site roped off and quarantined before you can even blink," said Ellie, her voice low and serious. "This is our only chance, the way I see things."

"Even if we do manage to climb down, who knows what could be inside of that Noah thing?" argued Franklin. "There could be a bomb in there! It could be a failed attack on the country! We could blow ourselves up, not to mention the entire state of Connecticut along with us!" He had only just thought of this possibility and the idea was making him sweat profusely.

"We'll vote, then. This is America, democracy is supposed to be our thing, right? All those in favor of climbing down and poking around?" Ellie demanded, raising her hand high.

The two boys remained still, their faces sullen and disappointed at their own cowardice. Perhaps Joey would have gone down if it weren't for the necessary leap of faith, but it was what lay below, the vessel known only to them as Noah, that kept Franklin's arm down along with his courage.

Ellie looked back and fourth between the two dejected boys, her eyes finally resting on Franklin, at whom she stared intently. She looked at him hard, harder than anyone had looked at Franklin since he had failed that math final two years ago. Her eyes seemed to pierce through his face and straight into his skull, pounding at his brain like a battering ram unleashed on some ancient, besieged castle's gate. He didn't know why she looked to **him** for help; he was no more complacent than Joey on the matter.

But Ellie saw something the boy did not. Deep in the eyes of Franklin Freeman, deeper than could be seen by a casual glance or even by a very discerning one, was a glimmer. She had spotted it, though. She had spotted it the instant she saw him as she emerged from the moving van just the day before. Ellie couldn't tell what the glimmer meant, whether it was one of hope, excitement, or even a secret, shimmering courage. But it was bright enough that she spied it, even so sunken into his retinas, and recognized it as a genuine, honest glimmer, as one that she could trust, even though the boy himself was completely unaware of its existence.

Franklin could bare the girl's gaze no longer and bashfully hung his head, breaking the stare. Ellie remained still for a moment, quietly regarding her new friend. She reached out and gently took his chin in her fingers, lifting Franklin's head so his gaze looked again into hers. This time it was her eyes that glimmered. They did not plead or beg, they did not demand, and they did not search for compromise. Ellie's eyes, at that moment, seemed to have become like stars in the sky, like two windows into the grander scheme of things. They had become part of something much larger than themselves, much larger anything the children could comprehend in that instant, and the request they spoke could not be denied, even by Franklin's trembling heart.

"Franklin," she whispered. "Please."

Slowly, like a suddenly activated rusty old cog that had not turned in centuries, Franklin's hand rose into the air, adding another vote to their invisible ballot. He turned to look at Joey who, rolling his eyes and heaving a great sigh, followed suit and stuck a reluctant hand towards the sky. He and Franklin had long ago sworn to stick together, and friendship runs thicker than blood.

And so it was, as the three children sat in the dirt with their legs crossed, arms raised, and nervous smiles upon their faces, that a unanimous vote was cast to embark upon a journey that would spirit the young souls further away from home than any of them could have possibly imagined.

Elie shook her feet out a few more times, swinging her shoulders as she did so. "I'm ready," she told her two worried friends confidently. Taking careful, deliberate steps, the bold girl approached the ledge and bent over it for one last peek at what fate potentially awaited her if she didn't land her jump: a dizzying plummet that could end in nothing but a shattered body. She audibly swallowed whatever fear threatened to grip her and faced the pole, locking eyes with it like a pitcher intent on a faraway mitt. As if to steady her aerial approach, she swayed back and forth and pivoted from her hips, searching for the best angle of assault.

"Wait!" Joey cried out suddenly. "Just wait a second." He snatched a small, fallen branch about as long as his arm off the ground. He stepped forward and pitched the stick at the pole. Bark collided with metal as the branch clattered down into the pit, letting out a series of loud *clangs,* like a little wooden Jacob on a little wooden ladder. "Okay, go ahead," he sighed. "I thought it might have been electrified. I didn't want Ellie to get, you know, fried. Who knows with stuff like this!"

"Good thought, Joey," said Franklin, who hadn't even considered the possibility and was massively relieved his friend had. Ellie stepped forward once again, ready to make her jump.

"Be careful," the boys whispered nervously from behind her.

"Don't worry about me," she exclaimed. "I've been waiting my entire life-" without warning, she sprang forward with frightening speed and leapt into the pit, latching onto one of the pole's rungs, swinging around it like Gene Kelley on a lamp post, and finally stopping to face them in an odd, pirouette-like flourish, "for something just like that!" she finished, panting through the adrenaline that had seized her limbs.

Franklin and Joey clapped quietly; already reassured and ashamed that Ellie had outdone them yet again. She clambered down the rungs as naturally as a chimp in a tree, and then stopped, waiting just out of sight below the rim of the crater. "Come on in," she taunted, "the water's fine."

Franklin turned to Joey, whose head was hanging. "Y'alright, Joseph?" he asked, poking the boy in the shoulder.

Joey looked up at his friend, his eyes beginning to brim with tears. "It's just so far down, Franny." He stifled a nervous cough. "You know how I am with heights... I'm not sure I can do it, jumping across and all that. I couldn't even climb the alpine tower at camp, you remember." One of the tears bubbled out of his lower eyelid and slid down his cheek, falling to the soil below.

Franklin placed his hands on Joey's shoulders and gave him a vigorous shake, forcing his friend to look him in the eye. "I'll go first. I'll wait for you on the pole and catch your hand if you fall," he said forcefully.

"But-"

"No buts, Joey. Have I ever lied to you?"

"There was that time with Santa-"

"That was in 4th grade and I only said that so your Christmas wouldn't be ruined. That's not what I meant."

"But Franny-"

"No buts, Joseph. Have I ever let you down?"

Joey didn't have to think about that one. "Never."

"I **will** catch you if you slip. I swear on Ho-Hum's grave, I will catch you," Franklin pledged. Ho-Hum was an injured hummingbird Joey and Franklin had found on the playground, named, attempted to nurse back to health, and then embalmed and interred with full funeral rights when their medicinal efforts had failed.

"Do you trust me, Joseph?"

"I trust you, Franny."

Franklin nodded solemnly and turned, back to the crater. He flexed his legs and fixed his eyes on his tall and slim target. The gap between him and the pole wasn't inconsiderable, and the distance to the ground below was even more intimidating. He glanced at Joey, gave a nervous wink intended more to bolster Joey's own courage than his own (his courage, at that instant, had nearly drained out of his feet), and made ready to leap.

"Hurry up, boys. Don't leave a girl hanging," Ellie piped up from below. Obnoxious.

Franklin rolled his eyes, ignoring the girl's attitude, and with one final huff leapt forward into the air. The minute his feet left the earth, his belly lurched downwards as if it wanted to exit his body down through his lap and plummet into the pit below. For an instant, he felt he was about to drop, but quickly his outstretched hands caught onto the rungs and arrested his fall.

He breathed a great, deep sigh of relief as he clung to the pole, glancing down to ensure his feet had not landed on Ellie's hands. She smiled up at him from below. "Well done," she said. She was not smirking at him this time, but genuinely smiling.

The surface of the rungs and the pole was not steel, as Franklin had thought. Instead, it felt entirely unfamiliar in his hands, a foreign texture he had never before encountered in his life. It was some sort of alloy, to be sure, but it felt strangely like a very fine velvet or fabric. Odd, very odd. Franklin was at once convinced this was some sort of new material the government had invented in secret, designed to protect the craft from all manner of atmospheric harm. Never had he felt something so smooth and soft to the touch but at the same time as sturdy as a rock.

He turned, carefully positioning his feet as he maneuvered around the pole, and faced Joey, stretching his hand out to his friend. Joey nodded in response, took a deep breath and closed his eyes. After a few minutes of encouragements from both Ellie and Franklin, he winced and took a terrific leap into thin air. Franklin snatched the boy's hand and yanked him towards the pole, throwing his free arm around Joey's back and drawing him in. Joey remained motionless for a moment, eyes squeezed tightly shut, and finally began to laugh great breathy laughs of relief from deep within his belly, pleased beyond measure he had survived the leap.

"See, Joey? Not so bad," said Franklin, patting his friend on the back.

"Well, at least the hard part's over. Thanks, Franny," Joey laughed, beginning to descend a few rungs in pursuit of Ellie who had impatiently begun her climb into the pit. Franklin wasn't so sure: the jump seemed trivial to what potentially awaited them below.

Ellie scrambled down the fifty odd feet of rungs in what seemed like an instant, going hand over hand, foot over foot as naturally as any trained circus acrobat does. The boys followed, Joey above Ellie and Franklin above him, as quickly as they could climb. The dirt heaped at the sides of the crater became increasingly dark and then suddenly light in hue as their eye levels descended, the result of their "entering a new layer of strata" as Joey found time to point out.

Finally, the three friends touched down upon solid surface beneath their feet. The pole (it appeared to be a telescopically extending device) stuck up directly out of the red sphere, and the sides of the pit were steep all around them, so the children had no choice but to disembark the pole directly onto the top of the craft (or whatever it was), a notion Franklin feared as he remembered Joey's remark about possible electrification. Ellie was first and stepped out onto crimson, shining metal, walking over its sloping surface a few paces to make space for her companions to descend. They followed in suit and came to rest, standing silently atop the mysterious craft.

The curious began to prowl about, searching for any outstanding features. First she inspected the white lettering, but that was so plain, she lost interest in it quickly. The glass viewing panels were caked with dirt and entirely impossible to see through, so she quickly abandoned those as well. It was when she moved behind the colossal red fin that tapered up off the spherical ship that she cried out, "I've found something!"

Joey and Franklin, who had been methodically scratching at the metal and poking at the glass to determine what exactly they were, much like a pair of infants might do, came hurriedly to her side. There, below the fin, was a sort of circular hatch. There was, however, no dog wheel upon the hatch like one might find in a submarine, and no visible way of prying the thing open - which Ellie had been exerting herself trying to do.

"Look," said Joey, pointing at a small, metal box attached to the sphere just next to the hatch. He knelt down and opened it, though his hands trembled as he did so. Inside the box was a black slate of glass, the outline of what looked like a human palm etched into it.

"It looks like your supposed to put your hand onto it," said Ellie. "It's got outlines for all five fingers, so maybe this is a human craft after all."

"Nobody ever said that aliens don't have five fingers," pointed out Joey, wiggling his own digits.

Ellie shrugged, reached forward, and laid her hand flat across the smooth, black surface. Nothing happened. Joey mimicked her only to produce the same, disappointing reaction. They shrugged 'worth a try'.

As his two friends scurried about to inspect other areas on top of the sphere, Franklin remained, staring blankly down at the hatch. His mind wandered, inventing both horrors and wonders that could exist within the ship. Absentmindedly, he stretched out his arm and touched the tips of his fingers against the black glass of the palm print scanner. The instant his fingers brushed the smooth surface, the scanner lit up, blinking on and off with a greenish glow.

Franklin, alarmed, glanced sidelong to see if either of his friends had noticed the reaction; they were still quite distracted. Gulping, unsure of why the device had responded to his touch,

Franklin stretched out his fingers and laid his entire palm across the glass, ensuring his hand fell into boundaries of the outline. The scanner emitted a low hum for a moment and then beeped. It lit up a solid, persistent green. Suddenly, the hatch hissed like a freshly opened soda can and slid open, startling Franklin so much that he fell back on his haunches. Ellie and Joey heard the noise and dashed back to find Franklin, his mouth hanging agape, staring at the open portal.

"How did you do that?" demanded Ellie.

"I- I just put my hand down on the scanner like you two did! I didn't think anything would actually happen," he managed to stammer.

"Huh. Maybe we weren't pressing hard enough. That or it's malfunctioning from the crash," conjectured Joey. He helped Franklin to his feet and the two moved to join Ellie who was already peering down into the open hatch. Below, all was darkness, but the scent that wafted up from within the vessel reminded Franklin of a dentist's office. Beneath the rim of the hatch was a rung, the top of yet another ladder that ushered them deeper still.

"Shall we?" asked Ellie rhetorically, disappearing down into the dark portal quick as a wink. Franklin and Joey exchanged the same, baffled look they had been sharing all the day long and followed her into the blackness.

They climbed for a moment only and dropped quickly onto a metal floor, their footfalls echoing like gongs through the dark interior of the ship. Franklin could hardly see an inch in front of his face and stumbled in the blackness, casting his arms out in front of him to steady his balance. Suddenly, the hatch above them hissed again and slammed shut, choking out all the light that remained in the chamber and shrouding the children in an absolute darkness. The sickening sound of a bolt sliding into place and presumably locking the hatch echoed above them. Franklin felt as if he was going to puke.

"Oh dear. Oh dear. Oh hell. Now we've done it," whispered Franklin, afraid to awaken whatever horrors lurked within the blackness. "We told you, Ellie. We told you this was dangerous. Now look! It's locked and we're trapped down here! No one goes into Cankerwood- **no one!** We'll starve and **die** before anyone finds this damn thing, let alone goes crazy enough to drop into this crater like we did. And who knows if they'll get lucky enough that the damn thing opens up for them? Good God! We're done for! Good God, we've really done it. Joey and I have been in tight spots before, but nothing as bad as this! Locked in a spaceship buried in a hole in the middle of a dead forest? Oh hell. Ellie! We're doomed!" Franklin had begun to babble, his panicked voice faceless in the pitch dark.

"Easy, Franklin. We've only just gone down the rabbit hole, we're not doomed- yet," said Ellie, voice steady and calm. "I don't suppose anyone remembered to take a flashlight out of the bag?" she asked sheepishly. The flashlights were, of course, safely tucked away in the bag back up on the surface; they had so responsibly remembered to pack them the night before and then all but forgot them as they descended into the massive crater. Faced with a possibly **permanent** pitch dark, Franklin felt the puke becoming a very real possibility.

They stumbled about, searching for anything they could possibly recognize. All of the forms that loomed up at them in the darkness were unfamiliar and bizarre. After what seemed like minutes of groping about in the pitch black, a general idea formed in Franklin's head as to the geography of the cockpit: it was circular, as he had expected given the spherical shape of the craft, and the interior seemed to be situated around a central column of some kind, the same one they had climbed down when they descended into the ship.

At one end of the room there was an elevated dais Franklin had blundered into several times, but the dark shapes that sat on top of it seemed intimidating and he was wary to tread too close to them. Beyond them, Franklin could make out what he assumed to be a sort of windshield, but black soil was heaped so thickly against it that not even the faintest pinprick of light had found its way through.

As he muddled about, Franklin could do nothing but think

of his poor parents returning home to an empty house and a half starved Monty. They'd search for him for weeks, he was sure, till some ambitious hiker would discover the pit and the police, or maybe the FBI, would drag the boy's bones all the way down Sachem's Head and into Pendel Circle for his poor mother to see. He supposed she'd cry quite a lot to imagine the boy, her only son, slowly losing his mind in the utter darkness, succumbing to hallucinations and voices. He envisioned her wishing she could have at least tried to rescue him, brought him some food before he succumbed to starvation before death rattled through his helpless body. He resolved, then, to make a pact with Joey: whoever died first would be the first to be eaten, it was only natural.

He chided himself for a moment, disappointed he was already considering cannibalizing his friends, and then gave the notion a second thought as the darkness seemed to close in even tighter around him.

"Franny," Joey whispered from behind him, "we're gonna get out of here, right? I'm due back for supper by six, and my mom will kill me if I miss it again."

"Joey..." Franklin was about to unload all the morbid and dismal thoughts in his head on his friend, but thought better of it and offered up encouraging words instead, words designed to comfort himself as much as Joey, "I'm sure we'll figure something out. It's an advanced something-or-other, isn't it? It's sure to have an emergency lights switch. We've just got to find it before- well..." His voice trailed off.

"Right," Joey agreed, and moved away to continue the search. Joey's voice, optimistic, concise, and without alarm, brought Franklin back to sanity and snapped him out of his chaotic, internal panic. Joey was concerned about missing supper, not dying a slow, painful depth. 'Perspective, Franklin!' he thought to himself. He drew in a deep breath like his mother did when she performed her morning yoga. Gritting his teeth, he returned to the search for any means of escape. The investigation brought him several times around the circular chamber, but each rotation yielded the same, disappointing results: strange, dark shapes that seemed to have emerged from some twisted Star Trek convention.

"This-" muttered Ellie and then paused, "-this isn't looking so good, boys. I can't find anything; it's just too dark. What if there isn't a way to restore the power-"

Suddenly a disembodied voice seemed to buzz over some unseen intercom, interrupting the girl, though the voice sounded more like the speech synthesizer on Mr. Freeman's laptop than a human one. "Request confirmed, it announced. "Auxiliary power activated." Whatever the voice was, Franklin assumed it had heard Ellie say the word 'power' and responded accordingly.

The children shielded their sensitive, inflated pupils as a brilliant flash of white drove away the darkness in the chamber and the lights flickered to life. Looking into the brightness pained his adjusting eyes. Still, Franklin couldn't resist peeking through his hands. The chamber was, indeed, in the shape of a great sphere, and laden with all manner of complex looking technology in whichever direction one happened to glance. The entire place was clearly a cockpit of some kind. There several steering mechanisms and apparatuses, along with a number of seats in front of them, arrayed before a great pane of glass that was curved like the outside of the ship, overlooking nothing but a whole lot of piled up dirt.

Set in the central column they had climbed down was an arching, silver door with no knob or handle. At the opposite end of the cockpit were a series of large, complicated pieces of equipment with wires streaming out of them in every direction; these were surely the ominous shapes they had seen in the darkness. Franklin could make neither heads nor tails of what any of the several devices surrounding them were for.

"Thank God," breathed Ellie.

"Got a little frightened there for a second, didn't ya, Ellie?" teased Joey.

"I'm just glad that computer voice heard you," said Franklin. He was relieved and about to let his shoulders relax-till he laid eyes on something that made the vomit he had been feeling at the base of his throat for so long nearly shoot up like a rocket. There, at the opposite end of the chamber, crumpled on the floor next to the pilot seat, was a slumped over body.

CHAPTER EIGHT

THE STALO

"**I**s it a robot?" a voice echoed far away, as if spoken through a tunnel.

"Could be," said another. "It certainly looks like one."

"Could be somebody in a space suit. Can't very well see his face with that big helmet on, though. Maybe we ought to pry it off."

"Don't touch it."

"You think this is was what spoke before, when the power came on?"

"Doubt it. That voice seemed to come over a speaker above us. At least that's the way it sounded. And he doesn't' look like he can do very much talking right now. He looks dead, whatever he is."

"Should I touch it?" A girl's voice this time.

Images began to drift above Hess's groggy eyes, though they were only blurry figures that bobbed in a hazy, dreamlike way

"No. Don't touch it. For God's sake, Ellie."

"I'm just gonna' tap it with my foot."

"Don't, Ellie!" the protestor cried out.

"I'm gonna'. Just hush, Franklin."

"Franny's right. It could be electrified."

"What is it with you and everything being electrified?" quipped the girl's voice.

"Better safe than burnt toast."

"Joseph's right, Ellie. I'd rather you didn't end up burnt toast," pleaded the worried boy's voice.

"Chickens. Watch."

Something nudged the torso of the HESS Suit. Hess. That is what he had been called. Yes, he had asked Mozi to call him 'Hess' not an hour ago. Or was it two hours? Three? A day? How long had he been out? His head felt so faint, so foggy, that he could barely gather enough focus to fully open his eyes, much less piece together a cohesive account of what was going on.

"Didn't move. Must be dead," mumbled the girl.

No. Not dead. Not dead. Hess wanted to scream it. One of the shapes that loomed above him stooped down closer to his limp body. Perhaps these were some sort of gremlins intent on devouring him, or worse, melting his suit into scrap metal with him inside. In a feeble attempt to drive the pest away, Hess clumsily swatted at the figure, which leapt back in panic.

"It moved! It tried to touch me!" the girl's voice screeched.

"See! It isn't dead. We told you to be careful!"

Hess groaned. Doing his best to shrug aside the bleariness, he fully opened his eyes. The heads-up display plastered across his visor was fraught with activity: several alerts indicating the Noah's system failure and Mozi's emergency shutdown, bright red circles that hovered over the three blurry figures identifying them not as gremlins but as humans, and, of course, the year indicator that read 2012 AD. So the Noah had made it out of the time stream successfully. Of course, not into the correct year, but he'd deal with that later. What had caused all the trouble? That's right, he thought to himself, the mysterious silver figure that had chased the Noah and nearly destroyed it. He coughed; it felt like he hadn't taken a good, deep breath in ages.

"It made a noise!" Franklin yelped.

"Not a robot noise, either. There's somebody in there. Or something," proclaimed Joey, backing away from the metal body. But Ellie remained firm above Hess, hovering nervously over him, half in concern and half in a tense readiness to attack.

"Can you hear me?" she asked gently.

Hess's vision was beginning to clear; these 'gremlins' were no more than young teenagers, at least his own age. What did these kids want? How had they gotten aboard the Noah? Mozi was only supposed to admit him and Dr. Burke, not random strangers from nearly a millennium ago. He groaned again as he realized the system must have malfunctioned quite badly to be making such mistakes.

"Is that a yes?" inquired Ellie. Never afraid.

"Yes, yes. I can hear you," Hess said weakly. He did his best to prop himself up on one armored elbow but failed miserably and crumbled back onto the floor. Ellie knelt beside him.

"It talked, it talked!" squealed Joey and Franklin, receding even further away from Hess's limp form.

"And in English, too. So you speak our language, Mr. Roboto! Does that mean you're from earth?" Ellie asked.

"For heaven's sake! Yes, I'm from earth," replied Hess weakly. "And I'm not a robot, this is just a survival suit. Now what the hell are you kids doing on my ship?" He tried again to sit up bat Ellie shoved him back down.

"Wait just a minute. You don't sound like any human. You sound like Darth Vader or something," she crabbed sternly.

"It's my suit's breathing mechanism! It distorts my voice! Hands off!" bellowed Hess, swatting Ellie's arms aside as he sat up.

"So what, is this a failed NASA experiment or something? What are you, FBI? CIA? NSA? Air force?" demanded Franklin, approaching Hess and Ellie with Joey following cautiously in tow.

Hess had no idea what any of these strange acronyms stood for. "Listen. I'm only gonna' ask one more time: what the hell are you kids doing aboard my ship? What do you want?"

"Listen, mister," Ellie growled, "You're the one who crashed into our neighborhood. We just came up to investigate. You're the one who's got some explaining to do."

"You mean to say I crashed here?" asked Hess.

"So far as we can tell," piped up Joey. "We saw something fall from the sky last night and, when we came to take a look this morning, we found your ship buried in a deep hole in the middle of the woods."

"In the woods?" echoed Hess.

"That's right," the children nodded in unison.

"So no one else knows I'm here? No one has seen the ship but you three?"

"We think so," muttered Franklin. "We hope so, anyway. We think we're the only ones who spotted the ship when it crashed."

"Good," Hess sighed in relief. The words of Dr. Burke echoed in his head, warning him to have as little unnecessary influence on the past as possible. "Let's keep it that way. It's time for you kids to get off my ship. Just forget this ever happened." Hess began to stand but Ellie moved to stop him.

"We're not going anywhere and neither are you," she snarled in her most intimidating fashion. "Not till you've explained what it is that's going on here."

"Listen, kid," he snapped at her, "This suit's got enough firepower built into its wrist to vaporize an elephant." Hess indicated what looked like a miniature cannon built into the armor, attached just above his hand. "Don't get on my bad side," he warned. "I haven't got any explaining to do, especially to the likes of you kids. Move aside."

Ellie raised her arms indignantly and allowed Hess to stand. Franklin, though the threat had given him quite a scare, couldn't help but smirk a little to himself; someone had finally managed to intimidate the dauntless Ellie Mars.

Hess steadied himself, still reeling from the aftermath of the electric shocks, and looked upon his cockpit. It was in a state of absolute disarray; important pieces of equipment strewn across the floor and others singed and fried beyond repair. "How did you kids get the power on?" he asked.

"By voice command, I guess," replied Joey. "Ellie-that's her-" he pointed to the girl, "-accidentally activated it."

"That means at least something's still working on this thing. Mozi, you there?" called Hess into the open air.

"Mozi Bot operating system offline. Basic functions active. Input command," answered the same disembodied robotic voice that had activated the lights only moments before.

"Who's this Mozi? There's another one of you in here?" asked Franklin, thinking perhaps Mozi would be the 'good cop' of the pair and perhaps treat the children a bit more gently.

"Hush," shot Hess. "Reset system functions. Access code zero twelve," he ordered, squeezing his eyes tightly shut behind the visor and crossing his armored fingers behind his back where the children could not see. He wasn't sure if the Noah would still work at all after the damage it had taken during the chase and subsequent crash.

The lights flickered and then went off; all was silent for a moment. Franklin cursed quietly; they were back to the pitch black again. Suddenly, a great rumbling from deep within the ship sounded out, followed by a series of high-pitched whines that reminded Joey of the sounds harbor porpoises make to communicate. As if they had never been gone, the lights returned in full but this time joined by the mechanical cacophony of all the other gadgets and gizmos aboard the ship powering to life as well. This bleeped and that blooped, this hummed and that buzzed; everything was whirring busily.

"Mozi, you there?" demanded Hess into the air.

"Affirmative, Mr. Hess. Mozi Bot Operating System fully operational," buzzed the friendly computerized voice.

"Thank God," whispered Hess. "Full systems report, please." He walked to the pilot's seat and began pushing buttons, glancing up occasionally at the monitor as Mozi spoke.

"Though the exterior of the Noah endured several carbon scars during the assault and then various dents upon impact, the craft is fully functional in all mechanical regards. The weapons system has suffered a complete system failure and internal nano-repairs will take several hours to remedy the problem. Weapons system aside, we are completely operational."

Had the bodiless computer voice said 'assault'? Franklin began to twiddle his thumbs worriedly.

"Life support systems seem to have been survived the affair intact and all basic and auxiliary functions respond to the mainframe in the positive. Though some of the onboard equipment is no longer useable, the backup functions implemented in the mainframe of the ship can replicate their operations successfully," Mozi chirped cheerfully along.

"And what about the Shard? Was the Shard damaged in the crash?" demanded Hess. A sudden panic had come into his voice. Without the Shard, the Noah wouldn't be able to do the one thing it was supposed to: travel through time.

"According to my calculations, the Shard is intact and unharmed, Mr. Hess. There is no need for alarm," the AI reassured him.

"Good, then it sounds like we're all set," exclaimed Hess, quite relieved.

"I noticed we have guests, or perhaps intruders," observed Mozi. "You have not identified them as hostiles. Please display a visual cue if you are secretly being held hostage and I have spoken on, unawares. Please scratch your wrist if you are their prisoner."

"We can hear you, you know," huffed Ellie.

"Preparing to incinerate hostiles," buzzed Mozi cheerfully. The children panicked and dove for cover.

Hess chuckled. "No, Mozi, they're not hostiles. In fact, they were just leaving. Would you show them the door, please?"

"Of course, Mr. Hess," said Mozi. Nothing happened and Mozi spoke again. "Mr. Hess, the main entry hatch is blocked with several tons of dirt. It seems to me our guests climbed down to the ship via the emergency beacon."

Joey looked at Franklin and winked; they had been right about the pole's function all along. It was indeed an emergency signal, just as they had thought.

"Courtesy dictates we at least, as one colloquially puts it, 'give them a lift' to the surface of our impact crater so they do not have to make the climb again," said Mozi. "It is only polite, after all, considering they did not kill you while you slept, consume you for nourishment, or steal any of my equipment."

Hess grumbled and then nodded begrudgingly. "Yes, alright," he relented. "I'm going to bring the ship up out of the hole and drop you kids off on the surface. As thanks for-" he paused and sighed, "-checking up on us."

"That's it?" exclaimed Ellie, putting her face in between Hess's helmet and the controls, restricting his view. "You're just going to drop us like a bag of rocks? No explanation? No introduction? Not even a souvenir? And what on earth is this ship for? Have you come from some sort space mission with all that robotic gear on? What's that 'shard' thing you were so worried about a minute ago? And who is this Mozi you keep talking to, your secretary or something?"

"I am Mozi Bot Operating System Type-" began Mozi.

"Shut up, Mozi," Hess barked. "Are you all this belligerent or is it just her?" he asked, turning to Franklin and Joey. They couldn't help but laugh, much to Ellie's dismay.

"No sir, just her, really," admitted Franklin.

"Don't call him 'sir', Franklin!" cried Ellie. "Why, as tall as he is, he couldn't be much older than you or me! That or he's some sort of midget astronaut."

"Don't be ridiculous, Ellie," chided Joey.

"Actually, she's not far off. What are you kids, thirteen? Fourteen?" asked Hess.

"Something like that," admitted the girl ruefully, shooting her still giggling companions a disapproving look.

"Yes, well, you could say I'm something like that as well," said Hess. He had been confined to Burke's lab while he was there and these were the first people his own age he had ever met (at least that he could remember meeting); he couldn't resist sharing his secret youthfulness with them, even though he'd likely never see them again.

"You mean to say you're a… A kid? Like us? For real?" stammered Franklin.

"As I said: something like that."

The children stared as Hess continued to push buttons and pull levers, mouths agape. Who on **earth** was this mysterious, masked boy and what had he come for?

"Are you surprised I'm so young?" Hess asked? He couldn't resist.

Ellie's vigor returned. "It's time for you to get explaining now, **kid**," she commanded. "You can't just keep us in the dark like this!"

"Actually, I can," he replied. "Mozi, take us up to the surface."

"Affirmative, activating vertical liftoff thrusters," answered the computer's voice.

"Wait, I'm serious! Why is a kid flying a spaceship?" began Ellie, but the Noah gave a sickening lurch and leapt into the air, throwing them all to the ground, save Hess who clung to the control panel. The ship seemed to shake herself free of the dirt she was buried beneath, like a dog excitedly drying off. She began to hover slowly into the air up through the hole. Though the ascent was slow; the Noah felt unlike any plane Franklin had ever been inside of; she rose the way a he figured a bumblebee might, in quivering spirals.

"Seems to be flying smoothly," muttered Hess. "Now to just get it up out of this crater." Handling the steering yoke with the delicacy of a mother to her child, he carefully guided the craft to the lip of the hole and set her down, the spherical form of the vessel coming to rest perfectly balanced on Sachem's Head Peak. Franklin watched, entranced; he had always been fascinated with pilots and aircrafts, and this ship was unlike anything he had ever laid eyes on before, even in the movies. It made his model airplanes back home look like a two-year old had made them.

"Open main docking portal, Mozi" ordered Hess.

A large section of the curved wall to the children's right emitted a hiss and creaked open. A gangplank extended out of the newly opened portal and came to rest on the soil below. As the ship's drawbridge lowered, the dim light of Cankerwood streamed into the cockpit and tickled their faces. Franklin breathed in the forest air with a huge, grateful gasp. He had never been more relieved to see gloomy old Cankerwood in his life.

"Alright, kids," exclaimed Hess, "out the hatch and down the stairs. By my calculations it's June of 2012 AD! Shouldn't you be out enjoying your summer? Come on now, out you go."

Franklin and Joey eagerly complied and moved towards the exit, relieved at the prospect of being out of harm's way, but Ellie stood at the center of the cockpit, her feet stubbornly planted.

"So that's it? You just crash-land in the woods. And when somebody finally finds you, climbs into a dark hole, turns your lights on, and wakes you up, all you can think to do is kick them off your spaceship? Just like that? With not so much as an explanation? How ungrateful!"

"I'm sorry, I really am," replied the armored boy." If I could explain all this to you, I would. But I can't for reasons I'm not really allowed to say." He waved his little wrist canon around impatiently and gave it a metallic tap with his fingers.

Ellie rolled her eyes, gave the ship one last look, and went to join Franklin and Joey at the exit. Hess followed close behind making sure she didn't make a surprise maneuver and hijack the Noah.

It seemed that hours had passed since the children last looked upon the sun as it had rounded most of its arch about the earth and was preparing for its final descent behind the horizon, gilded with an amber light.

The four descended the metal gangplank, gazes intent on Hess, who ushered them down. "I suppose you'll never see me again," he said. "So I might as well tell you- this isn't really a space ship, so to speak."

Franklin and Joey's eyes lit up. Surely the craft was one designed for travelling through space; it looked just like something you'd find in a science fiction story.

"Then what in the world is it?" yelled Ellie, climbing back up the stairs rapidly and standing on her tiptoes to meet Hess at eye level (though in his case it was really visor level.)

Before Hess could answer the girl, Joey caught his breath and tapped Franklin on the shoulder. "Look, Franny," he whispered. Franklin, along with the others, turned to see what had startled Joey so.

There, across the clearing, standing at the tree line and shrouded with twilit shadows of Cankerwood, was a menacing figure. It stood at least fifteen or twenty feet tall, towering above the children, its head nearly touching branches above. A bipedal, with two arms and two legs, it had a figure like that of a man, but at the same time horrifically different. Its skin was silver and grey, a motionless automaton, like a statue made out of steel. And its body was entirely featureless, save a strange symbol etched into the center of its otherwise blank head. The symbol resembled a many-pointed star and glowed a deep, intimidating red.

Its arms and legs, which were unnaturally long compared to the rest of its figure, tapered down into blob like hands and feet with no fingers or toes to speak of. With the sinking sun behind it, the figure cast a queer shadow; a shadow so long that it reached all the way across the clearing and licked at the children's feet.

It stood silently, as if it were a statue and had stood rooted to that very spot since the beginning of time. But its glare, which wasn't really a glare at all considering it had no eyes to speak of, was locked on the Noah and the children with a sense of menace, a sense of glowering, smoldering danger that plagued Franklin to his very core and sent icy chills and trepidations running up and down his spine. None of the children dared to speak or even dared to breathe; they were afraid of breaking the oppressive silence, a silence full of terror that seemed to strangle the clearing.

Hess was frozen, paralyzed by what the figure he saw glowering before him. This was the same being that had attacked the Noah in the time stream, the same monster that had nearly electrocuted him to death and burned his vessel to a crisp. But now it stood silently, stationary and brooding. How had it found them? How had it managed to follow them out of the time stream?

"What the hell is that?" shouted Ellie, undeterred by the figure's icy presence.

As if awakened from a deep and nightmarish slumber by the girl's noise, the silver giant slowly raised its tentacle-like arms till they pointed directly at the companions. The limbs sparked, like live wires exposed to water, and began to crackle nosily, glowing red. Hess recognized the hue, a deadly crimson color he had seen once before in the form of lightning bolts blasting out of the apocalyptic cloud in the future.

In a hollow, metallic voice that sounded like an ancient, rusted, iron door scraping slowly across a stone floor, the figure screeched:

"STALO"

Hess broke free of the figure's deadly, invisible grasp. In one swift, calculated motion honed by months of Burke's training, he raised his right arm and fired, the children ducking in alarm at the *bang* the miniature cannon emitted. A little rocket fluttered quickly out of the armor's wrist and blasted across the clearing, reminding Franklin of some of the smaller fireworks he and Joey would often light on the Fourth of July in Pendel Circle. The projectile bounced off the creature's chest and dropped to the ground like a tennis ball that had seen too many days with a disappointing *clink*. The silver giant didn't even flinch.

"Some firepower," Ellie quipped under he breath.

"Back onto the ship," Hess yelped. No one moved. "Now!"

he roared as loud as his young lungs could manage. He seized Franklin and Joey by the backs of their shirt collars and, screaming for Ellie to follow, dragged their paralyzed forms back up the gangway and into the ship. Ellie, who sensed the chilling fear in Hess's voice, scrambled up after them. The crackling sound of lightning grew louder behind them.

"Mozi, close the main hatch and seal it tight! For God's sakes, activate emergency protocols," cried Hess, darting to the control panel and leaving the children to flail wildly in confusion.

"Affirmative, Mr. Hess. What is the nature of the emergency," asked Mozi calmly as the gangway sealed shut with another hiss of air, obscuring the ominous and foreboding view of the metallic giant towering in the afternoon shadows of Cankerwood.

"It's that thing-**again!** It's found us! I have no idea how. Just get us in the air," answered Hess, who sounded like he had begun to hyperventilate, even behind his survival helmet.

"But sir, our guests-" began Mozi.

"Just do it!" exclaimed Hess desperately.

Mozi's alarm began to wail, but Ellie shouted over the racket, "You said 'that thing again'! You mean you've seen this monster-looking-thing before?"

Hess ignored the girl and began to yank on the yoke in agitation. The Noah barreled to the right and to the left, as if she were rolling across the ground like a ball, and then shot into the air with a tremendous rumble.

The children, who were already sprawled on the floor in confusion, slid across the cockpit like loose baggage in an overhead compartment.

"Sorry!" yelled Hess over his shoulder. "There are some seats here behind me. Come and strap yourselves in. Quick!"

The children did as they were bade and crawled across the shifting cockpit to buckle themselves into the seats at Hess's rear. As he stumbled forward in a foggy haze of confusion, Franklin could barely comprehend what was happening to him and his friends. Images of the frightfully still and ominous silver colossus were ingrained in his mind, and he could not shake the feeling that whatever it was, it meant them serious ill.

Hadn't he and Joey been fishing only the day before? Eating dinner with the Mars family? Hiking to the peak only that very morning? Panic seized the poor boy's innards and he began to feel quite sick again as he looked out the little portholes that studded the walls of the ship and beheld Cankerwood splayed out below him like a map; there was Pendel Circle, peculiar and quaint, and there were the marshes, and there his own little home with the ugly yellow garage doors. But all the familiar sights were rapidly shrinking as the craft vaulted into the clouds. If Franklin had experienced such a view under less tumultuous circumstances, he imagined he'd have quite enjoyed seeing his home from so high up; but all he felt now was the sickening feeling he wouldn't ever lay eyes upon the little seaside town again. Dreadful.

"Why are we flying? Why are we flying? Why are we flying?" Joey repeated again and again to the back of Hess's helmet. Ellie gave him a sharp nudge in the ribs, gesturing for the panicking boy to be silent.

"We're on the run, Joey. So far as I can tell, anyway," she whispered.

"From what? From that thing?" stammered Joey.

"Yes. What'd it say? I think it said Stalo," recalled Ellie, shuddering at the thought of its awful, screeching voice.

"We're on the run from the Stalo," said Franklin grimly, eyes glued to Hess, praying the mysterious stranger knew what was he doing.

"Mozi, is it following?" called Hess, focus fixated on his controls.

"I'm afraid it is, Mr. Hess." The monitor came to life. There, in the brilliantly orange sky above Cankerwood, was the Stalo, posed like Christ on the cross, gliding along behind the Noah. It weaved in and out of the sun-speckled clouds as easily as any bird might.

"It can fly, too?" groaned Franklin.

"Damn," cursed Hess under its breath. "It's too fast. We'll

never lose it at this rate. Mozi, can we increase thruster output?"

"Thrusters at maximum, I'm sorry to report. If we increase our velocity anymore, the thruster core could explode!" Even the AI was beginning to sound worried.

"Damn. Damn damn damn. What are we going to do? What **can** we do?" Hess cried out.

"Can't you outfly it?" suggested Franklin rather halfheartedly. "Maybe you could do some maneuvers or something and shake it. Lose it in the clouds, you know?" He felt completely at a loss, like a helpless worm on a hook; there was simply nothing to be done but to wait and pray the fish wasn't hungry.

"Not at the rate he's going," exclaimed Hess, tapping the image of the Stalo on the monitor.

"Are you kidding me? At the rate **we're** going, we'll be in Canada before the sun sets!" declared Ellie. "This Noah of yours can fly a helluva lot faster than any airplane, it seems to me! I've never seen a ship like it before! Besides, even if that thing does catch up to us, what could it possibly do? The Noah's ten times its size, at least."

"You don't understand," muttered Hess grimly. "That creature, the Stalo Monster; it's what caused me to crash land here in the first place. It attacked the ship! It's got powers like nothing I've ever seen. It can bend electricity to its will; it fired some sort of crimson lightning at us and completely shorted out all of the Noah's systems. And it's trying to again; didn't you see the red glow?"

A giant silver robot that fires lightning bolts out of its hands and can fly, thought Franklin. What had they gotten themselves into?

"It'll destroy us," said Joey plainly.

"It seems that way," agreed Hess. "Unless... There is another way."

"Negative, Mr. Hess," boomed Mozi very seriously. "Dr. Burke explicitly stated that the course of action you are currently considering was the only one you **absolutely** could

not follow. I cannot allow such a plan. It contradicts several of our prime directives!"

"What other choice have I got? If we slow down and try to land, the Stalo will catch up and vaporize us before these kids can even disembark. And we can't very well drop them out of the hatch midflight! They'd be killed by the fall," Hess protested.

"No. You can do the first bit: land and let us off," said Franklin, smiling weakly. "I'm sure it won't catch up. Besides, what's this alternative you're talking about?" He wasn't sure he wanted to hear the answer.

Hess didn't respond. He was sweating profusely beneath his helmet. Eject the three children in midair? No, far too cruel. Attempt a landing? They'd have to drop their speed far too much; they'd be caught in no time and fried by lightning. Try and lose the Stalo? Didn't even seem possible considering how rapidly the creature was gaining. There was only one option left... But Dr. Burke had cautioned strongly against it.

Below them, trees, lakes, shorelines, cow pastures, cities, and all manner of landscapes sped by faster than any of them could comprehend. The state of Connecticut that Franklin and Joey had lived in for so long was rapidly reduced to a dizzying blur, if they were even in Connecticut anymore (Ellie reckoned they might have reached her Maine by that point).

The Stalo, whose silhouette was plastered against the orange-pink sky, had loomed ever larger behind the Noah. It raised its head and stretched its arms out in front of its body like Superman. Again, its limbs began to crackle and glow red.

"The weapons system, Mozi! Is it repaired yet?" demanded the panicked boy.

"Negative, Mr. Hess"

"Then we've got no other choice,"

"Negative, Mr. Hess. I cannot support this decision."

"That's why Burke sent me; I can make the decisions that you can't."

"Even if you **do** follow through with this ridiculous course of action, the Shard needs time to recalibrate the destination information," argued Mozi. "Launching so suddenly could cause a dangerously unpredictable direction of travel. There really is no telling where we could end up, so to speak."

"Then dangerously unpredictable it is." Hess hung his head, sighed, and turned to face the children. "Remember how I said this wasn't a spaceship?"

They gulped and nodded.

"Well, the Noah is really more of a time machine," he said grimly, and then cried out, "Forgive me! I never meant for any of you to get mixed up in this." He pulled a lever and the Noah leapt away from 2012 AD and into the shimmering blue fog of time travel, leaving the cantankerous Stalo, and everything the children had ever known, far behind in the dim shadows of Cankerwood.

'A time machine?' thought Franklin. 'Time travel?'

'Who's going to feed the cat?'

CHAPTER NINE

THE LEGACY OF DOCTOR BURKE

"**W**hat's going on?" inquired Joey meekly. It sounded as if he wasn't sure he really wanted to hear the answer. All around them instruments buzzed and whirred, humming with activity. The skies of Connecticut had vanished as if they had never been there at all, replaced instead by a strange azure mist that whirled and glowed outside of the glass viewing panels.

"We're travelling through time," replied Hess bluntly.

"No. You don't understand. I've got a curfew. I- I can't up and leave home like this. My mom will have supper on the table! You've got to take us back!" exclaimed Joey, his eyes beginning to water.

"I can't," mumbled Hess, hanging his head. "I'm sorry."

Ellie was silent. She hadn't yet bothered to begin worrying and instead stared wide-eyed at the portholes, entranced with the brilliant blue light that swam and shimmered outside the vessel. But Franklin merely hung his head, eyes comatose and blank. Franklin Freeman knew **exactly** what was 'going on' and could not face the truth of it. Surely this was another bizarre dream like the one he had wandered into the night before. Surely. He could only hope against all hopes that it was, so he prayed:

'God, let it be a dream.
I'll never fail a math test again.
I'll do community service till my hands bleed.
I'll even become a monk and live alone on an island
Celibate.
Even though I've only just hit puberty.
That's how serious I am.
Just let it be a dream.
Please...'

Of course, Franklin didn't really know to what God or Gods he was praying, as he didn't particularly believe in any one of them any more than the others. Mr. Freeman had raised Franklin without any religion, or perhaps as an 'agnostic' as Mrs. Freeman so often put it (Mrs. Freeman had abandoned her Christian upbringing in the seventies to learn Buddhism and do a great deal of yoga). No, Franklin wasn't quite sure what he believed; but he had prayed as a shot in the dark once in the past, the night before an extremely intimidating algebra test, and emerged with a passing mark, so with no other discernable options, prayer would have to do.

"Temporal status check, Mozi" commanded Hess, trying his very best to ignore the way Joey's voice quavered, to ignore Franklin's whispered pleas.

"Unfortunately, due to the abrupt nature of the launch and lack of prior calculations, our destination, level of progress, and direction of travel are indeterminable at this point in time," admitted Mozi. "We can only hope the Noah retained our destination information from before and is acting upon it. There is no way to verify this, however. At this point, we have quite literally been set adrift in the time stream. When we shall wash ashore I cannot be certain. Let us hope the wormhole does not set us down beneath a dinosaur's foot or in the middle of some medieval siege."

Hess had no choice but to agree with the computer; the year counter display on his visor was blank. Mozi was right, he had no idea where (that is to say, when) they were travelling to. After Ellie had coughed impatiently a few times, he swiveled around in his seat and faced the children.

"Let me begin by saying I'm sorry," he announced. "Before I explain the situation you've just fallen into, what I've accidentally involved you in, I want you to know it was never my intention to bring it upon you and that it was merely chance, bad luck, and circumstance that drew you kids in."

"Oh God," Joey let out a little whimper and hid his face. Ellie reached out and patted the boy on his back, but even her bold eyes had begun to water. Franklin offered no comforting gesture. Not now. He remained stone-faced, his every thought hinging on Hess's next words.

"You might find a lot of this hard to believe - even though it shouldn't be, considering you're seeing it first hand- but just follow along and take my word for it: I'm being as honest as I can," Hess told them, as calmly as he could.

"As honest as you **can**?" echoed Ellie, though her words were choked.

"There are certain things I can't tell you because I don't really know the truth about them myself," admitted Hess. "But what I do tell you, the information I'm going to share with you about where I'm from, this ship, my mission- all of it- you'll have to bring to your graves. It has to stay a secret. You can **never** speak a word of what I'm about to say to anyone so long as you live. If you do make it back, that is."

"What do you mean **'if'**?" Ellie could barely produce the word but forced it out angrily all the same.

"Just let me try and explain first," said Hess, raising his hands as if to ward off an attack from the emotional girl. "Chiefly, we might want to get introductions out of the way. We're going to be stuck together for quite some time, it seems."

"How long is awhile?" asked Joey; again, it sounded as if he wasn't all too keen on the answer.

"I'm not sure yet, kid. What's your name?"

"J-Joey. Joseph Jensen. Sorry I'm freaking out- I just..."

"It's okay Joseph. It's alright. And you?" Hess pointed at Ellie.

"Elaina Mars," she answered gruffly. "You can call me Ms. Mars. Once I've decided I'm not going to **kill** you, we can discuss friendlier terms."

"Fair enough, Ms. Mars." Hess nodded. The girl didn't seem like she was just blowing hot air. Hess was glad for the helmet which masked his face; without it, Ellie might see just how much she actually intimidated the youthful time traveller. "And last but not least?"

Franklin made no move to answer. He simply stared at Hess and folded his arms across his chest. The armored lad cocked his head expectantly.

"This is Franklin Freeman," said Ellie. She was no longer the only one to be giving their new acquaintance such an icy treatment. "And **he** isn't going to let you just shanghai us like this."

"Franklin Freeman," muttered Hess. He paused and looked at the reproachful boy. His face reminded him of something far off, something he couldn't quite place his finger on; perhaps a dream he had once had or a painting he had seen. Maybe it was only his brain being nervous, but Hess felt as if he recognized all the children's faces. Had one of them grown up to be famous, with his or her image plastered all over the history books of 3012 AD? He could not recall, but the thought of abducting a potential celebrity troubled him greatly. "I'll keep that in mind, then," he muttered. "Now, I'll get on to explain-"

"Wait," interrupted Franklin, breaking his stony silence. He pointed at Hess. "You. What do we call you?

"Well-" Hess scratched the back of his helmet. "I suppose you can call me Hess. That's what Mozi calls me, at least. See, it's written here across my armor."

"Don't you have a last name?" asked Ellie.

"Well, that's the tricky part about all of this. You see: I haven't really got a real name to begin with."

"What do you mean you 'haven't got a real name'? What are you, some sort of space clone? Do you have a serial number instead?" demanded Franklin, arching his eyebrows sarcastically.

"Not quite. I'll explain. All in good time."

"You explain **now**," ordered Ellie.

"All in good time please!" Hess implored them. "Just call me Hess for the time being. Now that introductions are out of the way, I'll contin-" Mozi interrupted Hess with what sounded like a forced cough, although quite a strange one coming from a voice synthesizer. Hess sighed. "My apologies. I seem to have forgotten my travelling companion. Would you like to introduce yourself?"

"Affirmative, Mr. Hess!" chirped the computer. "I am Mozi, system administrator and the first mate aboard the Noah Temporal Navigation Vessel. The voice you hear above you is mine, a synthesized replication of human speech patterns. Whenever aboard the Noah, should you need assistance, feel free to call my name; I can hear you from any section of the ship. It is very nice to meet you 'Franklin Freeman', 'Joseph Jensen, and 'Ms. Mars'." Mozi played back recordings of the children introducing themselves.

"Mozi runs the ship, for all intents and purposes," explained Hess. The children mumbled a halfhearted greeting into the open air and turned back to the pilot.

"Alright. You certainly deserve an explanation," he said "You see: I've travelled from the year 3012 AD, exactly one millennium in the future from your time. I'm sure you don't need me to prove it; the technology you see around the cockpit, not to mention the Noah in its entirety, should speak for itself."

"The technology's all fine," interjected Joey, whose appetite for the bizarre had temporarily driven away his tears. "But I've read plenty of science books on this kind of thing and there's one big, gaping hole in what you say. Before you continue to peddle your mumbo jumbo nonsense, and setting aside all the obvious scientific impossibilities of time travel that I won't even make you explain, I'll ask you this: if time travel has been invented in the future, why haven't we been getting visits from other time travelers all this time? Surely, if it were even possible, someone would have gone back to add their name to the Declaration of Independence or save Kennedy or prevent the Holocaust or steal a tyrannosaurus egg or **something** like that. Can you explain that, Mr. Hess?"

At first, the armored boy didn't know how to respond; Joey had pointed out quite a logical fallacy in the concept, but the answer became quickly and depressingly obvious to Hess.

"I'm sorry you have to hear this when you're already so

distressed, I really am, but I suppose you ought to know if we're going to be together," said Hess. He leaned forward in his seat and placed his hands on his armored knees. "In 3012 AD, time travel is invented only **moments** before the entire earth, along with everyone on it, is destroyed. I am the first, last, and only time traveller in the history of mankind. When it comes to time travel, I am its first test subject and at the same time the last person ever to make use of it."

A silence fell over the children as they stared at him in disbelief.

"There've been no other time travellers because I'm the only one, and this is my only trip. Minutes after I left, all the other potential time travellers from the future were killed. The earth was completely eradicated." Hess had not meant to put it so bluntly, but he could conjure up no pleasant way to relate such dismal news.

Franklin's head spun. His hearing seemed to fade away. Joey's quiet sobs echoed like a dull pounding drum in his ears, and his body went numb.

'Let it be a dream
Just this once
Please.'

"The earth…" Ellie whispered.

"Destroyed?" Joey finished for her, his voice choked and miserable. "You mean to say…?"

"I'm afraid so," said Hess. "Complete and total Armageddon."

"But- but how? And why? What on earth do you mean?" Ellie's composure snapped like a twig and she joined Joey in weeping. Though Franklin had only known the girl for a short while, he had never thought he would see her cry. Not Ellie. Then again, he had never expected to be given news of the apocalypse, either.

Hess sighed. What a dismal speech to give. He wished Mozi would pipe up and just do it for him, but the AI would be no more compassionate than he.

"In 3011 AD, scientists began to notice some sort of cosmic mass approaching the earth," he explained. "Most passed it off as a solar storm or some kind of comet; very few saw it for what it actually was. But when it **did** arrive in 3012, it descended upon the planet in great black clouds like nothing you've ever seen. Over the course of a couple days, it obliterated anything and everything. It shot some sort of horrible red lightning, lit humongous fires, and eviscerated life wherever it was. I saw it with my own eyes, vaporizing whatever it came over: trees, people, buildings, mountains, you name it. It quite literally flattened the world into a dessert. It took humanity unawares and massacred us without mercy."

"So it's some sort cosmic thunder storm that destroys the planet?" asked Franklin glumly.

'Just a dream.
Please.
I'll never ask for anything.
Ever Again.'

"Well, that's what Burke thought... at first," answered Hess.

"Burke?"

"That brings me to the next part of the story," he continued. "I came to your time on someone's else's behalf. I've come to represent Dr. Hodel Burke."

"Never heard of him," murmured Ellie.

"Of course not!" cried Hess. "He won't be born till nearly a thousand years after you all die. But everyone in 3012 knows of him. He's really quite famous, you know. At least in his earlier years he was; towards the end people saw him as an eccentric lunatic."

"So he's a doctor?" asked Joey, sniffling.

"Yes. A brilliant scientist. He invents all kinds of useful things in the late 90's."

"The 90's?" echoed Franklin, confused.

"Excuse me," chuckled the armored boy. "The 2990's. If only you could see some of his inventions: robots he created, of all shapes and sizes, and computers ten thousand times smarter than man, toothpaste you can eat- though I shouldn't say too much. He even invented Mozi here. Mozi's been his assistant, secretary, and essentially his wife for several years. Isn't that right, Mozi?"

The AI buzzed, annoyed. "Though I have assisted in several of Dr. Burke's engineering and academic pursuits, I have shared no romantic words or relationships with him."

Hess chuckled. The children did not. So he continued. "But Burke was a real... How might someone from your time put it? Ah yes. He was a real renaissance man, a jack-of-all-trades, if you will. If you can think of an academic discipline, he tried his hand at it at least once. Even the disciplines that haven't been invented yet, in your time anyway. Physics, biology, archaeology: everything really. Lord, how many **books** he must have read. He lost several wives to his career; it seemed to have a habit of gobbling up marriages. But his favorite thing to do, above his wives, above even his many pursuits, was a simple hobby, really. Dr. Burke liked to sit out on the grass and look at the stars. I can't say much about space travel in 3012 AD as I don't know a great deal about it myself, but it's not as advanced as you might think. Certainly no contact with extraterrestrial life or anything, I can assure you of that. But Dr. Burke was disappointed in mankind."

Hess fiddled anxiously with the controls as he spoke. "He figured by such a late date, the stars should have been at earth's doorstep. It's because mankind was too enamored with itself, at least that's what he always told me. Too enamored with its creeds and causes, and too busy squabbling over petty trifles to look past the atmosphere and into the heavens, like he often did. He insisted mankind 'just had to get **over** itself and unite'. Easier said than done, I suppose. So Burke took it upon himself to keep his eyes skyward. He studied the universe meticulously, even taking several trips to the moon to get a 'closer look' as he put it, and observed every supernova, every new galaxy, every black hole he possibly could. It was while he was canvassing the cosmos that he first noticed the phenomenon I mentioned earlier: the cosmic storm. When he spotted it, it was about three years away from earth. He wasn't worried initially, but kept a close eye on the thing. And over the course of the year, Burke realized the phenomenon was full of a dangerous energy, one he reckoned could obliterate the planet. As it drew nearer and nearer, he decided to present his findings to the scientific community so that the rest of the world might become aware of the impending apocalypse. But they dismissed his findings as harmless. And then there's the church. I can't tell you too much, but I can share with you this: the churches and religions of the world become a lot more powerful than they've ever been before in the future. They marked Burke as insane, casting him from his position as a reputable intellectual into that of an obscure pseudo scientist operating on the fringe. A lunatic."

"Which churches?" wondered Ellie aloud, but Hess ignored her.

"Burke shrugged off the harsh words of the human race, the same race he was so desperately trying to save, and continued on tirelessly. He launched special interstellar probes of his own design to investigate the mysterious mass. Only a few returned, the rest were destroyed. But the ones that made it back brought news he never expected. The storm was immensely powerful, more powerful than even he had expected. In fact, he realized, there was no technology man possessed, or would possess for some time, that could neutralize or divert the threat in any way. But he would not be deterred; Burke always found a way. He discovered more than just the storm's power level, however. The probes had picked up, inside of the cloud, a sort of electromagnetic pulse. The more the doctor examined the pulse, the more he realized it reminded him of something: a brainwave. And as he investigated further, he concluded that's exactly what it was: a thought pattern of some kind. He couldn't be sure if it resembled that of an animal or man, though, as the pulse was wild and chaotic at times, ordered and steady at others. Whatever it was, Burke realized the storm had within it some sort of sentience, some sort of self-awareness, guiding it along.

"He was startled. Even Hodel Burke, wielder of the world's most open and thoughtful mind, couldn't believe this encroaching disaster was actually the doing of some sort of colossal life form. But the facts couldn't be ignored. He studied the pulse more and more and quickly realized there was a radioactive signature within it. This thing, whatever it was, had a kind of individual signature unlike **anything** Burke had ever seen before. Essentially, it had a genetic code that identified it. Made it unique. Made it distinct. Something like the DNA we organic beings have.

"Of course, these claims were even more outlandish than his first—a self aware, apocalyptic storm-- and he was pushed even further into the fringe for purporting them. But Burke was indefatigable. He scoured the earth for anything like the signatures he had observed in the storm. And soon enough, he found something similar. In the backroom of a museum, a museum one of his ex-wives owned, was a mysterious shard of glass, a relic from ancient times. It had been in her family for a long time, according to her. By mere chance, Burke discovered that this artifact, this piece of glass, possessed traces of the same signature as the cosmic storm. But the artifact was thousands of years old and the radioactive traces on it seemed to be even older. Burke arrived at an unbelievable conclusion.

"Whatever this storm was, it had visited earth before, long before mankind even began formally recording its own history. It had come to earth, interacted with the civilization that created the shard of glass, and then disappeared. Whoever that civilization was, Burke reckoned they must have possessed knowledge of a method to drive the apocalyptic anomaly away. But the civilization had all but disappeared! What good would their method do for the present if it were buried in the dusts of time? And so Burke took the artifact home. It took some arguing, according to him, as his ex-wife was very protective of the Shard, but he won out eventually. He studied the artifact day and night, hoping to learn its secrets.

"One evening, as Burke was just beginning to doze off, the artifact lit up like a star and something extraordinary happened. The way he described it to me, an object actually **emerged** from out of the Shard, as if it were a reflection coming out of a mirror. Something from another time, from the past, plopped right out of the Shard and onto Burke's laboratory floor. The artifact had served as some sort of mysterious, radioactive portal to the past, and to the time stream, the blue area we're travelling through as I speak."

"What came out of the artifact?" asked Franklin, who had momentarily forgotten his woe and sat enwrapped in the tale.

"I'll get to that last," answered Hess, wholly intent on finishing his story. "Burke discovered that this artifact, this Shard, perhaps through the ingenuity of the lost civilization that had created it, could serve as a means of travelling through time! A gateway to the past and the future! A portal through space and time."

The children were awestruck. It was like something out of a fairytale: a shard of glass that doubled as a portal to other eras in the history of the world. Franklin wasn't even sure he could believe the story, though he desperately wanted to.

"But he couldn't use the artifact on its own," continued Hess. "Its energy was unpredictable and fluctuated wildly when he conducted tests on it. So he built a focusing chamber around it, a machine that could harness its power and bend time **around** the object, essentially sending it into the past. Or the future. That machine is the Noah, here. The artifact is housed in that central column there, above the entrance to the lower deck," Hess gestured towards the silver pillar in the center of the cockpit.

"Shall I show them?" asked Mozi, who sounded delighted to show off the ship's accouterments. Hess nodded and at Mozi's command a silver panel slid to the side at the top of the column. There, housed within the column just below the hatch the children had originally descended from, was a strange shard of reflective glass. There were, of course, several wires and devices attached to the artifact, but the children could still see it quite well. It was about as tall as Franklin was, and just about as wide too. It was tinted azure, much like the time stream outside, and glowed in a similar manner, pulsing like a beating heart.

"Alright, so how do **you** fit into all of this?" demanded Ellie, who paid the artifact little heed. "Don't tell me you're the magnanimous Dr. Burke under that mask of yours and you've just been puffing out your own feathers this whole time."

"Ms. Mars," said Hess sadly. "Please don't speak harshly of him. As things stand right now, he's dead and gone, incinerated with the rest of the planet. It's hard enough to talk about him as is. Besides, as I told you: I'm really around the same age as you all under this armor."

"Fine. I'm-" Ellie struggled to force out the words, "I'm sorry. But where do you come into play in this tragic tale?"

Hess sighed. "You remember how I said I haven't really got a name? Well, I suppose I technically do. I just can't remember it. I'm an amnesiac, you see. I haven't got any memories prior to the moment I met Dr. Burke."

"And what moment was that?" asked Franklin.

"The moment I fell out of his mysterious artifact and on to his laboratory floor. I was that same 'something' from the past that had emerged out of the portal in the Shard and into 3012 AD."

"Unreal," breathed Joey. Franklin and Ellie nodded in agreement, disbelief and wonder palpable on their faces. Had Hess really come from the past and emerged from a portal in that strange, glowing shard of glass?

"Apparently," Hess went on, "I hit my head pretty hard when I flopped out of the artifact and all my memories went out like a light. And I mean all of them. I couldn't even remember what language I spoke! I emerged dazed, confused, lonely, and mumbling. But Burke bandaged my head and nursed me back to health. He put me in a capsule he invented that taught me English—our language. I had mastered it within a night, that's how effective his machine was. What an inventor, right? Since Burke couldn't figure out where—or perhaps **when**— on earth I was from, given I didn't speak any particular language and had no memories whatsoever, he had to do some guesswork. He surmised I must be from the same civilization that created the artifact and presumably defeated the apocalypse all those thousands of years ago - from the distant past. This idea was more tantalizing to him than anything he could think of! I really can't say whether or not he's right, I still don't remember a thing.

"So Burke took me on and let me live in his laboratory with him and Mozi. He trained me to live inside this survival suit, the Hess Suit and to operate the Noah. He also taught me how to use this." Hess produced a small device that looked like a pocket watch. "It's called a Rok Counter. Burke designed it to be able to detect certain radioactive signals. He tuned this one in particular to the frequency of the apocalypse anomaly."

Franklin suddenly nodded in understanding. "I see. And so that's why he sent you back,"

"Wait a second, did you pick up on something I didn't, Franklin?" muttered Ellie, bewildered with Franklin's sudden calm and understanding. "I don't get it. So an apocalypse happens in the future, but you travel back in time to the past?"

"No. I get it too," Joey put in.

"You see, Ms. Mars," said Hess, "Burke's ultimate goal was to prevent the end of earth, to prevent the apocalypse anomaly, the cosmic storm, from destroying humanity. The way he saw things, the lost civilization he supposed I came from, the one that created the artifact, had discovered a way to accomplish the solution he sought, to defeat Armageddon. He figured I had been sent forward in time by that same civilization to help the future defeat the storm, too! So, he sent me back into the past just as the world was on the brink of complete obliteration. Even Burke, the finest optimist there was, became hopeless towards the end, I think. He was afraid that his life had been purposeless in the overwhelming face of death. He instructed me to use the Rok Counter to seek out and locate the apocalyptic cloud in the past and see what I could learn: whether or not there was some secret to deflecting its power. Essentially, I'm on a mission to see why it is exactly the storm didn't destroy the earth when it had the chance in ancient times."

"And with that information, you'd return to 3012 AD and use it to help Burke fight off the apocalypse," finished Franklin for him, leaning back in his seat and casting his eyes towards the ceiling, barely able to digest the enormity of the tale. The enormity of what it meant. Would the world, so full of life and ideas, truly be snuffed out so suddenly one day? Could so much be reduced to nothing, just like that? Was mankind merely dust to be recycled and cast into space as the world crumbled? How dreary! Hopelessness began to eat at Franklin's insides, double teaming him with the help of the already chaotic panic raging in his stomach.

"Alright." Ellie took a deep breath, steadying her nerve and her quavering voice. "Alright, so what's that silver monster? What's the Stalo and why was it attacking the Noah?"

"That's one of the questions I don't have the answer to," admitted Hess ruefully. "Burke, so far as I know, was never aware of the Stalo or anything like it. What I can tell you is this: whatever the Stalo is, it has close ties to the apocalypse anomaly; it's composed of a very similar energy signature. That might explain why it was able to travel through the time stream without being ripped to bits."

"But why did you have to come to 2012?" Joey cried out! "Is our civilization the one that defeats the apocalypse anomaly and then fades away? Surely you can't mean that suburban Connecticut rises up and defeats the apocalypse! Believe me, we have some nice beaches and stuff, but I don't think we're capable of anything like that!"

"No. 2012 was an accident, really," said Hess. "The Stalo attacked Mozi and me while we were travelling back in time and the Noah shut down. We had to make an emergency landing in your year. Or perhaps a 'crash-landing' is a more appropriate term for it."

Ellie waved her hands dismissively. "That's all well and good. That's fine. But please, just take us **back** now. I'm sure we've outrun the Stalo, and it won't do him much good to hang around Cankerwood, so you don't have to worry about running into him. Just pull your lever there and return us. I understand why we can't tell anyone what you've revealed to us, I really do! It could alter the future! I get that, I've seen the movies. We're honest kids, really. I'm an honors student, you can trust me. I'll keep these two in line: we won't repeat any of this to a **soul**. Please, just return us.

"I can't. Not yet," stated Hess firmly.

"WHY NOT?" roared Ellie.

The armored boy took a deep breath through his ventilator and turned his visor-covered face away from the angry girl. "The Noah is only capable of travelling through the temporal stream a few times. If it travels too many times, the Shard will shatter and the ship will likely explode! Burke said it was due to the time travelling process putting a great deal of strain on the artifact. I've already wasted two of those opportunities thanks to that damn Stalo monster; I can't afford to risk wasting another, even by returning you lot. As things stand, I've only a handful chances left to get it right. I need them **all**. I can't take **you** back till I'm certain I've completed **my** mission! "

"Oh God." Joey choked back a sob.

"So we're **never** going home?" screamed Ellie, grabbing Hess by his metal collar and shaking him vigorously.

"Not anytime soon, no," yelped the harrowed boy apologetically. "But if I do succeed in all of this and if the artifact doesn't shatter, perhaps Burke can use the Noah to return you to your own time. I really am very sorry!"

Ellie only shook him more, though she slowly slumped over onto his shoulder and began to cry softly.

"Well, where are we going now?" croaked Joey raggedly. His voice was hoarse and worn out. He sounded like Franklin had never before heard him; completely and totally hopeless.

"We're supposed to be going to 3,000 BC," said Hess, patting Ellie on the shoulder as she wept into his. "That's the year Burke sent me to. 3,000 BC is the year he believes this lost civilization of his to have thrived in. But, like Mozi said, I launched the Noah suddenly after a system failure. I'm afraid we could be going almost anywhere at this point. We didn't have time to map out a route, you see. As things stand, we could be going to almost any year in the history of the world."

The words echoed in Franklin's head and he could hear his own heartbeat pulsing in his ears.

'NEVER GO HOME'
'almost any year in history'

'only a few times'   'I need them **all**'
'the end of the world'

And

    Just

        Like

           That

                Franklin

Freeman

Snapped

And went

bananas

He screamed, "You mean to tell me we're trapped aboard a time machine powered by radioactive piece of glass created by a dead civilization, going to God knows what year, stuck with an amnesiac in a suit of armor and his computer sidekick, on a mission to prevent the apocalypse for a man who won't even be born for another millennium, while being chased by some sort of insane, flying robot?"

"That about sums it up," said Hess weakly.

"Do you have an onboard lavatory?" asked Franklin politely.

"Yes, through that little door there. It's a-" Hess couldn't finish; Franklin had already disappeared into the bathroom and begun tossing up every single cookie he had.

The children, who Hess insisted ought to have some privacy and rest given the shock of their plight, retired into the cabin situated on the lower deck through the central elevator. They cringed as they rode the lift down, knowing full well they were directly beneath the mysterious pulsating Shard that powered the time machine known only as the Noah.

Franklin, who had gone quite weak in the knees, flopped gratefully onto one of the lower bunks and lay face down, breathing slowly. Joey and Ellie sat on the steel floor with their backs against Franklin's bunk, pulling their knees close to their chests and huddling together.

"This can't really be happening," whispered Joey.

"It is," groaned Franklin stormily into his pillow.

"We can't really be... travelling through time," Joey went on. "It's not possible. We just can't be. Not only is it against all the rules of physics, but... Well, this kind of stuff isn't supposed to happen to people like **us!** This nonsense only ever happens to people in the movies! We simply can't be travelling through time!"

"We are." Franklin grunted.

"What will our folks think when we never come home for supper tonight?" asked Ellie.

Joey's face brightened. "Well, theoretically, when we make it back we should return to the very same hour we left! No one will have even known we were gone!"

"That's if we make it back at all," added Ellie gloomily.

"You guys think we won't?" stammered Joey nervously.

Franklin lifted his face from the pillow, looked very hopeful for a moment, and then frowned and shrugged. He could come up with nothing particularly encouraging to tell his friends.

"This guy- this Hess character- doesn't seem very competent at the whole time travel thing," remarked Ellie. "Only a few chances to use the Shard to travel through time and he's already botched two of them? And he's an amnesiac?! What kind of idiot sends an amnesiac back in time as the future's one and only hope? Give me a break. No matter how genius this Dr. Burke is supposed to be, he sounds like he's a real fool when it comes to decision making."

The children were silent for a moment. Ellie was right; the whole mission seemed like a shoestring operation at best. Hess was hardly a dashing hero from the future with a ray gun in one hand, a damsel in the other, and a lot of Crisco in his hair. No, Hess came across as what he was: a bumbling, amnesiac lab assistant with a penchant for failure crammed in a stuffy suit of futuristic armor.

"Do you think he's telling the truth?" murmured Franklin, heaving a sigh and nuzzling his head back into the pillow.

"About Burke?" asked Joey.

"Yes, about Burke and the Shard and all of that. But more importantly, about the... you know."

"The apocalypse anomaly?" Joey guessed.

"Yes. Do you think the world really comes to a complete end? Just like that?"

"It doesn't," said Ellie.

"But he said-" started Joey.

"I know what he said. And he's maybe telling the truth. What reason has he got to lie? But it's not really true, you know? Not for us, anyway." The girl folded her arms.

"Not for us?" they echoed.

Ellie huffed. "The year 3012? Our grandkid's grandkids will be worm food centuries before then! Sure, maybe the world ends, but not for us. Our world keeps on going until we die sometime around 2080 or something like that. Then it's all over. When we die is when our world ends. Who cares if the earth gets destroyed a thousand years from now? This apocalypse is so far flung, so distant from us and our lives, that it might as well not even happen at all. And hell! It hasn't come yet and it won't for a millennium! It doesn't even exist so far as I am concerned."

"I can't tell it that's comforting or depressing," said Franklin.

"Maybe a little bit of both." Joey cast his eyes down and shrugged. "On one hand, we don't die in a cosmic storm that zaps everything with lightning bolts. On the other hand, we have to live with the knowledge that the earth gets completely obliterated someday."

"That is, unless Hess saves the day," Franklin reminded him with a weak grin. He had developed a kind of fool's sympathy for the underdog time traveller.

"Right. And we're going to watch him blunder around time and try to save the day," quipped Ellie. "He's going to use that little stopwatch of his to locate the ancient apocalypse and figure out how King Solomon or Jesus or Julia's Caesar or heaven knows who defeated the storm once before? Sure, and I'm the queen of France. You understand if Hess screws up, even a little bit, we never go back to our time, right? If he fails, we'll end up spending the rest of our days out in some backwater, dirty, little prehistoric village in the woods thousands of years ago. We never see our parents again, we never go back to Connecticut again. Hell, we probably never even get to use a toilet again. A toilet! Or take a hot shower! Can you imagine? Our very lives, everything we know or have ever known, all in the hands of that armored twit who's just kidnapped us. And you just know that Stalo is nowhere near finished with us! So if we don't end up trapped in the past, we'll maybe end up dead!"

The children were silent again. Exactly what Hess's possible failure implied had not fully occurred to them before that moment. Franklin was beginning to lose his sympathy yet again. The notion of never seeing his parents again, of never watching his mother sketch in charcoal or playing baseball with his father, struck him like a kick to the gut. They had been walking merrily along in Cankerwood only hours ago; could the gravity of the situation, the stakes of their lives, have truly increased so drastically in so short a space of time? And what about poor old Monty the cat? Who would feed him and water the plants and make sure no one burglarized the house?

"That's dismal," said Joey, breaking the silence. "What happened to all that courage, Ellie? Was it just hot air?"

"It wasn't just hot air, Joey," she replied. "But this is different from going into Cankerwood. This is different from taking a chance for a little adventure! There's a line between bold and insane. This is the kind of thing you don't come back from!" she exclaimed, waving her hand around.

"Is it so different?" Joey raised his eyebrows.

"Of course it is! And what about you? You were sobbing not five minutes ago," she pointed out.

"I know," admitted Joey brusquely. He looked at the floor. "I... I just miss my folks is all. And I wasn't the only one. Franny was ralphing in the bathroom just a few minutes ago."

"Yeah" agreed Ellie. "Franklin. You okay?"

"Fine," he mumbled.

"You're being quiet, Franny," observed Joey.

"Just-" Franklin paused, "comprehending? I'm comprehending."

"Comprehending all of this nonsense?" Ellie smirked.

"Exactly."

Mozi's voice buzzed over the intercom. "Miss Mars, Joseph Jensen, and Franklin Freeman! Mister Hess has asked me to check up on you and ensure all is well."

"Thank you, Mozi" said Joey. He had immediately taken a liking to Mozi. The two were very similar, both of them brimming full of facts.

"Can I assist you in any way to make your stay more comfortable? I can offer up several forms of nourishment in the form of dehydrated meal supplements!" offered the computer.

Franklin groaned.

"I don't think we're really in the eating mood right now, Mozi," snapped Ellie. "Kind of just kidnapped onto a suicide mission through time, you know,"

"Affirmative," chirped the AI, oblivious to the girl's sarcasm. "Might I make a suggestion? At your command, I should like to dim the lights. It will encourage a more peaceable rest cycle and encourage your natural circadian rhythms. On a purely aesthetic note, the time stream is much more easily viewed in a dark chamber, and quite beautiful, so I am told. I conjecture you might find it interesting to watch as you sleep!"

"No-" began Ellie.

"Yes please, Mozi" Franklin and Joey said in unison. Even though their situation was dire, they weren't going to pass up a chance to see something so spectacular as the fabric of time bending around them.

"How exciting for you. A real look at the time stream!" exclaimed Mozi. The lights went out. The brilliant blue shimmering outside the ship exploded with intensity and shone brightly into the cabin. White, almost hexagonal shapes, danced across the walls, reminding Franklin of the patterns the underwater lights had cast at the local aquarium.

He could not help but feel a tingle of excitement as he realized that each moment the time stream passed by the window, there was a chance he briefly inhabited the same year as the grand players of history's stage. Perhaps in that ripple of blue was Winston Churchill, and maybe in that shimmer of white lived Charlemagne or William Shakespeare. Maybe even his own grandfather, who had passed away so long ago, lived in one of the millions of dazzling glimmers outside the porthole. For a moment, and just a moment, the glum thought of the loss of his parents, his home, and maybe even the world itself, evacuated his mind and the ephemeral spirit of adventure replaced it. Set adrift on the sea of time, Franklin felt quite important. Certainly more important than he had ever felt before.

"Will that be all then?" asked Mozi.

"Yes, thank you," answered Joey.

The children sat quietly and watched the azure waves of light speed by the portholes. Franklin found himself wondering what years, centuries, and perhaps even millennia, raced so speedily past them. Could all of time truly be traversed through this blue tunnel, through this 'time stream'? In that moment, light returned to his heart. "We're going to watch him?" he asked.

Joey and Ellie turned to him. "Eh?"

"What you said before, Ellie," Franklin reminded them. "You said that we're going to blunder around time and watch Hess try to save the day. We're going to watch him?"

"Yes, I suppose so," replied the girl. "While he searches for the apocalypse anomaly or whatever he called it."

"I figured we'd just stay on the ship," sad Joey, scratching his chin thoughtfully. "It's really not so bad here. Why, Franny? Why do you ask?"

"It's only… It's only that I thought we might- you know- help him out. Give Hess a hand finding what he's looking for."

Ellie and Joey swung their heads around and looked at the boy incredulously.

"Are you delirious?" demanded Ellie with a completely straight face.

"Franny, you must still be nauseous. Shall I have Mozi get us some water or something? Maybe an aspirin? You think they've got aspirin in the future?" said Joey, reaching up and feeling Franklin's forehead.

"No, no! Hear me out!" cried out the boy, shaking Joey's

hand away. "You said it yourself not a minute ago, Ellie! Hess is incompetent! And you're absolutely right: he is. Do you really want to leave the fate of the earth in the hands of a buffoon like him? He gets given a time machine and almost immediately crashes it! Then he kidnaps three innocent kids on board! Let him wander around the past unsupervised? He'll maybe muddle things up even worse."

"You can't be serious," groaned Ellie, Joey joining in.

"Listen, he'll maybe do something awful and make it so someone important was never born or the dinosaurs never went extinct or something like that! We can't just let him go out there alone."

"What would be awful about having dinosaurs?" interjected Joey.

Franklin sighed. "All I'm saying is this: wouldn't you, Ellie Mars, honors student, and you, Joseph Jensen, expert on all matters of flora and fauna, rather not leave our lives, not to mention the lives of an entire world, an entire timeline, in Hess's hands?"

Ellie snorted. "It's like I said before. What's the point of trying to save a future you're never even going to experience? We've got nothing to do with any of this and we shouldn't put our noses into it. This apocalypse Hess told us about is not ours, it's not our grandkids', its not their grandkids'. What's the point? We'll be dead and gone a thousand years before it even happens! Who cares if a storm destroys the earth? It's not our problem! It's meaningless. It's meaningless just like everything else! Just don't worry about it, Franklin." She rose suddenly and crossed the cabin. Without a word, she rolled onto a bunk, facing away from the boys and went quiet.

Franklin looked at Joey who only shrugged.

"I... I guess you're right, Ellie," he murmured, and resigned.

"We ought to get a little rest," muttered Joey, occupying another bed.

Franklin was left to his thoughts. Meaningless? Could it truly be a meaningless mission? A dismal thought, indeed, but he couldn't argue with Ellie's logic. He and everyone he knew would be dead and gone before this terrible apocalypse even reached earth. And how terrible to think each and every person could be blown away as easily as a grain of rice set against a tidal wave of might. How awfully insignificant Franklin felt as he tossed and turned in the little bunk. How random and cruel it all seemed. He recalled sitting beneath the stars the night before and feeling like an ant stranded in a desert. The awful sensation had begun to return.

It was quiet, extremely quiet, in the cabin. The buzzes and whirrs of the machines on the deck above were blocked out entirely, and now all he could hear was the sound of the time stream racing by. It sounded like a soft breeze steeling through the boughs of some quiet forest.

'Meaningless'

Ellie's words plagued him in the quiet again and again in his head till a restless sleep claimed his weary mind.

"It seems our guests are soundly asleep on the lower deck," announced Mozi as Hess sat bent over the Noah's controls in the cockpit. "It should be an interesting experiment to observe the temporal navigation's effect upon human circadian rhythms. Shall I log their breathing patterns, Mr. Hess?"

"No, Mozi. Just leave them alone," the boy grunted as he reached across the control panel for a little tool.

"It is an unexpected pleasure to entertain guests on our journey," admitted Mozi. "Though Dr. Burke warned us very specifically against admitting taking anyone with us on our travels, it seems we had little choice in the matter. I suppose difficult choices must be made in difficult circumstances! I'm quite pleased with the measures you have taken, Mr. Hess."

"Let's not talk about it," the boy huffed as he tightened a

screw absent-mindedly.

"Are you feeling quite alright? Has the sudden leap through induced nausea?" Mozi sounded concerned.

"No, it's not that."

"Then what troubles you? If you don't mind my asking, I find the observation and analysis of human emotions to be a relevant study and a crucial one to my operations."

"Yes, Mozi. I understand." Hess working stopped and drummed his fingers on the control panel. "I feel guilty, is all. Really guilty."

"And what induces this guilt, Mr. Hess?"

"Those kids."

"Our new travelling companions?"

"Right," said the boy. "See, they have no desire to be our 'travelling companions' as you put it. They were living perfectly happy, little lives and now they've been drawn into all of this. It's entirely my fault, Mozi! Did you see the way they all looked at me? The way that girl- that Ellie- looked at me? Staring daggers, you know? And how she yelled! And how they all of them cried? Good God, they're only kids! Not ten minutes on board and I've already scared one of them so bad he puked! I've dragged them away from their lives onto a dangerous trip; a trip from which they might never get to return! I've put the lives of a bunch of goofy teenagers in mortal danger. They're only kids, Mozi."

"As are you," interrupted the computer.

"I am what?"

"Only a child, as you say."

"Yes, but-"

"But nothing," Mozi interrupted him. "Even given tremendous responsibility you have taken on, you must take care not to forget that you are only a child yourself. Whatever sympathy you give to them, our guests, you must also grant yourself. Fault is a mysterious human concept I find difficult to grasp. Often, your kind finds it necessary, if not paramount, to find someone-or something- to blame for whatever trouble has arisen. And it is unfortunate indeed, Mr. Hess, that you heap the lonely notion of fault upon your own shoulders. You could never have foreseen the Stalo's appearance, nor done much at all to fend it off. Circumstance, it seems to my sensors, is the true culprit of all the unpleasant turns our journey has taken thus far. The children did react a bit harshly, I'll admit. And considering the magnitude of their predicament, perhaps this was not an inappropriate reaction. But in time I believe they will come to realize our Mr. Hess is a good-natured fellow without ill intention."

"Nevertheless, I still feel guilty," said Hess.

"Try to keep your guilt at bay, for the time being," suggested the computer. "When the children have come to adjust to their new circumstances, I'm sure they will become more agreeable and perhaps a bit more sensible. They are an inquisitive lot, so far as I can sense, and we do owe them a great deal."

"We do?" asked the armored boy incredulously. "What do we owe them? We've only just met them!"

"Why yes, indeed!" exclaimed Mozi. "It seems they woke you up and reactivated my operating system just in the nick of time. If they had arrived even a few minutes later than they did, the Stalo might have very well located the Noah while it was derelict and you were unconscious. Imagine, if you will, how simple it would have been for the strange creature to destroy our little vessel in such a scenario, if that is, in fact, what the Stalo seeks to do. We'd have been 'sitting ducks' as Dr. Burke sometimes said. Those children really..." Mozi paused. "Saved our bacon." The AI then did its best to imitate a laugh in response to its own stilted joke.

Hess rolled his eyes beneath his visor and sighed. He hadn't even realized the children had potentially saved his entire mission, and his life, by waking him when they did. Now he felt even guiltier than before. "You're right, Mozi. I'll- I'll try and be positive," he managed to say.

"Excellent. I am encouraged to hear this! Now the only thing you've got to worry about is our destination."

Hess had momentarily forgotten about his most recent

blunder. He slapped his helmeted forehead.

"Good God, Mozi. Where **are** we going? Or maybe I should say 'when.'"

"I suppose we will only come to know the answer to that question when we arrive," admitted the computer. "It could very well be our intended destination, the year 3,000 BC, or it could be another time entirely; either the future or the past, only time will tell. Whenever the Noah leaps into the time stream without proper preparation, it is almost impossible to say what year it will travel to. Perhaps we'll return to our present, the year 3012 AD. Though Dr. Burke instructed us absolutely not to do so without completing the mission, it would be enlightening to ascertain his analysis of the Stalo situation. And I do think he would enjoy the children's company; he never had any of his own. Besides you, of course, Mr. Hess."

"Besides me?" Hess sounded surprised.

"Why, yes! While not the genetic offspring of the Burke lineage, the Doctor often shared with me the fact he considered you a sort of adopted son of his."

Despite the predicament of their mysterious destination, Hess couldn't help but smile beneath the helmet. "All the same, I'm worried," he said. "If we don't end up in 3,000 BC, then we've really haven't got many chances left to get it right, and then there is the return trip to consider. The Noah can only travel through the wormhole so many times without the Shard breaking to bits Damn! Only a handful of chances to save the human race, and if I strain the Shard too much, it'll shatter and then the earth will be really and truly sunk."

"Indeed, it seems to be quite a stress inducing conundrum," buzzed Mozi. "Perhaps you too should seek sleep while we travel. You endured quite a shock when our vessel was attacked; your person certainly needs time to recover."

"You have no idea how much I'd like to, Mozi. But- well it's just that I'd feel strange going to the lower deck and sleeping in the same cabin as... them. I feel like they wouldn't want me there. At least not while they sleep. You know?"

"I'm sorry to say I do not, in fact, know," answered the AI. "You are circumspect about slumbering in such close proximity as our guests, so instead might I suggest you sleep on this deck?"

Hess nodded glumly and retired to the back of the cockpit onto a small cot. For some time he tossed and turned until the exhaustion of his chaotic journey battled away his nervous thoughts and laid him to rest.

"Hullo, Franklin," a familiar voice said cheerily. "I'd been wondering when you'd come to visit!"

"Who's there?" asked the boy. All was dark and, upon inspection, Franklin could not even make out his own hands in front of him, nor his feet below. Perhaps his eyes were closed; he couldn't really tell.

"You've forgotten me already? Tut tut, Franklin Freeman!" clucked the voice chidingly. "Didn't I see you only yesterday?"

"Is it you again?" asked Franklin. "The girl from my dream? The glowing girl?"

The girl's voice rang out in mirth and cheer. "Why yes! So you have remembered! How splendid! I'm sorry about that little fiasco in the theater. I imagine that might have been a little harrowing for you."

"So I'm dreaming again, am I?" sighed the boy into the darkness.

"And what's wrong with a dream?" She sounded taken aback.

"Nothing. It's only that... I just... I wonder why I keep dreaming of you, you in particular I mean. I've never met you in real life, so far as I can remember. And I think my mind, given the situation it's in right now, would be more concerned with all the nonsense going on in my real life than some strange girl I've never seen before," Franklin muttered as politely as he could. It was disconcerting trying to be polite to a disembodied voice in the middle of a black abyss.

"You're right, Franklin Freeman!" the voice cried out, both elated and mysterious at the same time. "You've never met me! You've never seen my face nor heard my voice! You don't know to whom both those things belong, yet! But despite all this, you and I have known each other for years. Years and years. Longer than I can count!"

"You understand that doesn't make any sense, right?" asked Franklin, pausing. "What the hell am I talking about? I'm asking my dream hallucination if it knows it doesn't make any sense. Good God. I think I need professional help."

There was a long, awkward moment of silence, which was suddenly split by another peel of delighted, girlish laughter. "Oh, Franklin..." she whispered. In the midst of the darkness, a little white light began to shimmer. It grew and grew, drawing nearer to where the boy reckoned himself to be. It slowly took the shape of a white bird whose brilliant, pale feathers glimmered and shone in some invisible light, piercing through the darkness. A pigeon, Franklin figured. No, no, not a pigeon. It was too graceful, too pleasant for a pigeon. A dove. A white dove.

"Please," he begged the bird. "Please just explain all this to me. I've got so much to worry about in the real world. I don't want to have to figure out my subconscious on top of all of this! Is this puberty or hormones or something? Because this is not how they described it in health class."

"Hush, hush," breathed the girl's voice from within the dove, though its beak did not move. "Rest... rest." The bird, which seemed to be flying in a kind of serene, slow motion, landed upon his shoulder and nestled there, cooing softly into his ear as doves are want to do.

"Please just tell me who you are! I'm confused on all these levels, I'd at least like my dreams to be a relatively straightforward place!" he pleaded.

"How handsome you are! And you don't even know it, that's the best part. How handsome you were when first we met," she murmured. "How boyish and befuddled. And those clothes! Like none I had ever seen, oh dear. My darling, Franklin. And when you burst in, sopping wet from head to toe, on that frightful evening. Why even then, with your hair bedraggled and your poor face so drenched that you could barely see, you were still beautiful to me."

Franklin ignored all this. He hadn't the foggiest idea what this apparition was referring to. "I really don't know what you're talking about. I don't remember anything like what you just said. You must have the wrong person! So are you a dove or a girl? Or are you an albino pigeon? I never got to see your face before, last night when the stage burned and when you... When you kissed me. It was shining too brightly. I couldn't make it out."

"Hush, hush. So troubled you always seem! So worried! Alas, the poor boy that carries upon one shoulder the weight of the world and upon the other a face he has not yet come to recognize. Oh, woe."

"C'mon, dream lady. Enough of this!" he cried out.

"It is a shame we could not have met amid more pleasant circumstanced and had more time to dance in the sun. Now hush, sweet Franklin," she cooed.

"But..." his voice trailed off as the dove that nuzzled his shoulder seemed to transfigure slowly into that same girl's head, the one flowing with silver hair that shone like starlight. Again, the angelic girl's face glowed so brightly that Franklin had to look away, but she buried her nose into Franklin's neck and hid away the light. Everything went dark. Everything went quiet.

She began to sing:

"O, the captain of a ship in long flown days
Further from home each day he strays
Lost and lost again upon the waves
Where lies his star?

Hence came a storm that shook the earth
Lit the sky and smote ship's berth
From the singing crew was drained all mirth
For they saw no star.

The first mate of the captain calls to him
'Why must we bend to each wave's whim?
I have such love for you, but hope grows dim!
Where lies our star?'

The captain turns to mate and offers smile
'My dear, sweet boy, lend thine ear for a while
You have endured brave through each dire trial
But hope yet lies afar

For the storms that toss our ship have not pity
Sudden and indifferent is the sea
We are doomed to sink, no more to be
On comes our star!

Now take my hand, my lad, and hold it tight
As the waves cast us into frigid night
You and I as one will fight our fight
For you are my star!'

And so as the ship was dashed to dust
Into the sea they were flailing thrust
They did as true friends always must.
Shining bright, two stars."

Franklin faded away from the vision and the dove and into a deep, and thereafter dreamless, sleep as the lullaby wrapped him in a warming calm.

CHAPTER TEN

THE WORLD UNDONE

"I do hate to interrupt your slumber, as you seem to be partaking of it so peacefully, but I really must insist that you wake up this very moment," announced Mozi's disembodied voice over the intercom. For a brief moment, Franklin thought he was still nestled in blankets in his little room on Pendel Circle, but the reality of his surroundings sank in rapidly and the pleasant illusion vanished almost instantly.

Ellie, it seemed, had already roused and was shaking Franklin vigorously, repeating again and again, "Wake up. The computer wants us to wake up, Franklin. The weird, floating robot voice wants us to wake up. You should wake up or it might zap you. Who knows?"

Franklin couldn't tell if she was being facetious or if she was just delirious. Her eyes were bleary and her face blank; she had clearly hadn't slept very well.

"I can hear it, Ellie, thanks," he groaned, shooing her incessant hands away. "Is Joey up?"

"I think he's dead," said the girl plainly and then shrugged.

Franklin stared at her blankly. "I tried waking him up. He wouldn't budge," she exclaimed. "Probably dead. Wouldn't surprise me, not at this point." Across the cabin, Joey was buried beneath his blanket and audibly snoring.

Franklin squinted at the groggy girl, annoyed that she had frightened him unnecessarily. "You're a real peach in the morning, aren't you Ellie?"

She shrugged again. "I thought I was back home when I woke up."

"Back on Pendel Circle? Yeah, me too. Kind of jarring," he agreed, patting the girl's shoulder.

"No, not on Pendel Circle, you dolt. I slept there **one** night. Stony Creek isn't exactly what I'd call home, yet. Maine's still where my heart is. I was already bummed about leaving my old house; and now with all this time travel nonsense I'm beginning to feel positively homeless! Set adrift, you know?"

"Oh, Ellie!" exclaimed Franklin, sitting up at once. He had been so caught up in his own grief that he had entirely forgotten the poor girl's situation, a situation much more stressful than his own.

Taking Franklin entirely off guard, Ellie leaned forward and threw her arms around him, almost collapsing against him. There she rested, leaning her weight upon his. She pushed her head into the crook of his neck and sighed. Franklin had been nervous and shaking when they had, the two of them, first met; now he was positively breathless.

She began to mumble into his shoulder, "Just promise me we'll all stick together, through whatever happens. I know I was kind of, well, snappy last night. And I'm still so confused by it all. And angry. But I really do need you two, right now. I know we're only very new friends, or maybe renewed friends if you prefer that, but I was new and lonely when my parents made the move and you both helped me out a lot. I know I can be a bit... Overbearing sometimes."

"An honors student? Overbearing? Never," chuckled Franklin.

She stifled a little laugh and gave him a gentle smack on the back of his head. "Yes, sometimes," she admitted wryly. "But I was worried I might not make friends changing schools and everything all of a sudden like I did. But you two put that fear to bed. And now I'm twice removed, once from my old home in Maine and once again from my new one on Pendel Circle. I just need to know we'll all stick together. Promise me that, Franklin, okay?"

"Okay, Ellie," he whispered, patting the back of her head. Her hair was soft, softer than any he had ever touched, and felt like velvet beneath his fingertips. He was at once reminded of the silvery dream girl who had nuzzled her face into his shoulder in much the same way Ellie Mars was doing at that very moment.

"Children!" Mozi chimed over the intercom. "Please join us on the command deck as soon as possible. It really is an urgent matter."

Ellie broke hastily away from the embrace and returned to her bunk to fix her hair. Franklin went to take on the complicated and vexing chore of waking Joey. Normally, when Joey slept in his own bed next to his own reliable- not to mention extremely loud- alarm clock, he woke up on time without a struggle each day. But Franklin, having been with the boy on several camping trips and vacations, had always found rousing his friend nearly impossible to do without the obnoxious clock's buzzing.

"Joseph, get up," he said, shaking him. Futile. The sleeping boy hadn't even stirred. "**Wake up**," Franklin insisted into his friend's ear. Nothing. "Joseph, we **have** to get up. Mozi says it's urgent!" Joey mumbled something incoherent and burrowed further into his blankets. "Your cichlids are dying! We're late for the algebra exam! Sally Walkens is downstairs and she says she'd like to ask you out to the Halloween Dance! Good grief, man. Wake up!" Franklin cried.

Ellie, who had been observing the exchange, half amused and half annoyed, strode over, licked her index finger, and inserted it promptly into the sleeping Joey's ear. He jolted up from out of the sheets, scowling and rubbing the side of his head. When he had recovered from the shock, he glanced around in a daze and managed to mutter, "So we're still here, huh?"

"That we are," answered the girl, wiping her finger dry on her shirt.

"I thought I might have just dreamed all of this. Oh well. Could be worse, right?" said Joey as he slid out of the blankets and down onto the deck.

"That's quite an attitude change from yesterday," observed Franklin.

"If we're stuck here, we might as well make the best of it, right?" Joey smiled; and though it was only a halfhearted smile, it was a true one nonetheless. "I've read there's all sorts of species that have gone extinct since 3,000 BC. Maybe we'll get to see a couple of them."

"Children, now that you're all awake, if you would please," begged Mozi as the elevator doors opened expectantly. Each of them, still quite tired and grumbling, shuffled into the lift and ascended to the command deck.

"Thank goodness, you're all awake!" said Hess from behind the Noah's controls.

"What's all the fuss about?" demanded Ellie, still impatient with their ironclad companion.

"The Noah has just begun to slow its movement through the time stream," Hess told them. "We should be arriving at our destination any moment now."

"And just to be clear," Joey said as he began poking about the cockpit with a renewed sense of curiosity, "we're still not sure where, or perhaps **when** that destination is, exactly?"

Hess nodded. "You're right. But we can only hope for the best! If we get lucky, and if the navigation system retained the coordinates we put in before we crashed in your time, we'll end up in 3,000 BC just like we planned. Is it fashionable to cross your fingers for luck in your time?"

"Yes," answered Franklin, though he didn't really know why the people of his time, much less the people of the 3012 AD, practiced such an odd superstition; however, the strange habit had apparently outlived his time and into the distant future.

"Superb. Well then, you really ought to start crossing them now." Hess fumbled to follow his own advice with his clumsy, armored digits.

"I believe your time would be better spent strapping yourselves in," advised Mozi. "There's no telling what kind of conditions the Noah will enter into."

The children quickly took their seats behind Hess and fastened their restraints, none of them particularly wanting to roll around the cockpit like loose luggage again. The glass windshield before them still yielded only a view of the luminous, blue time stream, but it seemed to ripple and pulse with less voracity than it had before.

"I have a question about this time travel business!" said Joey, and Hess turned to him. "You said that we'll be, hopefully, popping out into 3,000 BC. That's all well and good, I suppose; but are we going to be exiting the time stream in the same location we entered it? Geographically, that is."

"Good question, Joey," said Hess.

"Call him Joseph, please," put in Ellie with a bitingly passive aggressive smile.

Hess bristled in agitation for a moment, though the children could not see it beneath the suit. "Good question, Joseph," he relented. "Mozi, you could probably explain it better than me."

"The Noah's primary function is that of a temporal navigation device," began the AI. "However, its original design was that of a self propelled locomotive vessel intended for several earthly climes, various extra-terrestrial planetary atmospheres, and even some regions of outer space. This ship, manufactured as a T-Class Orbic Runner Spacefaring Pod, was selected to house the artifact, the Shard, not only because it is a suitable and comfortable container for passengers such as Mr. Hess and myself, but also because it is able to propel itself through the air. The Artifact displaces the time flow around it and launches the Noah into the vortex through which it travels. In order to do this, the craft must be at a high enough altitude that it does not accidentally displace the ground beneath it with the vortex, which can be quite large. The vessel must also be travelling at a relatively speedy velocity in order to phase through the semi permeable skin of that vortex. In short: a degree of light travel is necessary to enter the time stream. Recall, if you will, the rapid flight in which we exited your time, children. Because of this, we will exit the time stream in the approximate geographical region of our departure, but not the same precise spot. Essentially, in order to travel through time, we have to be flying fast enough, first."

"Great Scott," mumbled Ellie.

"Pardon me?" Hess looked at her, confused.

"Nothing," she replied.

Franklin had followed the lecture as best he could. "So it'll look the same? Cankerwood and all of that?"

"If 3,000 BC is, in fact, the point in time we are racing towards, then yes." answered Mozi. "Although perhaps more heavily forested and sparsely populated, given the relatively thin distribution of human beings in North America in that age."

Franklin looked at Joey excitedly, forgetting their peril for a moment. He had an immense fondness for ancient peoples and cultures, Native Americans in particular, and was thrilled at the prospect of perhaps meeting a true denizen of the ancient earth in the flesh. Joey shared in Franklin's gleeful little glance, but imagining quite a different vision, one swimming with miles and miles of untouched, verdant green and dense, luscious forests brimming with animal and plant life. Ellie scowled at the two.

"But North America isn't where we're ultimately headed, is it Mr. Hess?" she asked obstinately.

Hess couldn't conceal his surprise. "How on earth did you know that?"

"A lucky guess," replied the girl. She had reckoned that whatever this lost civilization was, it probably hadn't been located in ancient New England.

"Well, well," chuckled Hess. "Actually, we're headed-" the Noah lurched suddenly and cut him off.

The blue glow of the time stream before them was extinguished with a flash. They were no longer traveling through time, it seemed, but through some sort of brown, unfamiliar looking sky. The shuttle rattled so violently that Franklin, clinging to his arm rests with rapidly whitening knuckles, thought the entire ship might fall to bits right then and there. A great brown and swirling mass obscured the cockpit windshield, hammering the glass and the rest of the ship with a thunderous *ratatatatat*.

Hess desperately jerked the controls back and forth but to little avail; the Noah simply would not level. "Something's wrong!" he cried out.

Mozi's siren, the same that had trumpeted when the Stalo had first appeared, began to wail again. "Warning! Warning! Thrusters jammed and unresponsive. Thruster core mechanism in potential danger! Rudder propulsion system offline! Warning! Warning!"

"I can see that, Mozi!" barked Hess, tugging ferociously on the yoke. The Noah rocked rapidly back and forth around them and, as each of their hearts dropped into their stomachs, she began to fall, spiraling downwards, though towards what they could not make out through the brown tumult outside.

"What's going on?" Hess demanded.

"Our instruments are blind. It seems we've entered a dust storm, which is battering the Noah quite badly," stated the AI.

'A dust storm?' thought Franklin, alarmed. 'That kind of thing happens in the Sahara, not Connecticut!'

"Our systems are clogged and we are in free-fall; brace for impact!" announced Mozi. And indeed they were; the Noah was plummeting in an out-of-control descent that could end in nothing but calamity.

"Pull up, you idiot!" shrieked Ellie, boxing Hess on the back of his helmet.

"I'm trying! I'm trying, but the controls aren't responding!"

"If you're such a fancy future man, why does your all your

technology seem like a such pile of junk?" she demanded. "Are you really going to crash your ship twice in the same twenty-four hours?" She scowled. "You blithering dimwit!"

"Hasn't this thing got a landing gear?" yelled Franklin.

"In the future we don't need them. The ship just kind of hovers and touches down!" explained Hess. "Unless, of course, you're shooting towards the ground at a couple hundred miles an hour!" Hess hastily pushed buttons and pulled levers in a panic. The children collectively gulped.

Through the torrential dust that ceaselessly battered them, Franklin could dimly make out the dark and ominous black mass that he supposed was the ground looming up before them, as if to swallow the little ship whole.

"Impact in five, four, three, two-" Mozi couldn't finish the countdown. The Noah collided with the ground in a tremendous crash, emitting an ear shattering sound much like what Franklin imagined a thirty-ton bowling ball must sound like when rolled across a rocky plain and straight into a phalanx of mountains arranged like pins.

The Noah somersaulted across the ground, head over teakettle, bouncing up into the air dozens of times like a stone skipped across choppy water. The children, suspended by their restraints in the center of a giant, spinning sphere, could do little but let the blood slosh back and forth inside of them from their heads into their toes, as they rolled, their hair whipping up and down, left and right.

Hess, ignoring the chaos, continued to wrestle with his controls, trying in vain to bring the Noah back into the air. But she would not cooperate. The ship began to slide; grating against the ground beneath it, and at last came to rest, tipping onto its side like Franklin's bike did when his kickstand had come loose.

Silence claimed them all for a moment as the alarms began to fade and their pounding hearts to slow. Despite the great ruckus, they had stayed anchored safely to their seats in a high speed, aerial crash.

Ellie's hair hung in loose strands, strewn about her face and shoulders as if she had been electrocuted in a cartoon; she looked mad and quite disheveled. Joey's glasses sat crookedly on his nose and he wiped away a little saliva that had rocketed out of his yelping mouth and onto his cheeks. Franklin's shoes, which had been tied on only very loosely, had come loose sometime during the crash been flung to the other side of the cockpit in the commotion. Hess appeared quite sound, but even though this wasn't his first crash landing, he was still shaking like a leaf beneath the metal suit.

"You're a real flying ace, you know that? A real Red Baron," bellowed Ellie between ragged gasps as the adrenaline slowed its pump within her. They could not help but chuckle, even Hess. All of them were simply relieved to have survived the incident intact. The floor, along with the rest of the ship, was askew, much like an old-fashioned rake stage, and the children sat at the head of the slight slope.

"How'd we do, Mozi?" asked Hess as he began unstrapping himself.

"I've begun performing a preliminary scan on the system. Results pending in three-to-ten minutes."

"Roger." Hess dropped to the floor, stumbling on the incline and falling flat on his back. His body, elevated off the floor by the suit's massive metal torso, rolled comically across the sloping cockpit, arms squirming pathetically by his sides. The children, unable to filter their mirth after near demise, began to laugh.

"I actually think seeing that made the crash almost worth it," chortled Ellie. Hess went red in the cheeks; he was quite thankful the children couldn't see him through the helmet. He cleared his throat, quite embarrassed.

Joey and Franklin relented, unstrapped themselves, and went to lift Hess off the floor. Ellie remained by the controls, however, doing her best to peer out the windshield and see what lay outside the Noah, but the glass was too caked with the dust of the storm to make out much of anything.

"Do we know where, or when, we are?" she asked over her shoulder.

Hess brushed off his suit. "Shall we find out? My visor hasn't zeroed in on a time reading yet, and it sounds like the dust storm, or whatever it was, has died down or passed us by. Maybe it's safe to peek outside. Mozi, open the main hatch."

The portal hissed and the gangplank lowered. Franklin could not help but feel uneasy as a rush of stale, moldy smelling air rushed into the cockpit from the world outside; it reminded him of how the attic of his house smelled when he first discovered it many years ago: abandoned and musty. Hess, the children close behind him, strode down and out of the Noah to take in their new surroundings.

Franklin caught his breath in his throat. This land which he now surveyed before him was no primitive earth bursting with verdant, green life. It was no forested paradise for the Indians of old. It was no Eden.

No, this was a dead place, a place so far removed from anything Franklin had ever seen he really had nothing to compare it to. As far as the eye could see, the land was flat; no mountains rose in the distance and absolutely nothing dotted the empty horizon. On the ground, if one could call it ground at all, was not dirt and soil, not grass, but a sort of ashen dust of the type one typically finds in a fireplace. There were no trees, no buildings, nothing to stand out against the maddeningly quiet and empty landscape. And nothing to fill the air: no bugs, no crickets, and no birds, just like a snowy day.

The air, which yielded no breeze unto them, felt neither hot nor cold, warm nor cool; it seemed thin and empty, as if there were barely enough of it to go around. Franklin could not summon a deep breath, there simply didn't seem to be enough oxygen for it. And what small breaths he could manage stung his lungs and made him choke. This was as inhospitable a place as he could imagine.

Most disturbing of all was the immense and cloudless sky. It was not brimming and blue, nor was it dusky and gray. No, the sky was a sort of disquieting opaque, as if one was looking through glass with absolutely nothing to see on the other side.

And the only thing that stood out against it was a great black mass that resembled a cyclone moving slowly away from them; Franklin reckoned it was the dust storm that had grounded the Noah only moments before. There were several of them, actually, dotting the horizon: colossal, dark twisters of dust that swirled chaotically and randomly about.

The sun was so dim it seemed almost a great, dreary puddle in the sky, although the entire landscape was covered in a constant matte of bleak gray light, almost fluorescent in its strangeness.

Ellie, after only a few moments of the new surroundings, turned with an angry face to Hess. Joey, on the other hand, was doubled over as if he was sick, breathing ragged and shallow breaths. Franklin could do nothing but gaze out in horror at this strange, alien terrain.

"What is this place? What is this awful place?" demanded Ellie, body visibly shaking. "Are we on another planet or something?"

"Oh dear," breathed Hess. "Oh dear, oh dear, oh dear." He fiddled with a dial on the side of his helmet. "Oh no."

"What is it, Hess?" asked Franklin, though he was quite sure he knew the answer.

"We haven't travelled to the past like we were supposed to," breathed Hess grimly. "We haven't jumped back. We've jumped forward into the future. **Far** forward."

"How far?" asked Joey.

"Too far. Much further than any human ought ever to go?" Hess sounded grave.

"What do you mean?" said Ellie. "Are you saying?-" her voice trailed off.

"I'm afraid so."

"Good God," muttered Franklin. "You mean we've gone into the **post** apocalyptic future? It's already happened, at this point? That's why everything is so... My God. So desolate?"

"Yes," sighed Hess. "The Shard seems to have skipped over the apocalypse entirely and brought the Noah accidentally into the future, into a time after Armageddon; into an earth where all life has been obliterated. This must be all that's left."

"I can't see this, I'm sorry," said Joey and retreated back into the Noah. The bare plains stripped of life had proved too difficult a sight for him to behold and had banished him indoors where he could take deep breaths of the Noah's ventilated air, a welcome relief to the breathless, doomsday exterior.

"There goes another chance to get it right. You've only got a few left before the Shard explodes, Hess," chided Ellie, though her gaze was too distraught by the barren earth before her to muster much sarcasm.

"**We've** only got a few left," reminded Franklin, and the girl nodded glumly.

"You kids don't need to see this, and frankly neither do I," said Hess. "It was a silly accident, but we don't need to spend anymore time here than is necessary. Come on, let's get back into the ship. The air out here is thin and I think staring out at these dreary plains for too long could drive us mad. Just pray another one of those dust storms doesn't come and blow us away, although I think it ought not to bother the ship so much while it's grounded."

"So we'll be leaving this time now?" asked Ellie.

"Yes," replied Hess. "At once if possible. My helmet can't seem to determine how many years after the apocalypse we've actually travelled, though I don't think it'd make a difference if it were ten or a thousand. This is a dead place now and there's nothing we can do to help it, at least in this age. We've certainly got no business here. Come on now, you all." He climbed back up the gangplank. Ellie followed and disappeared into the Noah, but Franklin remained transfixed, rooted to the spot.

"Aren't you coming, Franklin?" Hess looked at him worriedly.

"Don't you think we ought to look around?" he asked with blank eyes.

"At this?" Hess shook his head. "No, Franklin, it's best you don't. We haven't got any business here now, never had any to begin with." He returned to the bottom of the gangplank and placed a metal hand on the boy's shoulder.

"This is our earth, Hess," whispered Franklin. "Stripped bare. Licked clean. I know you told us about the apocalypse, I know you said it was horrible, but those were only words to me; I suppose I just couldn't comprehend it in my mind. But now I'm looking at it with my own eyes. To think that people and trees and animals once lived here, that there were hills and forests, lakes and cities, and now—this. How awful! I'm so sorry, Hess. So sorry." Franklin hung his head.

"Why are you sorry?" Hess was perplexed and pitied the boy the disturbing sight.

"I'm sorry we gave you a hard time!" cried Franklin. "To lose your world like this, be tasked with saving it, and then get dumped on by a bunch of kids certainly isn't a day I'd want to live through."

"Though it may not be my time, it certainly is my world, at least I'm sure of that," said Hess. "And I'm determined to save it. I won't let this happen, Franklin," he assured the boy. "Not permanently, at least. I know I may not seem like the most competent man for the job, and I'm admittedly maybe not. But I will not fail the Earth; it was too precious to Dr. Burke for whatever reason. And so I will not fail you either, Franklin Freeman." Hess reached out and squeezed the boy's hand. "Come inside." With that, Hess advanced up the steps and was gone.

Franklin lingered for a moment more, his mind stinging with guilt. Hess had no more allegiance to this future than he or his friends; he was, after all, a sort of timeless fellow with his amnesia and all, yet still he fought for it and cared for it while Franklin could do nothing but feel sorry for himself and bemoan his predicament. Earth after the apocalypse stared him down and he felt as if he could hardly look past the tip of his own nose, much less glower back over it. How pathetic.

"Get us out of here, Mozi," ordered Hess as soon as Franklin had boarded and the door been shut.

"Mr. Hess-" began the AI.

"No, no, Mozi," interrupted the armored boy. "We can't

dawdle here. I don't want to stay to soak up this forlorn place and neither do our guests. It's better we pretend that we never even came here. Now get us up into the sky and send us to 3,000 BC before the damn Stalo falls out of the air again or another dust storm hits us or something."

"But, Mr. Hess-"

"No buts, Mozi! We really must be going this very moment. Look how afflicted our guests have become! It isn't healthy to stick around such a gloomy place!"

"Mr. Hess, you really must-"

"Just do it, Mozi! I'm beginning to feel sick just being here. I should like to forget about it all as soon as possible and get the process back on track!"

"Mr. Hess, if you would please!" exclaimed the computer. "Indeed, I am just as agreeable to the prospect of departing this age as any of you. Though I am a virtual creature and immune to grief; frankly, even I feel a simulated twinge of despondence in observing this dreary place, and it serves our mission no purpose to remain. But I have only just completed the scans of our vessel and a problem has been located, a problem that would hinder and, indeed, obstruct our departure completely!"

"Oh dear," muttered Hess. "What kind of problem?"

"The thruster core, the device which directs our flight patterns and controls our liftoff and landing procedures, is missing."

"Missing?"

"Yes. It is my suspicion that the thruster core was torn from the keel of the Noah when we entered into that frightful dust storm upon arrival."

"It was **torn** off?"

"The winds were quite fierce, I'm sorry to say," admitted Mozi. "Much faster than any wind speed ever measured before on planet earth. I conjecture the strange atmospheric conditions of the post apocalyptic planet must be affecting its weather conditions, among several other changes, as you have clearly observed."

"Oh well," Hess waved his hand. "How long before you can fix it? Or do you need me to climb down and reattach it manually?"

"That's just the thing, Mr. Hess." Mozi sounded sheepish. "The thruster core is quite lost. It fell from the ship some twenty miles or so back, as far as my calculations can tell."

"Twenty miles? That's ridiculous! We've only just crashed and we weren't travelling **that** fast," said Hess.

"You are correct. The Noah's thruster speed was very low, but it seems the dust cyclone has whisked us quite a distance in small amount of time," said Mozi.

"Just like Dorothy," mumbled Franklin. Hess looked back at him, not understanding to what the boy was referring. Franklin shook his head and gestured for Hess to continue.

"Well, alright then," sighed Hess. "Haven't we got another thruster core, Mozi? A spare?"

"Dr. Burke had inventive foresight and supplied us with counter-measures and solutions to several problems he determined we might encounter," said Mozi. Franklin really was getting tired of hearing people gush about this Hodel Burke, no matter how brilliant he might be. "But," continued the AI, "thruster cores are really quite expensive, especially for a craft as large as the Noah is. Being designed for aspects of interstellar travel, she requires the most advanced and high-end accouterments available. And, as you know, the doctor's finances dwindled almost to nothing toward the completion of this vessel. I assure you, there is a replacement part for every apparatus contained within the ship, except the thruster core and the Shard, that is."

"You mean to say," said Hess, anger beginning to burn his forehead and make his hands shake. "You mean to say that Dr. Hodel Burke, renowned genius, inventor and scholar, was too cheap to buy us a replacement thruster core?! One of the most crucial pieces of equipment aboard this flying scrap heap, the one without which we cannot fly, let alone **take off**, and we haven't got a spare? Damnit, Mozi! The Shard is useless unless we can get this thing into the air!"

"We really must forgive the poor doctor!" proclaimed the computer. "Though he accumulated quite a fortune over the years, equipping the Noah to travel through time was not an economical process! Most of his finances were floundered attempting various methods to house the artifact and induce its time bending effect within a controlled environment. Please do not think ill of him! A second thruster core simply couldn't fit into his already meager budget."

Hess sank into his chair dejectedly. "Oh, hell."

"You mean we're stranded here?" cried Ellie from the peanut gallery.

"It seems that way," grumbled Hess. "How dismal! Cast away and stranded on a desert planet!"

Joey hung his head and Ellie looked as if she was going to stride across the cockpit and strangle Hess through his metal suit, like crushing a soda can. "So that's it?" she demanded. "That's it? We're done? The ship lost a part and so now you're not saving anyone and we're never getting home?"

"How anti-climactic," mumbled Franklin. Somberness took them all again as the potential reality settled in: they'd grow ancient and withered aboard the Noah, trapped at the center of a desolate wasteland, feeding off of Burke's boring food substitutes and listening to Mozi ramble, till one by one they dropped dead from either old age or, even more frightening to Franklin, extreme cases of boredom. Surely Hess would rust inside his suit and become immobile; that is when Ellie would finish him off for good and use his silly armor as a steel drum like she had been wanting to all along.

Suddenly, a memory came to Franklin from a very long time ago. When they were nine, or perhaps ten, Joey and he had tried their hands at a sort of orienteering called geocaching. They had been given a series of map coordinates at which several treasures were located, all hidden quietly away in the woods. They had then, in between Joey's sporadic visits to the undersides of rocks and banks of streams, used a little GPS device to find their way to those coordinates and unearth the surprises.

"Wait!" he exclaimed, reaching out to stop Ellie's hands from wrapping around Hess's neck. "Mozi, you said the- what did you call it- the thruster core fell from the Noah, didn't you? Several miles away?"

"That's correct," replied the computer.

"I don't suppose there's any chance that it would have survived the drop?"

"I suppose that is a possibility. I cannot say at what altitude we were flying when the thruster core detached, but our particular version was a high-end model and quite sturdy. I surmise it might have survived the fall intact and even, dare I suggest it, in working order."

"Is there any way of locating it?" asked Franklin. "Like GPS or something?" Perhaps, he thought, they could locate the core in manner similar to geocaching.

"Mr. Freeman, I am a proud computer of the third millennium. Suggesting I utilize GPS to track something is much the same as I telling you to fetch dinner using a wooden club and a rock."

Franklin cleared his throat. "Sorry."

"All the same, the thruster core, just like many other machines aboard this ship, contains within it a transmitter that, if not destroyed by the drop, I should be able to lock onto. Excellent suggestion, Mr. Freeman," announced Mozi cheerfully. Franklin was glad he wasn't in trouble with the AI, who seemed to be nearly omniscient aboard the Noah and could conceivably make his time therein quite miserable if it saw fit.

Machines began to whir, devices to hum, and whistles to blow as the computer attempted to locate the renegade core.

"Please, Mozi, I **know** you don't need to make all that noise," groused Hess, rubbing his metal forehead. He turned to the children. "He really does it all just for show. I don't know why Burke programmed him the way he did, but he ended up being quite a show off. Likes to toot all his little devices here every time he does something important."

"You really are quite a smart fellow, aren't you Mr.

Freeman?" exclaimed Mozi suddenly. "Why, it might have taken me hours, if not days, to come up with such an excellent and admirable solution! I have indeed located the thruster core. It lies approximately twenty miles from here, in a southerly direction. I only presume it is a southerly one, of course, as the apocalypse anomaly seems to have all but eradicated the magnetic poles of this planet, effectively rendering my digital compass entirely useless."

"Twenty miles?" asked Hess. "And you're sure this tub can't get even a little ways off the ground? Not even a little hover?"

"Without the thruster core, such an action could be extremely dangerous and ill advised," warned Mozi. "I'm sorry to say, in order to retrieve the thruster core you'll have to walk several miles, Mr. Hess. We haven't got any other means of transportation besides the Noah."

Hess sighed, "That's alright." He smiled beneath the visor, threw his head back and laughed in great relief. "It certainly is a lot better than being stranded here for all eternity, isn't it?"

Franklin, Ellie, and Joey all had become quite morose at the news of the mission's early demise and their chances at getting home along with it, but they began to dance a little jig at the prospect of the thruster core's retrieval and their salvation, too. Even Ellie, who hardly so much as smiled since climbing onto Sachem's Head in Cankerwood, looked delighted. Franklin could not help but laugh as he watched her, shimmying excitedly, her smile so white and clear in such a stark and lonely place. She caught him staring and smiled even wider, but this made him bashful and he turned away. Joey, who did not often dance, was performing a kind of intense shuffle, and Franklin joined him. They knocked their feet noisily and happily together, high-fiving and letting out little, victorious, Indian whoops.

"See that, Franny? See that?"

"Yes, Joseph. We're not sunk!" They danced a merry little circle into which Ellie soon joined, taking both their hands, relieved at the chance to be giddy, if just for a little while. Hess, who was looking on and quite lonely, cleared his throat and began to speak tepidly. "I ought to start getting ready, then," he announced. "Twenty miles is no simple distance to be walked in a heavy suit like this, even if it does have cybernetic limbs. I suppose the core shouldn't be too hard to find in such featureless terrain, though; it ought to stick out like a sore thumb." He entered the lift and descended down into the lower deck to gather supplies. Franklin frowned.

"What's wrong, Franny?" asked Joey and then furrowed his eyebrows knowingly. He had seen such a look upon Franklin Freeman's face before. It was, thought Joey, two looks, actually: a combination of the sparkling eyes Franklin had worn when the lust for adventure seized him in Cankerwood, and a guilty sort of look, one that had claimed the boy several times when he lied to his parents about test grades and missing algebra homework. An amalgam of guilt and wanderlust? Surely, thought Joey, nothing good could come of such a look.

"Nothing, Joseph. Nothing to worry about," muttered Franklin absent-mindedly.

"None of that, Franny. I know **exactly** what you're thinking and that is a **terrible** idea. Franny, don't be ridi-"

"Why, what's he thinking?" interrupted Ellie.

"I'll tell you exactly what this maniac is thinking! He's thinking-"

"Children," interjected Mozi before Joey could finish, "I'd like to ask a favor."

"Yes, Mozi!" exclaimed Franklin, disengaging from his prying friends at once.

"I need you to fetch something for me. It's inside the compartment located directly above the control panel, if you would."

"Of course," replied Franklin scurried over to the front of the cockpit and located the compartment. Written in plain white text across it were the words PROTOTYPE HARDWARE. Franklin opened it to find several odds and ends of varying shapes and sizes located in side. "What am I looking for, Mozi?"

"Inside there ought to be a small, green colored box with a

monitor on the front of it, approximately the size of your fist," said Mozi.

Franklin grabbed the said object, which was quite smooth in his hands, and brought it into the center of the cabin. Now, Hess emerged from the lift laden with sacks and bags. His eyes fell quickly upon to the gadget which Franklin had retrieved for Mozi and at once began to shake his head vigorously.

"No, absolutely not," he groaned. "Not a chance, Mozi. This is already going to be hard enough! Why would I want to bring that insufferable little piece of junk?"

"Why? What is this?" asked Franklin. The little box didn't seem like it would cause much trouble at all. It looked like almost like a cellphone.

"Don't worry about it, Franklin. It's not important because I will **not** be taking it along." Hess seemed quite stubborn about this.

"Mr. Hess, do be reasonable!" protested Mozi. "My little brother is designed for situations just like this!"

"Little brother?" echoed the children.

"No, Mozi!" barked Hess.

"Mr. Hess, I've conducted a test on the signal strength of our communications system in this area and I'm sorry to say it's quite abysmal. Transmissions would be irregular, infrequent, and lacking in quality," said Mozi. "I would have very little means of staying in touch with you and ensuring you are safe and healthy along the way! My little brother can serve as my substitute in your absence from the ship. He can help you out of any trouble you might find yourself in!"

"**He** can't help me out of anything and you know it!" cried Hess.

"Who is this 'he'?" asked Ellie.

"The box which Mr. Freeman currently holds is one of Dr. Burke's final creations," answered Mozi. "It is, symbolically of course, my little brother: a miniature CPU emulating my operating system, only at a fraction of the processing power, of course. I am known as Mozi, so Dr. Burke called my miniature counterpart the Mozi Box. Quite catchy, really! If it helps you, think of me as an eagle and my little brother as a swallow. Both birds, yes, but one is contained in a much smaller package and not quite as powerful as the other."

"And why does Hess hate him so much if he's just like you?" wondered Joey.

"While my little brother does possess a similar knowledge database and internal problem solving function set to myself, he and I are not one in the same. Because of Mozi Box's small size, he lacks the personality programming I myself so proudly use with you now. His disposition is, to put it politely, more childlike in demeanor."

"Childlike?" scoffed Hess. "Try downright obnoxious! That thing would make a better blender than an artificial intelligence. I think Dr. Burke made it that way intentionally, I really do. He loved little kids and how impossible they are. And this thing is no different."

"Nevertheless, he can act as my eyes and voice while you are away," pointed out Mozi. "I really must insist upon this, Mr. Hess. It is a non negotiable situation."

Hess sighed dejectedly and took the little box from Franklin and affixed it to a rectangular opening on his metal chest plate. The moment the box was in place, its screen lit up and a little pixelated face appeared on it with beady little eyes, smiling wildly.

"Hello! Hello! Good morning, world! Mozi Box is awake! Happy birthday," the little computer squealed from Hess's chest with a falsetto voice that sounded like Mozi's but laced with helium. "Yes! Yes! Hello! Mozi Box loves all of you!"

"Oh, God," Hess held his helmeted head in his hands.

"Good morning, little brother. Are your systems up to date?" cooed Mozi affectionately.

"Big brother is here? Bother. What trouble. Boo! Boo! Big brother is a bully! Mozi Box doesn't need a big brother. Dr. Burke likes Mozi Box best of all!" chirped the excitable little AI.

"Just update your system, you little cretin," groaned Hess.

"At once! At once! Anything for Test Pilot Zero! Mozi Box

loves Test Pilot Zero!"

Hess, even encased inside the inch thick armor, looked as if he was going to begin screaming any moment.

"Preferences updated! Goodness gracious, what a great lot of changes! Mozi Box sees personal preferences have changed too. Test Pilot Zero is now to be called Hess, the namesake of the very suit he wears! Or perhaps, with this latest name change, the suit has begun to wear him, hmm? What fun! What fun! Hess! Hess! Hess!" it chanted.

Franklin furrowed his eyebrows. He was beginning to get a headache, but Ellie seemed positively enchanted with the miniature computer. She put her head very close to Hess's chest and smiled at the little screen, grinning at the small pixelated face projected across the monitor which contorted itself every few seconds into different, adorable expressions like a baby might.

"Why hello, there! I'm Ellie," she introduced herself.

"Miss Mars! Miss Mars! Big brother's system says Mozi Box should call you Miss Mars! Boring. Boring."

"Oh, that's alright. **You** can call me Ellie. You're a cute little fellow, aren't you? This is Franklin Freeman. And this one is called Joey Jensen," she said sweetly, indicating the two boys who stood behind her. They nodded courteously to the miniature computer but did not approach him; his 'cute little' voice had already begun to wear upon them as it did Hess.

"Franklin Freeman and Joey Jensen. Mozi Box can help you! Mozi Box is at your service! Nicknames are Mozi Box's favorite! Nicknames! Nicknames!"

Joey could not help himself. "Call him Franny," he snickered.

"Franny! Franny! Franny canny fo-fanny!" squeaked Mozi Box delightedly.

"Please, don't encourage him," pleaded Hess.

"Little brother, you're to be embarking upon a brief away mission alongside Mr. Hess, here," announced the more mature Mozi from the intercom. "In my absence, you are to advise him concerning difficult situations and offer any assistance you are capable of in his service. Record the mission for my future inspection and performance evaluation."

"Bother! Bother! Big brother will be watching? What fun's to be had?" Mozi Box groaned on.

"Do be quiet, or I'll leave you for scrap metal out there in the desert," said Hess. At this, the Mozi Box became quite timid and hushed.

"Supply check, Mr. Hess," ordered the elder Mozi. "Portable all terrain tent?"

"Check."

"Automatic kindling kit?"

"Check."

"Miniature compressed oxygen supply?"

"Check."

"Hydraulic Exoskeleton Survival Suit?"

"Yes, Mozi. Clearly I'm wearing the damn HESS suit."

"Weapons systems?"

"Yes, I've got them, but they didn't even scratch the Stalo. Another financial point I'm sure Dr. Burke skimped on. I don't think he imagined us doing much fighting. Especially against, well, whatever on earth the Stalo was."

"Extra rations?"

"Check."

"Portable 'Multi Operational Zeno Intelligence' box system?"

"That's me! That is Mozi Box! Present and accounted for, big brother!" squealed the little computer from Hess's chest.

"The Rok Counter?"

"What would I need that for?" asked Hess. "I'm not looking for traces of the apocalypse anomaly out there, this entire planet is sure to be entirely oversaturated with them by now. "

"I've temporarily recalibrated your Rok Counter to track the Thruster Core and point you in its exact direction. For the time being, it will show you your way, and then when you've found it, it will bring you straight back to the Noah."

"Right. Good thinking, Mozi. Check." Hess patted his waist where the Rok Counter was stored.

"Internal water supply?"

"Check."

"External water supply?"

"Check."

"Good. It's quite dry in this barren country; you'll become parched in no time," said Mozi.

"How on earth are you going to carry all of that?" asked Joey, indicating the enormous sack slung over Hess's shoulders.

"The suit will bear most of the weight. It uses artificial limbs, you see, and makes me a helluva lot stronger than I'd be without it," answered Hess, flexing his robotic muscles.

"It seems you've all that you need, Mr. Hess. Are you prepared to depart or would you rather wait till tomorrow?" asked Mozi.

"I'll go now," said Hess. "There's no use in waiting, especially given that the Stalo could pop up any moment if he managed to follow us. Who knows with that thing?"

The children quickly realized that the same event, the reappearance of the Stalo, could very well befall them while Hess was away. They began to worry and twiddle their thumbs nervously, though Franklin for a different reason than his two friends.

"You are, in fact, prepared to embark at this very moment then, Mr. Hess?" asked Mozi.

"Yes."

"Very well. I would, of course, give you a more thorough briefing on the terrain at hand, but admittedly, you know just as much about it as I do. Be advised, you ought to avoid those dust cyclones, as they are clearly quite powerful. I will be very worried for you while you're away, Mr. Hess. Do take care of yourself. Dr. Burke would have my hard drive reformatted if anything happened to you under my watch."

"Dr. Burke can't do much of anything to you in this day and age, Mozi. He's dead, remember?" said Hess somberly. He pulled a lever, which lowered the gangplank to the gray world outside. "I'll be going, now," he announced. "I should be back in no later than a day or two, if the terrain stays so flat as it looks here." He gazed out the Noah's entrance and shook his head at the despair of it all. "Wish me luck." Now, he descended the steps and went out into the barren earth.

"A trip! A trip! A trip! A trip!" chanted the Mozi Box till. Hess was nearly out of earshot.

Joey turned to Franklin and saw 'the look' return to his friend's face, that combination of a lusty desire for adventure and two sympathetic, puppy dog eyes. "Franklin, don't you dare," he threatened.

"Joey, when will a chance like this **ever** come again? And he looks so hopeless and sad out there! Just a lonely little speck of dust on the horizon!" exclaimed Franklin.

"Wait, that's the look you were talking about before, Joey?" asked Ellie.

"Yes. That's the look. God help us."

"Surely he doesn't mean to-" She couldn't even say it.

"I'm afraid that's **exactly** what he means to do," sighed Joey.

"Franklin, don't be ridic-" She couldn't finish. Franklin had already disappeared down the gangplank, chasing after Hess and waving vigorously as he went.

"Hess, wait! I'm coming with you! Slow down! I want to come along!"

"Damnit, Franklin," cursed Joey under his breath, watching his friend race across the wasteland after the armored amnesiac.

"He didn't come off as the impulsive type!" exclaimed Ellie. "Franklin Freeman seemed like more of a worrywart! Has he done this kind of thing before?" She was quite flabbergasted by Franklin's sudden change of heart.

"All the time," grumbled Joey. "He gets all excited for an adventure and then chickens out when push comes to shove. Just like in Cankerwood."

"That must get annoying," the girl remarked.

"You have no idea," he hissed. "Well, what are we supposed to do now? They've left us all alone."

"And the Stalo could come around at any moment," remembered Ellie, eyes widening. They looked at one another and gulped.

"So long, Mozi! Be back soon! We hope so, anyway!" called Joey over his shoulder as the two raced down the gangplank and out into the wasteland, chasing after their bothersome friend.

CHAPTER ELEVEN

ACROSS THE WASTELAND

And so it was; they set out across the empty earth that was to be. Franklin, Hess, the Mozi Box, and the begrudging Joey and Ellie, all trudged their way slowly across the vast expanse of nothingness; they all of them reduced to tiny black specks upon a great, bare canvas.

The going was quiet and Franklin was left to his thoughts, silently enduring the guilt brought on by the smoldering glares borne into the back of his head by Ellie and Joey, who walked a ways behind the rest of the party so that they might grumble and whisper angrily about their somewhat unwilling recruitment into the trek across the plains. Ignoring them, Franklin contemplated the terrain before him, though it was nothing like the planet he had known, more closely resembling pictures of the surface of Mars he had seen in his books.

The thin and nearly airless atmosphere that stung their lungs as they walked was hauntingly quiet. Not quiet like Cankerwood; no, this place had to it such an oppressive silence that several times Franklin stuck his finger into his ear to ensure he hadn't gone deaf. The sky above them yielded nary a cloud to shade them, though the sun was so bleary and tepid it offered very little to shield them from in the first place. Far across the horizon, north towards where the Noah had crashed, Franklin spied the towering cyclones of dust that had grounded them earlier that morning. They were few and far between, but even from such a distance, their tremendous height and ferocity were not lost upon the travelers. Franklin could not help but to see these twisters as solitary, black ghosts wandering the horizon without aim. How lonely they seemed.

Hess had spoken very little and only mumbled a halfhearted thanks to Franklin upon the boy's abrupt entry into the journey. He now walked ahead of the children, silent and somber. Franklin was quite confused, though this was the state he had spent most of his young life in so he was used to it. He felt as if he simply couldn't win; Hess was ignoring him to his front, Ellie and Joey were ignoring him to his rear, and he walked quite alone between the two parties without anyone to talk to. He quickly realized he was just as socially inept when time travelling as he was in the high school lunch line. Rats.

"Mozi Box would like to say something! Oh please, oh please let Mozi Box speak Mr. Hess! Mozi Box will be brief! He promises, he promises," begged the miniature computer. Hess said nothing, so it continued, "We've travelled approximately one half of a mile nearer to the thruster core! Mozi Box loves Mr. Hess for carrying him."

"Only a half mile?" demanded Hess. "We've been walking for nearly an hour! Surely we've gone further than that."

"Mozi Box is certain. Mozi Box is never wrong!"

The going was slow as it was quiet and the children lagged behind Hess, stopping periodically to linger and draw deep breaths.

"What's taking you all so long? You're lollygagging!" called Hess back to them, addressing them for the first time since their departure from the Noah. Franklin looked back to his friends, but they glared expectantly at him as they panted, ragged and worn. It seemed Franklin was to be the designated speaker for when it came time to address any of their shortcomings.

"We're sorry, Hess. We haven't got breathing helmets like you and the air's thin out here. It's slow going," he explained.

Hess bristled angrily for a moment, but quickly had a change of heart as he cast his eyes across the stark and featureless world; how very alone he would be without the children, without his new companions. "I'm sorry!" he cried out. "How selfish of me to forget. Take the time you need, we're not exactly pressed for it at this point." With this, the armored boy dropped into a slower pace to accommodate the rest of the group.

Quite relieved, Franklin, who had been powerwalking in a futile attempt to keep up with Hess, fell into step with Ellie and Joey. They had been making no attempt to keep up; in fact, they had been dragging their feet in a rather childish attempt to spite Hess and embarrass Franklin. Begrudgingly, they allowed him to walk with them.

"I'm sorry, guys," Franklin whispered sidelong to his friends. They rolled their eyes. "No, I really am," he insisted. "You didn't have to come along! You could've stayed with the ship."

Joey allowed himself a frank, though still annoyed chuckle, "And let you have all the fun?"

"I told you this morning, we're all sticking together, Franklin," Ellie reminded him. "Joey and I weren't going to let you go out into this terrible place with only Hess to help you. You'd maybe have already gotten sucked up into one of those tornados if we weren't here to keep an eye on you and it was just that bucket of bolts leading you on! And we certainly weren't going to let you leave us on that creepy old ship alone out in the middle of nowhere. Especially with that Stalo monster potentially lurking around."

"Yes, I'm sorry for that," said Franklin. "I really was hoping you'd come along. I figured you might. So thank you."

"I just want to know why!" exclaimed the girl, who was quite bewildered. "Why were you so eager to come out here and look for this thing?"

"It's just the way he is," said Joey. "Franklin's always had a tendency to go looking for trouble, even when it's clearly already found him. "

Franklin shrugged. "I suppose Joey may be right. But I usually chicken out when it comes to stuff like this! Real stuff, I mean. You remember how I was on Sachem's Head yesterday? All excited at first, but then a real yellowbelly when things came down to brass tacks."

Ellie smirked. "I do remember. So what's different now? Eager to show off for Hess?"

"No," admitted Franklin. "No, that's not it. I don't think Hess wanted us to be out here any more than you two did. We're only slowing him down, so far as I can see."

"Then why?" she pried.

"I guess I was feeling too self centered," admitted the boy. "Here's Hess with the literal weight of the world on his shoulders and all I can do is moan about my own problems. I guess I felt a sort of duty to him, if that makes any sense."

"A duty?" prodded Joey.

"Yes, though I'm not sure why." Franklin scratched his chin as he watcher their armored companion striding on ahead of them. "He's so alone on this mission of his, with nothing but computers to keep him company. No name, no memory, and such a massively important task to complete, one that I wouldn't wish on anyone! It's got to be hard as hell, and I don't envy him that. I figured I'd just do what I could to give him a hand. Better to expend my energy helping rather than hindering and whining. And even though it is a terrible state to see our planet in, so empty and desolate, I wanted to make sure I saw it. I'm not sure why, really."

Joey and Ellie nodded and sighed. It was indeed a dangerous undertaking, and not one of the kind they would easily accept again, but they agreed it would certainly occupy their minds and distract them from their own miserable misfortune, which would surely would have eaten eat away at them incessantly while trapped aboard the Noah.

"We'll forgive you for now, Franklin Freeman," sighed Ellie. "But we're going to have a long talk about your decision making skills when we get back to Pendel Circle,"

"When we get back," echoed Franklin. Yes, he liked the

sound of that. They all did.

Hess had slowed his cybernetically enhanced trot to a methodical lope, allowing the children to meander along behind him at a more leisurely pace.

"This place," said Joey as they walked on, "it reminds me of the Cambrian."

"The Cambrian?" asked Ellie.

"You're an honors student, Ellie, shouldn't you know about that kind of thing?" chided Joey. Franklin smirked at this and Ellie pinched his arm till he grimaced instead. "The Cambrian," continued Joey, "was the first geological period of the Paleozoic era, the first era of the earth. Life hadn't really begun to evolve yet, except in the sea, but even in the ocean it was only fairly simple life. The land, however, was a lot like what we're looking at now: rocky, barren, dry, and, most importantly, completely devoid of life. There weren't any trees in the Cambrian, and I've read the oxygen was quite thin back then because of it, just like now. Of course, this all happened hundreds of millions of years ago, long before even the dinosaurs, before even fish came to be. But isn't it interesting to see how the earth has come full circle? Like all the natural progress it's made, not to mention human progress, has been wiped away in the blink of an eye. Evolution, forestation, even geological formations like mountains and hills, all blown away, just like that!" He snapped his fingers.

Hess had overheard this and stopped a moment. With his back to the children, he began to speak, "The Cambrian came to be as earth was created, a process of nature, an innocent action void of intent or meaning, if you don't believe in God, anyway." He then gestured to the wasteland around them. "This is something else entirely."

"You don't think the apocalypse was a natural occurrence? An act of God, so to speak?" asked Ellie.

"I'm not sure what I believe, to be perfectly honest," he replied. "But the way Dr. Burke always talked about the apocalypse anomaly, the way he described its patterns... Burke was always convinced that the storm came to earth with some sort of intent, with some kind of sentience. For whatever reason, he refused to believe that nature could be so frighteningly thorough in its eradication of life. And there were scientific reasons for his beliefs too: observations he had made, but they were much too complex for me to understand."

"So you think this phenomenon could be some sort of being? Like an alien or something?" wondered Franklin.

"It could be. Dr. Burke was a very smart man, but he had a wild imagination, too. I suppose it could be some sort of entity from outer space, but I certainly hope it isn't."

"Why do you hope it isn't?" asked Joey.

"If this thing can think, it's going to be a hell of a lot harder for me to kill," muttered Hess, taking up his gait again and leaving the children to scramble along behind in his dust.

As the day wore on and the milky sun fell lower towards the horizon, the great emptiness and unchanging, consistent nature of the landscape began to wear on Franklin's mind. Though the Noah was only a speck in the distance, and though Mozi Box had insisted again and again they had travelled several miles already, it felt as if they had been standing still. There was nothing, not even a far off mountain or cloud, to measure their progress against. Everything looked the same.

During one of the several breaks which Hess had begrudgingly allowed them, Joey knelt to scoop up a handful of the abundant dust that carpeted the wasteland and pocket the stuff, but Hess stopped him sharply. "I wouldn't do that if I were you," he warned.

"Why not?" Joey looked indignant; collecting samples of this and that in nature was his greatest love in life.

"Mozi Box?" Hess called out to computer. There was no response. Hess groaned and tapped the little monitor attached to his chest. "Wake up you worthless waste of circuitry. He won't shut up all morning and then, when I need him, he goes into sleep mode!"

The miniature, pixilated face appeared suddenly on the screen and smiled widely. "Mozi Box loves to take afternoon naps, just like Papa Burke used to! What is it, Mr. Hess? What can Mozi Box do for you?"

"What can you tell our friend Joey here about the post apocalyptic matter he's about to put into his pocket?"

Mozi Box furrowed its little, digital eyebrows, scrutinizing the dust in Joey's hand. "Transportation of this matter is ill advised. It is saturated with the energy signature of the apocalypse anomaly, an energy composed of substances unknown to my database and therefore highly unstable and potentially dangerous. Prolonged exposure to large amounts of this energy, which I can only refer to as dark energy, could result in severe genetic mutations."

"Mutations? Count me in!" Joey was positively bubbling at the thought.

Hess swatted the dust from his palm sternly. "You can't take that stuff out of this time period and into another. God knows what trouble it could cause. We're already risking radiation poisoning just by walking on it!"

Ellie and Franklin had become quite antsy at the mention of radiation poisoning and were both hopping from one foot to the other. "So we're going to get mutations by being around this stuff?"

The AI laughed a little laugh that sounded like a parakeet's. "Mozi Box loves your dancing! Not to worry, it would take years to do you any permanent harm. But my sensors detect there are places upon this planet with much more severe concentrations of the dark energy, concentrations that could affect you very quickly. We should proceed with caution."

Night came upon them quickly, though it was an unusually sudden change from day to dusk and took the friends off guard; the sun did not dim in its lackluster intensity, and only when it began to disappear behind the horizon did the children realize how late it had become.

Hess, noting the hour, held up his hand for the troop to

stop. The children did so gratefully, panting hard, worn nearly to exhaustion from the breathless trek across the empty plains.

"That's far enough for today," he said, and then held up the Rok Counter to inspect it. "The Rok Counter says we've gone about half the distance, and we should arrive around this time tomorrow if we maintain our pace."

"Mozi Box concurs," chirped the AI.

"We'll set up camp here and stay the night," announced Hess. "Normally, I'd camp on high ground or beneath a cliff or something; an advantageous position, you know? But given the nature of this territory, or lack thereof, we'll have to make do."

Franklin nodded. "It won't be so bad," he said hopefully. "It'll be just like the pioneers camped when they used to wagon train it across the Great Plains."

They set to work quickly in erecting a makeshift shelter for the evening, though Hess's futuristic gear did most of the work for them. The ugly, orange tent, which was nearly as large and spacious as Franklin's garage, sprang out of a small container no bigger than the average matchbox. Inside there were several, inflatable accommodations: a line of air mattresses, a table set in the center of the tent, and even what looked like a long, rubber sofa. All of this had come to take shape in only a matter of moments, inflating as fast as most balloons popped, and without a single human breath, only the push of a button. Joey and Franklin, who were quite enamored with the hobby of camping, could not contain their awe for what seemed to them a mansion compared to their raggedy old pup tents.

A few meters outside the shelter, Hess set down a small, black cube, which burst into flames at his command. It stayed there burning just as brightly as any campfire might, and with just as much warmth. The children came to stand around it and toast their toes as the balmy day waned into a chilly night.

Next, Hess produced a compact, silver cylinder that resembled a thermos, which he stood on the ground, and laid several regular looking mugs next to it.

"What's that?" asked Ellie.

"It's fifty gallons of water." Hess gestured to the cylinder.

"Drink up," he ordered. "You'll need it to wash down the meal supplements. They're pretty dry."

"Fifty gallons in that little thing?" the girl demanded.

"Compressed water. A real lifesaver when space is sparse. Still weighs just as much though," said Hess, shrugging his shoulders.

And weigh just as much it did. Franklin found he couldn't even knock the cylinder over with his foot, much less lift it into his arms. "That suit of yours sure does make you strong," he panted after several pathetic attempts to heft the water container. Hess had been effortlessly carrying the thing, along with several other packs, all day. "How much do you think you could lift?"

"A lot more than I'd ever need to," conceded the armored boy. "But hell, maybe it'll come in handy someday."

"You haven't got an extra one of those laying around back at the Noah, have you?" wondered Ellie. Hess laughed and shook his head.

"Like I said, Dr. Burke didn't give me a lot of replacements for all this gear."

"Doesn't it get stuffy inside the helmet?" asked Joey. He imagined it would be maddening, like being trapped in a locker all day long.

"No, not really," Hess admitted. "It's got all kinds of breathing and hydration apparatuses. It's even got one to eat. And there's all sorts of information displayed on my visor here. Although, sometimes it can be a bit distancing. Sometimes I feel like a robot, like I'm not really here, like I haven't got a face."

"What does your face look like?" asked Franklin. He reckoned Hess looked perhaps a bit like them under all the armor.

"I don't really remember what my face looks like," Hess told him. "I wouldn't be able to pick it out of a crowd, anyway. With the amnesia, and with being inside the suit so much, I guess it's just kind of lost to me."

The children pitied him this and asked him to speak on the

topic more; they could not imagine such a feeling, nor did they wish to.

When the sun finally disappeared, night rolled over the little camp like a storm. But, unlike the dismal day hours, the nighttime was beautiful, and Franklin could not seem to turn his eyes any other direction but skyward. The stars above seemed as close as they could possibly be without causing some sort of cosmic collision. Without any city lights or clouds to diminish their splendor, they shown and sparkled with an intensity the likes of which the children had never laid eyes on before. Because no mountains, buildings, or even trees encircled them upon the horizons, the sky seemed to blanket them unhindered, as if they stood inside a glass dome and gazed up and out of it and into the universe around them. Franklin had never felt so close to outer space in his life; it seemed nothing separated him from the dusty earth below and the grand symphony of the cosmos above.

"I've never seen anything like this before," he whispered as he sat down with the others who were lounging by the artificial campfire. "It's nothing like the view back home on the roof of the garage. I feel like I can see the entire solar system, maybe even the entire galaxy." They were all indeed startled and pleased with the glimmering night sky, which so radically contrasted with the gloom of the day.

"With approximately zero light pollution from artificial light sources, we are now viewing the sky as it might have been observed millions of years ago on a more primitive earth," remarked Mozi Box.

"Just like the Cambrian," breathed Joey. "I guess we should be at least a little glad; we'd certainly have never seen anything like this back home, and we're likely to never see anything like it again."

"I have a feeling that's going to be the case for a lot of sights on this trip," muttered Franklin, and a shiver went down his spine.

Now, Hess distributed to them Dr. Burke's patented meal supplements, which came in the shape of grey, little rectangles.

They were glad for the water, which they drank greedily, as they were parched from the day's march and the meal supplements really were very dry and tasteless; although, they were quite filling. Soon, all of them sprawled about the fire and picked their teeth clean of the chalky dregs left over from the sorry excuse for a meal.

"A thousand years in the future and they still haven't figured out how to make health food taste any good," groaned Joey, filling his mug for the seventh time that evening.

"I'm sure someone did," chuckled Hess. "These supplements are typical Burke, though: completely devoid of any unnecessary bells and whistles. They'll fill you up and satisfy all your nutritional needs, but they won't taste any good. To him that kind of thing was unimportant, I guess."

"What is the future like, Hess? Or should I say the past, given our current lot?" asked Ellie.

"I'm really not allowed to talk much about it, Burke's rules, you see?" he replied. "But even if I was allowed, I wouldn't have very much to say. I only spent a few months in that time period, and I hardly left the lab while I was there- or then, I should say."

"Well what **can** you tell us, then?" asked Franklin. Part of him was aching to know, and the other part would rather such knowledge remain a surprise like it ought to.

"I can tell you what I told you before," answered Hess. " Dr. Burke was none too pleased with his present. He felt that humanity should've come a lot further by that year than it had. According to what he said, people were still so bogged down in the past, in old, petty conflicts, that they couldn't seem to look ahead. He worshipped progressive thinkers, people from your time: Hume, Voltaire, Da Vinci, Newton- you know, the intellectual leaders of your people."

"Not quite our time. All of those guys are a little further back, but do go on," said Ellie, rolling her eyes. She wasn't sure it was a good idea to have such a haplessly ignorant fellow as Hess operating a time machine with the fate of the earth in his hands.

"He saw it as his duty to help humanity onwards," attested Hess, shrugging.

"Why him?" asked Franklin.

"Why not him?" The armored boy leaned back on his elbows and looked up at the stars. "He saw himself as setting an example. If **he** couldn't meet the lofty standards he set for his planet, why should he have expected **others** to? It's just the way he thought: very globally. He couldn't help it, he had such high hopes for the future, and he didn't have time to bother with misgivings about the past. He simply kept moving forwards, unattached to what lay behind. I suppose you could say I'm the same way, although not by choice."

Silently, the children chewed on their thoughts and their tasteless suppers for a few minutes whilst they watched the grand dome that was the night sky above them turn slowly through space.

"It's not so bad at night," admitted Ellie, crossing her arms comfortably behind her head any lying back.

"Mozi Box knows several campfire songs!" squealed the computer suddenly. "But, Mozi Box knows only how to sing in binary code."

"Spare us," groaned Hess, reaching up to smother the AI with his metal hand.

Ellie shot him a dirty glare, though, and he conceded, allowing the computer his voice. "I think we'd all very much like to hear one of your songs," she cooed, and waved her hand. "Go ahead, Mozi Box."

The little AI began to trill with a garbled and simulated, albeit melodious and sweet voice. "One Zero One Zero," he chanted in various combination and arrangements, sometimes elongating his notes or racing through them with staccato beats. The melodies were none Franklin had ever heard; they seemed otherworldly and strange, but they were pleasant to hear nonetheless as the shimmering stars wheeled overhead. Even Hess, though he regretted allowing the obnoxious, overgrown calculator any pleasure whatsoever, began to find himself falling slowly to sleep as the digital melodies filled the silence.

Franklin, too, began to doze, but not for long. Suddenly, in the middle of one of Mozi Box's songs, something moved in the corner of his eye, just on the periphery of the campsite where the fire's light dwindled into darkness. At first, he dismissed it as nothing but a trick of the night preying on his weary mind, but then it moved again. Something, or perhaps someone, seemed to be scuttling along just to the right of their tent. In fact, thought Franklin as he squinted into the darkness, there seemed to be several shapes, shadowy forms about chest high, mulling about where they could just barely be seen and skulking low to the ground.

"What in the hell is that?" he shouted, rising and pointing into the darkness. The others roused at once and leapt to their feet. Hess held out his wrist, shushing the children, and a small spotlight folded out of his armor, casting a beam of light onto the spot in question.

For a moment, the shapes seemed frozen in the light like nervous deer upon a road, but then vanished into the darkness, scurrying off till their commotion could be heard no more. Franklin wasn't sure, but he could have sworn he had seen deep-red eyes glowing in that beam of light.

"Holy hell, what on earth were those?" cried out Ellie, but Hess motioned for her to whisper.

"Did anyone get a good look at them?" hissed Joey, intrigued. "They looked like mutant cockroaches, the way they scuttled. Did you see what I saw, Franny? Did you see the eyes?"

"God I hope not," whispered Franklin, shuddering at the image burned into his mind.

"It seems," announced Hess gravely, "we are not so alone as we thought."

After retreating inside the tent to where they felt less vulnerable than their exposed position out the open plain, they began to conference about what was to be done concerning the strange, unblinking and blood-red eyes that had peered out at them from the darkness.

"Are we sure we saw anything at all? It could have been an optical illusion! A trick of the wind," offered Franklin, not wholly wanting to believe what he had seen.

"First of all: what wind, Franny? It's as dry as a bone yard out here," retorted Joey, who rather wanted to believe the earth was not quite so empty as they had previously thought.

"And second of all," continued Ellie for him, "we all saw it! Even Hess saw it. That doesn't sound like a mirage to me. Speaking of which-" she turned to Hess who was fidgeting nervously by the tent flap, "-did your sensors have anything to say about it? Couldn't they tell us something about what we saw?"

Hess shook his head. "No, the suit's sensors didn't get anything, oddly enough. Neither did Mozi Box."

"Mozi Box is very sorry, but Mozi Box was singing and intent upon completing his tune. The moment you raised the alarm, Mozi Box was overtaken with a case of stage fright and went into sleep mode!" the little computer chirped apologetically.

"You see what I mean? Useless." Hess crossed his arms and smothered the AI.

"See, Franny!" exclaimed Joey, wiggling his fingers like worms. "We all saw those things! All of us."

Franklin nodded and swallowed hard. "Yes, but maybe it's best we forget about them altogether. They didn't bother us all day; surely they won't come skulking around again. Hess scared them off."

"That won't do at all." Ellie slammed her fist down onto the inflatable table around which they stood, resulting in rather a more comical effect than she had desired. "You're just trying to make the problem go away by pretending it's not there. That's denial, Franklin, and it simply won't do."

"Franny thought he could get our sixth grade bully to go away by closing his eyes every time he walked by," snickered Joey. Franklin scowled at him.

"Ellie's right. It won't do. We can't ignore a potential threat," said Hess. "But we've got a long walk ahead of us tomorrow and you all will need your rest; I don't want anyone dragging their feet. I'll keep watch outside the tent during the night. In case whatever those things were should come again, I'll raise the alarm. You three get some shuteye."

Ellie, who was still quite unhappy with Hess and saw no reason he shouldn't take a full watch, found this suggestion agreeable, and Joey was beginning to nod off, so the two shrugged and began to head towards the inflatable beds. Now it was Franklin's turn to become indignant.

"Now, **that** won't do at all!" he cried, following his two friends and seizing them by the shoulders. "Hess needs his sleep just as much as us, if not more. We can't let him stay up all night while we sleep all safe and sound in here. Besides, I don't think I'll be able to sleep much anyway tonight, not after that scare." He looked at his friends scornfully and they relented. Franklin's eyes had a tendency to grow soft and penny colored when he pleaded with them, and they found it difficult to refuse the bright faced boy.

"Fine then. We'll take shifts keeping watch," sighed Ellie. "You'll go first, Franklin, since you seem to be so eager. Then Hess, then me, and Joey last, since he's hard enough to wake up already." She gave Franklin a challenging look.

"It's alright! It really is. I'll take the watch by myself," sputtered Hess, but Franklin would have none of it. He marched boldly past Hess and out the tent flap and into the night.

Suddenly, at the prospect of waiting alone outside while dark forms might have very well been lurking about, Franklin's spurt of courage abandoned him and left him cursing at the hauntingly beautiful sky, wishing the morning's sun would hurry up and rise already.

There he sat, huddled close to the fire and shivering quietly for a long while. He had no problem keeping himself awake; his eyes darted nervously to and fro, scanning the terrain for any sign of movement, and the cold bit into him with sharp, frostbitten teeth. Just as he was beginning to feel as though his toes were going to freeze and fall off, Ellie emerged from the tent with bleary eyes and a blanket draped over her slender shoulders.

"Why aren't you asleep?" he asked, his voice trembling with chill.

"I was," she said bluntly, "but then I woke up. I guess I was a little obstinate before and I'm sorry. I forgot all about you out here, you must be freezing." Her voice, though it sounded tired, was tender. With this, she removed the blanket from her shoulders and arranged it upon Franklin's so that all of his extremities were comfortably, not to mention, warmly, contained. Pausing, she draped her arms down over his neck and let them dangle there, warming them in the light of the artificial fire. She began to fake snores playfully and Franklin chuckled. He could only hope the sound of his pounding heart, a throbbing brought on by her touch, did not make his voice quaver.

"Thank you, Ellie," he whispered into her ear, afraid to disturb the silence. He could feel her cheeks contort into a smile against his shoulder. He nearly melted. After a quiet moment, she stood and retired back into the tent without another word.

The rest of Franklin's watch passed uneventfully, and he entertained himself by watching the dazzling stars above. Dozens quickly turned into hundreds, and hundreds into thousands, till he lost count and at the same time lost himself in their grandeur, having quite forgotten about the mysterious shapes lurking in the shadows.

Just as he began to nod off, Hess came clanking out of the tent and sat down next to him.

"Seen anything?" he asked Franklin.

"Nothing."

"Heard anything?"

"Not a peep. No wind, no crickets, nothing whatsoever. It's deadly silent out here. It would've driven me crazy if it weren't for the stars and the crackling of that fire cube of yours." He hugged his knees closer to his body.

"It's not quite time for my shift yet, but I couldn't sleep. I can take over for you now, if you like," offered the armored boy.

"Thank you," replied Franklin, "I'll sit up with you for a few minutes more, if you don't mind. I'm not sure I'm quite ready to sleep yet myself."

"Fine with me." Hess leaned back on his metal elbows. There they sat in silence for a while, two lonely little specks illuminated by the fire, quite solitary upon the vast, arid plain.

"Franklin," Hess said suddenly, turning to the boy. "I appreciate what you did for me before. I want you to know that."

"What, with taking the first watch? Don't worry about it."

"No, not the watch, though that was generous of you. I'm talking about earlier."

"Earlier?"

"Yes." Hess fidgeted. "Earlier in the day, when you-" he cleared his throat,"-decided to join me on the trip. You didn't have to do that, and don't think you ever have to do it again; I don't expect you to."

"Oh good," sighed Franklin in relief. "I thought you were mad at me. Mad that I joined you and, well, slowed you down."

"At first I was a bit mad, to be completely honest," confessed Hess. "This mission is so important, and any weakness or disadvantage could mean its ruin, could mean the difference between the earth's survival and, well, this." He spread his hands out, indicating the ruined planet before them. "But it would have been a lonely day without you all. It's been lonely for a long while. I've never met any people my own age like you three are, and it's been..." He paused. "I guess I can say it's been a relief to have a little company along, even if you do all walk a bit slower than me. It may be a weakness in the mission, but at least it's a pleasant one."

Franklin chuckled and nodded. "We'll try and keep up tomorrow. I promise."

"Don't worry about it." Hess waved a dismissive hand, and then stared into the fire. "I'm not sure either of your two friends would have done the same - joining me, I mean. I don't think either of them is too fond of me. They didn't seem too thrilled about coming along with you, either."

"We're all still in a bit of shock, I'm afraid, But give yourself time to grow on them and I'm sure you will," reassured Franklin. "Once we all get past the fact that all of this is actually **happening**, Ellie will soften up. I'm positive."

"That's nice to hear," said Hess. "Now, if we could just figure out what the hell those things were before, we'd be peachy king. Got any hunches?"

"You'd know better than me," laughed Franklin. "Joey was saying something earlier about mutant cockroaches. That'd make sense, I guess; I've heard they can survive all kinds of calamities: nuclear holocaust, floods, hurricanes, and maybe even whatever this storm was."

"Maybe," Hess agreed. "I certainly hope that's all it is. You ought to go in now, you've been out here long enough as is!" He gestured to the tent. "Get some rest."

"I'll try," replied Franklin. "No promises, though."

Hess extended his great metal glove. "Thank you again, Franklin Freeman." The boy accepted the gesture and the two shook hands, Franklin's smile spread across his face and Hess's grin hid beneath his helmet.

Without another word, Franklin crept inside the tent and curled up beneath his blanket in between Joey and Ellie who were already fast asleep. Hess was left to his portion of the watch, which he conducted dutifully. Franklin was restless and fitful as he thought on all the strange things that had befallen him; but, soon, listening to the gentle rhythm of Ellie's breath and the clockwork consistency of Joey's snores, he fell to sleep and dreamt of nothing but the stars, which shimmered so brilliantly above.

They set to work early the next morning. There was a great deal of grumbling as Hess bustled busily about, deflating the tent and stowing away his various instruments. Apparently Ellie had informed him that he 'ought to take a long walk off a short pier' when he had tried to rouse her for her shift. A tumultuous, albeit hushed argument had ensued which Franklin and Joey had slept soundly through. And yet another shouting match had taken place when Ellie tried to wake Joey, who slept like a bear in the middle of December and was not easily dissuaded from his rest. Franklin, thankfully, had not woken during the tumult.

The sun, where it might have been orange or pink in the early morning back home, simply popped up without any warning, still quite bleak and dreary, and began to climb the sky lethargically.

As soon as there was enough light, Joey and Franklin began to circle the campsite with eyes carefully trained to spot animal tracks, snooping across the ground to see if they might find any evidence of their late night visitors. There was none. Whatever the creatures were, they seemed to be extraordinarily light on their feet and had vanished without a trace. This was not helped by the fact that any footprints, when first laid into the ashen earth, vanished almost instantly in the shifting dust underfoot. Nothing was missing from the campsite, and there clearly wasn't any scat or other markings for at least half a mile around the shelter; it would've stuck out like a sore thumb against the stark and empty ground. Dejectedly, the two boys rejoined their companions and finished packing away the camp.

"You really think it was cockroaches, Joey?" asked Franklin, folding a blanket and depositing it into one of Hess's sacks.

"Could be. It'd make sense," replied Joey, chewing on a meal supplement thoughtfully. "Then again, I've always had theories about the durability of crabs in situations like this. Of course, there's not a lot of water around here, so they must've evolved to live without it and just scuttle around on land instead."

"Why crabs? I thought you said roaches."

"I dunno. I guess I've always fantasized about gigantic, toddler sized rock crabs scooting around Stony Creek."

"You've got some strange fantasies for a kid your age, Joseph. What would they eat?"

"I'm not sure. There doesn't seem to be a helluva lot for them to feed on out here. They could pick minerals out of this dust." He scooped up a bit of the ash and rubbed it between his fingers. "It doesn't seem to be very rich with nutrients, though. I could've told you as much. Maybe they just sit around all day and filter feed. There's got to be all sorts of tasty contaminants floating around in the air. Or maybe they photosynthesize! Wouldn't that be something?"

"I'm just surprised there any life at all," put in Ellie as she stacked their mugs and stowed them away. "This place is as inhospitable as the moon! What could possibly survive here? Besides us, anyway." She smiled then, quite proud she had not yet been disintegrated or evaporated.

"Maybe it's not life at all, " said Franklin, suddenly wide eyed.

"What do you mean?" She looked at him, puzzled.

"Hear me out on this one," he began.

"Not more of this bologna, Franny," groaned Joey.

"Just hear me out!" exclaimed Franklin. "What if, whatever those things were, they weren't alive? What if they were... ghosts?"

Joey and Ellie snorted derisively and returned to tidying up. "Every time something freaky happens, Franny blows the ghost whistle. He's been doing it ever since we were little. The toast comes out of the toaster because a spring pushes it out, Franny, not because the ghosts are hungry," Joey chided, reminding Franklin none too kindly of some of his more outlandish childhood superstitions. Franklin went quite red in the face as Ellie let out a long and ringing peel of laughter.

They left the site as bare as they had found it and re-embarked upon their journey to locate the missing thruster core at once, following the Rok Counter's needle towards their hopeful destination. The trek across the plains went faster that day, and there was liveliness in their step and pace, as if their spirits had been renewed in spite of their apprehension that mutant cockroaches or toddler sized rock crabs could be lurking nearby. On and on they marched and even, at times, sang those sorts of songs that they had so merrily trilled in Cankerwood. Of course, Hess did not know the words but still he hummed the melodies lightheartedly through his breathing apparatus. And when the children's voices tired, Mozi Box took over and played out his little binary tunes.

Their pace went uninterrupted for nearly half the morning till Franklin, who had been squinting far ahead, hoping to catch a glimpse of something or other in the empty wasteland, spied a far off mote. It was only a dark speck in the distance, quite small to his eyes, and he could have well mistaken it for a lonely bush or a solitary rock in any other circumstance.

"Look there," he said, and pointed out that which he had spotted. The companions slowed their stride and cast their gazes out to the horizon like fishing lines searching for a bite. Franklin continued to point and gesture till at last they discerned what only his eyes had comprehended before.

"Do you think it could be one of those things from last night?" wondered Joey aloud.

"Dubious. It's not moving. At least I think it's not. It's so far away," observed Hess, scratching at his helmet.

"Exactly!" cried Joey. "What did I say before, Franny? Photosynthesizing! It's one of the mutant crabs sitting and soaking up the sun!"

"Whatever it is, it's no concern of ours," shot Hess. He held up the Rok Counter and pointed to the far away speck, "Look how far off course we'd have to go to see it. No, I think we'll stick to our current path and let whatever that is be. We have to keep heading south! There's no point in sidetracking now. None at all." Hess bustled ahead and resumed his trot.

"Woah woah woah," shouted Joey, rushing behind him with the others in tow. "You're not serious?"

"I am, in fact, and I won't be compromising on this. My

mission is to acquire the information I need from 3,000 BC and get back to Dr. Burke with it as soon as possible so we can destroy that apocalyptic storm. Just because we've gotten a little sidetracked with fixing the ship doesn't mean we can dilly-dally around to our random whims out here."

"But it's the only thing we've even seen in this desert!" exclaimed Ellie. "You're not just going to leave it, are you? What if it's a clue? Something to do with the apocalypse anomaly? I'm sure Dr. Burke wouldn't be happy to hear you ignored the chance to improvise a little and ended up dooming the world."

"That was low, Ellie," Franklin whispered into her ear.

"I know, just bear with me," she hissed back. "What's more," she continued with renewed volume, "what if that's not a clue or a cockroach or even a mutant crab! What if that's actually the thruster core and your little counter there just isn't pointing directly towards it?"

"But the Rok Counter is 100% accura-" Hess began weakly.

"But nothing," Ellie cut him off. "Thus far your instruments have crashed your time machine twice in one day! We're marching over there right now and investigating. Don't be a chicken. It's out in the open! It can't hide from us. And even if it's one of Joey's monsters, there're three of us and only one of it. And one of us has got 'enough firepower to drop an elephant', remember?" She raised a smug eyebrow.

Hess sighed and turned to face the other two children. "And you boys agree with her?" Joey nodded with ardor and Franklin, after a moment of hesitation followed by an angry glance from Ellie, did too. "Alright, I guess I'm outvoted. Just this once, though," Hess conceded.

Ellie led them proudly across the plain. However, the speck was quite far away, at least a mile and a half, and her confident stride soon slowed and Hess reclaimed the lead, leaving the children behind to drag their feet. The closer and closer they drew, the more strangely shaped the speck appeared. At first, Franklin was sure it was nothing more than an old rock, but then it seemed more like some sort of disfigured, hulking gorilla. No, not a gorilla, but something with the same relative shape.

"My God," declared Ellie. "Why, it's a man. That's a man kneeling there!"

"No, not a man. Not like any I've ever seen," breathed Franklin. They came upon it now, though they hovered cautiously a few yards away. Its skin was not rotting or flaking like Franklin had expected to find, but rather it was covered in metal from head to toe. It's head was like that of an overturned bowl and two lifeless, green eyes peered out from beneath its upside down lid. It indeed had the shape of a man, but bulkier and squatter in stature. It knelt on the ground, head bent as if deep in prayer, but its arms hung motionless at its side. It looked as if it had simply given up some very long time ago and kowtowed, submitting to the barren land that had apparently defeated it.

"No," said Hess again. "That's no man. It's a **robot**, albeit a long dead one. How sad, the poor fellow must've run out of power years ago and simply keeled over on the spot. And what a meaningless place to finally stop! How open and empty it is with nothing to see for miles. Perhaps he was wandering, though I couldn't guess in search of what. God knows how he ever survived the apocalypse, nothing else clearly did."

The children, who had never seen a robot of the future in their peaceful, suburban lives, gazed at the poor, artificial creature wide eyed. Franklin thought it looked rather like the HESS suit did; a series of metallic barrels and limbs brought together with slim, silvery joints.

Dust lay caked in layers all over the dead automaton, and his limbs looked as if they had not budged in a very long time. Nothing, it seemed, had disturbed the derelict machine in ages.

"So this is what robots look like in the future?" asked Franklin, sad and intrigued at the same time.

"No, actually," remarked Hess. "This is an old model, at least for 3012. Most of the robots I saw with Dr. Burke were entirely indistinguishable from humans, save their mannerisms of course." He approached the figure and wiped some of the thick dust away from its chest plate, indicating the words written upon it. "Utility-Bot 400," he read. "See? Nothing but an old maintenance model. Then again, I'd wager to the clunky old utility bots would last a lot longer out here than any of the more human looking ones would. Still, it's awfully sad that he died out here all alone."

"Not dead! Not dead!" squealed Mozi Box suddenly. "Battery rechargeable! Battery rechargeable! Mozi Box can resurrect this dead cousin. Mozi Box can be Dr. Frankenstein. Mozi Box can give life to the lifeless!"

"Hush," hissed Hess. "We'll have none of that."

"But Mozi Box can-"

"No!" commanded Hess. "He clearly can't be recharged, he's been powered down for years, maybe even centuries. The acid is sure to have leaked out of his battery and corroded his system. And even if you could recharge him, why bother? He'll do us no good. We're supposed to leave the other time periods alone! Remember what Dr. Burke said?"

"Dr. Burke never discussed meddling in the future, only the past," protested the concerned little computer. "Mozi Box will be positively devastated if his sleeping cousin is left to rot!"

"I won't hear it," spat Hess. "Let's move on now, if you're all ready, that is."

"We certainly aren't ready!" growled Ellie. She strode slowly to the rusting metal man. "He looks so sad, all alone out here like this. Like he just couldn't go on anymore." She placed her hand gently upon its head. "See? He can't even lift his eyes to look at the sky. He passed away all by himself in this awful, empty place; there was no one to hold his hand or tell him it was alright!" She looked as if she was about to begin crying.

"It's a robot, Ellie," said Hess bluntly. "He didn't need anyone to hold his hand. He hasn't got any feelings!"

"But he's the only sign of life we've seen in this dead place. And he's likely to be the last one, too," pointed out Joey as he and Franklin joined Ellie to look sullenly down on the pitiable metal man. "The least we could do for him is a small favor and give him a bit of a jumpstart. Maybe he'll even get to wherever it is he's going with a little shove in the right direction. Think of it a last service to the future before we leave, a last service to all that remains of society."

"**Nothing** remains of society!" cried Hess, exasperated with the overly charitable children.

"Except him. He's all that left," protested Ellie, kneeling before the robot and caressing his still face.

Hess groaned. "Are you seeing all of this, Franklin? You can't possibly agree with these two! What if the thing wakes up and it's hostile? What if it attacks us and someone gets hurt? What then?"

Franklin shrugged his shoulders. He didn't want to give Hess a hard time and further slow him down, especially after the armored boy had confided in him the night before. But, at the same time, he could hardly bare to see the lonely old android sitting so glumly out in the middle of nowhere. And he certainly didn't want to get on Ellie's bad side.

"Mozi Box really must insist!" piped up the miniature computer. "It would be a great insult to my kind to leave this fellow here when we would so readily assist any human being in need. Oh please, Mr. Hess. I beg you, oh please! This model of service bot would only need only a small portion of energy, a negligible fraction of what courses through your survival suit."

Hess wished he could stick his thumbs straight through his abominable metal prison of a helmet and jam them into his ears, blocking out the begging lot. But after a great deal of pleading (even Franklin joined in eventually) Hess relented and produced a plug and a long cord from somewhere around his rear end. After a few minutes of searching and dust brushing, which the children eagerly helped him to do, he located the utility bot's outlet and plugged the statuesque fellow in.

For quite a while, nothing much happened and the robot didn't budge. Ellie grew increasingly morose as a disheartening proposition began to dawn on her: perhaps there really was nothing left of civilization upon the hopeless planet, nothing left of life, even artificial life, it seemed. As the automaton sat still as a stone, the girl bit her lip and blinked back tears. Franklin reached out to pat her on the shoulder, but she shrugged his hand away and turned her back on the unresponsive robot.

Finally, Hess sighed and went to remove the power cord. As he wrapped his hand around it, though, a long moan that sounded like a washing machine dragged across asphalt seemed to belch fourth from within the stationary figure. Hess withdrew and leapt backwards, alarmed.

"Taaaaaaaaan yooooooooo,"the robot seemed to groan.

"Did it just speak?" demanded Franklin, eyes wide with disbelief.

"Taaaaaan yooooooooo," it moaned again. Ellie spun on her heels and knelt again to look at the android face to face.

"Are you alive, then?" she asked as gently as she could.

With what looked like a tremendous effort, accompanied by several rusty creaks and groans, the robot slowly lifted its head to stare at Ellie. Deep within its sad, worn out eyes, which looked like dusty gemstones set into its head, they could all make out what appeared to be the faintest glimmer of an emerald light, as if a bright green flame veiled by centuries of dust burned somewhere inside the robot's cranium.

"Taaaaaan yooooooo," it repeated. Ellie leapt a joyous little leap and threw her arms around the waking metal man. With an earsplitting screeching sound, the robot crumpled backwards under Ellie's weight and fell flat upon its back, taking the girl with it. Ellie clasped her hand over her mouth; her face had gone quite red with a mixture of embarrassment and the most extreme of worries.

"Oh no!" she cried. "I've killed him! Now I've done it! We only just revived him and I've killed him already" With a tremendous heave, Ellie attempted to right the robot and bring it back to its kneeling position, but to no avail; it was much too heavy for her. Franklin and Joey soon joined in the effort, but even with their strength combined, they could barely heft the hulking metal body an inch off the ground. Hess, whose rear end was still connected to the prostate automaton, rolled his eyes beneath his visor and gently herded the children out of his way. In one fluid motion, he grasped the robot by its wrists and hauled it to its feet, bringing it to something of a standing position; though, its arms still dangled at its sides and its head remained quite bent.

"Mozi Box's scans indicate this cousin will be charged and operational in a matter of minutes," announced the AI. "Please, allow him silence! And try not to tackle him again, Ms. Mars. It is very rude, artificial intelligence or not, to knock someone over!" chastised the computer.

Ellie looked very red again, and Joey and Franklin snickered, but she silenced them quickly with a shake of the fist, a fist they knew she was more than willing to use.

Gathered about the mysterious utility bot in a huddle, the four of them watched as slowly its joints creaked and began to flex. Basic motions at first, starting with the opening and closing of its palms, the twisting of its wrists, the bending of its knees, and so on.

"Brought down by a cyclone and now we're watching the tin man come to life, huh?" muttered Franklin. "This place really is like Oz, then."

"What was that?" asked Hess absent-mindedly.

"Never mind," replied the boy.

Finally, the robot turned its head from left to right, shook it a bit, and then raised it to look them peer at them all. Its eyes were glowing in full now, emerald and fiery. Its gaze fell upon Ellie and it peered at her. There was no mouth upon its face, but words came out anyway.

"Greetings," it croaked. Its voice was much deeper and much more rudimentary than Mozi's or even Mozi Box's. It sounded a bit like Franklin imagined an alto opera singer would sound if he were trapped inside an oil drum. "Call me Lazlo, for that is my name and proudly do I wear it. Lazlo Utility Bot, B-Model. Manufacture Date: March 16th of 2,962. Patched to version 2.4," it recited. "Call me Lazlo, for that is my name and proudly do I wear it."

"Hello Lazlo," said Ellie, though she shrank back a bit

before the full and somewhat intimidating height of the resurrected automaton; it stood at least two heads taller than Hess.

"Might I inquire, miss, if it was you who took pity upon this lonely, miserable creature and offered such generous charity?" it asked.

"Well, it was my idea," she replied breathily, still quite in awe of the figure before her. "I mean, Hess charged you up, but it was my idea."

"How fortuitous for me that an angel was stalking these parts and happened upon my forgotten, lifeless form," it proclaimed. "Forever am I in your debt. My life and operations shall be henceforth dedicated to doting upon your every whim. Your wish is my programmable function, forever more."

Ellie blushed hard. "Oh, well, I don't know about all that. And an angel? Oh my, Mister... Mister Lazlo, was it? Oh my," she giggled nervously.

"Would you grace my auditory receptors with the heavenly lilt that is your moniker?" asked Lazlo, bowing his head.

"Greetings, cousin!" sang out Mozi Box. "This one we call Miss Mars, though perhaps she would prefer Ellie. We are happy to have located you and offered assistance!"

"Miss Mars," echoed Lazlo, and Franklin could almost swear he said it dreamily. "Such a musical name to befit such a miraculous character. You have given life to my limbs and spring to my step. Without your charitable spirit, I should have remained frozen here in this accursed wasteland indefinitely!"

"Oh, Mr. Lazlo. Stop all that!" laughed Ellie again, hiding her face in delighted embarrassment.

"Hess," whispered Franklin, "don't you think we ought to start- you know- asking questions?"

"And miss this?" Hess stifled a laugh. "She's flirting with a robot, so far as I can see. He's awfully suave for a utility-bot, isn't he? They're usually just for fixing machines and sweeping up!"

Joey, too, was snickering through his hands at the peculiar scene. Franklin really didn't know what to make of it, so he crossed his arms and shut his mouth.

Lazlo bowed low, now. "Indeed, forever am I in your service, Miss Mars," he repeated. "That such a bright angel should be delivered to my salvation, even in this dark place, is a miracle. Name your desire and I will do my best to grant it you." He extended his metal hand gracefully, which she bashfully accepted. He lowered his artificial face down and pushed it gently against the back of her palm, as though he were a suitor in mediaeval times, slyly kissing his fancy's hand. "My mistress," he murmured.

Ellie could do nothing but giggle, quite taken with the android. Franklin tapped her on the shoulder and she spun suddenly, snapping out of the trance. He gave her an urgent look to which her eyes widened in response and she nodded vigorously.

"Yes, yes of course. Right," she stammered and turned back to Lazlo, who was still bent over in a humble bow. "Actually, Mr. Lazlo, there are a couple things you could help us with. Me and my friends here, that is."

Lazlo straightened and then swept gracefully into yet another bow, this time offering a little flourish of his hand to the boys. They nodded in return. "Any friend of Miss Mars is a friend of mine," he said. "What can I do for all of you people?" Lazlo paused for a moment and glanced at each of them individually, as if he were counting them. If he could have worn an expression, it would surely be one of befuddlement.

"Why, there are several of you, and I have not laid eyes on any of you since the time of my activation. It seems you do not travel from whence I hail. Might I inquire from wither it is you come that you wear such strange clothes and such youthful, fair faces? Never have I seen such faces! They are like those of the people of the past we have so often seen in the projections! Pale and plump! Where have you come from, o bright-eyed travellers? I thought nary a soul existed anymore save those from my homeland! Please, tell me! Are you from the fabled realm to the north?"

"Actually, we're from-" began Ellie, but Hess cut her off

with a nudge in the ribs.

"That is our business and ours alone," he said in the most serious tone he could manage. "We wish it to be kept that way, if it's all the same,"

"Er, yes," Ellie corrected herself. "I'm afraid we're here on important business. Confidential business, you see? You'll have to forgive us our secrecy."

"Of course!" exclaimed Lazlo, placing his hand on his chest plate. "Who am I to question such generous heroes? If it would please you, I'll even erase the memory of such a query from memory banks that I should not even dwell on the selfish thought for another moment."

"Oh, no!" said Ellie. "That won't be necessary, Mr. Lazlo. Please leave your - what did you call them - your memory banks just as they are.

"Please tell me then, my mistress: what can the humble Lazlo Utility-Bot do for you?"

Ellie glanced at Hess, who nodded and stepped forward. "For starters, you can tell us what year it is," he said.

"Year? My good sir, the term 'year' is an archaic one and has little meaning these days," replied Lazlo, taken aback. "If I'm not mistaken, the last time such a phrase was used was in the Green Time, long ago."

"The Green Time?" asked Franklin.

"Indeed, young master," exclaimed the robot. "The Green Time! Is this era not familiar to you? It is an epoch of history well studied in my homeland."

Franklin looked to Joey, who shrugged. "I'm sorry, it's not," he admitted.

"My apologies," said Lazlo. "The Green Time is how my people refer to the 'years', as you put it, before the dread Bhasma Cloud came upon the earth and rendered it thus, as you see it now."

"The Bhasma Cloud? You mean the phenomenon that destroyed the world?" asked Hess. He could understand calling the apocalypse a cloud, but the phrase that had preceded it sounded queer to him. What in the world was a Bhasma?

"Destroyed the world?" inquired Lazlo. "My new friend, look around you! The world is not destroyed! It is spread out before you here quite plainly. But I can discern your meaning! Forgive my impudent reply and let it not vex you; we who dwell after the end of days must find what little pride we can in this, the barren earth. Indeed, the Bhasma Cloud wiped away most all things that drew breath or danced in the sun; all that was green or depended upon those green things. To answer your question from before, I was activated and put into service a decade after the cloud ravaged this planet. It has been two-hundred of your 'years' since that day."

"Two hundred!" breathed Franklin. "Two whole centuries after the apocalypse. The Noah really did overshoot! That must mean we're somewhere around 3,212 AD right now!"

"Wait a moment." Hess silenced Franklin with a wave. "You said 'my people'. There are more of you robots out here?"

"Yes! Many of us," answered Lazlo. "At least I believe so, or I hope so, I should say. I ran out of power and became hopelessly stranded out in this forsaken spot nearly two of those 'years' ago. Who is to say whether my fellow robots have survived this long or not?"

"What were you doing out here when you ran out of power?" asked Hess.

"I was sent upon a mission by my people, they dwell south of here, to see if I might seek out other signs of civilization or life in the north. For days I walked and toiled in the sun, but to no avail; there was nothing to be found and no one to be heard. As my power cells began to grow low, I doubled back and began my return trip, quite empty-handed. But I had overestimated my endurance, and upon this spot, only a few short miles from my destination, from my home, my energy ran dry and I collapsed. Were it not for all of you, surely I would have become fossilized and been forgotten entirely."

"Your home isn't far off, then?" asked Franklin.

"Quite near, really. It sits a ways down south, like I said before, in that direction." Lazlo pointed off into the vast, empty plains; the wastes in that appeared just like they always had, stark and stripped of any landmarks. Perhaps, thought Franklin, Lazlo's people hadn't survived and their home had crumbled into the dust; he certainly couldn't make out any outlines of buildings or other structures in the distance.

"Are you going to return there?" asked Ellie worriedly; she too was concerned that Lazlo might find his home erased from the world like so much else.

"Not till I have paid my debt to this mysterious angel of mine," said the robot, and bowed to Ellie again. "How can I aid you, oh fair queen of this desert place? Oh ye oasis in this sea of sand!"

"Could you answer one more question for me, please?" Joey piped up. He had been quiet throughout the exchange up till now. "Last night as we rested, sometime after sun fall, we spied glowing red eyes on the periphery of our campsite. They disappeared as soon as we raised the alarm. You have any idea who or what they belonged to?"

Lazlo looked taken aback, if a robot could look so at all. "Red eyes, you say? Yes, I'm afraid I do know to whom those sinister orbs belong, and I am most displeased to find they have ventured so far outside their usual prowling grounds. They belong to a sort of creature with very long ears, though, so it is better not to utter their name out in the open like this. If given the chance, I shall speak to you of them in closed quarters when their mischievous and probing ears should not drop us any eaves. Please, tell me, what is it Lazlo can do for all of you? Name it and Lazlo will do his very best!"

Now, Mozi Box began to speak excitedly. "Sir Lazlo! Mozi Box knows an elegant cousin when he sees one, and this android speaks with poise Mozi Box can only dream of! If it would please the good Lazlo, might Mozi Box communicate our urgent needs to you in the language of computers in order to expedite the trivial process of human conversation?"

"Anything for a cousin." Lazlo nodded.

"Mr. Hess, if you would hold up the Rok Counter and show it to Lazlo for me," said the little computer. Hess did as he was bade and Lazlo inspected it. Soon, Mozi Box began to speak quickly in a rapid sort of gibberish composed entirely of ones and zeroes, like his songs before, which Lazlo chattered back at him in turn. This exchange was only very brief, though, and Lazlo soon nodded knowingly.

"How awful! A lost thruster core! And in so large a place to lose it," the robot exclaimed, but then tapped his metal face right where his nose ought to be. "I have little idea what one could hope to do with a thruster core out in these parts given that spaceships are a thing of the past, but it matters little. Regard yourselves as lucky, though, my new friends! The coordinates of your thruster core, imparted to me by good Mozi Box here, match the coordinates of my home nearly identically. It seems the device must have fallen straight upon my doorstep! We are headed towards quite the same place."

Hess couldn't believe his luck and nearly leapt for joy. "You mean to say our thruster core is in your homeland? Would you be our guide to this destination, then, and help us locate our lost apparatus? Surely, you know the terrain much better than us - not that there's much to know - and could help us pinpoint the thruster core's exact location."

Lazlo looked to Hess and then to Ellie. "Is this what you wish, Mistress Mars?" he asked very seriously.

"Oh yes!" exclaimed Ellie, and glanced at Hess quite smugly. It had been her decision to recharge Lazlo, a decision that had just given them a great advantage in the search for the thruster core. She intended to lord it over the armored boy. Hess shrugged and gave her a little, submissive nod. Perhaps, he resolved to himself, these children weren't entirely without their uses.

"Please then, let me guide you and show you the hospitality of my people," offered Lazlo. "We haven't had a visitor in, well… We've never had a visitor, actually! Cousin Mozi, are my cells quite charged?"

"Fully, Cousin Lazlo. Mozi Box sees you are ready to complete your prolonged trek home."

"Let us depart this empty space, then. I have certainly

lingered here longer than ever I intended, and I would like very much now to stretch my legs," said Lazlo, and plucked Ellie softly by the wrist. With the stride of a gentleman he began slowly to lead her away down south, talking to her and even, at times, singing little binary tunes like the ones Mozi Box had played before.

The three boys meandered leisurely along behind the pair, pleased not only that they had a friend to aid them in their quest, but that they had found life, even artificial life, and the promise of more of it to come, in such a dead place. Franklin watched Lazlo as the robot strode, watched his hypnotically artificial gait and marveled at all the wiring which ran up and down the automation's legs. He was immensely relieved to have met the robot, though he couldn't be sure why. Perhaps it was because Lazlo seemed an adult, if only an artificial one. Perhaps it was because the robot was the only one among them who was in exactly the place and time he was supposed to be.

CHAPTER TWELVE

NEW HOLLOW

"The green time, huh?" mused Joey aloud. "I always hear people complaining in our time about how we're losing all the green in the world. But it looks like the people of the future lament the loss even more and look back on **us** as the green ones. Imagine that. Funny, I always thought mankind would be its own undoing, not some terrible cloud flung from the far depths of space."

Franklin did not abide by this. "I never thought mankind was going to do ourselves in, not really," he said. "I'm sure we'd have gotten our acts together eventually if it weren't for, you know, the end of the world."

"That was always Burke's hope, at least," agreed Hess. "You two think this Lazlo guy has got a home to go back to?"

Franklin and Joey scrunched up their eyes and squinted as hard and as far as they could past Lazlo and Ellie, who walked ahead of them, but they could see nothing.

"Probably not," said Joey. "It looks completely flat whichever way you look, unfortunately. Imagine, though, a colony of robots living in the post apocalyptic earth! Wouldn't that be something? I wonder how it is they all survived. And why do you think he was so cautious about talking about those red eyed things?"

"He spoke about them like they would understand what he was saying," remarked Franklin. "But surely that cant be right. Maybe it's just some sort of weird robot superstition."

"Robots tend not to have superstitions. They're logical beings, you know?" Hess reminded him. "So if Lazlo says to keep our wits about us, we'd better do just that."

"Hess, what does 'Bhasma' mean?" asked Franklin. He had been wondering about the strange word for several minutes. It had a menacing sound to it.

"I'm not sure. It's what Lazlo called the cloud, as he referred to it. It's what he called the apocalypse anomaly. Any ideas, Mozi Box?" Hess tapped his miniature companion.

"Mozi Box can find no results in any of his several dictionaries and logic databases containing or referencing the term 'Bhasma.' However, Mozi Box enjoys synthesizing this phrase. Shall we say it together, Mr. Hess? Bhasma. Bhasma. Bhasma," it began to chant obnoxiously.

"I'm sorry I asked," Hess groaned.

"It's got an evil sound to it, hasn't it?" observed Joey.

"Sort of like something you know you're not supposed to say, but can't reckon why," agreed Franklin. He had noticed it too.

"Yes, exactly. It's eerie sounding. I barely want to say it out loud. Bhasma." Joey spoke the word under his breath, as if uttering a curse.

"And well you shouldn't speak that name aloud!" called Lazlo over his shoulder. "Please, refrain from mentioning those bothersome creatures or that terrible dread cloud till we are safely tucked away inside my home. Doing otherwise could draw... unwanted attention."

They did as Lazlo bid them and turned their attention instead to more menial topics. "Do you think the Noah will be alright with all those dust storms swirling around, Hess?" asked Franklin.

"I'm sure it will. It's a resilient craft. And a reliable one, despite its track record so far." Hess chuckled. "You know, it's funny, I haven't seen any of those twisters today except in the distance from where we came."

"Yes," called Lazlo again, "they do not generally wander these parts and stay to the north. Legend has it that they patrol the space where the ocean once lay, but this is only a legend. It is difficult to prove such talk. Occasionally, those tornadoes have flown off course and rampaged across my home, but we haven't been wiped out yet."

Franklin was on the verge of pointing out that it looked like Lazlo's home had, in fact, been wiped out; but he stayed the harsh words and held his tongue, not wanting to offend or trouble their friendly guide.

"He's awfully enamored with Ellie, huh, Franny?" whispered Joey.

"For a robot, he's very poetic. Not that I know much about robots. Or poetry, for that matter," admitted Franklin. "But this is the happiest I've seen her since we left Cankerwood."

Joey nodded in agreement. "I think she just needed to feel in charge of herself again. She made a lucky decision by insisting on recharging Lazlo, and it's helped us out. She did a brave thing, just like we know she loves doing, and it's put her back into high spirits. We can only hope they stay high, though. When she's down she's not so friendly, biting even, and I think our friend in the suit of armor here has taken the brunt of that bite on his big metal chin."

"You should've heard her last night when I woke her for watch," agreed Hess, shivering at the memory."

Suddenly, Lazlo, who still walked ahead of the group with Ellie, stopped his robotic stride and tottered for a moment. After nearly falling several times, he clumsily regained his composure and planted his cybernetic feet. "You'll have to excuse me," he said. "My joints are still a bit creaky from the prolonged hibernation. There's far too much dust in them to be healthy for my system."

"Too bad we haven't got the oil can," joked Franklin, but Hess didn't hear and Joey just rolled his eyes. Franklin had seen that movie far too many times for his own good.

"How do you fix a problem like that, Sir Lazlo?" asked Ellie, concerned for her new friend.

"If it wouldn't bother you, I should like to run a bit," suggested the robot. He flexed his legs so that they creaked and groaned for the children to hear. "Only a few hundred yards, you understand; just to loosen up my poor, weary joints."

"Of course!" exclaimed the girl, delighted. "In fact, I think a bit of running would do us all some good." She looked slyly back at the boys. "Game for a race?"

Franklin and Joey, who were really no good at running, groaned. "At least you're feeling better, Ellie. All right, if we have to," Franklin conceded, and nodded halfheartedly.

"Yes, a race will clear our lungs of all this dust!" she cried happily. "Alright, Mr. Lazlo, run ahead and set a finishing line for us. There's little else out here to use as a landmark, so you'll have to do, if that's alright."

"For Mistress Mars? Anything!" proclaimed the robot and launched into a spirited gallop. He sailed across the plains in loping, mechanical strides and finally came to rest some three hundred yards away.

"Right then," said Ellie. "First one to Lazlo doesn't have to take a watch tonight, or any other night, ever again."

"But we need equal rotations, it's only fair-" began Hess, but Ellie cut him brusquely off.

"No buts. You won't be competing, Hess. I'd imagine you wouldn't be able to run very fast in that suit of yours anyway." Hess nodded sadly, left out once again. "So that means it's just us Stony Creekers," the girl went on. "Come on, boys, come stand near me on the starting line so we can begin. Don't forget to stretch a little, you'll need it. I ran cross-country in Maine almost every day," she boasted, beckoning to Franklin and Joey.

Reluctantly, they dragged their feet over to where the excitable girl stood, cursing their luck. They had been tricked into racing a seasoned cross-country athlete.

"Hess, would you do the honors?" Ellie inquired politely after Joey and Franklin had performed some lackadaisical, rather comical stretches.

"Take your marks," ordered Hess, eager to see the competition. "Get set. Go!"

The runners exploded off their line like dynamite and entered into a rapid bolt across the wide plains. Franklin, who had spent the past few days either walking or sitting (like most people in the sedentary year of 2012 so often did) felt the blood gushing through his arteries and racing back to his heart through his veins. It felt good. His breath was clean and the lead was all his. It was unusual to run in such a place as the wasteland; the dust below his feet was springy and soft, not a shrub or rock impeded his step, and there was nary an incline to speak of. The earth was so entirely flat and slopeless that they glided across it like a plane does above smooth cloud. His lead was short-lived, however, for Ellie and Joey soon gained and began to lick at his heels.

"Here I come, Franklin," panted the girl, reaching out and poking him in the elbow as it bounced up and down. Joey, who was equal in league and stride with the Ellie, said little and devoted his focus to his breath. Joey was a small boy, much shorter than either of his two competitors, but his legs were spry and he pumped them with ease. Franklin had forgotten how fast his old friend could run.

Suddenly, Ellie sprang forward and swerved in front of Franklin, making him stumble and nearly fall to the ground.

"Watch it, Ellie," he snapped in between heaving breaths. Now he and Joey dashed quickly along behind the girl. Franklin looked to his friend with an exasperated huff, frustrated with the impossibly competitive girl, but Joey just smiled a wry little grin and, suddenly, leapt ahead as well, outpacing even Ellie and sprinting forward, leaving the two to eat his dust.

"No. You. Don't!" gasped Ellie raggedly, and her stride intensified. Franklin followed her along as they chased behind Joey, and soon they came into pace with him. There they ran, shoulder to shoulder, rushing across the wasteland to where the silhouette of Lazlo stood, outlined against the gray and cloudless sky.

In that moment, as he rubbed shoulders with his two friends and as his breath came shorter and far less often, he felt happier than he had been in some time; at least since their departure from Sachem's Head Peak. Though he began to foam a bit at the lips, and though his lungs felt as if they were about to explode and his heart to pound its way straight out of his ribcage, he smiled. And, as he looked to each of his competitors, he saw Joey and Ellie smiling too. For a brief moment, all was well.

But, as it is with all fleeting moments of peace, it soon came to an end. With a grim and nearly psychotic roar of determination, Ellie furrowed her brow and began to pump at the earth with a new and rapid vigor she drew from some hidden spring of energy within her. Forward she flew as her arms, being completely unable to keep up with her wheeling legs, simply flailed uselessly behind her.

'Damn,' thought Franklin, though his mind was becoming dimmer and blurrier with every exhausted step, his vision nearing total blackness. 'The girl can run.' He and Joey could do nothing but watch in a sort of elated despair as she sailed past Lazlo and tumbled, laughing and panting, to the dusty earth below.

With less of a flourish, they crossed the finish line after her and doubled over, panting and gasping for the air that was hardly there in the thin, unforgiving atmosphere.

"Miss Mars takes the day and victoriously so!" cheered Lazlo. "How splendid! How splendid! Such a race I have not beheld since the youngest years of my activation! Triumph belongs to all, but especially to Miss Mars upon this most auspicious and luckiest of afternoons! How perfect that, not only should I be saved by this angel, but see her compete to her fullest and seize victory by the horns."

Franklin and Joey, who were very near to dry heaving in exhaustion, were beginning to wish Lazlo would shut his loud mouth (though he did not really have one to shut in the first place, being a robot and all).

"Good race, boys," sang Ellie cheerily as she came to stand with them. Already, her voice sounded quite recovered from the endeavor and she further emasculated them by standing straight and tall, with only the hint of a pant in her rising chest. They, of course, were still quite bent in the middle and close to collapsing.

"Yeah," wheezed Franklin. "Good race."

"That wasn't really fair, Ellie," gasped Joey. "Making us race a trained runner and all."

"But who's complaining?" she asked, laughing. "You still liked it and you know it. I saw you smiling, Franklin Freeman. Even though I whooped you, you still enjoyed it."

Franklin looked up and offered her a weak smile, but a genuine one nonetheless. He clasped hands with Joey, with whom he had tied for second, and they chuckled breathlessly. "Why didn't you ever run that fast for coach back in the day? Back when we were in Little League?" Franklin demanded of the boy.

"Beats me." Joey shrugged. "Puberty, maybe?" But Franklin knew this was not true. Joey simply would not put his all into anything unless he was sure to enjoy it, or at the very least be interested in it. And, apparently, baseball had never lit the boy's flames like dashing across a post apocalyptic earth had been able to do.

"Hurray for Miss Mars, an Olympian among us! Hurray indeed! Shall we celebrate, then?" cried out Lazlo, and he hefted Ellie up onto his great metal shoulders. Now, he piggybacked her about and paraded her victory in elated little circles upon the empty country. She waved her arms and laughed delightedly. Even Joey and Franklin, two smarting urchins still stinging with defeat, watched the strange sight of a robot carrying their friend and managed a chortle. Hess's laugh, too, rang out; he had been striding briskly across the plain and now joined them at the finish line.

"I'll need a break now, I think," groaned Joey, straightening at last and drawing in another gulp of air.

"Yes," agreed Franklin. "I'm bushed. You'll have to give us a moment, Hess, if you can spare it."

"I can spare you two, and more if you should need them," replied the armored boy, and sat on his haunches in the dust. Out came the bottomless thermos and mugs, and they all gathered round to drink and rest. Lazlo, who complained his joints were quite tired of sitting, elected to stand and offered them a brief shade from the milky sun with his hulking form.

When he had drunk his fill and leaned back comfortably on his elbows, Franklin resolved to ask the question that had been gnawing at his mind. "Lazlo, I know you say your home's only a few miles south, but I don't see anything! Wouldn't a house, even a small shelter, be visible in all this emptiness, even at so great a distance?"

Lazlo pivoted and gazed into the south. "Indeed, friend of Mistress Mars, my home does not appear silhouetted against the horizon. I guarantee you, however, that it is there all the same; though I cannot guarantee anyone resides within it anymore."

"Is it invisible?" asked Joey. "Does it have some sort of cloaking device?"

"A cloaking device?" Lazlo chuckled. "I believe I learned about those in the projections, once. I'm afraid not, Master Joseph! Such complicated technology is sparse in this time; nigh all of it was obliterated with the coming of the Bhasma Cloud."

"Then why can't we see it?" pressed Joey.

"It is quite a sight to behold, my little world, and I'd rather not spoil it for you in the telling," admitted the robot. "Please, if your patience can hold, wait till you can look upon it with your own eyes."

Joey sighed and looked skyward, disappointed yet hopeful.

"I must wonder aloud again," mused Lazlo. "Since you did not allow me to strike the query from my mind, and since you are so full of questions about this place, I must wonder where it is you all come from that you know so little of this wasteland

and all its shortcomings. Could you hail, perhaps, from the north, from that place I sought and failed to find? Legend keeps that the north is flowing with prosperity and green, but no one among my kind has ever been able to travel so far as to find it and return home alive. That would certainly explain your fair faces and plump cheeks. Why, you look almost like the children from my projections, from the green time!"

The three looked to Hess with questioning eyes, to see whether or not they might reassure the quizzical robot they hadn't come from some promised land in the north but from the actual Green Time itself. He shook his head 'No.'

"Forgive me," said Lazlo. "It is not my business. Normally, I am not so impolite as to pry but, you see, among my people we rarely see others whom we have not seen before. It is a small community, you understand. And, when we do see strangers, they have red, spiteful eyes and we afford them a wide birth." Joey's ears pricked at this. "But all in good time," Lazlo continued. "I am not so articulate and versed in this language to tell you of such things. I am better accustomed to the whirs and beeps that Master Mozi Box and I so amiably share. There are those among my people, however, who will well slake your thirst for knowledge of this place, its going-ons, and particularly its less savory denizens, those individuals you reportedly spied last night." Joey drooped disappointedly back down.

"Right, then," said Hess, collecting the empty mugs and stowing them away, along with the thermos. "I think it's about time we started heading to this home of yours, Mr. Lazlo. We need to locate our device and be on our way as soon as possible; we've got a worrisome computer waiting for us and he'll start to get impatient if we're not home by tomorrow night at the latest. On your feet, everyone!" he ordered. Franklin and Joey rose and dusted off their trousers, but Ellie remained, for Lazlo had placed a massive hand upon her shoulder.

"Lazlo shall only move when his mistress is prepared," he declared sternly. "Are you quite rested enough to move on, Mistress Mars?"

Ellie gave Hess a sly look and slowly rose. "I am, Sir Lazlo," she reassured the protective robot. "Thank you kindly

Hess grumbled and began to trot ahead towards the southern horizon. The others followed obediently behind. The sun was now just a bit past high noon. Franklin could not help but feel this earth spun a bit slower than the one he was used to, or perhaps faster- he couldn't be sure. With so little to measure time against, the entire planet seemed like a topsy-turvy abyss into which one could sink hours in moments or seconds in days.

"Where do you figure we are, Franny?" wondered Joey as the two strolled, side-by-side.

"What do you mean?"

"Geographically. You think we're anywhere near home? Or at least where home was in our time."

"I suppose we could be. Then again, we could very well be walking along what used to be the bottom of the ocean. It's impossible to say! No landmarks, you know?"

"You're right," said Joey. "That Bisquick Cloud, or whatever Lazlo called it, must have been a helluva storm to flatten everything like this. You know how hilly our neighborhood was, and New England in general. It made riding bikes a real chore."

"It did," agreed Franklin. "But I'd trade this place for hilly old Connecticut any day. What Lazlo said got to me: I miss all the green. I miss seeing the mountains in the distance and the clouds in the sky. I miss the smell of the ocean on the breeze and the sun, sun so bright it could burn your skin, not like this bleary stuff. I reckon there's a layer of dust in the atmosphere blocking it out. And I miss birds chirping and bugs and cicadas. I even miss the sound of cars going by in the night and their lonely headlights shining through my window as they pass. Who knew I even liked any of those things? But I miss them now. I really do, Joseph"

"The sea breeze, you said," muttered Joey, sniffing at the bland air. "Yes, I miss that more than anything. And hearing the gulls, and even those noisy Canadian geese." He looked up at the cloudless sky and frowned. "I've been thinking: as things stand, we leapt forward into time and left our home without a trace. Do you suppose our parents just figured we were dead, or kidnapped, or hopelessly lost?"

"I'm sure they formed search parties and fanned out across Stony Creek, searching and sniffing for any clue as to our whereabouts," said Franklin, again beginning to picture his mother weeping quietly next to the window and his father, hopeless but determined, picking through the woods till his feet failed him and he collapsed, quite defeated by his poor son's apparent disappearance. The thought made him sick to his stomach and he at once abolished it from his mind. Joey seemed less bothered by the prospect and more fascinated with what their lives, or the world with the lack thereof, would be like, exactly.

"I wonder if they made little statues in the town square-like, memorials in our honor," he conjectured. "Wouldn't that be neat? 'The Lost Children' they'd call us. When little kids misbehaved, their parents would say 'Don't you go into those woods again, lil Timmy. The ghosts of the Lost Children will get ya' and eat your heart out!' And lil Timmy would run off yelping and squealing. How scared he'd be! Or maybe they'd name something after us. I should like a sort of louse named after me: JoeyJensonus, it ought to be called. Not a head louse, you see, but another sort. Yes, I'd be happy if they at least did that. But still, the Lost Children, Franny? That's us! Lost little ghosts."

Franklin was beginning to feel physically queasy. "I think we should talk about something else, now, Joseph," he gurgled.

"The time for idle chat is quite passed now, friends of Mistress Mars!" announced Lazlo. "Behold! My home!" He gestured forward at what appeared to be only more empty ground. Franklin's heart sank. The robot really was delusional, senile in his corroded circuit boards.

"Still nothing there," said Joey, though his tone was both chiding and hopeful.

"Perhaps not from where you stand," said Lazlo. "But the

earth is so flat, as you said before, and often those things which dip below its surface are hidden from even the keenest of eyes. Come forward and stand by my side. Take care, though, that you advance not a pace further than I, for you could indeed take an unfortunate tumble."

Intrigued and befuddled, the children approached Lazlo like timid young sheep, and Hess was their bold but cautious shepherd. Suddenly, vertigo gripped Franklin as he realized Lazlo stood not on a piece of unbroken, flat ground, but on a steep ledge. "My God," he breathed. "My God."

The home Lazlo had been pointing out had indeed been quite hidden from their view. Not by a mysterious cloaking device or some strange, voodoo spell, though. No, the place they looked upon now was shrouded from sight by more conventional, rudimentary means. There before them was a bowl, deep and wide, hollowed into the flat earth on which they had traveled all day, forming an unbroken, circular shelf around its lip. At least several miles in diameter, the crater extended nearly as far as the eye could see, but Franklin could make out where the flat earth resumed and continued on into oblivion on the other side. This hollow in the ground was so perfectly concave and sloped so suddenly down from the surface that it had been concealed from their view entirely, even as they had approached.

The immense crater, however, was completely unremarkable when compared to its contents. Scattered in several massive clusters about the crater, dotting its sloping sides and clumping at its base, were buildings - what remained of buildings, anyway. They were scorched and ruined, bent as if they had been squashed into the sunken earth along with the ground itself. Not like any buildings Franklin had beheld, they seemed to be futuristic (even in their dusty ruins he could make this out), complicated and needle-like in their architecture, though some were spherical and warped in appearance. They looked almost like sculptures he had seen at the modern art museum in his town.

"What is this place?" asked Hess, who had dared to breathe

first.

"Look there and read, if you have literacy to do so," said Lazlo, indicating a crumpled metal sign which was dug into the bowl's slope just below the ledge where they stood. Hess began to read it aloud, but Joey and Franklin spoke suddenly over him in unison.

"New Hollow City?" they cried out in disbelief.

"Get out of town," hissed Ellie.

"Why, what's New Hollow City?" asked Hess, for he could not comprehend whatever had made his companions so excited.

"It's a city not far from Stony Creek, the town where we all live," explained Franklin, eyes wide and mouth still agape. His eyes darted about like a gadfly, unable to settle on one thing for very long, unable to process what lay before him. The buildings were clumped densest at the base of the bowl. Here, what were once tenements, now scorched and abandoned, appeared as vacant bee hives, honeycombed with dusty and hollow apartments. Rising from out of the center of these former neighborhoods were what once had been skyscrapers, Franklin was sure, but now they stooped low to the ground, drooping like wilting flowers. It seemed they had been hammered down towards the earth with cosmic blows delivered by some divine and punishing hand.

This was New Hollow City, the same city where his mother had brought him to watch plays and cheer at parades in front of City Hall. Where the great, tall Christmas tree every year was lit upon the city's green. Where he had attended his cousins' commencements in grand assembly halls thronged with thousands of people. The city in whose hospital he had been born nearly fifteen years before! Yes, New Hollow had been a busy place; there had always been a constant flow of bustling pedestrians, cars, buses, and commerce. The city had always been abuzz with energy.

New Hollow City had been so busy and crowded, remembered Franklin, that even the traffic lights had seemed confused by the mobs of chattering people going about their lives like hummingbirds, buzzing from one flower to the next without ever missing a beat. But now it lay quite still, solemn and quiet, its urban splendor humbled and bent like a decrepit, old corpse.

Though the millennium had changed the city, dressing it in advanced, technological infrastructure, which now lay crushed into its pavement, Franklin could still make out a precious few landmarks. Though several spiraling towers branched up out of its top, the old city hall, Elm Hall it had been called, was visible just near the center of the basin. Like any good city hall, this one overlooked Main Street. Franklin recalled he and his father driving up and down that same street, searching for a dentist's office or some well camouflaged restaurant at which they had pressing reservations, several times. It still ran snaking through the heart of the city, though it was wider than he recalled and littered with fallen streetlights and various other bits of wreckage. Of course, this all lay miles away and hundreds, if not thousands of feet down the sloping sides of the crater. The 'Hollow' in New Hollow city's name had taken on a new, more functional meaning.

"You have heard of this place then, hmm?" inquired Lazlo as the children gawked. "Yes, this was once the great slum of New Hollow, a place so ridden with crime and dirt that it was nearly vacated entirely towards the end of the second millennium."

Franklin was taken aback. New Hollow City, like any other urban community of its time, had had its issues with crime and pollution, but never anything so severe as what the robot had described. In fact, he remembered it to be quite a clean place and a safe one too, though he had very little way of proving this.

"Yes," continued Lazlo. "Only a few ragtag communities made their homes here before the Bhasma Cloud arrived undid so much of what was. They are gone now, murdered by the cloud's malice, and the city is empty save my people who dwell here and those foul creatures that dwell below. The city was mostly spared the sky's wrath, thanks to an otherwise fatal flaw in its design. Beneath New Hollow, engineered to combat its constantly spreading muck and filth, was constructed a tremendous sewer system: a series of cavernous catacombs the likes of which you have maybe never seen. Like cathedrals, they were, a network of massive tunnels that wound their way around one another in patterns and designs more complicated than even the most chaotic anthill.

"When the Bhasma Cloud came and the earth began to shake, most of these artificial caverns collapsed and brought the city down into this basin you see now; though, many of the deeper tunnels still lie undisturbed by the collapse, haunted and infested by the red eyed devils. So perfect was the collapse in its roundness that the buildings, save the tallest among them, were spared destruction and bent inwards instead, as if they were bowing towards the center of the city."

"And no one survived?" asked Ellie, though the answer was quite plain.

"All those who made their home in New Hollow City - that is to say, all those who dwelt here under everyday circumstances - were taken by the cloud in one way or another," sighed Lazlo. "My people have quite a different story, however, but you will learn it soon enough."

Hess, who was less disturbed by the harrowing sight than the children, held up the Rok Counter and inspected it. "Well, whatever this place is, the thruster core is somewhere down in that pit where all the buildings are. Bother. The one spot in this whole wasteland where it won't be easy to find, and it falls smack dab in the center of it."

"I'm pleased to know your device has ended up here!" exclaimed Lazlo. "Perhaps my people have already found it. They're quite handy at scavenging, you see, and would find a tidy purpose for such a piece of technology in no time. It's not often that something so unusual falls into the lap of New Hollow, so they're sure to locate it in no time."

Hess recoiled, startled. "You don't think they've taken it apart or destroyed it, do you?"

"Mozi Box detects the thruster core is intact!" announced

the little computer happily. Hess sighed, relieved.

"I should hope it remains that way," remarked Lazlo. "Though my people are quick to locate potential equipment, they are slow in repurposing it: there is always a great deal of debate over what ought to be done with salvaged technology. We should be hasty, nonetheless, in making contact with them; that particular device sounds useful to their ways and might soon be dissected if we do not intervene."

The children had heard very little of this exchange; their attention was irresistibly affixed to the calamity which lay before them. Each of them had their own memories in this city and though, for the most part, it had been changed not only by the apocalypse but by the centuries of progress, it reeked of an unwanted familiarity to them and they could not shake the feeling they had lost an old friend of sorts. How many field trips to the science museum had they all taken together there so many years ago? How many excited rides to the airport and fancy city dinners had they partaken of? Each of them was born in the city's hospital, they knew this much.

"I hate it," whispered Ellie. "I hate seeing it like this. The rest of this wasteland was easier to stomach; it might as well have been another planet. But this - this hits too close to home. Literally."

Joey and Franklin nodded quietly in agreement. New Hollow had been smote and spared at the same time; they secretly wished it had just been wiped away with everything else. Now, it was an audacious sore, a boil on the face of the barren earth which only served to remind them of everything that was lost, inducing within them the most wretched sort of nostalgia imaginable.

"How do we get down into the crater?" asked Hess. The sides of the basin were steep and looked perilous, to say the least, heaped with loose dirt and debris that threatened to break free of the wall at any moment and go thundering down the slope. Lazlo pointed his artificial finger to indicate a crude path carved into the side of the crater near to where they stood. A rudimentary staircase, it seemed, and hastily carved some hundred years ago. It was ill worn and showed little signs of use; whoever Lazlo's people were, they seldom came in and out of New Hollow City, at least by this road.

"We can descend there," proclaimed the robot. "It is known as the Lamentable Step, for none who have ascended it have ever returned. I suppose I am the first, actually. Seldom do we stray out of the city and into the wasteland. I will caution you here: the way down is risky business. Several footholds have decayed with age and the steps are sure to crumble in certain places. Take care that you afford yourself enough balance that you should not slip and count one less life in this already sparse population."

"Yes," agreed Hess, "it's sure to be a dangerous descent, and I don't want to begin it till you're all ready." He looked at the children. "We wouldn't want anyone getting lost in a daydream and end up becoming a daydream themselves. You kids ready or should we wait and rest a while? I'm sure it'll all sink in eventually, and it'll be easier to stomach."

The children exchanged glances and a few hushed words. Franklin turned to Hess and said, rather glumly, "We're alright, Hess. We've made it this far, and we're ready to go a little further. Lead on."

"If I might beg your pardon, Mistress Mars," said Lazlo. "I should be quite a lot happier if you would allow me to carry you down the slope. My footing is sure to be sturdier than a human's, and even should it break, I can shield you with my metal frame. It is considerably stronger than yours, though infinitely less graceful and elegant."

Ellie smiled sadly and declined the robot's polite offer. She had no appetite for fun now.

"Let's get moving. We're losing precious daylight; at least, I think we are- it's very hard to tell," said Hess, scratching at his helmet.

Lazlo led them for a few hundred yards along the ledge until they came to where the staircase began. A small sign stood, dusty and untouched. "Welcome all ye who enter here with intentions good. Mites: stay out! Signed: The Lonies," read Franklin aloud. "Who are the Lonies?" he asked.

"My people. You will doubtless meet them soon," replied Lazlo. "They live at the center of the city, where we are headed."

"And the mites?" inquired Joey, intrigued. "What are those?"

"Come," beckoned Lazlo, ignoring the boy's question. "Let us begin the descent." And so they did. Franklin followed Hess, who tailed Lazlo closely down the steps. Ellie was behind him, and Joey took up the rear behind her. The going was quite steep and more than once Ellie tripped forward and steadied herself on Franklin's shoulders, grasping him gently at the base of his neck and sending tingles down the length of his spine. He swayed, at these times, nearly plummeting forward into the abyss himself, but he relished the moments nonetheless. He found himself secretly hoping she might stumble again, and at once chided himself for the thought. Joey, who was ill at ease around heights, walked slowly, with his eyes half closed and thrust up towards the sky; he was doing his best to pretend the incline wasn't there and he was instead romping in some far off salt marsh where he could relax.

Hess had some difficulty with the steps, too. His suit constricted his knees and he could really only goose step sideways down the path awkwardly. Ellie found this quite amusing and found the time to make several remarks about the boy's odd gait.

"Planning on serving the Reich, Hess?" she asked coyly. This joke was lost upon the amnesiac, though, and he only looked blankly at her, befuddled. Franklin, who had a passion for history, would have at any other time explained the joke to Hess, but he didn't feel like talking about such a dark time in such a dismal place as New Hollow City.

"The Lonies, huh?" murmured Franklin, changing the topic. "Some meaning behind that name? Or is it as self explanatory as it sounds?"

"Indeed, the name of my people is quite clear in its origin," replied Lazlo. "Our language is a bit different from yours, I'm sure you will soon see. It is less refined, a bit more colloquial. The title of Lonie seemed a natural choice given the solitary lifestyle we eke out here in the wasteland. Not that we have much choice in the matter, mind you. You must forgive my kind if they are quite taken aback to see you; strangers are unheard of and we have never encountered friendly ones before." He stopped then, as if some thing had just occurred to him, and turned to Hess. "You do have friendly intentions, do you not?"

"Of course," the boy reassured him hurriedly.

"I knew as much," proclaimed Lazlo, spinning on his heels, and resuming his climb down. "Surely no companions of such an angel as Miss Mars could have anything but amiable intentions. What a ridiculous question for me to ask, do forgive me again, if you've not already tired of the practice."

"Not at all," laughed Hess. "I understand your misgivings. Protecting your people, your loved ones, is not a task to be taken lightly! I would be skeptical in your shoes too."

The sloping dirt walls around them were speckled with the ruins of buildings and other structures, though they were bent sideways and jutted out horizontally over the pit, like the teeth of a Venus fly trap. Sometimes Ellie, who rapidly grew bored with the slow and steady descent, would leap up on top of one of these leaned over structures and walk upon it like a massive balance beam. This made Lazlo quite nervous and he fidgeted; Franklin had figured robots would be one of the only creatures he'd meet not to fidget, but Lazlo was more man than machine, it seemed.

As they climbed lower and lower into the basin towards the city, an unfamiliar sensation began to tickle above their lips: scent. Since they had left the Noah, few smells had wafted their way in the desert save the stale odor of the wasteland. But now, faced with the decay of civilization and the dregs of a failed city, the odors and stenches nearly overwhelmed their sensitive nostrils.

"Like death and burning rubber," groaned Franklin,

pinching his nose.

"What is it?" asked Joey. "It's like nothing I've ever smelled."

"I've smelt it before," said Hess. "It's a scent you would be unfamiliar with, given your origins in the past. You all still use those...What did they call those wheeled devices, Mozi Box?"

"Automobiles! Vroom-vroom! Beep-beep!"

"Yes, automobiles."

"We don't drive cars, but our parents do," said Ellie.

"I recall reading that these 'cars' of yours ran on an archaic fuel system, one composed of fossils and black muck."

"Not quite black muck, but close enough," Joey chortled

"The land vehicles of Burke's time ran on another sort of fuel entirely," explained Hess. "I do not recall what its name was or what composed the stuff, but I recall its stench when the tanks broke. It seems the scent has lingered, even after all these years."

"Perhaps that is **one** of the odors which permeate this city," Lazlo admitted. "But I have oft been told that the smell of death and decay is that which most powerfully plagues the air here. We Lonies have not forgotten the stink of the dead and forgotten."

✦

Soon they came down into the low-lying lands of the pit and stopped to rest. Here, the buildings stood vertically, but they were like stumps, with their tops clove deftly from their bottoms. The windows were all but gone from these vacant structures, shattered by earth tremors long ago, and Franklin could not help but peer inside them. Most of the rooms he looked in offered up brief glimpses into the life that was and the life that was to be, in his case. Although they were gutted from head to toe, by the Lonies he reckoned, still he could see remnants of family life scattered about their interiors; lives that had been abandoned in a flash and doomed to live forever on as a morose still life in this dead place.

Scenes flashed in his head. Pedestrians strolled by, car horns honked and taxi drivers hollered. Chapel bells boomed and tolled the afternoon songs, yet now there was nothing to be heard save their own quiet footsteps plodding down the Lamenting Step. 'New Hollow' the bells seemed to sing, but slowly their song diminished and simply whispered 'hollow' instead, again and again.

For one brief moment, Franklin could hear his mother's voice ring out against the din of traffic, ushering him over the crosswalk. 'Hurry up now, Franky. The light's about to change and we're already late for your cousin's recital.' He wanted to call out to her then, assure her that he was all right and would be coming home as soon as he could, apologize for going missing so abruptly like he did, tell her he loved her. But her voice was gone as soon as it had come, and he was thrust bluntly back into the quiet ruins.

Franklin would have quite broken down then and fell to the ground weeping but for Ellie who, noticing Franklin's distress, began to hum softly and again placed her hands on his shoulders behind him. The tune was calm and familiar, though he could not immediately place it. It soothed his nerves and made him remember trees, made his breathing slow and his intense grimace lessen into only a little frown. Then she began to sing:

"Oh Shenandoah, I long to see you.
Away you rolling river.
Oh Shenandoah, I long to see you.
Away, I'm bound away, 'cross the wide Missouri."

Franklin, too, began to hum and soon Joey joined in. For a moment, they were all back in Cankerwood, climbing eagerly to Sachem's Head, unaware they were actually climbing down into the belly of a long dead metropolis.

"Your song," remarked Lazlo when their humming had faded. "It moves through me. Its lyrics do not exist in my database; it must be really very old! It seems you too have lost a home that was dear to your heart. Pardon me: what else can a home be if not dear to your heart? Even one so dreadful as this." He spread his hands out and gestured at the city. "Mistress Mars. Once our business here is concluded, and if I am able to convince my superiors to allow me leave, I will do all in my living power to return you to that Shenandoah of yours."

"That's very sweet, Lazlo," she said. " But I wouldn't want to take you away from your people."

"Nonsense! You found it in your beating heart to take pity upon a rusted metal man and help him to his long lost home; the least I can do is offer you the same grace. Please, allow me to deliver you to that sacred place from whence you come, and safely so!"

Ellie smiled. "I think that place is a bit further away than even you could walk, Lazlo. But you've made me feel better by offering. Thank you."

Lazlo pushed no further after that. He was quite secure in the knowledge that, however strongly his Mistress protested, he would see her home and happy no matter what he had to do.

Now, they came to the bottom of the Lamentable Step and into the heart of the city. Here, they went beneath an arch, an arch which all the children remembered well. It was hewn of stone and marble, and stood at least twenty feet high. Though its surface was dusty and faded with years of exposure, still they could remember the emblem etched into its keystone: the silhouette of an elm tree. This had been New Hollow's crest, and they had all walked beneath it and through the arch several times.

"So the arch is still standing, after all this time," observed Ellie.

"I always liked this old thing," muttered Joey. "If I remember right, this was at the entrance to the city green. It should be right through this way." He pointed through the arch. "Remember going to all the Christmas tree lightings here,

Franny? When we were little? And the hotdog carts? And even that crappy little softball field?"

Franklin nodded and stepped through the opening. The green, unlike the rest of the planet, was not so entirely far-gone. The space was largely free of buildings and extended across the way for at least a half a mile. There was no grass and there were no trees, of course, but the dust that blanketed everything in the wasteland and the city was not quite so abundant here. In fact, as Joey was quick to point out, there were patches of darkly colored soil here and there, scattered sporadically across the area.

"The Lonies keep clear of this place," remarked Lazlo grimly. "It is big medicine to us, for legend says it is the largest graveyard in the city. Bodies lie beneath its surface, victims of the Bhasma Cloud. I am sure by now they have decayed almost to naught; but still, we only pass through this place when he have great need to do so."

"Do you know why there might still be soil here?" inquired Franklin. "There's only dust everywhere else."

"I'd guess because of the corpses underneath the ground," remarked Joey. "If everyone really did get vaporized by the cloud, like Lazlo and Hess have told us, but these people under the green got buried instead, for some odd reason, then their decomposing bodies have maybe kept the earth here at least semi-healthy."

Lazlo shrugged, which was quite an awkward action given his metal frame. "I can't answer to any of that," he said, "but if you don't mind, I should like to keep moving. It may just be a superstition, but ever since the time of my activation, a wariness of this place has been everyday instilled into my circuitry. I know what you think now: how comes an automaton by such illogical beliefs? Of course, the robot's ideal man is an entirely rational one, free from frills and unnecessary notions. But I have come to learn that life often loses so much of its luster when we approach it without these wild thoughts and fears of ours. Please excuse me, but we should be moving on."

All of them nodded, sympathetic to Lazlo. Even in Stony Creek there were places rumored to be haunted with the ghosts of the dead that everyone steered clear of, Cankerwood being chief among them.

Leaving the arch behind, they plodded hastily across the former lawn and quietly, too. City Hall and the rest of the urban skyline, though it was only a very short one, loomed up before them.

Joey nudged Franklin and pointed. "See there? That's where the New Hollow Historical Museum used to be. The one you liked so much. Remember the field trips? And remember eating lunch under that tall old tree with Mr. Whiffin in the third grade when the field trip was done? I think the tree was thereabouts." He moved his finger a little ways to the right.

"I remember," said Franklin. "Mr. Whiffin loved that place, with all the Pequot artifacts and such. I did too. I wonder what he'd say to see it all gone now."

"I wonder what Mr. Whiffin would have to say about a lot of things," remarked Ellie. "Forget the museum, I wonder how he'd react to all of this. How any of the adults in our lives would react, actually. It's a mystery to me."

Hess spoke up for the first time in a while. "Given the circumstances, I think you've all handled it very well. Especially for people of your - er- our age. I'm sure the adults of your time would be just as distraught as you've been, if not more."

Franklin found this to be a comforting thought and, for a moment, took pride in what little courage he had showed under duress.

"It appears to me you are quite unfamiliar with such a difficult location as this one. You must have travelled quite a ways," exclaimed Lazlo. "To undertake such a massive journey is certainly an impressive feat for a group so young as yours. But I have faith you will carry out whatever mission has been entrusted to you honorably and with care. You seem a trusty bunch, at least to me, and I'd say whatever trouble ails you now does not play across your faces so obviously as you might believe. Such a remarkable lot! And so generous! Especially the young Mistress Mars! How refreshing!"

The children were all beaming, quite impressed with themselves as they ventured out of the old city green and onto the remnants of Main Street, over which City Hall once towered. Joey, in need of a rest, stopped and knelt by an ancient, rusty manhole. Lazlo yelped and snatched up Joey by the shirt collar, dragging him away from the manhole cover.

"Do not peer so closely at those portals which would take you to the deep places of this city, for a claw might reach up and do just that," warned the robot. "Take my word; you do not want to be dragged down those slimy tunnels. Though they are caked with grime and filth, what awaits you at their bottom is far more awful."

"The mites, then?" asked Joey, rubbing the back of his neck.

"Hush! Hush!" Lazlo pleaded. "Take care not to call them by their name, for should they answer, we are likely doomed! Please, hold your queries till we are safely tucked away indoors! I really must insist."

Joey apologized, though his curiosity still burned within him, and they hurried across the street and ducked into a side alley. The walls that glowered over them on either side were laden with brick, although they were unlike any bricks Franklin had ever seen before. They were silvery in hue and even through the dust they had a kind of shine to them. At least some things were chrome in the future and glimmered, if only a little bit.

"Why don't we travel along the main roads?" asked Ellie. "Wouldn't that be quicker?"

"The foul things I mentioned before often take up small outposts on the outskirts of the city," replied Lazlo, ushering them further into the shadowy alley. "Were we to stay out in the open for too long, mischievous eyes would surely spot us and all manner of trouble would ensue. We will snake our way through the side roads and alleyways, for the present, till we come to safer ground in the heart of the city. It is there that the Lonies patrol and will see us safely home."

There were objects here and there, mostly squat cylinders, which lay, knocked over or leaned against walls. Franklin would have thought they were trashcans, but they seemed much too small.

"Energy cells, all used up," said Hess, pointing to the things, which puzzled Franklin so. "The main source of power for Burke's time. At least that's what I think they are."

Quietly, they navigated a labyrinth of alleyways and side roads, following Lazlo as he peered cautiously around every corner they encountered. Turning to them, he said, "I have not been back for some time now. Things might have changed, you see. When I was last here, the Lonies ruled over most of this place and their presence was palpable. I can spy none of my people now, though, and that makes me believe they have since lost ground to the enemy. I would hate to blunder upon an encampment of the monsters mistakenly, so we must proceed slowly and quietly while we are able."

As they pressed deeper into the city, the buildings above them grew taller and taller as if they were stretching out their lithe fingers to the bleary sky above. Some were familiar to Franklin, though only vaguely, and the others were strange and foreign, like metallic trees and tendrils jutting up from the ground.

The day wore on, and still they trudged; the city looked much smaller from above than it actually was. Strangest of all was the lack of any sort of perspective to the rest of the world within the crater. When they were afforded a rare chance to peer into the spaces between buildings and out towards the outskirts of the city, they could see no mountains in the distance, no sky, and certainly no horizon, just the dust that was heaped along the sides of the gargantuan crater through which they travelled. The only clue they were on the surface of the earth at all was the grey sky above, which they had to crane their necks upward to look upon.

"Yes, yes," murmured Lazlo. "This is all very familiar, and little has been changed. We shall rest up ahead and shelter in that small home there." He pointed to what looked like a former store, or perhaps some business of sorts, and lead them to it.

They entered through its shattered glass doors and found themselves in what once must have been an exquisite lobby, lined with satin curtains and fine rugs. Not a store, Franklin corrected himself, but a bank. Lazlo beckoned them over to what Franklin supposed was a teller's counter and beyond it, and into a back room.

"When travelling the city, the Lonies take great care to rest in only safe spots where they will not be preyed upon," remarked Lazlo. "Of course, most of the security measures of the year 3,000 were energy based and have long since died in their functions, rendered useless to our purposes. Still, some more rudimentary means of protection remain from ancient times. Behold!" He swung out his metal arm. There, at the rear of the little antechamber in which they stood, was a colossal metal vault much like the ones Franklin had often seen in exciting heist movies.

Lazlo approached the huge metal door and took the small lock-dial on its front between his fingers. Rapidly, his robotic hands entered a combination that flew by so fast none of them could recognize even a single number, and the lock clicked. Lazlo seized the massive handle and swung the door open, which was no small feat given its size. It did not creak or moan, like Franklin had expected it to, but glided quietly across the tiled floor. Evidently, the Lonies often sought refuge here and kept the area well maintained.

Clambering inside at Lazlo's behest, they entered a comfortable vault that was surprisingly well kept. Lining the walls were hundreds of small lock boxes, some much larger than others. At the rear of the chamber was a series of barred doors behind which there were more boxes. In its center were two benches with velvet cushions. Joey and Ellie flopped down onto these gratefully.

Lazlo shut the gate behind them with another stupendous heave and secured its lock. "The enemy, though strong indeed, would have great trouble overcoming such a solid barrier as this," he explained proudly. "And they are certainly not clever enough to discover its secret mode of entrance, that is to say: its combination. The Lonies discovered that secret many year ago thanks to my enhanced robotic hearing, I take pride to admit. This building is centuries old and quite archaic in its enterprise, but those who came before left it undisturbed for whatever reason, and we give great thanks for that. We use this place as a sort of outpost, a spot in which to leave messages for one another should someone end up cast out on a lonely night. Here!"

He opened one of the lock boxes by the benches and withdrew from it what looked like a crushed soda can. "It is a sign from my people, though I cannot say how long ago it was left. This particular item means for us to take caution; the enemy have been spotted in this neighborhood recently and could very well be still prowling about."

"I do not recognize this sort of place from Burke's time," said Hess. "What is it for?"

"It's from our time, actually," whispered Ellie to him so Lazlo would not hear and question them again about their strange origins. "It is a bank, I think. A place for keeping money locked up and secure. This is a safe that we're inside of, a vault really, and the majority of the cash is kept here where nobody but the bank workers can get at it."

Hess turned to Franklin and raised an eyebrow beneath his visor, though Franklin could not see this. "Is she pulling my leg? Did people really used to keep money in a big metal box like this?"

"Yes, actually. Ellie's telling the truth," replied Franklin, who was busy searching the other lock boxes for anything of interest.

"Such a strange custom that must have been for you, then," said Hess. "In Burke's time, all the money existed solely in computers. You couldn't hold it in your hands, it was all digital."

"I suppose that's not unreasonable," mused Ellie. "Our time is heading down that road pretty quickly, too. I guess it was only a matter of years till cold-hard cash disappeared completely."

"Good riddance," scoffed Joey. "With inflation, deflation, hyperinflation and God knows what other kinds of 'flation,' we were killing more trees than we could count with all that 'cold-hard cash'."

"You see!" exclaimed Hess. "At least some things improved! The future isn't all that bad."

Ellie looked at him like there was something terribly disgusting on his face. "You've been seeing what we've been seeing all day, right?" she demanded. 'This most certainly is all that bad! It's much worse than anything I'd ever imagined. When I thought of the future, I imagined hover boards and field trips to the moon, not a planet completely starved of life and color!"

"If I can do anything to make this admittedly terrible time more comfortable for my mistress, all she needs do is ask!" said Lazlo politely. He had overheard the bickering and come to make what peace he could.

Franklin was caught up at first in Ellie's fiery eyes as she glared at Hess. How ardent and audacious she could be at one moment, and how sweet and gentle the next, like the night before when she had brought him a blanket and draped her long arms over his shoulders as if to shield him for a moment from the troublesome world. But soon his thoughts wandered to her words. He could not deny it, the world was a dire place as they saw it now, and he could not live well knowing that such a time was to come even though he'd be long gone when it did, should he survive the mission at all in the first place. Joey glanced at him and grimaced.

"Franny," he murmured. "You've got that look again and I don't like it."

Franklin shook his head and smiled. "It's nothing this time, Joseph. Just a passing thought, really. Have you got any more water, Hess? Just looking at this city's made me parched with all its dried out ruins."

Joey frowned but let it pass; worrying about Franklin's

inner antics was not high on his list of priorities at the moment. Hess poured them each a drink and they moistened their dry throats which had been caked with dust all afternoon. Franklin, having inspected nearly all of the lock boxes and found very little that caught his eye, wandered now into the center of the vault and sat down with Joey and Ellie. Hess stood quietly behind them, conversing softly with Mozi Box.

"Can you establish a connection with big brother?" he asked.

"Mozi Box can try. If nothing else can be said of Mozi Box, let it be remembered he always tried, at least," replied the computer. A series of beeps and whistles ensued, and then radio static began to blare from Hess's chest.

"If you would please!" begged Lazlo. "Turn all that racket down, would you? These walls are thick, but the enemy's ears are tall and would pick up on such a noise in no time."

Hess gave an apologetic wave and adjusted a dial on his chest. The static noise sank down into a dull roar.

"It seems big brother has been trying to reach us for some time!" squealed Mozi Box excitedly. "He has left for us several transmissions, though they are all quite muddled with interference, most likely from the dust storms. Shall I play them anyway?"

"Yes, play one for me. Maybe it's discernable."

The static suddenly began to waver, and the elder Mozi's garbled voice came over the speaker, though it was broken into chunks and shrouded with a din of static. "Mister Hess... mission progress... **stay**... I repeat... **stay**... at all costs...**stay**... Mozi out."

"I didn't get much of that," remarked Hess. "He seems to want us to 'stay' put somewhere. Maybe he spotted another cyclone moving in our direction and was recommending we take shelter. I suppose that's no problem now, though." He shrugged. "Ole Mozi must be worried about us. We should have been back by now. Mozi Box, send a transmission to big brother and make it as clear as you can. Tell him we're safe and give him a full mission update."

"Again, Mozi Box shall try!" the AI repeated.

"How're you holding up, Franklin?" asked Ellie, and took his hands into hers for a moment to grip them tightly. This made him weak in the knees. That all too familiar, noodle-armed sensation returned to his limbs, and he could only stare at her, not answering for a few dumb moments. "Well?" she looked at him kindly.

"Good, Ellie. Better than I ever expected I would be in a situation like this. I'm beginning to trust my resolve a bit more than I used to," he said honestly. She abandoned his hands and took Joey's now, allowing Franklin to breathe normally once again. Joey did not seem nearly so phased by the girl's touch.

"And you, Joey?"

"Just fine. Tired, though. I think it's the low oxygen levels. I'm surprised there's any air to breathe at all around here! I certainly haven't seen any trees or plants to turn carbon dioxide into oxygen. Maybe we're just breathing in whatever was left after the cloud rolled over, if that's even possible; I really don't know."

"And you, Ellie?" asked Franklin. "How fares the intrepid traveller from the northern wilds of Maine in this faraway place?"

She smiled. "She fares well, but she misses her home."

"Misses Maine?" Joey raised his eyebrows.

"No, not really. Home is where the heart is, you know? And Pendel Circle is where my parents are, along with my bed, my dog, my clothes, my brush, my pillow, my fridge, and… You two are there as well. And I'd rather like to be around you two for a while. You promise we'll stay friends through high school?"

"If we ever make it back to the damn place! Personally, I wouldn't mind if we never did," snorted Joey. "I'd take the wasteland over homeroom any day."

Franklin laughed and looked Ellie in the eye, holding her piercing gaze for as long as he was able. He extended his hand. "I promise. Unless you get all caught up with your shiny new honors friends, Joey and I will always be there for you at school. And, even if you do get bogged down with scholastic and social success, we'll always be there for you at home. Only across the street." Ellie shook his hand then, and they huddled close and shared a smile.

Lazlo approached them. "We ought to be pushing on now, if you've finished your beverages and are feeling refreshed. The sun is dropping low and the enemy hunts by night, so we should be along swiftly before the hour chimes too late."

Hess collected their things and, after Lazlo had again opened the vault door and then secured it behind them, they wandered out through the bank lobby and onto the street.

Suddenly, Joey froze in his tracks and the others followed suit. They followed his bewildered gaze across the road and located the sight that had startled him so. There, peering out of a ramshackle old factory's window not twenty meters away, was a pair of glowing red eyes much like the ones they had seen the previous night. As soon as they had been noticed, however, whatever creature the eyes belonged to scuttled hurriedly away and retreated into the darkness of the factory, vanishing entirely into the shadows.

"We have been spotted by one of their scouts," hissed Lazlo. "Come, we must hurry along before the devils return in greater numbers and ambush us in the dark, for that is their way, cruel though it might be."

"Which way?" asked Hess urgently. He wanted to avoid any fighting at all costs. His encounter with the Stalo had left him smarting and he had begun to doubt just how effective in combat his suit actually was. Then again, he thought, perhaps it was the measly boy inside it and not, in fact, the armor that had contributed to his failures.

"Follow in my steps," commanded the robot. "But you should abandon all pretense of caution now that we are sighted and focus instead on haste. If night falls before we reach our destination, we are surely done for. Their numbers will only increase as the light dies."

With that, the companions began to bolt down the street, racing past the ruined structures without paying them much thought. Lazlo was stomping hard now, propelling his heavy body forward, and his feet clanged out against the ground, their beats echoing off the labyrinthine web of thoroughfares through which they raced. The robot made sudden and sharp turns around corners, often surprising the children and causing them to swerve suddenly to keep up. "Quickly! Quickly, now!" he roused. "Hurry, danger is at our heels."

This pace was well maintained till suddenly Ellie tripped and crumpled into a heap upon the pavement. Lazlo spun on his metal heels and came quickly to the girl's side.

"Mistress Mars?" he demanded. "Are you alright? Have you been injured because of me? Oh, how I would curse my hasty march if it had done you any harm."

"No, I'm fine!" exclaimed Ellie. "I've only bruised my ankle a little."

"I will have none of that," said Lazlo stubbornly. "Thanks to my Mister Hess, there is power enough in this suit to carry two." Without another word, he scooped Ellie into his arms and spun her onto his back in one fluid motion. She clung there, uncomplaining, and Lazlo began to run again.

Hess, Joey, and Franklin followed swiftly, though now the two unarmored among them began to pant and heave. Lazlo seemed panicked for the sky was becoming palpably darker. His robotic pace doubled and the boys began to stumble along behind him.

He turned to them, trotting quickly backwards. "Soon we will rest for we have almost arrived!" he informed them. "Only a little longer, I promise you. But you must keep in stride till then! Hurry! Hurry!"

They came into a large, empty area. It was void of buildings and circular in shape, like an ancient, stony arena. Franklin recognized the spot at once; it was where the circus had performed every year and, over the summer, a farmer's market had been held each Sunday morning, followed by a less dignified flea market in the afternoon. Images raced through his head of sun-worn vendors pedaling corn and potatoes, squash and carrots, turnips and all other manner of earth-grown goodness.

The market ground was bare now, though and looked like it had been repurposed long ago as some monument to the past. Phony looking cobblestones lined the ground and here and there were statues depicting personages Franklin did not recognize.

Lazlo froze in the center of the circle and Ellie clambered off of his back. "What's the matter?" she asked.

"It is too late," the robot muttered. "We have hastened but not speedily enough, it seems. Do you not see?" He gestured at the buildings which encircled the market ground. To his horror, Franklin laid eyes on that which Lazlo had indicated. All around them, in each available broken window he could, see, were hundreds of sets of glowing red eyes. They bobbed up and down, as if shuffling against one another in the darkness to claim a better view of the vulnerable companions. The eyes looked hungry and Franklin could almost hear invisible lips smacking in his head. Terror seized him and his breath, which was already ragged, began to quicken.

"What do we do?" demanded Hess, his voice suddenly stern and willing. "Can we stand and fight them? You and I could take a few apiece I'm sure, Lazlo."

"Keep your voice low. Do not alarm them or provoke them even nearer," shot the robot over his shoulder. "Even if you and I were to combat them, we would be endangering these children here by engaging open battle. Besides, there are far too many to handle, even for metal beings such as you and I."

"Then what's the plan?" stammered Franklin, quite uneasy to be standing in the circle with so many beastly eyes upon him.

"We shall run and, doubtless, they shall follow," said Lazlo gravely. "Your feet must fly here like they never have before. There only lies a little ways yet, but their pursuit will make the going difficult. They are a frightful-looking sort to those who have not laid eyes on them before, so I beg you not to halt or falter when you see them. On the count of three, follow me and run as fast as your feet will carry!"

Franklin swallowed hard and glanced at his friends. Ellie looked indignant, almost angry, as if she were ready to fight the mysterious enemies right then and there. Joey, who was quite exhausted from running, was squinting to see if he could catch a glimpse of the creatures, but they were still shrouded by the shadows in which they hid. The sun was nearly gone, now, and the whole city was blue in dusk.

"Three...two...." They all bent forward like runners taking a mark, preparing to sprint. "One!" Lazlo bellowed and they dashed off behind him. Quickly, he guided them out of the market ground and into another side street. Franklin could hear what sounded like the scraping of hundreds of claws against cobblestone behind them, though he did not dare to look back. The sound grew and grew till it seemed to be thundering, as if an army of the scuttling monsters gave them chase. Still, he kept his head forward.

Lazlo darted around another corner and quickly doubled back, finding only a dead end there for fallen rubble had blocked the way. To the right, Franklin could see a great black, wavering mass composed of hundreds of hunched over, dark forms bubbling with the frightful red eyes, though he refused to look directly at them. The mass was rushing towards them down the cramped alleyway and would soon be upon them, but Lazlo waved them all back onto a main road and they sprinted onto it.

Joey pointed up now, and Franklin followed his finger. Upon the low-seated rooftops above them were even more of the creatures, dozens of their red eyes glowing in the darkness above as they raced along the rooftops, parallel to the frantic companions. They seemed to be crawling now out of every nook and cranny Franklin could spot, and the city was full of such tiny crannies.

"Eyes ahead, children! Eyes ahead! Pay them no heed! They

cannot harm you while my circuitry yet runs!" shouted Lazlo. "Look there!" He gestured wildly. "Our destination at last!"

Franklin wasn't quite sure what he was supposed to be looking at. The building Lazlo had indicated looked almost like chrome colored Easter egg that had been sliced at the middle. It was similar to a dome, but more elliptical in shape and taller too. It sat quite plainly between several other more normal looking structures, a bizarre sort eyesore. It had probably brought the block value down a lot, thought Franklin, given its ugly appearance. It had no outstanding features to speak of really, save a large window situated close to its top and several smaller ones that speckled its shiny surface. Close to its base, where it appeared to almost sink into the ground and continue indefinitely into the earth, was what appeared to be a massive, sturdy garage door.

When they had drawn near enough to it, Lazlo rushed forward and began to bang on the gate vigorously. "It is I, Lazlo!" he cried out. "I have returned with friendly strangers in tow. But the Mites have given us chase! Oh, do open up now! Open! Open!"

Suddenly, a little slot slid open above the door Lazlo was banging on and, to Franklin's shock and delight, a human head popped out. Even amidst the confusion and chaos, the children found time to rub their eyes in disbelief and gawk at the face. It was a living human being in the flesh, here in the wasteland city of New Hollow! The head was quite far above them, but Franklin could see it was a man's head, and quite a dirty looking one at that, with only an eye patch and a scraggly, unkempt red beard to adorn it. A tall, strange looking hat sat awkwardly upon his brow.

"Who's that, then?" the head called out in a raspy voice.

"Why hullo there, Jamjar!" Lazlo called out. He sounded relieved. "Lazlo is my name and I wear it proudly! I have come back! Do not think me trick or illusion, for it is truly I! These are new friends of mine. Be quick and allow us entrance, a horde of Mites is close at hand!"

The man did a triple take between Lazlo, the children, and

the rampaging mob of creatures drawing ever nearer behind them. He looked back to Lazlo, bewildered. "The name, again?"

"Lazlo! Confound this nonsense! It's me, Lazlo!"

"Lazlo?" The man sounded astonished. He reached up and tore off his eye patch, revealing what looked like a perfectly healthy eye beneath it, and peered down at the robot. "Lazlo!? Is that-ee, then? It is! It is! My head balls have not lied to me! Why, we haven't seen headises nor feetsies of-ee in nigh half a dook-ade!"

"I will explain my adventures soon. Open this gate at once, Jamjar! The mites are nearly upon us!" Lazlo begged, exasperated.

"Who are these queer looking folk behind-ee?" asked the man suspiciously. "I've not ever seen such an oddly dressed bunch in all me days, methinks. And their skin is mighty-purdy like!"

"Jamjar. Do not take this as a threat, but if you do not open up this door at once, I will see that I plant your head firmly inside my metal armpit and give it a great squeeze," bellowed Lazlo. "I can crush steel with my fingers, mind you."

"Alright, alright," grumbled the man. "Hold your hammers." He disappeared back into his hole. Suddenly, the gate began to rise. It stopped about halfway up and Lazlo hurriedly ushered the children and Hess inside, one by one. Before Franklin ducked his head beneath the gate, he dared to take one final glance back at the oncoming horde.

The mites, as Lazlo had called them, were an ugly lot. They only stood about four feet tall, but there were a rare few among them who rose above even Hess's height. Their legs, arms, and faces were scaly and dark blue, like a lizard's might be. Atop their heads and covering their torsos and ankles were thickets of black, matted fur. They had vicious looking claws where their hands ought to be. Upon their faces were pig-like snouts and below them snapped toothy jowls that were lined with razor sharp fangs. Their ears were like those of bats, massive and triangular. And then there were the eyes: red and hateful, and engorged so large they looked almost like saucers on the ugly things' faces.

They were chattering and hooting, whooping and snarling like a pack of hungry, rabid hyenas. But, above all the commotion, Franklin could make out their hideous chant, which many among them seemed to sing incessantly. "Bhasma! Bhasma!" they howled and sang. "Bhasma! Bhasma!"

"We have come so far! To dawdle now and be eaten whole would be an unhappy twist of fate, I think!" cried out Lazlo, grabbing Franklin by his shirt collar and dragging the terrified boy under the half open door. With a clang, it slammed shut and everything went dark, blotting out the frightful image of the pack of horrific monsters.

CHAPTER THIRTEEN

THE LAST GARDEN

It was dim inside of the strangely shaped building. All around them the children could hear hushed voices murmuring. As their eyes adjusted to the gloom, they began to make out several human shapes that were slowly encircling the children, coming closer in a ring around them.

Suddenly, a shape thrust out of the darkness and came very near to Franklin's nose. It seemed to be a spear point, albeit a rather ramshackle one; it was really only a long knife of sorts tied to a rusty, metal pole: a tool improvised from what few resources remained in the desolate city. Lazlo reached out and swatted the weapon away.

"Lower your sharps, Lonies!" Lazlo implored the shadowy figures. "There is no need for any such inhospitable behavior."

But the spear tip soon came back up and was quickly joined by several others. Franklin's eyes had fully adjusted now and he peered about the crowd of figures that encircled them, half in wonder and half in fear. There were at least a dozen of them clustered about the children, Hess, and Lazlo. Several were humans, like the gatekeeper had been, and just as dirty too.

There were only two women, so far as Franklin could see, but their faces were so smeared with dust and grime, and their hair so greasy and unkempt, they very well could have been men, or not humans at all. The rest of the circle consisted of a smattering of males who were all rather grimy looking, with mostly unshaven, dusky faces. Among them were a few robots, like Lazlo, but all with different colored eyes that glowed in the dimness.

There was a clatter above and Franklin looked up to see a man clambering his way hurriedly down a ladder from the top of the sealed gate. This was the gatekeeper, that same disembodied head from before, Franklin quickly realized, but now there was a body to go along with it. The odd looking man reached the bottom of the ladder and shoved his way through the circle of spear wielders, coming close to Lazlo. He touched the robot's face and looked deep into his green eyes.

"Why, it really is-ee, Lazlo!" he exclaimed suddenly after what seemed like an eternity of scrutinizing the robot's face. "Bless Old Bess and call me paprika! I had figured-ee for dead a whiles-way back!"

"It is I in the steel," reassured Lazlo. "How relieved I am to see you're still tending the gate, Jamjar. You mind the door so very thoroughly that we were nearly eaten alive thanks to your dawdling!"

The man Franklin supposed to be Jamjar let out a great guffaw, saliva leaping from his mouth and spraying over the children like a dribbly little rainstorm. Ellie nearly gagged. Jamjar turned to the circle and gestured at the long lost robot beside him. "Look-ee, Lonies! This be Lazlo, for it is his name and proud he wears it! Member-ees? Member ole' Lazlo? Come back, he has!"

The crowd murmured and slowly the spears began to lower again. Some of them smiled, quite delighted to see who Franklin assumed must have been their friend of old, a friend they had long thought dead, suddenly standing alive and well before them.

"Not so fast, all of you! Spears up!" barked a harsh voice from behind the circle. The wielders did as the gruff command had bid.

"This does indeed seem to be our lost brother Lazlo, and soon he will regale us with the tale of his prodigal, somewhat suspicious return," continued the voice. "Speak you now, o lost Lonie, and speak you quick: tell us who these queer persons are that you bring them uninvited into our home and sanctuary!"

The owner of the voice stepped forward through the crowd. He was a tall man, that is to say, tall when standing next to the rest of the Lonies who were all rather small in stature. He was wearing what appeared to be a pair of red Long Johns, which covered his body head to neck. His feet were stuffed into sturdy, leather-hiking boots and he wore upon his head a tall, straw hat like a farmer might wear. His face was gaunt and ancient looking, intensely lined with deep crevices and wrinkles the likes of which Franklin had never seen. His mouth was hidden behind a bushy white beard, which dipped all the way down to his hips. Most peculiar of all were the several burlap sacks that were tied all over his body with twine, forming a kind of makeshift tunic to cover the Long Johns.

This queer looking fellow held not a spear but a long staff. The staff was, of course, really just an uprooted parking meter, another makeshift Lonie contraption. A machete was tucked into the rope belt around his waist, the same belt that held his sack tunic taut.

"Old Sacks! Why if it isn't our leader, Old Sacks!" Lazlo greeted the elder happily! "My poor cybernetic heart is near bursting at the sight of you! How long your beard has grown and how tired your eyes look. It seems you have much to tell me of these unkind years in which I have been lost and away."

"Indeed," answered Old Sacks. "There is much to tell; but, first you must speak your story that it might fall upon the ears of us Lonies and allow us to decide whether these strange-ees be friend or foe." The old man was much more articulate than the gatekeeper and when he spoke he did so quickly and with authority so that the other Lonies bowed their heads to him in silent deference.

"Foe? Never have I seen a label placed so ill upon someone's head before," exclaimed Lazlo, waving his hands about and smacking away the spears again, but the blades would not yet yield. "These are friends in the truest sense of the word!" he declared, gesturing at the children and Hess. "They are my rescuers and come here only with the friendliest of intentions!"

Suddenly, before Lazlo could say anymore, a great cacophony began outside the gate. Shrill and beastly voices howled and snarled, and Franklin could hear the creatures clawing at the gate and chanting again, "Bhasma! Bhasma!"

"As you can see," continued Lazlo, "we have been chased all afternoon and come to you now, ragged and worn. I do apologize for bringing the Mites to the gate, but it is nothing that hasn't happened before. My friends are quite exhausted, and frightened too; might we bring them to a more peaceable spot and converse safely away from this racket?"

"Very well" allowed Old Sacks. "We will hold council now, but the strange pale faces shall not be allowed to wander and peer into the Sacred Chamber! I am not yet ready to reveal to them such secrets as we so dearly keep. They will need to be held in confinement for the time being. Take them to the pen!"

"The pen?" pleaded Lazlo. "Sir, there is no need for such wanton cruelty! We have not used the pen since we captured that Mite nearly twenty circles of the sun ago! Never have we encountered friendly life besides our own! We ought not to treat our first visitors so poorly!"

"What's the pen?" stammered Franklin.

"You're not throwing us in with those monster things, are you?" asked Ellie, a stubborn look of defiance beginning to creep across her face. Joey stayed quiet. The angry adults around him scared him much worse than any snarling creature ever could.

"So, they do talk after all? I was beginning to worry you'd brought us a bunch of mute-ees, Lazlo!" Old Sacks chuckled. He leaned forward towards the children and looked at them very close, as if inspecting farm animals. His breath smelled old, almost like mothballs. "Have you got names, pale ones?"

Hess stepped between the ancient Lonie and the children and extended his hand, which Old Sacks only looked at, puzzled. "Call me Hess, sir. At your service." The spear wielding Lonies jumped in surprise at Hess's human voice and quickly began to yammer amongst themselves.

"That voice of yours sounds almost as real as mine, metal strange-ee," Old Sacks proclaimed. "Though it rings with the sound of iron, it is still very clearly the voice of a young boy!" He seemed unafraid of Hess, unlike the spear wielders. "What manner of creature are you? Person or machinery?"

"A bit of both, I suppose," replied Hess honestly. "Beneath this metal exoskeleton I am a human, just like you all."

"And you lead this sorry bunch?"

"I do."

"Hess, leader of the strange-ees. Very good." Old Sacks stroked his beard and turned on the rest of the children. "And have the rest of you titles, or shall I simply call-ees pale faces?"

Ellie was first to step forward. "My name is Elaina Mars. Call me Miss Mars, please," she said.

"A strange name, if I ever head one!" Old Sacks nodded.

Now it was Franklin's turn. "Franklin Freeman, sir, at your service." He gave a little bow.

"Your name. It is very strange, no?" asked Old Sacks. "As you have spake it, it is too difficult for me to pronounce; I shall call-ee Frankfurter instead. The crowd murmured in approval of their leader's new name for the pale young fellow.

Ellie nudged Joey softly. "I'm Joey," managed the timid boy.

"Joe-ee? Joe-ee. Very good, Mr. Joe-ee," said the gnarled old man. "Call me Old Sacks. I am leader of these Lonies and have been so for as long as anyone cares to remember."

"Excellent! Excellent! How merry!" cried Lazlo, clapping his metal hands. "Now that we've dispensed with introductions, let us allow our guests some rest and nourishment. I'm sure they're all quite-"

"Quiet, Lazlo!" barked Old Sacks. "I am not finished with these strang-ees just yet. Before you spin us the tale of your long journey, I should like to hear from the strange-ees' own mouths why it is they have come to this place."

The children were silent. Hess had warned them several times about the confidentiality of their mission and objective; they would not breach his trust so easily.

"Well? Will any among you speak of your goals, here?" demanded the badger-like old fellow. "You there!" he stuck a bony finger in front of Hess's visor and waggled it about. "You are their leader, no? Speak you and tell me whey it is that you have come and from what otherworldly place you hail!"

"That is our business and it will stay that way, I'm afraid. I assure you, we mean neither you nor your people any harm," said Hess as calmly as he could.

"I'll give you one more chance to answer," snarled Old Sacks, his eyes suddenly alight with fire. "Why have you come here to New Hollow? Where do you come from and what do you want?"

"As I said, that is our business and ours alone," repeated Hess, through gritted teeth this time.

"Will none of you break this silence?" Old Sacks implored the children. They didn't make a peep. Suddenly, he turned his nose up at them and sniffed loudly. "Spies for the Mites, no doubt," he declared. "Take them to the pen."

"But, sir-" pleaded Hess.

"And take special care to restrain this machine man! I like him not!" Old Sacks gave a dismissive wave and trotted off into the darkness.

Suddenly, the circle of figures enclosed around the children and they were seized by the arms, albeit gently. Many of the Lonies looked down on the children with kind old eyes that reassured them they would be quite safe, despite the old codger's harsh orders. Even the robots' grips were soft around their arms.

"Come-ee now, little ones," whispered one of them and smiled. "All will be well as parsnips and pee-tatoes, soon enough."

The children allowed themselves to be lead along, and Lazlo walked beside them. "Oh how sorry I feel, now!" he cried apologetically. "You rescue this poor lost robot. And what does he do in return? He brings you to imprisonment! Worry not, though! I will argue your case before the council and have you freed in no time. Meanwhile, do not resist the Lonies, it will only make your defense a more difficult one to argue."

The children nodded; they felt quite safe. They were, in fact, relieved to be around human adults again; it gave them a strange sense of reassurance and safety, though none of them would ever admit this and each of them maintained an indignant facade. Hess was not so comfortable, however, as two hulking robots, ones much bigger than Lazlo, had seized him by the arms and were marching him forward. He supposed his suit, laden with weapons as it was, most likely posed a greater threat than his unarmored companions did.

"Joey," whispered Franklin as they were steered on, "are we being taken prisoner?"

"Yes, it looks that way, Franny," replied Joey. "Why are you smiling?"

"I'm afraid," confessed Franklin, grinning weakly. "But I've always kind of hoped something like this would happen to me, getting taken prisoner and all that. I feel like I'm in some sort of action movie or something."

"Well, I don't like it a bit!" hissed Ellie. "Not a little bit. Being wrongfully imprisoned like this. It's un-American!"

"I don't think America's principles of democracy really apply in the post-apocalyptic future, Ellie," reminded Joey.

"All the same: this was an American city once! Haven't they ever heard of the right to fair trial? The writ of Habeas corpus?"

"Ellie," whispered Franklin. "I don't even think some of those things apply in 2012, much less whatever crazy year this is."

"Quiet, all of you!" hissed Hess. "We're already in deep

enough trouble as is! Don't upset them any further. I knew we shouldn't have recharged that damn robot. Now we'll never find the thruster core! And even if we do manage to escape them at some point or another, they'll hunt us through this accursed city and make it that much harder to find the stupid thing."

"Oh dear, oh dear!" cried Lazlo. "What a fool I am! Do forgive me. I'll get you all out of this pickle, yet!"

Hess lowered his head, shook it, and said quietly, "I'll maybe have to end up fighting our way out. I had hoped to avoid any unnecessary violence." The robots, who must have overheard him, tightened their grip on his arms and marched him hastily forward till he disappeared into the gloom.

The children could hear Mozi Box squealing in the distance. "Unhand Mr. Hess. He is my protector! Surely you would not detain a cousin like myself. Unhand us, Mozi Box demands it!"

"Think we'll ever see him again?" asked Ellie.

"Not sure, hope so," murmured Franklin. Now that Hess had been brought away, his fear overtook his excitement and he began to tremble.

"Do you really think Hess could fight all of these people off and get us free if he had to?" Joey sounded skeptical.

"Not sure. Hope so," Franklin repeated. Their captors herded them now into a long corridor, away from the dark antechamber they had been inside of. The lights were strange in this hallway, issuing out from luminescent mushrooms that grew out of the earthen walls on either side of them. At the end of the corridor was the distant flicker of a fire's light.

"Where are you taking us?" demanded Ellie.

Jamjar bustled up along side of them and strolled next to Lazlo. "To the council chamber, little Miss," he told her politely. "Thank-ee all for keeping such a placid att-ar-tude about-erselves. For a small bit of time, ees will be kept in the pen for inspection. Old Sacks is a good-un, but he protects his Lonies real fierce like. Ees have to excuse his precautions."

"Yes, children. Old Sacks is a wise old sage," added Lazlo.

"He may seem gruff, but soon he will see the good in you and relent. I am certain of it."

"Where have they taken Hess?" asked Franklin nervously. He wasn't sure if their metal friend would be afforded the same courtesy as them, given his rather odd position as a man encased within a machine.

"Old Sacks had to contend with a sort of robotic uprising many sun-cycles ago. He is weary of us metal folk, to say the least," replied Lazlo grimly.

One of the other robots escorting the children had been listening and piped up. "Of course, he still trusts the utility bots like Lazlo and my other brethren here with all his heart. It was the fighting androids that rebelled and were subsequently quashed. They are quite gone now, either broken down for spare parts or exiled into the wastelands."

"They won't hurt Hess, will they?" Ellie sounded legitimately concerned, despite her chilly feelings for Hess.

"I doubt it, Mistress Mars," replied Lazlo. "Excepting the Android Uprising, Old Sacks saves up any aggression he has to be used against those hateful mites. Otherwise, he disdains in violence and avoids it when he may."

"If I find even a scratch on that metal head of his, there'll be hell to pay, Lazlo," warned the girl, and she sounded frightfully honest. "Don't forget that debt you owe to us!"

"A debt from Lazlo to these strange-ees? There is much to tell indeed, aye Lazlo?" exclaimed Jamjar. "And we have bundles to tell-ee too, Lazlo! But behold-ee now, the council chamber is at hand! Hush now, strange-ees, and be peaceable in-er words as-ee have been thus'n far."

They were led into a large, circular chamber. It was illuminated by several torches that lined the walls and by an immense bonfire that crackled and roared in a stone pit at the center of the room. The whole area was like a sort of Greek amphitheater; there were crescent shaped benches ascending to the rear of the space upon which many Lonies sat, both robot and human.

At the base of these steps was a small circular stage where

the bonfire was. Two raggedy looking men emerged from behind a curtain. They were pushing a large cage made from metal bars and other scavenged odds and ends. They brought it to the center of the stage, in front of the bonfire, and opened up its door.

Now Hess was led out from behind the curtain, and he looked none too happy. They had affixed large blocks of concrete onto his hands and feet so that he could only shuffle across the floor with his weighted arms dangling uselessly by his sides. Unceremoniously, the two robots that had been escorting him pushed him into the cage and then did the same to the children. The door was shut and locked behind them.

"Now we've done it! This cage must be the pen! Damn!" cursed Ellie under her breath. She turned to Hess. "You alright? They didn't hurt you, did they?"

"No, I'm alright," he sighed. "I let them think these blocks of concrete would keep me incapacitated. I'm positive I can lift them if the need arises, though. Super strength, remember?"

"Right, we'll keep that in mind," whispered Franklin.

"Silence in the pen!" bellowed Old Sacks, who sat in the center of the forum. Peering through the bars, the children could see other Lonies and robots taking their places in the amphitheater, their sallow faces lit hauntingly by the firelight. Lazlo and Jamjar stood nearest the cage where the companions were held.

"Fear not, friends! You will be free again in no time," whispered their robotic friend.

"The defense will be silent as well!" commanded Old Sacks, and a hush fell over the room. "Now," he continued, "let us first welcome back Lazlo, our long lost utility bot. We feared he had perished, but he returns with eyes brighter than we have seen in a long time. Here, here!"

"Here-ee here-ee!" cheered the Lonies, and Jamjar clapped the prodigal robot on the back.

"My thanks, brothers and sisters. Were it not for my new friends here, I would not stand before you now so healthy as I am," said Lazlo. He bowed in the children's direction.

"Yes, yes, we will hear all of that soon enough," grumbled Old Sacks, dismissing the topic entirely. "Let us first hear how it is you have been so long disappeared and so suddenly resurrected. Shall I remind the Lonies how it is Lazlo came to depart from us?"

"Aye! Aye!" they cheered.

"Settle-ees, for I shall tell the tale now." The elder Lonie furrowed his brow and leant upon his staff. "Recall-ees some five sun cycles ago, now. The Android Uprising had just barely been defeated. The Mites, taking advantage of our momentary weakness, began running rampant about our borders. Never had we so little faith in our future here in New Hollow. Lonies were being killed by the bushel and it seemed all was lost. A council was held here in this great hall to decide how it is our misery would be dealt with! Voice-ees bantered and debated, shouting with mirth at times and with the deepest of grief at others. So low fallen were we then; it saddens me to remember it.

"Then Lazlo, who has always been brightest bot among us, came forward and spoke. His words did touch our hearts and made them soft again, for the Mites had made them hard like stone over time. Lazlo spoke of those pleasant things that we so often see in the projections of the past: of gentle fields flowing with grasses that dance merrily in ocean breezes. And of water as clear as crystal. But greater than a dream he made these notions out to be. 'To the north,' said he! 'Mightn't there be such wonderments to the north? For we have never been that way for fear of the dust storms. But perhaps those cyclones are guardians and protect the paradise we have so long sought!' And we hollered 'Aye, a lovely thought and a handy one, too. But how shall we seek them? We live here in New Hollow and have our own secret to protect. We cannot leave the sanctuary for the Mites to claim!'

"But Lazlo, who is bold in his robotic head, spake thus: 'Send me, your faithful servant Lazlo! I will travel across the wasteland to see what I may. I will wander as far as my power supply can take me, then return and fill your ears with what I have beheld. Surely you can spare my presence here for a few weeks.' I, leader of the Lonies, thought this wise beyond measure, but I feared for Lazlo so alone in the wasteland.

"'The road will be a dangerous one, bot brother!' said I. 'Between here and the north are many dust storms, and the Mites roam the wastes by night. If wander you do, return you might not!' But Lazlo would hear me not. 'Dust storms can do little to deter my spirit, and the Mites only rarely venture outside the city perimeter,' said he. Then the council cast its vote, as we are often wont to do, and it was decided that Lazlo would venture out to seek the fruitful paradise rumored to be in the north.

"The Lonies wept to see him go thus, alone into the wilderness, but cheered and blessed Old Bess for his bravery to act. I remember well his great, green eyes looking into mine own only moments before he left us. And that, dear Lazlo, is the last we saw of-ee for nigh half a decade! How we sobbed and how we spoke of-ee in that time when you were gone! 'Saint Lazlo' they called-ee, and a martyr too. Each evening we grieved your passing up the Lamentable Step. We were unsure how was that you vanished! Perhaps Mites overcame you while the sun was gone, or perhaps a cyclone ate you up and carried you to the edges of the earth. But here you are, and we smile to see-ee! Now give us your tale: how is it you have returned? And how do these strange-ees you have brought here fit into such a perplexing puzzle?"

"Your words are kind, Old Sacks!" said Lazlo, and took the stage. "First, let me remind you how sorrowfully I missed you Lonies while I was far and away. It is a trial to lose one's way, yes, but it tries the heart beyond any measure to lose one's friends and family. I count among you fewer numbers than when I departed, but of these missing souls you shall soon inform me, I am sure. Joy is upon me, though, to see those faces I can! I will recount now my journey to the north and all those troubles that befell me upon it. My trip through the city and up the Lamentable Step went quite unhindered. I would venture to say it was a pleasant walk, even! The wasteland, too, was kinder to me than I had ever expected. For some time I strode to the north and without interruption. During the nights I slowed my pace that my power supply might last me a while longer and afford me more time to explore the northern wastes. Soon, I surpassed Cyclone Row and went further north than any Lonie has e'er gone before."

"I regret to tell you this, brothers and sisters," continued the robot, "but the land there was quite bare and empty, no different from what we see in each other direction! Still, I pressed on, quite determined to find at least something to bring home, something to prove my journey had not been in vain. These extra days I spent in the north proved to be my undoing, though, for I quickly realized my power supply had diminished to a dangerously low level. I began to hurry across the plain, but was forced to halt my stride by a sudden dust storm. This was vexing, yes, but in time it dissipated and I carried on.

"Soon, the power in my legs had nigh evaporated, and I clawed my way across the wastes, pulling myself hand over hand. I came so close to New Hollow, so tantalizingly close that I could nearly taste it with my sensors. So I summoned what power was left in me and stood upon my two feet. I dashed, then, across the plains, homeward bound. But, alas, my energy reserves failed me and I froze on the spot, rooted to the earth, hopelessly immobile."

"Search parties were sent," assured Old Sacks. "We did not figure-ee dead till several cycles after your disappearance. I suppose we never thought to look for-ee so close to home."

"I do not blame yourselves for not being able to locate me. In such a wide, empty place," consoled Lazlo. "I must have appeared as but a speck in a sea of dust, for that is indeed what I was, and what we all are, in a way. But now, if Old Sacks will allow it, I should like to recount the tale of how it is I was found and rescued from my plight."

The leader waved his hand and said, "So touched am I with thy tale of determination and woe that I will listen readily to whatever it is my poor robot brother has to tell."

"I think it best, if Old Sacks will allow it, that my ill treated guests here should tell this portion of the tale from their own point of view," recommended Lazlo.

"For a time I will abide it," said Old Sacks, "but soon the strange-ees will have to reveal their purposes to me, or risk being held in the pen for longer then they wish,"

"We shall see," replied Lazlo. "Friends!" He turned to the children and bowed deeply before them. "Dear friends! Again, excuse this inhospitable welcome! It was never my intention. Understand, the Lonies have many enemies in this city and thus are forced to exercise constant caution. Will you tolerate this ridiculous trial for a moment more and share with the council the story of how you came upon me? Exclude what private information you will, I will not begrudge you that."

The children were silent, but Hess stepped forward and nodded to Lazlo. "I will tell the story," he said boldly, and he looked proud and defiant even with the concrete restraints that clung to him.

"Splendid!" Lazlo clapped his hands. "Please, proceed when you are ready!"

Hess nodded again and cleared his throat loudly. Now, he turned to the tribunal and began to speak. "Well met, Lonies, and well met Master Sacks." The old man waved for him to continue, sinking back into his seat. "I am called Hess, and he Franklin Freeman, and he Joey Jensen, and our female companion is known as Miss Mars." He indicated each of the children in turn.

"Have-ee a name by which thee all are called together?" shouted Jamjar, intrigued with the group of prisoners.

Hess thought for a moment then said, "Call us the Noahnauts, for now."

"Hail-ee Noahnauts," called the Lonies, but they stumbled over the complex word and butchered its pronunciation.

"Er... Hail," Hess answered them. "I'd like to first remind you that, while I understand your caution when it comes to outsiders, my friends and I are on hasty business and time is of the essence; this imprisonment will only be tolerated for a while more."

"Do not threaten the Lonies in their own hall!" barked Old Sacks, rising on his bench and banging the butt of his parking meter scepter into the ground.

"He meant no offense," assured Lazlo hurriedly. "Mr. Hess only speaks the truth."

"Continue-ee then." The grizzly old man motioned for Hess to speak.

"Thank you, sir. I meant no harm." Hess resumed his tale. "My companions and I have travelled long across the wasteland. Our faces are dusty and our legs weary. We were deterred by the great emptiness of this place and became hopeless in our search very quickly."

"From whence do you come that the wasteland seems empty by comparison? And what is that thing for which you search so hastily?" inquired Old Sacks suspiciously.

"Again, those answers I cannot share with you. Truly, I am sorry for it," replied Hess. "As I was saying, the plains were vast and we were lonely and lost upon them. We are wanderers, you see! Eventually, our Franklin here spied something in the distance, only a dark speck, really, but still the first outstanding feature we had noticed in days! I was against commencing an investigation, but Miss Mars absolutely insisted upon it as she is a curious girl if I ever saw one.

"Curious but generous!" added Lazlo. "How grateful I am that Mistress Mars saw fit to come to my aid." He reached his robotic hand through the bars and, kneeling, offered it to her. She took it and smiled, glad at least one among the Lonies trusted her. "See how her brilliant smile flashes in the darkness?" proclaimed the chivalrous robot. "Tell me, Lonies, ever have you seen so fair a creature in all your days? Surely a person of such divine beauty and grace could bring nothing but good tidings to our humble home!" Ellie's face became so red Franklin thought she might turn into a tomato any moment.

"Aye! Aye!" cheered the Lonies. "The strange-ee is fair indeed! Her hair is like the golden-brown straw we have seen waving in the projections, and her smile like a bright star in an empty night sky!"

"Anyway," Hess went on, "at Miss Mars's insistence, we deviated from our path and made out for the speck on the horizon. Soon, we found it not to be a rock or stump, like I had expected, but instead our robotic friend here. He was frozen in place, quite unmoving, and I suspected him dead. Surely, I thought, his circuitry must have corroded itself long ago. I demanded we leave his corpse in peace and return to our path, but again Miss Mars insisted we should investigate further. It was her wish to see life upon the barren earth, even if it were only robotic life. My assistant, Mozi Box, ran a diagnostic and told me it might be possible to save the derelict droid."

"Mozi Box wanted to save his cousin, too!" squealed the computer suddenly.

"Yes," agreed Hess, patting his chest piece helper. "But, again, it was Miss Mars who drove us to his aid. I plugged our Mister Lazlo into my exoskeleton's power supply and soon life sprang to his eyes! Even now it burns there."

Lazlo turned to the crowd and made his emerald eyes glimmer suddenly. They gasped and cheered in awe. "Thanks to these folk, and especially to the good nature of Mistress Mars, not only am I alive but healthier than I have been since my activation nearly two centuries ago!" the robot cried out to them. "This fellow's power is the purest which I have ever tasted and still my circuitry buzzes with its energy."

Hess felt the crowd succumbing to their charming story and his speech gaining momentum, so he continued with increased ardor. "When he had awoken fully, and after he had thanked us profusely again and again, we shared with Lazlo the objective of our search and he informed us that it was close to his home, here in New Hollow. Happily, he led us here and down into the basin, down the Lamentable Step. Our journey was pleasant and slow going, but soon the sun began wane and he hastened us onwards, warning of an enemy that lurked in the dark. Very quickly we learned how real this enemy was.

These Mites, as you call them, gave us chase through the streets right up to your front door. Thanks to Jamjar's expedience in opening it, we just barely escaped with our lives! The rest of my tale you have observed with your own eyes the same as me. Now, if you are satisfied, remove these shackles and free my friends and I from this pen!"

A few Lonies and Jamjar advanced forward to unlock the cage. They were quite satisfied with the story and enchanted with the pale-faced children. Old Sacks, however, would not relent so easily.

"Your account is inspiring indeed, and falls upon the sympathetic ears of a kindly people," he said. "My praise and thanks to you all, particularly Miss Mars who, first saw fit to offer our lost brother aid. But still I must insist-ee offer up explanation! Your search across the plains intrigues me! What is it that-ee quest for? And from where do-ee hail? Never have the Lonies encountered any others of the human sort. Only robots and Mites have we known! And though humans you may be, how came you by such strange garments and such clean, flawless faces?" Franklin and Joey found it rather refreshing to have their hormone-ridden faces referred to as 'flawless'.

"We have offered your long lost brother help, must we still offer you more?" pleaded Hess. "I can give you no more information than I have already! My mission is a secret one and can only fall upon the most carefully selected of ears!"

"And until my ears are among those selected, you will remain locked away!" bellowed Old Sacks. "Forgive me, but you might be tricky spies for the Mites or some other hostile force. Few can the Lonies trust! Mighn't your good will be only an illusion, one devised to bring down the Lonies' careful vigil? You will be well taken care of, to be sure, but-er cage will remain till you can tell more of your aims!"

Suddenly, anger and courage surged up from the depths of Franklin's being and a grandiose lie began to bubble therein. His eyes became fiery and full of vigor. "Wait!" he shouted. The crowd's heads spun towards him, surprised that the otherwise quiet boy had begun to holler so suddenly. "Wait," he continued. "Tell me, please: would you really detain messengers from the sky?"

The crowd gasped and recoiled. Joey and Ellie shot Franklin baffled looks, and Hess groaned within his suit, but the suddenly ardent continued his oration anyway. "You heard me right! We come from a divine kingdom in the sky! We are fair and pale, yes, for that is because we have lived so long in the clouds!"

"Yes!" Ellie had caught on and stepped forward now. "Would you really detain us angels? Our mission is borne in heaven and our search designated to us by a higher power. Should you hinder us, you hinder His purpose as well!"

Now the crowd recoiled again and began to rail and yelp. Old Sacks, however, remained quiet and placid where he sat. "Say-ee that you're angels then?" he asked. "And what do-ee angels search for?"

"A great treasure that has fallen from our kingdom of heaven and into your city," replied Franklin. "We need it back badly! Our mission is urgent!"

Old Sacks sat forward suddenly and his eyes were wild. "This... this treasure of yours fell from the sky? Into the city it fell?"

"Yes," said Hess. "And we have been sent to retrieve it, whether you would hold us or not!" With this, he grunted and stretched out his armor laden arms in front of him, lifting the tremendous concrete blocks that restrained him like they were feathers. With another grunt, he clapped the slabs together and they crumbled in his hands. Without losing a beat, he stomped his two metal boots and the slabs on his feet shattered, too.

The crowd began to yelp and shrink back in fear. Even Old Sacks seemed impressed. Hess stepped forward, grasping a bar of the cage in either hand, and bent them like straws, rending a gap into their prison. He hopped down through it and out of the cage, followed proudly by the children.

"Do you believe our story now?" asked Ellie smugly.

"Your metal man is strong indeed," said Old Sacks,

standing and striding down the forum towards them. "But it was not his strength that assured me of your honesty. Though your story is far fetched, and I believe very little of it, I do believe that you have come from the sky in search of a treasure that fell to earth. Come!" He beckoned them. "I will show you why." Old Sacks then turned and vanished down the corridor they had been taken through earlier. The other Lonies followed behind him, but they refused to make eye contact with the children and seemed very much afraid of them after Franklin's bold claims and Hess's feats of strength.

Now, only the companions, Lazlo, and Jamjar were left in the council chamber. "Good thinking, Franny," said Joey and patted the boy on his back.

"I didn't think it'd work so well," admitted Franklin. "It seemed to scare them, though, and that's not what I was going for. I only wanted to, you know, put them in awe."

"In awe we were!" declared Jamjar. "Eee've made a right mess of our pen, too!"

"An excellent fib you've woven indeed!" praised Lazlo, clapping. "We are taught in the projections that religion is a dangerous notion and powerful, too; it seems you selected just the right chord to strike at in the Lonies' hearts. I think it is instances just like this one that start religions in the first place, actually! Old Sacks is not so convinced by your story, however; but what can he do? Hardly can he shackle those who would so easily break their bonds. But I caution you, he is wary to the dangers of Gods and angels, and I would keep my preaching to a minimum, if I were you."

"Lazlo." Ellie looked at the robot. "What are these 'projections' you keep mentioning?"

"They'nt got projections where-ee come from?" sputtered Jamjar in disbelief. "How ever did-ees learn about the Green Time and the past?"

"Children," said Lazlo, turning to them. "Allow me to formally introduce Jamjar Brickbeard. He is an old friend of mine and sits upon the Lonie council. He is gatekeeper in this, our sanctuary, and oversees those going in and out."

"At-er service," sang Jamjar and swept into a low bow, so low that his strange hat fell from his head and onto the dirty ground. He retrieved it and, without even dusting it off, placed it back upon his brow.

"And Mistress Mars," continued Lazlo, "like so many other things, I believe Old Sacks might better be able to explain the projections than I. Come, he has summoned us. Let us follow and see what he has to say; then we will rest, I am sure, and all your questions will find their answers."

"Lazlo," said Hess suddenly. "I think it might be better if we just part ways now. Franklin, Joey, Ellie, and I will go and hunker down someplace in New Hollow for the night; we'll find the thruster core in the morning and be on our way. I wouldn't want to cause any more trouble than we already have and, frankly, we haven't been that well received by the Lonies!"

"Nonsense! Nonsense!" exclaimed the embarrassed robot. "Profusely I will apologize for this incident till the end of my days, but forgive the Lonies! They live in a dangerous place. And speaking of that dangerous place, you can hardly 'hunker' down in the city tonight. By now, New Hollow is sure to be positively swarming with those beastly little brutes. The Sanctuary here is the only safe place in the entire wasteland right now! Please do stay! How wretched I would feel if you were to depart me now and later I should only find your poor, mangled bones strewn across the street. And the search for that machine of yours could take weeks, if not months without Lonie aid! Old Sacks is quite a clever fellow and perhaps already has an idea of where your lost device might be hiding. Oh dear! Please stay! Please stay!" he begged.

"While I agree with Hess that our welcome hasn't been quite as warm as we might have hoped," said Ellie, "frankly, I'm bushed. I can hardly go another step without some food and rest. The whole day of walking killed me. And then, my god, that chase? I practically fell asleep while that whole council business was going on!"

"Ellie's right, Hess," agreed Franklin. "We can't go on anymore. And I'm certainly not pitching any tents where those

things can get at us. I could eat a horse, and I'm sure Joey
could too. And we could all do with at least twelve hours of
sleep. Isn't that right, Joseph?"

Joey was doing a little dance of some kind, squinting his
eyes and clenching his fists. He ignored the question.

"Joseph?" repeated Franklin.

"Yes, yes, we're all very tired and hungry. Old news!"
snapped Joey. "Lazlo, isn't there a bathroom around here
anywhere? I don't think I've gone since yesterday!"

"A bath-er-oom?" Lazlo sounded out the word, puzzled.

"A place to, you know, bathe?" offered Ellie.

"Bathe?" asked Lazlo, still confused. "I have learned of this
bathing in the projections and, let me tell you, it is not a
common practice of the Lonies."

Joey groaned painfully.

"A place to deposit his excess fuel!" chirped Mozi Box.

"Oh my! How rude of me!" Lazlo sprang into action and
ushered Joey into a small side room carved into the dirt wall. A
few moments later, the boy emerged and grimaced.

"What are bathrooms like after the apocalypse?" asked
Franklin, not quite sure he wanted to know the answer.

"Remember that outhouse at summer camp?" said Joey.

"The one on Deer Lake?"

"Yes."

"I'd rather not remember. That bad?"

"Much worse." Joey simply left it at that. Franklin quickly
decided he could hold it.

"Have I convinced you all to at least stay the night?" Lazlo
pleaded. Hess sighed and gave a nod. "Perfect! Oh, how
perfect! The first guests in the Lonie sanctuary and they are my
own! This will be a day well remembered, I am sure. Come,
Old Sacks is waiting for us. Once he has said his peace we will
find all of you lodging and nourishment and tuck you safely
into bed! Come!"

The children, who were very near collapsing from
exhaustion, nodded dumbly and shuffled out of the council
chamber with Lazlo and Jamjar. They followed the Lonie

crowd that had gone ahead of them on Old Sacks' heels. The mob whispered and muttered, casting frightened and worried glances back at the companions, particularly at Hess who towered above the rest of them in his suit.

"They's right afeared of-ee now!" chuckled Jamjar. "Eee've gone and upset a bunch of fearless warriors who fight demons every moon! Well done! I fear-ee not, however. If Lazlo trusts-ee then so does Jamjar."

They came into the antechamber where the main gate was. There were several dozen Lonies gathered there now; they had been peering down the corridor and into the tribunal. As the children entered, they shrank back and glared.

Old Sacks emerged from out of the group and banged his staff. "Let only the Lonies who sit upon the council join us. Let all the rest disperse!" he ordered.

Dejectedly, most of the crowd sighed and disappeared into nooks and crannies in the shadows. Only the council members remained. "Let me dispense now with the introductions, that the strange-ees might be familiar with us Lonies!" declared Old Sacks.

Now, two fellows stepped forward and bowed to the children. They had youthful, pleasant faces and they were garbed head to toe in black fur, fur that looked strangely like the kind the children had seen covering the Mites. "Call this'n Stingwhit and this'n Fluthers!" instructed Old Sacks. The two bowed again. "They are captains of our guard and a more reliable pair I do not know of! In a fight, anyway," the elder added.

"Welcome strange-ees," exclaimed the two warriors. "We are ever in-er service! Call upon us to fight and fight we will! Call upon-we to sing and all day we'll trill! We are happy with all and a friend to each, but the Mites lie far out of our loving reach. We will smite them here, we will smite them there, but we caution you now, stray far from their lair!" chanted the pair together.

"Have-ee just devised this song?" asked Old Sacks with an annoyed tone. Stingwhit and Fluthers shuffled their feet and coughed nervously.

"Apologies, sir. We thought we might sing like what is done in the projections!"

"Very well." Old Sacks shook his head and dismissed them. "Excuse these two: they are young yet and know not the gravity of the times in which we live. Let's see, who have we got next?"

A large man stepped forward. He wore a white apron, which was spattered in old, yellow grease stains. His face was ruddy and fat, but his eyes were beady and kind. "This'n is Chunk!" Old Sacks proclaimed. "His profession is most difficult of all the Lonies', for he is our chef and must scrape and scavenge all day long, finding what little sustenance he can and serving it to us each night. I cannot guess how well or how easily-ees eat in that 'sky kingdom' of your'n, but the pickings are mighty slim hereabouts! Far too often do we dine on the flesh of the Mites; one will never find a more unpleasant delicacy. But Chunk here can make most anything taste half good, and we bless Old Bess that he's here to do it for us!"

"Pleas'rd am I to see and meet-ee, but excuse me ees must! Tonight's supper is nearly finished and ready for the heaping on Lonie plates!" explained Chunk in a meaty voice, and then waddled away to go about his business.

Another man popped out of the crowd. He was lithe and tall, and his features gaunt and worried. "Call me Suds!" he stuttered nervously. "I am the custodian of this sanctuary and see to its cleaning and organization." He lowered his head bashfully. "Excuse me the mess. We have not been expecting visitors; we haven't had any in nearly four generations."

Old Sacks now indicated two slender, little women. They smiled and laughed. "Call her Mia and her Zaki!" he said. "The twins of our sanctuary. They make our drinkin' water, and they make it well!"

He listed the rest of the names off very quickly. "Here is Fopo, here is ParkPan. Next is Duckdon and after, Mousemick. Gulch and Lamps, Derps and Tot! This'n be Munster and this'n be Pepper Jack."

Now, Old Sacks pointed to a hard-faced man leaning against the wall. "Yonder is Nimrod, who tracks the dreaded Mites wherever they wander and monitors their inhuman movements," explained the Lonie leader. "He is chief among our hunters. You know our Lazlo, here, and Jamjar too. And I am called Old Sacks, if-ee haven't figured that out already. I am regent of these Lonies and inherited the position from my father before me, his before him, and Old Bess before the both of them. While-ees remain here, should you require assistance or help in any way, call upon one of these fine fellows; they are leaders each in their own right and well respected by the Lonies at large."

"Welcome, strange-ees! Welcome angels!" cheered the council, and then dispersed. Only Lazlo and Jamjar remained.

"Come," Old Sacks whispered to them. His voice was softer and kinder now that the crowd had flocked away. "Let me show you my secrets." Now that he could not be heard publicly, he seemed to have abandoned his strange Lonie accent and spoke instead in a way the children could better understand.

He brought them down another hallway. This was a manmade one, unlike the earthen hallway, which had brought them to the council chamber. Torches, not glowing mushrooms, lit their way. The air inside was quiet and discouraged speech among the companions. Old Sacks lumbered along in front of them. Though he was ancient indeed and leaned on his makeshift staff for support, he did not hobble or limp; his steps were proud and filled with strength.

"Ees are being given a great honor now, ye are!" whispered Jamjar to the children. "Only council members are allowed through this way, for beyond lies the greatest secret of the Lonies, one that's been kept for as long as anyone can remember. Hallowed ground, this place be."

Old Sacks turned to Jamjar and raised a bony finger to his withered old lips. The red bearded man went quiet at once.

The light at the end of the tunnel grew brighter and

brighter till at last they emerged from the corridor and out into what Franklin imagined was the chamber at the center of the sanctuary. It was another grand, rounded room, but it was much bigger than the council forum.

At least a few thousand feet in diameter, this was one of the largest rooms the children had ever set foot in, dwarfing even Franklin's visit to Grand Central Terminal in New York City, a place that had inspired almost nauseating awe and vertigo in him. The silver egg like structure the children had seen from the outside hardly looked like it could contain such a grand hall within it. In fact, it appeared like they now stood in the very center of that silver dome, as the ceiling arched sharply above them and climbed to a rounded vertex hundreds of feet in the air.

To their left was another gate; much like the one they had come into the complex through. This gate, however, looked like it had seen almost no use for centuries. It was rusted and worn, and several wooden boards patched various small holes in its surface. Far above the children, plastered sporadically across the curving ceiling, were window panels through which shafts of dim starlight fell.

Most peculiar of all, however, was what lay in the center of the massive room. Equidistant from the round walls that surrounded it was another dome in much the same shape as the Lonie's sanctuary. It was smaller, of course, only about twenty feet tall and fifty some feet across. It was not made of silver like the building, but instead of some thick, translucent glass through which the children could see what lay inside the dome.

The first thing Franklin noticed was the ground inside the structure: it was not laden with dust like the rest of the wasteland, but soft, green grass! Small bushes cropped up out of the grass here and there, and in the center of the dome was a little birch tree. A garden.

"My God!" whispered Joey. "What is this- some kind of terrarium? How did you ever get it to grow?"

"We didn't," replied Old Sacks, and took a step towards the

dome. There didn't appear to be any way in or out of the container, and the glass seemed several feet thick. Franklin wondered how the Lonies came and went from inside of it.

"No," continued Old Sacks, "we didn't get it to grow. Nor do we tend it. The life you see inside this tank has been growing therein for as long as the Lonies can remember. It was left to us by our first leader, Old Bess."

"How do you get inside it?" asked Franklin. "It doesn't look like there are any doors!"

"There aren't," replied the elderly leader sadly. "This garden is both our blessing and our curse at the same time. It is sealed very tight; there is neither a way in nor out of it, so far as I know. We can only look upon it, dote on it in our minds, and fantasize about the Green Time, but that is all. Should the plants ever become sick or die, we can only look sadly on and lament their passing."

"That's ridiculous," snapped Ellie. She was quickly tiring of the Lonies and their strange customs. "Why the hell would Old Bessy- or whatever you called her- leave you a garden, a garden with the last plants on earth growing in it, and not give you a way to get inside of it?"

"Old Bess," corrected Old Sacks sternly, "was no mere leader of Lonies. Nay, she lived both in the Green Time and this, the time after the end of days. Indeed, she survived the Bhasma Cloud's assault upon the earth."

"How?" asked Joey, indignantly. "And for that matter, how did all of you survive it?" The Lonies shouldn't be alive if all the horrible things I've been told about this cloud are correct."

"Again, this triumph over Armageddon's totality we must attribute to the tireless efforts of Old Bess, my greatest of grandmothers," said Sacks. "In her time, she was a wizard of sorts, a magician you see. There is a better word for it, and I have learned it well in the projections, but it fails me now. Lazlo?" he turned to the robot.

"She was a scientist, sir."

"Right-ee are!" exclaimed Old Sacks. "Yes, a scientist. She tinkered with the wise old earth and made it do as she commanded it! Well regarded was she in her time, for she was skillful and knew her craft well. But even she realized the threat of the Bhasma Cloud too late to do much to defeat it. Instead, she devised a way to preserve at least a small portion of the Green Time and quickly constructed two domes. One, the smaller that you see here before you, to preserve the plant life of the world. It is fed by the sunlight which filters down from those windows there." He pointed to the panes far above them. "How the tree acquires water I am not so sure; Old Bess must've reckoned some way to feed it by some pump beneath the earth; something like that."

"And the other dome?" asked Hess.

"The other dome is the sanctuary in which you now stand," said Old Sacks. "The home of the Lonies. It was created to not only act as an extra layer of protection for the garden here, but to house a select few humans whom Old Bess took it upon herself to shelter from the Bhasma Cloud. Both domes are composed of some material that is foreign to both my tongue and my mind; but she synthesized it to withstand the storm's wrath, and that it did. It is the only structure we know of to have successfully protected its inhabitants from the dark Cloud."

"Unbelievable," said Franklin in awe, again astounded by the scientists of the third millennium. "She alone managed to save a few lives from Armageddon. Unbelievable," he repeated. "But why seal the garden off?"

"At first, the garden was to be open to all those who wished to enter it; its seeds ripe for the replanting in the wasteland so that the earth might some day be restored," admitted Old Sacks. "But the first generation of Lonies were a frightened lot, and fighting soon broke out between them. So severe the violence grew that Old Bess became disgusted with the salvation she had given them, and threatened to destroy the garden altogether, dooming the earth to ruin and desolation for eternity. But she saw fit to grant the Lonies one last chance, and addressed them thus: 'This garden, this small oasis of life in sea of death, is a gift only for those that deserve it. If humans are to continue their violent ways, even in this dismal era, then I think it better that they should go extinct entirely and kill each other till there are no more. I will not give them the chance to repopulate the earth with my garden's help if they will only send it back into violent ruin. But if the Lonies can survive three hundred years without fighting in their own ranks, without killing one another, then this garden shall open for them and bear them all its wondrous fruits.'

"And so," continued Old Sacks, "we are doomed to wait another century before the glass dome around the garden opens and yields us the life therein. This is the greatest secret and ambition of the Lonies, and I would ask you never to speak of it outside these walls; should the Mites discover this information, their efforts towards our extermination would intensify tenfold."

The children and Hess were dumfounded. Who ever this Bess was, she sounded cruel and unusually stern. Would she really risk the fate of an entire planet on the tentative peace of a band of survivors? To set a timer on the dome and only allow it to open after three centuries had passed? To force generations of human beings to lust after a garden which they would never be able to walk through? How reckless, thought Franklin, could one's principles actually be?

"The action seems a tad wicked, we know," confessed in Old Sacks, breaking the sudden silence. "But it was effective! Since then, the Lonies have not fought amongst themselves except to quell arguments and rebellions. We save our violence for the Mites, who would have us dead and gone, garden or not. I could ramble on all day about this, our most sacred treasure, all night and into the morning if you allowed me. But that is not why I have brought you here!" Old Sacks snapped suddenly out of his trance. "No. I do not believe your story. You are no angels, I am sure. Your clothes and faces remind me more of some far off times I have seen in the projections. But I will pry no more; though your story is a lie and a tremendous one indeed, I'm sure you have your reason for telling it. There is, however, a small seed of truth to the tale, is there not?"

"What do you mean?" asked Hess, suddenly defensive and alert.

"You, boy!" Old Sacks swung around and stared at Franklin. "You spake and told us a treasure from your 'kingdom in the sky' had fallen to earth and into New Hollow, did-ee not?"

Franklin looked to Hess, who nodded. "Yes, I did say that, sir," he replied politely.

"So you do, in fact, seek something that has fallen from the sky?"

Hess nodded to the boy again. "We do," said Franklin.

"Though I can offer little more aid than this, methinks I might know where it is your 'treasure' might have flown to. Behold you and look there," he cried and gestured to the window panels far above. The children squinted as hard as they could, and Hess adjusted his telescopic visor to better make out whatever it was Old Sacks was gesturing towards. There, hundreds of feet above them, was a smashed window with a gaping hole at its center.

"Not two days ago a cyclone came rumbling above our sanctuary. It is an unusual occurrence for the storms to stray this far south, but not unheard of. However, something or other came whistling down from the sky, from out of that twister, and plummeted into New Hollow. It smashed through those windows there and fell further into the sanctuary. Nothing like this has ever happened before, so far as Old Sacks can remember," said the elderly leader.

"And a right mess it made, too!" added Jamjar. "I had to clean up the glass shards, I did. Nearly nicked my fing-ees off a few times, I is loathed to admit!"

"You mean it fell here? Into the sanctuary?" Hess sounded ecstatic. "What luck! I've never been so lucky! Where is it? Where are you keeping it? Oh God, you didn't scrap it for spare parts, did you?"

"Spare parts?" Old Sacks shot him a sly, knowing look. "My half-metal friend, what treasure from heaven could the Lonies possibly use for 'spare parts'? But your excitement is premature, I'm afraid. The object in question did indeed crash down through my irreparable, two-hundred-year-old window and into the most sacred place on this planet, but it did not come easily to rest upon the dirt here."

"No, of course not," grumbled Ellie. "Because that would be too easy."

"Where did it go, then?" asked Hess, though already his high spirits were sinking.

Old Sacks frowned and pointed to the gate on the left, the one that looked like it had not been used for centuries. "See the planks in the middle of that door there?" He gestured to the boards which covered one of the gaping holes in the center of the surface of the gate. "Those planks patch a hole which your treasure made when it crashed through the gate."

"Alright, so it's on the other side of the door," sputtered Hess, exasperated. "Just open it up and we'll be done!" He held up the Rok Counter, which indicated the thruster core did, in fact, lie in the direction of the rusty old gate.

"That gate looks awfully rusted, Hess," reminded Joey. "It looks like it hasn't been opened in a long while."

"And for good reason, strang-ee! An astute observer you are," remarked Old Sacks. "He's right. That gate has not been opened since Old Bess herself disappeared into it and sealed it shut behind her. That was after she closed the garden dome. She left the Lonies, you see, and vanished behind that gate; and she has neither been seen nor heard from since!"

"What's through it?" asked Hess, spirits sinking lower still.

"The Well," hissed Jamjar and shuttered. "The Well lies behind that ancient door. Such legends I have heard about it, I cannot help but to shiver at its thought."

"The Well?" repeated Joey. He sounded intrigued.

"A pit so deep, so dark, and so dank that I'm sure the even the sun's brightest rays have never penetrated its filth. It is black down thata-weez," explained Jamjar. "Blacker than the most awful patch of midnight-ee can imagine."

"But what is it, really?" insisted Joey.

"Remember how I told you all that New Hollow collapsed many years ago into an ancient, colossal sewer system?" asked Lazlo. "The Well is the only direct way to reach that forgotten, subterranean realm. It is a pit that descends nearly a mile into the earth. The Mite hordes dwell at the bottom of it in full force; some say it is where they were first born and from whence all their evil stems. No Lonie has gone down the well since Old Bess, and she never returned."

Hess groaned. "And that's where our - er - treasure has gone?"

"I'm afraid so," said Old Sacks. "And into a more dangerous, despicable place it could not have dropped. On quiet nights, when young Lonies cannot sleep and lie fitfully into the night, they can hear the horrible chanting, the moaning, the roaring, and the shrieking of the Mites all echo up from The Well. The sounds have cursed even the bravest children with unrelenting nightmares of the dark beneath New Hollow."

The children cringed.

"Look," Hess said, annoyed with what he perceived to be the old man's fear-mongering. He held out his wrist and the little flashlight popped out, casting a beam of light on the decrepit gate. "I've got lights aplenty, a suit of armor, and above all-" a burst of flame shot forward from the wrist cannon into the air, illuminating the dark room with a flash of orange and yellow, "-I've got weapons. Whatever's down there, I can handle it."

Jamjar had gone positively wide-eyed at the display of technology and applauded hardily, having never seen such tricks. But Old Sacks' face remained placid. "Were I not wiser, I'd believe you to be an angel indeed with such a show of force as that," he muttered. "But I am skeptical still and-"

Hess cut him off, "Listen, you stubborn old codger. I haven't got time to dawdle around and explain myself to you. Open up that gate, give me a few hours behind it, and my companions and I will be on our way and out of your hair."

"Hold your hammers!" cried out Old Sacks. "To open that

gate, even for a moment, is to put the Lonies at the greatest risk they have ever faced. Old Bess alone knows what could come surging up out of that pit. I'll tell you this only once: there are creatures much more awful than mites that brood in the dregs of the Well."

"Please, Old Sacks." Lazlo entered the fray, now. "If you cannot find it in your heart to open the way for these folk, then do it for me, your loyal servant. I owe them a life debt, you see, and as of yet it has been ill refunded."

"Aye!" crowed Jamjar suddenly. "And if it be a treasure like'n the strange-ees say it be, then certainly we cannot leave it in the hands of the Mites. Imagine what terror they could wreak upon the sanctuary with a relic of heaven. Makin' me shiver just to be thinkin' about it!"

"Yes, sir," added Franklin. "It really is imperative we find this treasure. More imperative then you know." Old Sacks arched his eyebrows skeptically. "Please, sir," the boy continued, "the fate of our entire world lies in your hands." Ellie nodded in agreement.

Joey said nothing; he had wandered off to peer through the glass and into the garden, muttering to himself the names of plants he could see inside.

"Your entire world, you say?" The elderly leader leaned on his staff as if a great weight had suddenly taken him. "Though you are liars about your origins, I see sincerity in your eyes now. Earnest eyes have you, young strang-ee," he observed, looking at Franklin. "Your entire world... Our world was long ago destroyed, and nothing is left but the ghosts of the past to haunt us, along with the faint promise of a greener future none of us will ever see. I would not wish such a way upon any lot, not even a bunch of false angels such as yourselves. Very well." He sighed. "I will do what I can to aid your search, even should it mean plumbing the depths of the haunted well."

Ellie gave Franklin a small high five, and Mozi Box began to squeal a little hip-hip hooray, but Old Sacks waved his hand. "This will be no easy task, however," he assured them. "First, I must convince the council that you are to be trusted, then I must convince them again, this time to open the Well's gate. That will be most difficult of all; the Lonies would barely be able to stomach such a dangerous proposition, I guess. But try I shall, nonetheless. Give me a few days time, and we will see what we can do. Meanwhile, flee you from this chamber here and do not return to it till the time is right; it is a sacred place and ought to be disturbed with idle chatter. Lazlo will see to your accommodations. Rest you easy while you may!" With this, Old Sacks spun on his heels and marched off down the corridor from where they had come.

Lazlo sprang towards them with delight. "Did I not tell you he was an amicable old gentleman at heart? Oh, happy day! He has agreed to help you, or at the very least do what he may."

Hess shook the robot's hand. "Thank you for intervening on our behalf, Lazlo." He shook Jamjar's hand next. "And you too, Mr. Brickbeard. You have no idea what you've done for humanity - er - heaven."

There was much cheer now, the first in some time. At last, the sleepiness that had been clawing at the children all the evening began to slink into them, drooping their eyelids and slowing their step.

Drowsily, Ellie and Franklin walked over to where Joey was standing, his face pressed unceremoniously against the sacred dome. "Did you hear that, Joseph? Sacks is going to try and open the gate for us," said Franklin.

"Or for Hess, anyway. Nobody said anything about us going down there." Ellie still had the chills from the various descriptions of the Well. Franklin shot her an incredulous glance.

"Something's scared you? Scared Ellie Mars?" he wondered aloud.

She shrugged. "Maybe I'm just tired. We'll see about it soon enough. But that's good news, huh Joey?"

"Yes," mumbled the distracted boy. "It is. I've always kinda' wanted to see what kind of biome a sewer system would evolve into if it were left alone for a while. Especially one as big as they say it is." He gestured inside the dome, drawing the two others' gazes. "See in there, Franny?" he asked. "It's an old, white birch tree, just like the one in Mr. Whiffin's garden. It looks nearly identical. But I guess all birch trees do. And there are some hydrangeas, some hostas, tulips, lilies, and chrysanthemums, even a snowdrop! God knows how they got any of these plants to grow, but they did!" The children all nodded and let their eyes wander across the garden.

Suddenly, a faint blue light caught Franklin's eye from the ceiling. He squinted in the gloom above, doing his best to make out what the light belonged to. As his eyes adjusted, he realized it was some sort of massive computer apparatus affixed to the ceiling, and there was not one but thousands of the blue lights plastered all over it. Stretching out like tendrils from the device were hundreds upon hundred of cords which snaked out across the ceiling, striking out in every direction. It looked like they travelled to several places all over the sanctuary.

"Lazlo," called Franklin to the robot who was still cheerily congratulating Hess. "What's that glowing thing up on the ceiling?"

Lazlo strode over to them and followed the boy's gaze. "Why, that is the projection database," he replied. "All the images and footage the Lonies view in the projections of the past comes from inside of it. You will see how the system works soon enough, perhaps when we retire to my apartment. Speaking of which, it's grown awfully late! I should be seeing to your supper and your beds, not standing around chitchatting! Forgive me. Come, let us take a meal, talk some, and slumber like we so well deserve."

The companions didn't have to be asked twice. Even Hess, whose every movement was supported by a series of hydraulic limbs, was beginning to stumble with each weary step.

Lazlo ushered them quietly down the hallway they had entered through and turned into another passage branching off from it. They passed dozens of man-sized holes carved into the walls as they walked. Through these holes, which were really just makeshift doors, the children caught brief glimpses of various Lonie homes within, lit by humble little fire pits. In some there were families of the strangely clothed folk, parents tending the fire while the children whispered and played, going about their innocent lives. Other rooms, noted Franklin sadly, sheltered what appeared to be widows; ancient old women who watched the fire, sad and alone.

"Robots have their own homes too, huh Lazlo?" asked Joey as they walked.

"Yes. The Lonies treat us artificial fellows no differently than those composed of flesh and blood. Not to mention, there's more than enough room to spare; Old Bess did not anticipate how many scores of us Lonies would be lost to battle and disease over the years. Many of these homes are vacant." And indeed they were. Some apartments they passed were laid quite bare, untouched; but, others clearly had once been happy homes and still housed various odds and ends their respective families had left behind.

"Here we are," said Lazlo, and led them into a spacious apartment with dirt walls. There were few things inside, and they were all covered in cobwebs. A sort of ramshackle table sat in the center of the room, and to its side was a fire pit. They were both dusty and hadn't been used for some time. At the rear of the room was a small, silver device. It looked like a pair of tinted ski goggles, but it was connected to a cord, which ran up into the wall and out of sight. The cord looked just like the ones Franklin had seen branching out of the projection database earlier.

"We left it just how-ee had it when-ee departed five sun cycles ago," said Jamjar, blowing dust and cobwebs off the surface of the little table and giving it a futile wipe with his sleeve. "Though there weren't much to move around, were there? Eee robots are simple folk and need not many earthly possessions to keep-ee contented, aye?"

"It certainly isn't much," said Lazlo, and then sighed contentedly. "But it's home to me, nonetheless. Living in a place like this for so long as I have, nearly two centuries now, one grows attached to his surroundings, no matter how humble they may be. Thank you, Jamjar, for seeing that the place was looked after."

"Welcome are-ee, for sorely I've missed-ee," said the gatekeeper. He snuffled for a moment and held a dirty hand up to his clay colored beard, dabbing at his eye with his filthy sleeve. "Thought-ee was dead I did! How miserable I've been without my old pally-friend, Lazlo! Welcome! Oh welcome-ee lost Lonie!" With this, Jamjar let out a manly little sob and threw his arms around the robot, pounding his metallic back with his meaty palms. No matter how comical the sight was, Franklin could not help the small tear which welled in his eye as he watched them; hopes were surging through his mind, hopes that he one day might return like Lazlo had and be so warmly welcomed back to his home.

After the robot and Jamjar had embraced a few more times, Lazlo brought out some chairs and set them around his table, insisting that the children sit down and let him tidy the place up bit. Hess' chair, being an ancient piece of furniture and quite unwilling to bear the exoskeleton's weight, buckled and collapsed beneath him.

"Quite alright! Quite alright!" bubbled Lazlo, sweeping up the pieces and disposing of them. Soon, the robot brought out a sturdier seat. "I often sit here myself, and since we are of similar weights much greater than our friends here, I reckon it ought to suit you just fine." Though the chair creaked a bit as Hess occupied it, it remained steadfast beneath his metal rear.

Chunk, the Lonie councilman they had met earlier that evening, appeared at the door to Lazlo's apartment and let out a tremendous belch to announce his presence.

"Ullo! Ullo Lazlo and Strangees and even-ee, Brickbeard!" He was carrying a large tray with several bowls on it. "I've brought-ee leftovers! Ee've missed supper, but I saved-ees what remained, and a right lot of it too! This stew's a good'n, methinks. Made it myself to celebrate our Mr. Lazlo's homecoming!"

Chunk entered the room and let the tray clatter down onto the table in front of the children; the soup sloshed about in the bowls with all the commotion and a bit spilled. The children leaned over the meal and grimaced down at the bluish, pinkish broths; they smelled repugnant, worse than even Mrs. Freeman's orange roughy.

"Is this all that's on the menu, Mr. Chunk?" asked Ellie. She was in no mood to be polite; her day, as she saw it, had been trying enough without being forced to swallow down a mouthful of god-knows-what.

Chunk scratched his head. "Well, I s'pose it is. I've seen three course meals in the projections of the Green Time, but we Lonies are really only a one course sort; eats quicker that way and saves more for later, it does."

"Are you sure?" She was persistent.

"We've got some food Ole' Bess left us all those 'undreds of years ago. We eats it sometimes when there's no stew to make."

"What is it?" Her eyes lit up.

"A bunch of none perishable garbage, if you ask me," scoffed Chunk. "Called Burke Brand Freeze Dried Meal Supplements. Taste a great deal like I reckon sand might. Ole' Bess had thousands of 'em for some reason."

The children groaned. Why, wondered Franklin, was mankind always forced to select the lesser of two evils? Freeze dried meal supplements or monster stew? A cruel world indeed. The three boys had completely exhausted their appetite for any more gritty Burke Bars, so they opted instead for the strange broth.

"Thanks all the same," said Ellie, "but I'll stick with the protein bars for now. Something doesn't smell quite right about that stew. No offense, Mr. Chunk."

"None taken by me!" chortled the chef. "You strang-ees must have delicate tastes indeed coming from the clouds and all. I'm honored to serve such a refined bunch. Truly, I am!"

He sounded quite sincere.

Franklin near gagged when he took a whiff of the broth. It smelled like something had crawled into the stew pot, died, and been ladled out as a liquidy mess of rot and decay. Doing his very best to be polite, he pinched his nose and brought the clay bowl to his lips, sipping on the lukewarm concoction. It didn't taste nearly so bad as it smelled, almost like a putrid variety of beef stroganoff, but it slid down his gullet like some sort of toxic sludge; oozing past his tongue and clinging to the insides of his throat. The sensation was atrocious and the soup nearly came right back out, but Franklin forced a smile and swallowed down the mouthful anyway.

Joey, taking note of his friend's culinary daring, did the same and winced. "What's this made of, Mr. Chunk?" he asked after trying not to wrinkle his nose.

"Few things we 'ad in the pantry. Some salt, some pepper, a sprinkle o' my special spices, and meat of course."

"What kind of meat?" asked Franklin, wondering if it was some sort of artificially preserved stuff the Lonies had kept fresh all those centuries.

"Mite Meat, of course!" replied Chunk, guffawing. "What else? I weren't going to feed-ee Lonie flesh, now were I?"

Franklin's hands began to shake and his stomach to gurgle violently. A cold sweat claimed his brow.

"You... You mean to say this soup is made of..." He couldn't even bring himself to finish the question.

"Those creatures we saw outside?" Joey finished for him.

"Indeed! Nimrod caught these'n fresh for us this very morning! Feisty little buggers they were too." Chunk smiled and began to stew the broth with a long metal spoon. "But, like I always says, feistier they are, easier they boil."

Joey had always enjoyed tasting bizarre foods. When he and Franklin had visited Louisiana with their parents, he had eagerly devoured alligator meat and all other sorts of swamp delicacies. Now, a smile crossed his face and he tucked immediately into the stew, savoring each spoonful and carefully analyzing its strange flavor.

Franklin, who was having trouble keeping down his first bite, pushed the bowl politely away and accepted a meal supplement from Hess, who had also declined the Mite Meat Stew. Ellie smirked at the nauseous boy. 'I told you so,' her eyes seemed to say. Chunk gave them a little bow, which he could hardly manage given his great, protruding gut, and strode out of the room proudly.

They ate in silence as Jamjar and Lazlo bustled about the apartment, dusting this and that, and eventually kindling a small fire in the central pit. Franklin hadn't realized how cold he was till the warmth of the flames began to seep into his weary bones; the Lonie sanctuary was sort of like a massive cellar, cramped and chilly. But, when all was said and done and the apartment was well lit and warmed, it appeared to the boy as the coziest place he had seen since his leaving his bed on Pendel Circle. His eyes began to droop.

When the unsatisfying dinner was finished and the dishes piled in a heap on the table, the companions sat around picking their teeth. There wasn't much to say; the thoughts of their exciting day simply stewed in their minds much like the Mite meat had been left to stew in the bowls. Hess, who had grown quickly bored, began to ask Mozi Box to try and re-establish contact with the Noah. For the second time that day, the little computer whined and moaned till at last the static radio noise blared over his speakers.

"Big brother's left another message," said Mozi Box. "It looks to be much the same as the last one: almost entirely incomprehensible. Shall I play it?"

"Might as well."

Mozi's voice came in infrequent patches through the static, garbled and uneven. "Mr. Hess... children... **stay**... **stay**... I repeat... **stay**... Mozi out."

"Damn," muttered Hess. "Just as useless as before. Poor old Mozi must be worried sick. Maybe he got the ship up and running and now he's looking for us but he wants us to 'stay' in place so he can find us."

"Difficult to say, Mr. Hess! Mozi Box hopes he'll see his big brother again someday!" Even the AI was intimidated by the daunting task ahead of them.

Just as the children were beginning to fall out of their chairs, nearly asleep, the scarecrow like Suds appeared at the door and ducked into Lazlo's apartment. As if on cue, he had brought sleeping rolls along. He laid these out on the floor near the fire for the children and Hess. He was not so friendly as Chunk, though, and would not make eye contact with the pale creatures he believed to be fearful angels sent from above.

"Y-y-y-your majesties!" he stuttered and made a hasty beeline out of the room. Eagerly, the children occupied their rolls and snuggled deep inside of them. Though they were ancient and smelled musty like Franklin's grandmother's closet, they wrapped the children in warmth and made their chilly toes tingle with delight.

"God," mumbled Ellie to her two friends as she sniffed the air. "You two stink. And I hate to admit it, but so do I. First priority tomorrow is finding a shower."

"Agreed," said Franklin. Joey didn't respond; he was in his natural, odorous state and loving it. Soon, as Franklin listened to the crackle of the fire and the quiet murmurs of Hess, Jamjar, and Lazlo who all sat around the table, his two friends' snores joined the quiet chorus. He was content to stay up a while longer, pleased to be with his friends and locked safely away inside the Lonie sanctuary. Having nothing better to do, he began to eavesdrop on the others who talked late into the night.

"Much has changed since-ee left us so long ago, Lazlo," whispered Jamjar in a hushed tone, afraid to awake what he thought were literally sleeping angels. "The battles have been many and the victories few for us poor Lonies. Not long ago, the Mites overwhelmed us, they did, and with a cowardly ambush of the kind only they are so wicked to execute. The Lonie ranks were forever thinned that wretched afternoon, and I'd say irreparably so. Pears and parsley! Curse them Mites! Curse'em says Jamjar Brickbeard! They kilt his friends and thieved his favorite hat!"

"We suffered great losses, then?" Lazlo sounded devastated.

"Aye, terrible'ns. Fifty mens, at least!"

"Fifty men?" Lazlo's voice synthesizer could barely choke the words out.

"How many Lonies are there, anyway?" asked Hess, thinking fifty not so great a number to lose when compared to some of the greater battles of history he had read about in books.

"Only a few hundred. As-ee can imagine, losing nearly a quarter of-er population don't work wonders on the morale," replied Jamjar, rubbing his eyes, which were tearing up. "We lost a good deal of ground that fateful day, and with our diminished numbers we 'aven't since been able to take it back! The tides have turned, Lazlo old man, and the Lonies are on the losing shore! Each day the beastly things grow stronger and bolder, encroaching closer to the sanctuary than ever they have ventured 'afore. Things look ill for us, Lazlo. I fear that we might fail and crumble'n their hateful claws. How ever can we hope to defend the sacred garden if'n we can't even protect our own borders? Ill indeed, Lazlo. Ee've come home to troubled times!"

"Troubles times indeed," Lazlo sighed. "But there is yet some good in this wasted world of ours, Jamjar. Our Mr. Hess here and his companions have proved this to me. See you that girl with hair like golden wheat who slumbers on the floor? No matter how says Old Sacks, she will always be an angel to me. Who knows? Perhaps these pale-faced travellers will offer us some unseen advantage over the Mites. Perhaps they will prove to be the Lonies' salvation."

"I'm sorry," said Hess sadly, "but I wouldn't get your hopes up. We're heading straight back to where we come from once we've recovered our device. I don't mean to be rude or ungrateful for your hospitality, but our mission is dire, even more hopeless than your grave situation here. But I'll say this: while we're here, my companions and I will offer what little help we may."

"Your words are kind," said Lazlo, and patted Hess's hand.

"But I'd sooner rust than see Miss Mars put to work!"

"I don't think you'd be able to stop her, Lazlo," chuckled the armored boy. "I've only known her for a short while, but she's one of the feistiest, most stubborn people I've ever met!"

Franklin rolled over and glanced at Ellie who was snoring quietly at his side; though her features were dusty and tanned with the wasteland sun, her face was serene and her sleeping lips were curled into a little, contented smile. How pleasant she looked as the fire danced gleaming patterns across her cheeks and made her eyelashes glitter in amber and gold, as if they were about to burst into flame. For a moment, her lids flickered and she rolled over and smiled sleepily at the boy.

"Go to sleep, Franklin," she whispered.

"Goodnight, Ellie," he whispered back, and nestled far down into his bedroll, shutting out the fire's light and encapsulating himself in a cocoon of warmth. Soon, as the muffled voices of the others faded slowly away, Franklin lapsed into blackness and fell peacefully to sleep.

Franklin awoke with a start in the middle of the night. He had been dreaming of the marshes back home, the smell of salt in the air, and the soft cries of gulls as they flapped overhead. But some far-off noise had pricked up his ears and sent a chilling tingle down his spine.

The fire had gone dead hours ago and its embers smoldered dimly in the pit; the apartment was a dark, deep blue. Joey and Ellie were still snoozing calmly, quite undisturbed, and Hess had lain down next to them. Lazlo sat in a corner of the apartment, plugged into an outlet, recharging. His emerald eyes glowed faintly in the dark, like two green will-o-wisps hovering happily in dusky forest. No one else had awoken, so why had Franklin?

The sound that had so jolted Franklin from his sleep came again and reassured the boy he wasn't imagining things. It was a faraway noise, but a powerful one nonetheless and echoed hauntingly through the sanctuary.

At first, it was unintelligible and reminded him of the buzzing of a bee or a whisper from across the playground. But soon it grew in his ears and its enunciation became more frighteningly clear to him "Bhasma. Bhasma. Bhasma. Bhasma." Franklin began to shiver as the chant grew in vigor and frequency. "Bhasmabhasmabhasmabhasmabhasma!" He buried his head beneath his blanket in a futile attempt to block out the ghastly song, but it only seemed to grow louder.

Being unable to bear it a moment longer, he shot up out of his sleeping roll and raced to the door, not even bothering to put on his shoes. He followed the long, dark corridor through which Lazlo had lead them earlier; it seemed a haunted place now in the dead of night, and each shadow upon its walls stretched out like a gnarled hand, as if it were going to grasp the boy and squeeze all the life out of him.

He wound his way slowly through the passages, shivering in the chilly night air and guiding his way with a hand placed gingerly on either wall. The noise was not coming through the main gate out to New Hollow like he had expected, though. No, it echoed from another source, one he hardly wanted to visit before he had to.

Soon, he found himself wandering into the sacred chamber, the one in which the garden dome stood. Starlight shot brilliantly down from the windows above and lit up the branches of the lone little tree with streaks of silver and white. But the garden was not what Franklin had come seeking.

Almost unwillingly, he stole across the room to where the rusted old gate was, the same one the thruster core had apparently crashed through. Yes, the noise was strongest here and had a terrible, biting ring to it. There wasn't a doubt in his mind anymore: the chanting was echoing up from inside the Well, the pit just beyond the gate, ringing so powerfully that it sneaked its way around the edges of the iron door and permeated the quiet of the sanctuary with its toxic melody.

Suddenly, a shape loomed up out of the darkness from

behind him and gave him a fright. Franklin whirled about on his heels and, rather clumsily, raised his fists and prepared to battle it out with whatever Mite had come to devour him. But he couldn't bring himself to open his eyes and look upon his assailant; he would simply have to endure a blind, painful death.

"So you can hear it too?" asked a creaky, familiar voice. Franklin opened one cautious eye and saw that Old Sacks, his white beard lit silver in the starlight, was standing behind him, bent wearily upon his staff.

"Yes," sputtered Franklin, suddenly embarrassed and nervous. "I didn't mean to trespass in the sacred chamber or anything like that. Honest, I didn't."

"Of course you didn't." Old Sacks gave him a tired, gap-toothed smile. "But the creatures awoke you with their death songs and you couldn't stay away. I know that feeling well, the same thing has befallen me nearly every night since my childhood. It seems you are an honest faced lad, and susceptible to their call, just the same as I."

Old Sacks stepped past Franklin and placed a withered old hand on the gate, leaning towards it and bowing his head.

"They are at their strongest deep down in that hole, the Mites are. They breed and fester there like a colony of black mold and fungus; infecting each and every thing they can lay their slimy claws on. Those Mites who walk the surface here in New Hollow are merely their scouts, only peons to their deep dwelling brothers' malignant schemes. The true power of the beasts lies far beneath the earth, at the bottom of the Well, where the dark gives them pleasure and compels their wicked ways."

"Sir," said Franklin tentatively. After a moment of reflection, Old Sacks grunted for him to continue. "If you don't mind my asking: what are these Mites? I thought only the Lonies survived the Bhasma Cloud because of Old Bess."

"Mites?" Old Sacks huffed. "Mites. Oh dear, where to begin? Wherever it is you come from, Lad, I'm sure you have Mites there as well."

"No," Franklin admitted. "I'm glad to say we don't."

"Certainly you do," said the elder. "Mites are as old as mankind itself. This new form of theirs is only a very recent development; one brought about by Armageddon. By the Bhasma Cloud."

Old Sacks began to pace about, stroking his beard thoughtfully. "Mites is only what we call them for short, lad. Bhasmites are they called in full, but we Lonies try not to utter their whole name. Bhasmites, indeed." He trembled, half in anger and half in fear.

"They were human once in the Green Time, you see. Humans much like you or I. But humans of a certain kind, for they alone were singled out by Armageddon and affected by the Bhasma Cloud in a manner most peculiar, unlike the rest of the population. It is our belief that they were once particularly wicked and cruel human beings, heartless individuals who suited the Bhasma Cloud's malign taste and appetite for destruction. Instead of being vaporized and wiped away like all the rest, they were transmuted during the apocalyptic storm and corrupted, deformed into the creatures you see now by what means of hideous torture I cannot imagine. They slipped away into the deeps of the earth where still some sustenance was yet to be found. They soon forgot the sunlight altogether, for now they abhor it and will not readily walk beneath its rays, electing instead to prowl by night.

"But they did not forget the Bhasma Cloud, their master and tormentor alike. They are, in some strange, perverted way, devoted to it. They kowtow in its name, do penance to it, and worship it as divine. Often, on a quiet night like this one, you can hear them in the caverns chanting without end, 'Bhasma! Bhasma! Bhasma!' as if they so greatly desired its return and the resurrection of that chaos that reigned in the end of days."

"They're very violent, then?" asked Franklin. He was in shock. Could these twisted, goblin-like creatures really have been humans at one time?

"Indeed, they are of an aggressive sort. Though our compound is quite secure, they have conducted raids against us in the past. They were selected by the Bhasma Cloud to be the sole survivors of its wrath, you see; they have a seething hatred of all those who defied their master's calamity. A hatred of any who survived Armageddon. A hatred of the Lonies."

"And they all look like that, then?" wondered the boy.

"Not all. There are larger ones amongst them, though they are quite a rare breed. But large they are, gargantuan to their kind and indeed colossi, even to us. The tribe that lives beneath New Hollow is led by one of these giants; he is called Cherophobe and has sparsely been seen, save in acts of terrible defilement: rending the flesh of innocent Lonies and tearing them limb from limb. Just terrible. The Bhasmites flock to him and throng by his monstrous feet. If ever there were a Mite to avoid, I'd advise that you give Cherophobe the widest berth. He was selected specially by his terrible, apocalyptic master to lead these minions in the wake of his destruction."

"Cherophobe?" whispered Franklin, afraid to utter the name too loud."

"Cherophobe. A demon taller than twelve Lonies stacked one upon the other, and stronger than the most powerful automaton, too. I have seen him only once, and I was nearly smote by the encounter. He is truly the most wicked embodiment of the Bhasma Cloud's desolation."

Franklin tried at once to dispel the image of a Mite who towered above all the rest from his mind, for it was a beastly picture indeed. But a thought nagged at the back of his mind, one that had been troubling him for some time. "Where did the cloud go?" he asked suddenly.

"The Bhasma Cloud?" Old Sacks drummed his fingers on his staff. "This is difficult to say. Perhaps it spent itself in its hatred and evaporated. Or maybe it has since fled the earth to seek out new conquests in the stars. I am not sure, and would rather not know, so long as it never regresses here to earth. The planet could not endure such an offense again, already even the peace of the Lonies buckles beneath the mischief of the Bhasmites."

"How terrible!" exclaimed the boy. "Walking through that

barren wasteland, I would have never guessed there was such a ferocious war going on down here."

"It is no war, lad," said Old Sacks with a stern gaze. "It is a fight for survival. In war there are negotiations and treaties to be made; in war there is always some kind of end in sight, no matter how grave the conflict. But this wretched battle is one betwixt predator and prey. If our enemies are to be successful, we are to be no more: obliterated absolutely and made extinct. They seek the desolation of the last remaining life on earth. This is no war. This is an extermination."

Old Sacks looked towards the garden now and flashed a small yet determined smile. "But I will not let them succeed. Not while that tree stands and offers us a glimmer of hope, no matter how faint. While that tree stands, the world is still worth living in."

The ancient Lonie smiled and the two were silent for a while. In the quiet, Franklin realized the chanting had ceased and the air was quite empty of sound, now. "It's gone," he muttered. "I can't hear them saying 'Bhasma' anymore."

"And it is difficult to tell if they've really stopped chanting, or if they were never chanting on the first place," said Old Sacks.

Franklin was befuddled. "What do you mean, sir? Of course they were chanting. I've been hearing them all night! You just said yourself they've been waking you up since you were small."

"Aye," Old Sacks growled. "Certainly they often chant and sing down thereabouts. But I must wonder if our imaginations do not make the songs up themselves, sometimes. Surely even the Mites do not chant every night, but every night have I heard them! I am suspicious my mind has begun to sing a wicked song of its own."

"Why would our minds ever do something like that?" demanded Franklin, alarmed. Any notion of his brain making decisions without his input was terribly frightening to him.

"The Mites' call is infectious, lad. It is a sort of siren call, if you will; a summons to a brigand's lifestyle, one wrought with pillaging and cackling, killing and burning, an existence completely free of consequence. In each of us, even those with the purest of hearts, there festers a secret longing to embark upon such a carefree rampage and leave behind all our responsibilities, all our ideals. A little creature inside each of us gnashes its fangs and demands that we join the rabid hordes of the world. It is our savage instinct and most secret desire."

Franklin shook his head vigorously, positively appalled by the suggestion. "No! Not me. I'd never want to join a bunch of monsters like that. And, I guarantee you, there isn't some subconscious part of me that'd join them, either."

Old Sacks laughed and threw his head back. Starlight sparkled through his flaky beard. "Why, dear child! You have no access to your most principle motivations. A secret furnace blazing within your core compels you forward, and each choice you make is merely a branch stemming from that original, smoldering root. You are a force of will in many forms speeding in many directions, all at once, but coerced by that insatiable, hidden desire nonetheless."

Franklin didn't respond. He didn't much like the thought; something about it didn't sit right with him.

Old Sacks tapped the rusty gate with his staff. "Don't worry your head about this gate till you must. You'd best be retiring to bed now, lad. The sun will soon rise and you will wonder where the night has gone!"

Franklin nodded and, without a word, tore away from the strange encounter and headed down the corridor towards Lazlo's apartment; he wanted to put as much distance between him and that dismal gate as possible. Upon returning, he found everyone still soundly asleep.

He realized he was quite weary himself and, since the chanting had ceased, he laid his head down and snuggled beneath the bedroll. His sleep was fitful, though, and feverish nightmares plagued him, nightmares fraught with images of the Bhasmites and their piercing, red eyes glaring out at him from a sea of darkness.

He dreamt of a tremendous and towering beast, too; a

creature so vile and massive that it could only be the same Cherophobe that had been described to him. Old Sacks' words swirled tauntingly in his head.

"It is our savage instinct and our most secret desire."

CHAPTER FOURTEEN

LAZLO AND THE LONIES

"**F**ranny... Franny, wake up," muttered Joey, shaking the sleeping boy. Franklin forced open two bleary eyes and blinked groggily up at his friend.

"You're up before me? And without your alarm clock?" he yawned. "It must be late."

"I guess it is, though I can't really be sure." Joey frowned. "It's hard to tell all cooped up in this compound like this, but we've slept the morning away so far as I can see."

Franklin rolled over to see Ellie's bedroll empty and the room very much vacant, save Joey and himself. "Where are the others?" he asked.

"Ellie said something to me about finding a shower but I was still half asleep and she sounded grumpy so I wasn't really listening. I don't know where Hess went; he was gone by the time I got up in earnest."

Franklin sighed and stirred restlessly, squeezing his eyes shut and furrowing his brows. "I keep hoping I'll wake up and realize this is all a dream and we're all back in our nice comfy beds in Stony Creek," he murmured. "We're wasting away a precious summer break you know, Joseph. What do you suppose we'd be doing today if we were back home?"

Joey scratched his head and blinked. "Fishing again, I guess. Or maybe biking in the woods. Or helping Mr. Whiffin in his garden. Who knows? Stony Creek seems a long way away, huh, Franny?"

"It sure does. Don't you just wish we were back there?"

"Not really," admitted Joey. "And I know you don't wish that yourself, Franny. Sure, I'd like to get back as soon as possible. This whole ordeal's pretty dangerous, after all. But it has been nice to get our feet a little more wet than usual, you know?"

Franklin smiled at the pensive boy and nodded. "Of course you're right, Joey. It's just that- waking up in a bed other than my own always makes me homesick. Doesn't matter if it's here in the post apocalyptic wasteland or at summer camp; I miss it just the same."

"I miss waking up to the smell of waffles on Saturdays," stated Joey with a lamenting little chuckle. "Come on, Franny, let's go have a look around; there's no use lying in bed all day."

The two boys rose and dressed, but they allowed themselves a leisurely pace; for the first time in days, there was no need to rush and they could at least pretend their typical lazy summertime routine still applied.

After munching on a few dry Burke Bars that they assumed Lazlo had left out for them, they left the apartment and began to wander the compound. All of the Lonie homes that had bustled with family life the night before were now vacant and quiet. The embers of the fire pits inside of them were cool and smoldered softly; Franklin resolved they had been extinguished hours before and that the Lonies must have been early risers indeed.

The elderly widows, on the other hand, were still in their apartments. Joey and Franklin, being quizzical and curious, popped their head into one of these chambers to see if they might say hello. But its senior inhabitant was not to be bothered. She was an elderly woman, wrinkled and liver spotted like an old sausage. She sat in the corner of her room on a small, wooden stool. On her face, strapped in front of her eyes, was a pair of goggles of the same sort they had seen in Lazlo's room, cord and all. She was quite motionless and it seemed as if she was hardly breathing. Smote with curiosity, the two boys continued to observe the strange sight.

"What do you think she's doing?" asked Joey.

"Beats me," replied Franklin. "But that thing on her head looks like those virtual reality goggles you're always seeing in movies and stuff. We'll have to ask Lazlo later on." Joey nodded in agreement and the two abandoned their peeping spot and plodded further down the hallway.

They found the large room with Jamjar's main gate in it abuzz with activity. Lonies bustled about, hauling crates and leading flocks of squealing children hither and thither. The children, who had not seen the strange visitors the night before, watched the two boys warily with wide eyes. Franklin, having a sort of fondness for youngsters, shot the tots a grin.

"White teeth! White teeth! Angel's got him some white teeth!" screeched a little Lonie girl in delight. She bore her teeth back at him, which were so far gone from yellow they were almost brown, but her caretaker quickly whisked her a way and gave Franklin an ugly look.

"I guess not all of them like angels," he whispered to Joey.

"I don't think I'd like us much either, to be honest! I imagine your skin must hurt their eyes, Franny," Joey pointed out. "Lucky for me, Korean skin isn't so nearly as hard on the eyes as the skin of you pale faces!" The boys laughed and carried on in their wanderings. Soon, Jamjar called out to them from where he stood on a parapet above the gate.

"Oh, hello-ee fellows!" he hollered. "I fancy-ee snoozered so hard-ee might never wake, but here-ees are and pleasant faced as anyone I've ever seen."

"Hello Jamjar," they called back and waved.

"I'm about to open up the gate for the afternoon, would-ee likers to come up and assist Ole' Jamjar here?"

Franklin and Joey looked at each other, shrugged, and began to ascend the ladder, which the bearded gatekeeper had eagerly indicated. "That a-boy. Foot over foot, just like that," he coached them as they climbed. "Can't be too careful, now. We wouldn't want a fall; I imagine angel bones can be quite fragile. Brittle and easily broken, aye?" Suddenly his face became frightened. "Beggin' er pardon, masters. What do I know? For all Jamjar knows, angels could have bones like steel! Strong as a robots, aye?"

Franklin and Joey reached the top of the ladder and scrambled onto the parapet where Jamjar waited. He grinned at them and gestured to a wheel and crank, both of which sat on top of the gate. "The Lonies still have some electric power left over from the Green Time, and we conserve it well; but we still relies on Ole' Jamjar here to crank open the main door! Takes a right spot of muscle, it does." He flexed a sun spotted bicep.

"Grip that handle here, Master Jensen, and-ee that one there, Master Freeman," he instructed the boys. "There's a good lad. Now, on my signal, give it a great tug and then a heave and our gate here should start to creak. Music to my ears is the sound of my gate; like a purdy lady singin' in the mornin'. Right then, ready? Pull!"

The two boys gave the lever a yank and nothing happened. Again, they tugged at it but it only gave way a little then snapped back to where it had originally stood.

Jamjar began to laugh. "Where is the strength of strange-ee angels now, my hearties? Har har har!" Jamjar doubled over as he watched the two boys repeat their futile attempts. Breathless, he lifted his eye patch and wiped a tear away from the fully functional eye beneath. Franklin and Joey, being very much embarrassed, glared at the laughing gatekeeper.

"Oh, now!" he chuckled. "Pay me no heed! No heed at tall! Jamjar is a badger-like old spud! Remember-ee lads, there be an art even to something so simple as opening up a rusty ole' gate."

With surprisingly careful attention to detail, Jamjar rapidly explained to the boys that the gate's opening was no matter of strength and that it was, in fact, "rather a tricky process," as he had put it several times. After several demonstrations and lectures on theory, a process which ate up nearly half an hour, Jamjar offered them up another try.

"Now remember, chums, a flick of the wrist and a flash of the smile is all it takes to best this trial!" he sang. Franklin and Joey, the senseless rhyme pounded into their heads after the lengthy lecture, nodded and placed their hands upon the lever. Doing as Jamjar had instructed them and following a rather complicated series of steps, they at last gave the lever a final pull, a much more delicate one this time, and the gate began to slowly creak open.

"There it is, lads!" Jamjar cried. "I told you she's finicky, and that's the truth! But like any fine Lonie lady I've ever know, ee-just haft know how ta' treat her right!" Franklin and Joey were unimpressed with their achievement, but Jamjar's enthusiasm seemed genuine so they smiled nonetheless.

"About time!" sniped a voice from down below. The gatekeeper and his newly appointed wards looked down and saw Stingwhit, Fluthers and Nimrod trudging towards the open gate.

"Thought you'd never get the damn thing open," grumbled Nimrod, eldest and most grizzled of the trio. The three warriors were bent over under heavy packs laden with all manner of weaponry: spears, crude swords, hammers, bows and arrows, even clubs fashioned out of old lead pipes.

"Hullo there, oh ee-hunters of New Hollow! Excuse the delay, I were just showing these strange-ees here some of the tricks of the trade. Where you off to this'n mornin'?" asked Jamjar. He seemed proud to have his new apprentices to show off.

"Where do we always go?" snapped Stingwhit. "You are truly a wily old creature if'n-ee can't remember! On patrol, of course! Patrol through what few neighborhoods are left, anyway. The Hollow Hunt, obviously. I remember the days when it took nigh twenty strong Lonies to properly patrol and oversee all that territory we called our own, but alas, look at us now! Three hopeless beggars, a bunch of ragamuffins, wanderin' the streets. Poor excuse for a standing army, if'n yer ask me."

"Watch it!" bellowed Nimrod, turning an angry glare on the younger Stingwhit. "Three may be a small number, but a happy one is it anyway, and lucky, too! Three fellows, three strong and hearty Lonies, is all it should take to stand against the wicked Mites. Long have I hunted them! They're not a cunning bunch, easily tricked and simply smote, they are. The only strength they have over us is in their numbers. And quantity is a poor quality, if'n-ee ask me."

"Talk is all good, Nimrod, talk is all good," replied Stingwhit coolly. But talk like that'll do-ee little good next time we're running for our lives with one of them Mite mobs hot on our heels."

"That last time was your own fault and-ee knows it!" Nimrod shot back.

"Twasn't!"

"Twas!"

"Twasn't"

"Twas!"

"Would'n-ee both stop all this bickering!" barked Fluthers suddenly and silenced his two companions. "We're already late and we've got work to do. Now, thank our gatekeeper's new helpers and be on your way." Fluthers bowed, joined begrudgingly by Stingwhit and Nimrod, and the three trudged out the gate and into New Hollow.

"Those three," chuckled Jamjar as he watched them go. "Nimrod's an old fellow, older than me even, but certainly nowhere near as ancient as Ole' Sacks be. But he's saddled with them two wily youngsters. Har har, a more incompatible bunch I've never seen. Nor have I heard so much bickering! But they're warriors true as truffles and can best most any man here. I used to be in that sort of rank myself, once upon a time, but my talents lie more with gate opening and the general overseeing thereof, I think."

Franklin and Joey bid Jamjar a polite goodbye and climbed

down the ladder back into the main hall of the sanctuary. They peeked out through the open gate and into the milky sunlight outside. It seemed to be quite a mild morning, but they had experienced no other sort of temperature in the wasteland so they were not surprised. That same smell they had detected the previous afternoon, one of decay and death, wafted through the portal and stung their noses.

"Where do you suppose Ellie is?" wondered Franklin.

"Probably still trying to find a shower or a bathtub or something," snickered Joey. "Heck, I bet she'd settle for a spray from a garden hose at this point, but I don't think she's going to get even that lucky."

Laughing, the two boys wandered off and left Jamjar to his work. Seeing no other familiar faces and at a complete loss as how to occupy their time, they resolved to explore the sanctuary; but, beyond the apartments, the main hall, the sacred garden, and the council chamber, there wasn't much they hadn't already seen. There was a room labeled 'armory' but its door was bolted tightly shut. Perhaps this room was from where the hunters had gathered all their rudimentary weapons, thought Franklin. Suddenly, a shrill voice rang out and drew the boys near.

"Surely you can spare a little," pleaded Ellie. She was standing in front of a large, complicated looking piece of machinery. Barring her passage were the twin Lonie girls, Mia and Zaki, to whom they had all been introduced the night before.

"Deepest and sincerest apologies, angel! Truly deep are they," exclaimed the twins, flustered. "But we can offer-ee none for such purpose! It is not the Lonie way."

"You can't be serious!" Ellie shook her fists in frustration. "I'm not usually even this concerned with bathing and all that, and I must be coming across as very vain, but I haven't showered in almost a week and I've been walking around in a desert! My hair's so caked with dirt it feels like straw!"

"And it looks like straw too!" exclaimed Mia, beaming. "Golden straw like we have seen in the projections of the past.

299

Oh, how envious are we two homely lasses! Would that we had hair like your'n."

"Aye! Aye!" agreed Zaki and reached out to touch Ellie's locks.

"Please!" demanded the exasperated girl, pulling away. "Please don't touch it! Not like this. It's usually soft; I wouldn't want anybody to feel it when it's all hard and crusty like it is now. Are you sure I can't just take a bath or something?"

"A bath?" echoed the twins. "Yes, we have heard of such a thing in the projections! Oh, how lovely it must have been to soak in water pure and drain away all-er dirt and grime! How lovely to make-er hair smooth like silk, instead of coarse like sand. How lovely! If only, if only." The twins shook their heads. "But it is not to be," the chanted. "Old Sacks has limited each Lonie to but a few meager cups a day! This ole' machine here has enough trouble synthesizing our groggy drink as is without further draining it for 'baths' and such!"

Ellie hung her head. "I understand," she mumbled. "I feel selfish for even asking, but it was worth a try. Thanks anyway, girls." Disappointedly, she began to walk away, but the twins suddenly cried out to her.

"Please, miss Strange-ee!" called Mia, and Ellie turned to face them. "Please! Though to thee your hair might seem dirty and unkempt, to us it is beauty like no other. Please, allow us to touch it once and to dream on it when you are gone."

Ellie blushed and shrugged, embarrassed to have her messy hair played with, but flattered all the same. The twins came forward and gingerly took a strand each, caressing the locks between their fingers and rubbing them softly upon their cheeks. "How smooth! Like the silk so often spoke of in the projections! How delightful and soft. If only we could make ours like your'n. If only, if only. But it is not to be." With this, the twins let Ellie's hair fall and returned to their post.

Ellie, having noticed the two boys who were watching and smirking, came to them with her face shining bright red. As she approached, Franklin could not help but notice her beautiful hair that the twins had so coveted; it fell about her face in long, bright strands and tickled the base of her neck. Even when it was dusty and set against her crimson, blushing face, he still longed to hold it like the twins had done.

"You guys finally woke up, huh?" she asked, waving away Joey's snickers like gnats.

"Yes, and we've been wandering around all morning," replied Franklin. "No idea what to do. I see you haven't had much luck on the bathing front." This remark caused Ellie's already-red face to become redder.

"No. None whatsoever," she admitted. "And I feel completely idiotic for even asking them! A total girlie thing to do, and you both know I'm not like that." She certainly wasn't. "Whatever these projections are, the Lonies sure are enamored with them! But they never do anything about it! They just shake their heads and say 'it's not to be.' Oh well." she shrugged. "Might as well find something else to do, right?"

Suddenly, she sniffed the air and pinched her nose, glaring at the two boys. "I know they haven't got any baths or showers around here, but do you think they at least have deodorant? You both stink!"

Now it was their turn to be red in the face. "You don't smell so hot yourself, Mars," retorted Joey playfully.

Franklin thought she smelled like a bed of flowers, but he wasn't about to say that.

Still bored and with nothing to do, the three began to wander up a series of creaky metal ramparts that wound their way about the lofty spaces of the sanctuary, forming a series of beams that crisscrossed the ceiling.

"There you two are," called another familiar voice. The children whirled about to see who the greeting belonged to; they had not expected to find anyone loitering about up so high. Hess was kneeling at the tallest point in the sanctuary, a spot where all the ramparts converged into a vertex upon which a platform had been erected.

"What are you doing up here?" Franklin asked as they approached their armored companion.

"Still trying to get in touch with Mozi, unfortunately," Hess answered. "I figured if I got higher up maybe the signal strength would boost a bit, but no luck so far. This detour expedition was only supposed to last two or three days; at this rate, it looks like we'll be out here for nearly a week! And that's not taking into the consideration the time I'll be spending in the Well. Who knows how long I'll be down there looking for the thing. And whose to say it's still intact and hasn't been gobbled up by those monsters." Franklin shivered at mention of the black pit.

"Have you heard anything about the council's decision yet, Hess?" Joey was curious to see the inside of the Well.

"Not yet," replied Hess. "I ran into Old Sacks earlier, but he just sort of grunted at me. I don't think he cares for me very much. Chunk mentioned they'd be discussing the motion tonight, though. It might be a bumpy process; most of the Lonies really don't want to open that place up."

"And for good reason," Franklin muttered to himself. "If you open up a jar of bees, you're likely to be stung."

"Don't be so sure, Franny!" said Joey. "Remember what those hunters said? The Mites down there are dimwits. Even if they get the better of us with their numbers, we can still outsmart them. Like that time we outsmarted everyone in capture the flag last summer." He turned to Hess and Ellie and stated proudly, "We buried the flag. They never thought to look for it underground. We were CTF champions."

"That was against the rules and got us disqualified, Joseph," said Franklin ruefully. "Everyone hated us after that."

"Doesn't matter, they only disqualified us after we won. After that -who cares?" Joey beamed.

"Still," continued Franklin, "I think we may be underestimating whatever's down there. As I understand it, there're things worse than just Mites down below."

His friends gave him a quizzical look and he quickly recounted to them the story of his chance meeting with Old Sacks the night before, making sure to share with them the tale of Cherophobe and the hordes of Mites who lived below. The part about their song and how it drew people to it, however, he left out; even speaking about such an idea made him uncomfortable.

"Cherophobe, huh?" Ellie whistled, impressed. "That's a mouthful. And he's really that big?"

"According to Old Sacks he is."

"It's not unheard of," remarked Joey. "There are some rare Eurasian boars who grow to almost ten times the normal size of their species. I suspect they'd be the leader of their pig packs, too. I certainly would follow the one with the biggest tusks if I were a Eurasian boar."

Ellie took note of the boy's dreamy look. "You wish you were a Eurasian boar, don't you Joey?"

"I could certainly think of worse things to be," he admitted. "A gargantuan, mutated human-demon-thing born out of an apocalypse cloud, for example."

"That's all besides the point," said Hess, dismissing Joey's nonsense. "You're sure, Franklin? You're sure Old Sacks wasn't just making up legends to scare you or something like that?"

"He seemed awfully serious, and I don't think he'd do something like that." Franklin shivered, remembering how grave the old man's face had looked. "He even said he'd fought against Cherophobe once and it nearly killed him. He mentioned that Old Bess was the last person to go down into the Well after she closed off the garden dome, although she never came back out. I'm positive there are Bhasmites down there, I could hear thousands of them. But there are other things that have grown so deep down since then. Terrible things I don't even want to think about; even Old Sacks looked troubled when he mentioned Cherophobe."

"Well, it's pointless to worry our heads about any of it now," said Ellie. "We don't even know if they're going to open the gate for us yet; we might as well enjoy the time we have till they decide. How about we get some lunch? If I can't even enjoy a shower a day, I'd at least like to get three square meals in, even if they're those mealy old bars."

The companions all nodded and made their way off the ramparts where their small meeting had been held. As they strode back to Lazlo's apartment to take their midday meal, Joey interrogated Franklin further about his encounter with Old Sacks.

"What other kind of things live down there?"

"He didn't really say, besides Cherophobe anyway, but it seemed to frighten him."

"Maybe there's still hope for the mutant crustacean idea yet!" exclaimed Joey. "They could be down there! Crabs like dark, wet places."

"Would you stop it with the overgrown crabs, Joey?" shot Ellie over her shoulder. "It's not going to happen."

"You never know," mumbled the boy wistfully. "But I expect Old Sacks is right. With all that leftover waste and water in those sewers, it'd be an absolute breeding ground for all sorts of weird, creepy life. Right up my alley."

"I think this stuff is too awful even for your alley, Joseph," said Franklin. "Let's stop talking about it. Old Sacks has already given me enough heebie-jeebies as it is!"

Soon, they were ducking into Lazlo's empty apartment and sitting themselves down around the table, the children in their little chairs and the armored boy in his hefty sized one.

Lazlo still hadn't come home. "I'll bet he's got a lot of catching up to do after five years," said Hess. Hess reckoned that if he ever regained his lost memories and made it to wherever or whenever his home was, he'd have to do a lot of catching up himself. Should I be so lucky, he thought dryly. The notion sobered him and throughout most of the measly lunch he was quiet.

The children were coming into better spirits now that they had settled into an atmosphere at least a little similar to the one they had known in Connecticut. No matter how many oddities and quirks it had, the Lonie sanctuary wasn't all that different from Pendel Circle and the little seaside community of Stony

Creek; people went about their daily chores, took care of their children, lived in neat and tidy rows, and every evening they sat together and took supper. But something was off, and it disturbed the children greatly. At first, none of them had quite been able to place their fingers on it; perhaps it was the strange dress of the Lonies or their dusty faces or their queer manner of speech. But they quickly realized it wasn't the appearance or language of the people that disturbed them. No, they all knew what it was and eyed it suspiciously in the corner: the goggles through which the Lonies experienced these 'projections' they mentioned so often.

"Franny and I saw an old lady wearing them today," said Joey. "She wasn't moving an inch, just sitting and sighing."

"I saw something similar when I got up," added Ellie.

"So did I," said Hess.

"What do you think they're supposed to do?" asked Joey.

"They way they talk about them, it sounds almost like TV," managed Franklin through a mouthful of Burke Bar. "But a different kind of TV, like everybody watches the same channel. Projections of the past, they call them." Suddenly, a mischievous light came into his eyes. "You don't think we ought to..."

"No, Franklin!" Ellie's voice was sharp. "Those are Lazlo's goggles! We're his guests! Would you want someone coming into your room and touching all your things?"

"Joey does it almost every day and I get over it." Franklin shrugged.

"I agree with Ellie," said Hess. "It's not a good idea! What if they beam something odd into your head and you can't get rid of it. What if those projection goggles make you talk like a Lonie for the rest of your life with a bunch of ee's and er's. You wouldn't want that."

"I think it's kind of charming, in a weird sort of way," mumbled Franklin. "I don't think Lazlo would mind; and how dangerous could it really be? The Lonies all seem sane enough." His curiosity had gotten the better of him and, despite his friends' continued protests, he rose and crossed the room. The goggles were only the size of ski goggles and, upon inspection, there didn't seem to be any needles attached to them (or other kinds of objects which might pump some unwanted substance into his brain). "They look fine, just like the ones at the arcade," he observed.

"Don't!" commanded Hess sternly.

"Just a peek." With this, Franklin brought the goggles up to his eyes and pulled the strap around the back of his head. At first, all was dark and he couldn't see much of anything; but, after a few moments, a voice began to speak to him. The voice didn't seem to be coming through his ears, as there weren't any sort of headphones on the goggles; instead, it seemed to be coming from directly inside his head, just above his brow. But the voice wasn't his own.

"Hello. Welcome to the Spero Inc. Historical Education Projection series." The voice was soothing, that of middle aged woman who spoke clearly with a Mid-Atlantic accent.

"Are you guys hearing this?" asked Franklin.

"Hearing what?" asked Joey, befuddled.

"Good day," continued the voice. "I hope you'll enjoy the projection I've prepared for you this afternoon. Today's lesson is a special one! We'll be taking a trip into the ancient past, travelling nearly a millennium back in time to see how our ancient ancestors lived."

"What's it saying, Franklin? Can you see anything?" entreated Ellie. Her curiosity had been roused and she came and stood close to the goggled boy.

"Can't see anything yet-" Franklin paused, "-wait a moment. Here comes something now." A picture surged up into Franklin's line of sight as if it had been shot from very far away. The picture came closer and closer; it shimmered and trembled the nearer it drew. Now it completely obscured his field of view and even seemed to extend beyond the borders of his vision, as if the image had wrapped around the boy's head like a spider.

"I see," he muttered, and then shook his head. "No, I shouldn't say 'I see', that wouldn't do this justice; it's more like

I'm floating in a picture, floating through a movie, almost. It's like nothing I've ever done before. Completely surreal."

"Here we can see the city in which you currently reside: sleepy, peaceful New Hollow," narrated the voice. "But this New Hollow isn't so new!" The voice gave a stilted, little chuckle. "No, this isn't the New Hollow of the year 3,000. This New Hollow exists in a much more primitive age, one thousand years ago: 2,000 AD."

"Oh God," said Franklin. "Ellie! Joseph! It's showing the city as it was in our time. It's showing old New Hollow." The two clambered around Franklin and they began to trade the goggles on and off, relishing the familiar sights as the voice narrated on.

"The people of this year drove about in strange little metal boxes known as automobiles. These locomotive devices used fossil fuels to propel them forward on an axil attached to metal loops. These loops were known as tires. Look how speedily the little things zoom about!"

The image, which all three children did their best to view at once given that they only had one pair of goggles between them, swooped low into the city like a diving bird and soared slowly above a busy street as trucks, vans, SUV's, and taxis sped about below them. "People often walked to get around in those days, as well. See here: foot travellers called pedestrians use designated paths known as sidewalks to make their way through the city. How happily they bustle about! Before the advent of intravenous dietary fluids and meal freeze dried meal supplements, people relied on walking and other forms of physical exercise to keep their bodies lean and functioning; this practice was known as recreation."

"This is too weird," breathed Ellie. "I feel like we're a diorama on display in a museum."

"Much like today," the voice went on, "water and food was readily accessible to civilians, but in vastly different ways. The New Hollow we know today draws its water from the Mega Complex beneath the city using synthesizing machines to give us nearly an infinite supply. The New Hollow of yesteryear, on the other hand, relied on nearby lakes known as reservoirs to keep water pumping through their homes. This water ran through long, metal tubes known as pipes and was disposed of using sewers, much like today."

"The mega complex," whispered Joey as if he were at a theater and unwilling to disturb the performance. "She must mean the Well."

"This water was clean, and naturally so. Unlike now, when we must scrub and clean all our synthesized water meticulously to ensure it is palatable, the water of 2,000 AD was quite spotless and tasty, too. Let's look now at the entertainment of this ancient time-"

"Greetings," called out a voice suddenly from behind them. The children hid the goggles behind their backs at once. Lazlo had appeared at the apartment door. The emerald-eyed robot stooped and entered his little home, glancing at the children. "I see you've discovered my projection goggles. It's quite all right; you needn't hide them or be ashamed. Every Lonie family has at least one pair of them and they make it a habit each night to use them. I'm sure we've learned all the lessons at least a few hundred times by now, but still the Lonies use them whenever they have the free time to do so. It is a precious tradition and one of the only ones we have, I'm afraid."

Franklin, relieved Lazlo wasn't mad, placed the goggles back where he had found them and began to question the robot. "What are they for, exactly?"

"A number of things, I suppose," replied Lazlo. "Education and entertainment, primarily. Madame Bess left them to us before she disappeared into the Well. I remember that day very clearly. The Lonies were puzzled, unsure of what to do with them. All the images you see therein are routed from that projection database I pointed out before, you understand. But soon the Lonies recognized Bess's voice in the goggles and came to treasure them, visiting the past each and every day no matter how unattainable it is."

"I think I like that idea," remarked Hess. It was an attractive notion, at least to him; he'd have very much liked to have a pair of goggles with which he could peer into his own foggy history and learn of his origins.

"It's not so bad," said Ellie. "But it's a waste of time, if you ask me."

"Not for the Lonies," replied Lazlo. "We spend so much of our day at work, toiling in the sanctuary or out and about in the city, that whatever leisure time we can claim is precious and often spent with the projections, here."

"That's what I don't like about them," interrupted Franklin, agreeing with Ellie. "I figured they were some sort of historical education device, and I'm all for that. I think history is one of the only useful classes we take at school; it's definitely one of the only ones I can stay awake through. But this doesn't seem to be a history textbook. It's sort of haunting, sort of disturbing."

"What do you mean?" asked Hess, confused; he quite liked the goggles.

"They work just fine and showcase the past and all, but..." Franklin paused and scratched his chin thoughtfully. "I don't really know. The way the Lonies always talk about the projections; it's almost like they're lamenting them. 'If only, if only. But it is not to be.' That's what Mia and Zaki were saying before, remember?"

"So you have heard the Lonie lament," exclaimed Lazlo. "Yes, it is a phrase oft repeated with a heavy sigh. 'If only, if only. But it is not to be.'"

"Yes, exactly," cried Franklin. "It seems to me, because the Lonies haven't really got a history of their own, they spend all their free time envying someone else's. It doesn't seem healthy. Don't you think that time would be better spent thinking about their own future?"

"The Lonies haven't much of a future to think of, save the one which their descendants might enjoy when the sacred garden opens up," said Lazlo. "No. They are a people without a past, without a future, caught up entirely in a hopeless present. I'm afraid you're right, Mr. Freeman. The projections do little for the Lonies save a distracting them from the pain of now. But this distraction is not such a beneficial one. The dead hand of the past reaches out with cold fingers and inhabits the present entirely."

"Now," Lazlo suddenly sounded cheerier, "what have you four been up to all morning? I trust you have explored the compound some and that the Lonies have been hospitable to you?"

"Franny and I lent Jamjar a hand earlier with the gate," answered Joey. "We also met up with those two warriors - Stingwhit and Fluthers, were they? And their older counterpart, Nimrod, was there too."

"A merry bunch, though they are known to bicker," remarked Lazlo. "When I left, Stingwhit and Fluthers were merely rookies in the Lonie army, and Nimrod only a low ranking sergeant. But look at them now: the entire standing army and patrolmen to boot, wrapped up in one tiny package. How low have we sunken thanks to those Mites?" He shook his head. "And you, Miss Mars?"

Ellie began to blush again. "Nothing much, really. I, er, I tried to get some water earlier."

"My dear Miss Mars!" exclaimed the robot. "Are you thirsty? Have you not been rationed enough drinking water? Oh my! Oh my!" At once, Lazlo began to fawn over his self appointed charge.

"She wasn't looking for drinking water," snickered Joey. Ellie glared at him but he continued anyway. "She was looking for a bath!"

"A bath?" The robot thought for a moment. "I did not think humans took baths anymore. I could offer you an oil bath, Miss Mars! Robots need them at least once a month to keep our joints in working order. But I must warn you, they are quite hot and you might become uncomfortable."

"Thanks, Lazlo," sighed the girl, embarrassed and ashamed to have made a fuss. "But I think I'll pass. I'm not sure an oil bath would be very good for me anyway."

"Lazlo," interrupted Hess. "Have you heard anything about the council yet? Have they approved our request to enter the

Well?"

"Patience, Mr. Hess," cooed the robot. "All in good time. Because each Lonie works during the day- even Old Sacks himself fixes machines in daylight hours- they have woefully little time for politics, and the council process can sometimes be drawn out- painfully so."

"When will they decide, then?"

"When they can, Mr. Hess," sighed Lazlo. "We can ask no more of them then we already have. I will beg that they expedite the process, but when things need doing, the Lonies are the only ones on the planet who can do them! You must understand."

Somberly, Hess nodded and crossed his arms. "I do. Forgive me for being impatient."

"My dear fellow, think nothing of it," scoffed the robot cheerily. "I too became quite impatient as I baked and rusted for five years in the sun, but thanks to you all I'm on my feet again and moving about. I will not forget the debt I owe to you lot, especially to Miss Mars. Each and every day I will campaign your case before the council till they see fit to allow you access to the Well. Fear not, friends."

"You're a saint, Lazlo," exclaimed Ellie. "A real robot saint."

"Every saint serves an angel." Lazlo beamed at her. "Now, you all seem like you might be in need of something to do. I'd prescribe the projections to occupy your time, but something tells me wherever it is you all come from, you know more about the past than the projections do." The children could not help but smile wryly. "Perhaps you would not mind joining me on my rounds this afternoon?"

"Your rounds?" asked Ellie.

"Yes. There are several families and old friends whom I still must visit. My heart has been sick for them while I have been away and I'm sure they have missed me in my absence, too. I would be so very excited to take you all around to them; you have become quite the hot topic in these parts and I'd be proud to introduce you as both my saviors and my guests!"

The children, who became rapidly bored, nodded eagerly and agreed to join Lazlo in his visitations, thrilled to have something to do for the rest of the day. Hess was not so willing, however, and resolved to remain in the apartment for the remainder of the afternoon. He would brood there for hours, trying in vain to establish contact with the Noah, again and again mulling over in his mind what kind of precautions his daring descent into the Well would entail.

Hess knew better than the children; he knew that soon they would be leaving this place to never again return. Surely, the children would become attached to the quirky Lonies and find themselves sorely wounded upon the realization that they would never see any of them again. Hess, his demeanor hardened from his departure from Dr. Burke, decided he would simply save himself the grief. The Lonies would have to see him as aloof and distant, no matter how fond he grew of them. Such is the curse of a time traveller who hasn't the time to tarry. Such was the curse of Hess, who wouldn't allow himself even a smile while the threat of apocalypse loomed menacingly in the back of his head.

The depressing thought nagged at Franklin's mind too; all these Lonies, all these people, would soon only become a distant, unattainable memory to him, just like one of the projections. But his life had been a happy one, unlike the small fraction of a life Hess could remember living, and he disregarded the somber notions and allowed himself to enjoy the remainder of the day in the company of his friends despite the dismal thoughts.

Lazlo buzzed about with the children in tow, visiting nearly every apartment in the sanctuary at least once. Even the very eldest of Lonies, ancient creatures by even Old Sacks' standards, wept when Lazlo appeared. They told the robot how they had missed him and how kind he had been to them when they were only children. At first the children were taken aback by such a prospect; they had all but forgotten Lazlo's true age: he was nearly two hundred years old!

It appears, thought Franklin, robots do not age in the same

way humans do; they accumulate all the wisdom and experience, but (with proper maintenance) they do not decay or falter with time.

Lazlo, too, was elated to see all his old friends and compatriots; but even more elated was he to introduce the children to each and every family they visited. Some Lonies shrank back, afraid and wary of the 'strange-ees', hesitant even to allow them into their homes (although they did so for Lazlo's sake). Others were more like Jamjar, however, and revered the pale-faced youths, greeting them warmly and offering them their most comfortable chairs and even any extra gruel from the night before. The children politely declined these gifts.

Time and time again, Lazlo recounted the tale of his power loss, and then of his salvation, each version of the story with more exaggeration and flourish than the last. By the end of the afternoon, the children felt like national heroes returning from a far off mission, revered by the Lonies and feared by them too, all at once.

The Lonie children were the most polarized in their reception of the strange-ees. Some cackled with glee and demanded piggyback rides from the boys and a chance to fondle Ellie's hair between their fingers. Others shrank back into the corners of their home and watched them warily, afraid they might make something unnatural happen, or that they might be 'nasty Mites in disguise' as one audacious urchin had so boldly put it.

Franklin was quick to notice something was off with the children. Not in their behavior, though; something else. Then it came to him: they were all infants or toddlers, for the most part. Even the eldest among them were barely old enough for the fourth grade. There were no children, that is to say young teenagers, of the same age as Joey, Ellie, and he. When asked about this, Lazlo simply shook his head sadly and said, "Woe to them that art lost. The Lonies come to fighting age while they are still very young, and I am sorry to say many of them have been taken or defeated by the Mites. But their memories remain, that is to be sure. I remember those youths, tramping about the sanctuary halls with such arrogance and vigor, ready to conquer the entire wasteland. How marvelous they were to watch. But they are dead and gone, now. The casualties of a war fought by the young and lamented by the old. I will say no more of this, it grieves my circuits too sorely."

Soon, Lazlo finished his rounds and the children could hear the creak of Jamjar's gate far off in the distance. The end of the day had come and a calm swept over the complex like a sudden wave.

Exhausted from meeting all the faces, both new and old, the four companions tramped off to dinner where Chunk had prepared yet another odorous concoction for them: Mite Casserole with a side of salted Mite shank.

All the Lonies sat at a long table, which had been dragged out into the main hall for that very purpose. As the children ate quietly (forcing each bite down) and listened to Chunk's monologues about each dish, Stingwhit and Fluthers, both sweaty and bloodied from a long day's patrol, strode into the room, took their seats, and began tucking into their meals voraciously.

"How-ee like that Mite meat, strang-ee?" shot Fluthers across the table to Joey. The boy, table manners not being his strong suit, smiled through a mouth of food and gave the hunter thumbs up. Fluthers frowned, unfamiliar with the gesture. "Id very tathtey," reassured Joey through a mouthful of casserole.

"Tasty! Hear that, Stingwhit? Strang-ee says it's 'tasty!'" The two men began to laugh, spitting slop everywhere and banging their fists heartily into the table.

"Tasty indeed, says he!" Stingwhit gasped between guffaws. "Do-ees both agree?" He pointed a greasy fork at Franklin and Ellie. Both unsure of how to respond, they glanced at one another, and then back at Stingwhit who raised his eyebrows expectantly. Meekly, they nodded.

"They like the Mite meat!" trumpeted Fluthers and began snorting again. "Why I never! Come now-ee Strangees, abandon-er polite lies. What really think-ee?"

Reluctantly, the children shrugged their shoulders and rolled their eyes, indicating they were perhaps not so fond of the gruel as they had previously let on.

"There we are," said Stingwhit, wiping a tear from his amused eyes. "A polite bunch, and an honest bunch in the end. That's all that really matters, isn't it? Now," he stood and addressed the three of them all at once, shaking his fist like an enthralled politician, "as much as I'd like to say this meat is the finest tasting stuff around, given that Fluthers and I here have spent all the day laying down our lives to hunt it, alas- I cannot. It's true, my hearties, the stuff is tasteless on a good day and rancid on a mediocre one. Eee don't want to be around when all we has to eat is spoilt Mite porridge- it's truly a grizzly site and offends the nose like no other scent."

"But," declared Fluthers, rising as well, "tis all we can eat save those damned booger bars, and even the Mite meat has got more flavor than them. I'm sure, coming from whatever paradise kingdom-ee do, ee've sampled all manner of fine delicacies and lived in a constant lap of culinary luxury. But we Lonies have not known anything else all our lives, and grown right used to this putrid stuff! Ee will not offend us to stick out-er tongues in disgust, nor will-ee offend our efforts in acquiring the food. In fact, ee-might just humor us with a tale or two of-er kingdom's food so that we might at least dream upon a happier sort of meal."

Ellie, who was glad to have an excuse to push her bowl tactfully away for a while, chewed for a moment then spoke, "Well, I suppose there are far too many types of food back home to tell you about all of them, but I'll do my best," she explained. "You see, just like you we have lots of recipes: porridges, casseroles, stews, and all kinds of things. But unlike you, we have more than one ingredient with which we make them.

The crowd gasped and drew closer about the girl, shocked and intrigued. "How... how many ingredients?" asked Stingwhit, his mouth beginning to water already.

"Thousands!" exclaimed Ellie, a smile flashing across her face. In disbelief, some of the Lonies began to try and count that high on their fingers but quickly gave up. "Thousands and thousands," she continued. "In fact, you've probably heard about them in the projections." At this, the Lonies eyes became wide and the closed in even more.

"Have... have-ee got the **cheese**, then?" stammered Chunk.

"And the bread? What about the bread? Do-ee eat the bread where-ee come from?" Suds begged, his eyes lusty and full.

"Yes," answered Franklin. "Bread and cheese both. They're some of the oldest foods of our people." The sound of Lonies' lips beginning to smack became audible in the air.

"Do tell us. Do. Is the cheese as yellow and soft as it appears in the projections?" Chunk was drooling onto his aprons.

"And is the bread really fluffy like a cloud?" Suds licked his lips.

"Yes," said Joey like a preacher. He was amused by all of this fuss over mundane snacks. "Everything you've heard is true." The Lonies near groaned with desire and began to wriggle in their seats.

Ellie grinned. "There is even a very famous combination of these foods. It is very popular among angels our age. First, a sumptuous red sauce that tastes like summer is spread out on the bread, or crust, and on top of that is sprinkled the cheese. This concoction is all baked altogether in a fiery oven. When the meal comes out, the cheese has melted and glistens with moisture, bubbling hot, while the bread has risen and fused with the red sauce. This combination of flavors is then cut into triangles and served many times over. Sometimes we even add vegetables or meats on top, just to further improve the flavor. We call it pizza."

The image of glistening, bubbling white cheese in their heads, the Lonies nearly collapsed.

Chunk began to cry. "No more," he begged. "No more, please, I implore-ee. Poor old Chunk cannot bear it. The taste stings me tongue with a dull ache, but no matter how hard I lick, I cannot detect it in full."

"Don't bother with that old fool," whispered Fluthers, leaning forward in his seat. "Tell us more."

And so the children did, regaling the Lonies with as much information concerning the various cuisines of New England as they possibly could. From pies, fried calamari, hotdogs, hamburgers, pasta of all sorts, Chinese food, fried chicken, cakes, chips and salsa, tater-tots, mashed potatoes, turkey, gravy, cranberry sauce, stuffed breads, sausages, eggs, bacon, cereals, oatmeal, pancakes, club sandwiches, BLT's, salmon, tuna fish, potato salad, lobster, lobster rolls, clam chowder, corn chowder, beef stew, steak, tacos, burritos, empanadas, guacamole, grilled cheese sandwiches, pot roasts, prime ribs, pork chops, pickles, salads, to grilled asparagus, they rambled down the list.

When the children had finished, the Lonies' mouths hung agape, saliva dribbling down onto their chins. Breaking out of the trance, they sighed and wiped away the drool, shaking their heads and saying sadly in unison, "If only, if only. But it is not to be." With this, they collected their plates and retired for the evening. The children were left, drooling a bit themselves, to finish off their meager meals in silence.

On the way back to the apartment, Franklin tapped Lazlo on the back of the shoulder. "Lazlo," he whispered softly. "I can't help but feel we've done a bad thing telling them about all those foods that they can never have."

The robot turned and his green eyes flickered with happiness. "Nonsense, my dear child. If anything, you have given them something to talk about for the next five years. Entertainment comes to these people not often enough, and even the weakest of stories are told and retold to the point of exhaustion. But I'm sure the Lonies will look back on this night and remember a feast of splendor, instead of the gruel they are used to. You have given them a great gift, indeed: the gift of a fine story."

Franklin's guilt was soon further assuaged when Stingwhit and Fluthers appeared at Lazlo's door as the children sat with Hess, picking their teeth and digesting. Without much ceremony, they let themselves in, strode across the tiny apartment, and bowed low to the companions.

"Our mouths won't stop their watering. Look-ee here!" cried Stingwhit, sticking out a glistening tongue. "I should be very pleased to eat Mite gruel for the rest of my day so long as my memory doesn't fail me and I can continue imagining these illustrious feasts of-ers."

Fluthers nodded and stuck his tongue out too. "Quite! Quite! How ever can we repay-ee strange-ees for giving us something new to think about when the day draws long and our weary minds wander?"

"Not at all! Not at all!" laughed Ellie, waving her hands about, overwhelmed with compliments. Hess nudged Franklin discreetly in the ribs. The boy took his meaning at once.

"Actually," said Franklin, "you could vote in our favor before the council. Help us get down into that Well."

"Consider it done, young masters," they exclaimed in unison and bowed again. "But we were already planning on doing that anyway. Isn't there something else the captains of the guard can offer you?"

Hess shrugged. "Nothing comes to mind."

Fluthers began to scratch at his stubble and Stingwhit sat on his haunches by the fire. There they stayed, thinking silently for a few minutes, till at last Stingwhit started and sprang up like a firework. "I've got it I have! Hear-ee now, for Stingwhit has the idea of the century, nay... of two centuries! And that is a very long time for the Lonies, rest assured."

"Go on!" pushed Fluthers, intrigued.

Stingwhit turned to the children. "Despite how some Lonies may cower before-ee strange-ees, we both are bold and unafraid. In fact, after this excellent story of-ers at dinner, we've grown very fond of-ee. Do-ees really intend to venture down into that dank Well? Tell me true."

"We do," replied Hess bluntly.

"A dangerous quest indeed, if-ee truly intend to follow it." Stingwhit's eyes narrowed and his voice became hushed and low. "The Well and caverns below are rank with all manner of evil, some even ole' Nimrod has never encountered before. And I'm sure-eeve heard of Cherophobe already, though I'm certain he's dead and gone by now, only a myth, really. But still, Mite fighting is our expertise and we would be poor guardsmen indeed to allow our beloved strange-ees to enter the Well unprepared and ill advised against the wiles of the enemy."

"I believe I do see what-er getting at!" cried Fluthers and clapped Stingwhit on the back.

"Aye!" Stingwhit looked proud. "Since entering the well is forbidden for any Lonie by Old Sacks himself, we cannot come with-ee and protect-ee with our own hands, which we'd do at once if we could. But we can offer the next best thing: I officially propose that, till the council makes their decision, you lot come and learn from us. We'll teach-ee how the Mites operate, and teach-ee how to out-think the cunning little demons. Teach-ee how to use a weapon proper-like, in true Lonie fashion. Teach-ee how to navigate the tunnels and step softly upon-er feet so as to not alert the enemy."

Hess leaned forward, at last excited by the prospect bettering his tactics against the Mites. "That sounds excellent. Better than excellent! Absolutely perfect."

"What say-ee, angel lads and lassies?" asked Fluthers, his eyes agleam with the vision of thrilling days ahead. Ellie was first to nod and vigorously so (she had always wanted to learn how to properly fight), then Franklin (who fancied it might be a useful skill to have someday, maybe something to put on college applications), and last Joey (who was something of a pacifist but enjoyed a good rumpus as much as the next boy).

"Splendid!" Stingwhit applauded his proposal and danced a little jig. "Splendid indeed! How excellent! A chance not only to help our strange-ees but to pass our knowledge on, too! I have oft worried I'd never have a son mine own with whom to share my secrets, but now I might as well have three!" He cleared his throat. "Beggin' your pardon, miss. Two sons and one exquisitely purdy daughter." Ellie blushed and dismissed the mistake.

"It's decided then!" Fluthers gathered up his cloak about him and bowed again. "After our rounds tomorrow, come and meet us 'neath Jamjar's gate when the sun climbs highest in the sky! We will take-ee out and snag some of those sniveling ne'er-do-wells." With that, the two warriors marched triumphantly out of the apartment and left the companions to mull their situation over.

"They're an energetic pair," said Hess. "But I like them. They've just done more to help us than almost anyone in this whole sanctuary, besides Lazlo anyway. Finally a chance to do something useful around here."

Franklin's face suddenly took on a worried air. "You don't think they're going to make us kill anything, do you? I'd really rather not, if it's all the same."

"They're not going to make you do anything," reassured Hess. "They just want to show us what to do if we get ourselves into a pickle down there, which could very well happen if we're not careful."

"Who said anything about 'we'?" shot Ellie indignantly.

"My mistake. If 'I' get myself into a pickle down there, is what I meant to say," Hess corrected himself.

"Just think about it like taekwondo class, Franny," said Joey, aiming a playful kick at his friend's leg.

Franklin groaned. "We only lasted two weeks in that class, Joseph, and you're Korean!" The two laughed as they remembered yet another one of their many failures in the world of sports.

"How pleased I am to see you all getting along so well with the Lonies," exclaimed Lazlo, who had been quietly eavesdropping on the exchange. "I never expected you would charm them so fast, but behold! You have and their hearts belong to you now. Handle them gently, I implore you, for the Lonie life is not an easy one and even the most miniscule smidgeon of happiness is precious indeed."

"Will you be joining us in the training, Sir Lazlo?" asked Ellie, smiling at the robot.

"I am quite proficient already in the art of walloping Mites; I have seen my fair share of battles over my many years, and there is no greater teacher then experience. But I will watch with glee as our two guardsmen teach you fine folk how it is the Lonies stand up for themselves." Franklin couldn't really picture the agreeable robot locked in a fierce battle, but Lazlo's formidable size and long, bulky metal arms spoke for themselves.

CHAPTER FIFTEEN

THE HOLLOW HUNT

That night, the chanting of the Mites bothered Franklin no more and he slept soundly. It was not Joey who shook him awake the next morning, though. Joey's bedroll was empty; apparently the boy had risen early for once and sallied off to make himself busy somewhere in the compound.

No, it was a particularly long and elegant looking hand lying gently across his chest that had roused him suddenly from a placid dream. It appeared that Ellie, who was still snoozing quietly, had huddled close to him in her sleep after the fire had died away, her unconscious arms seeking to share in his warmth. Now she had drawn him close, like a teddy bear or pillow, and nestled her head deep into the crook of his arm.

Franklin wasn't quite sure how to react; he'd have preferred not doing anything and instead bask in the girl's touch and scent, her hair tickling his chin. But what if she awoke and, in alarm, falsely believed that he had been the one to snuggle up against her? Would she be angry? Would she push him away and yelp in disgust? Perhaps he could simply pretend he was asleep; surely she could find no more fault in his subconscious actions than he had found in hers. And where was Joey? Bother, thought Franklin, why did Joey always have to disappear when he needed him most?

Ellie stirred now, and nuzzled closer to the boy who was growing more and more frantic with each passing minute. Franklin was certain, no, positive that his pounding heart would surely wake the girl any moment; he could almost hear it beating out his chest like a tribal drum. But Ellie was quite still, a silent smile drawn calmly over her pink lips. What to do? What to do? Why couldn't he simply enjoy the moment? And what were these tremendous feelings of chaos and nervousness that seemed to overtake him whenever the girl was near? Rats. Rats. Rats. Rats!

Suddenly, as if she had heard his bickering thoughts echoing out of his skull, she opened her eyes and smiled at him. "Sorry," she mumbled, still half asleep. "It's just that you're really... warm. I can move if you want me to."

"No, that's okay," he muttered, pretending he was half asleep himself and not, in fact, in a state of gut wrenching panic.

"Good," she murmured, and with that, she cuddled closer to the boy and squeezed him tight. That was it, he wouldn't last another minute; surely, his brain would simply melt out of his ears and pool in ugly brain puddles behind his head. But no such luck.

There he was, Franklin Freeman, in the clutches of Ellie Mars. And he could not escape. Nor did he want to.

Joey had lumbered groggily out into the sanctuary about a half hour before the sun rose, having awoken from a particularly nasty nightmare in which all of his fish tanks had cracked at once and spilled all of their inhabitants onto the floor, forcing the boy to speed about his dream collecting as many flopping, suffocating pets as he could before they drew their final, fishy breaths.

The sanctuary was quiet at this early hour. It seemed that no one was around. Joey quite liked having a moment alone, and took the opportunity to visit the garden dome and see what other kinds of plants he might spot through the glass.

Peering into the dome, he began to count the different flowers. After several intensely focused minutes, he finally decided there were far too many smaller shrubs and flowers to catalogue in one session. But a voice from above startled him from his work. Half expecting to see the ghosts of his dead dream fish floating above him, cursing him for abandoning them, he looked up.

"Hullo there, master Strange-ee!" called Suds. The gaunt Lonie was balancing easily on an extremely tall pair of stilts and dusting the top of the garden dome as serenely as a maid does to the fine china cabinet, as if he wasn't balanced nearly twenty feet up at all.

"Mr. Suds!" exclaimed Joey. "You're up early! And you're up high, too."

"Ah yes, I see-ee've noticed my little invention here," said the Lonie. "I saw a similar pair of devices in one of the projections, something about a circus I think, but I rather like to take credit for the ingenuity of these two fellas here." He stooped and patted the stilts affectionately. "I hope-ee won't tell the other Lonies. Plagiarism is a touchy matter in these parts, it might surprise you to hear."

"You're secret's safe with me," said the boy, crossing his heart while still craning his neck to look up at the man and wondering how he had snuck up on him so silently. "We call them stilts where I come from."

"Stilts, aye?" echoed Suds. "Not bad. Not a bad name at all, really. I call them Lift'ems, but stilts is good too. It rolls off the tongue a bit better, ee'l notice. I take it they use these 'stilts' to clean in the hard to reach places of your kingdom."

"Something like that," Joey lied.

"How wonderful. What a picture of progress I am! Cleaning just like they do in the heavens! Tell me, is it very clean there?"

"You'd be surprised," said Joey, concocting an image of his own personal paradise in his head. "It's not so much clean as it is... overflowing."

"Overflowing?"

"Yes, with an abundance of life. Everywhere you look there are beaches and marshes, oceans and rivers, mountains and forests full of trees just like this one here." Joey gestured at the lonely birch inside the dome. "It's clean in its own special way, a sort of clean that keeps itself that way without any help. We just use the stilts to clean the, uh, palaces and places like that."

"Palaces? Oh my, how excellent! And forests and oceans? Just like in the projections? Oh my, oh my!" Suds was positively wide eyed. "How I should like to go into this blasted dome here and stroke the grass and caress the birch leaves with my fingers. If only, if only, but it is not to be. This tree is forbidden to us, and our children, too. But in a century, when it opens up and yields its wonders, certainly someone will be able to enjoy them! Perhaps you strange-ees will return then and watch the Lonies frolic and prosper 'neath the branches of an entire forest born from this very tree here. How delightful a sight that should be! I should like nothing better than to see it with my own two eyes, but I will be dead long before then."

Suds sniffed, dabbed his sleeve at his eye, and loped away with gargantuan strides upon his towering stilts.

Franklin felt like he was floating on a cloud. Ellie had soon fallen back to sleep and her soft, rhythmic breaths were almost hypnotic to him as her chest rose and fell gently against his side.

How badly he wanted to reach out and touch her fine hair like Mia and Zaki had, but his nerves would never allow him so daring a conquest. He couldn't count how many hours had passed by, but both Hess and Joey had left the apartment some time ago so he reckoned it must have been getting late.

To be alone with the girl, and so close to her, close enough to feel her breath on his skin, the flutter of her eyelashes against his neck like a butterfly's kiss, was not a chance he thought he'd get again any time soon, so he relished every moment of it. But all good things must come to an end, and soon Ellie stirred, sat up, and stretched her arms with a mighty yawn.

"Good morning," she mumbled, all the affection and warmth suddenly gone from her voice. "I'm going to go find something reflective to fix my hair in. I'm sick of it being such a mess."

She slithered out of her bedroll and lumbered out of the apartment as if nothing had happened at all. Franklin was puzzled. Had the exchange truly been an empty one, only an unconscious desire for a little body heat? Did the girl not remember her sweet words earlier and how she had nuzzled her head against him? Bother, he thought; with each step forward, another two back. Rats. Rats. Rats.

Suddenly, the boy shook his head in disbelief. What was he thinking? This was neither the time nor the place to be worrying about such trivial stuff. Besides, he wasn't even sure how he felt about the girl; the very thought of her made him confused and weak in the knees.

Suddenly, Hess's helmet appeared at the door. "Up and at 'em, Franklin. We've got to find the others and meet Stingwhit and Fluthers at the gate. It's training day!"

Franklin nodded dumbly and deposited the silly thoughts into the back of his head where they wouldn't bother him for the rest of the day.

It didn't take long to find their companions. Ellie had joined Joey by the garden dome, both of them peering into the glass, Joey lost deep in thought, and Ellie struggling with her hair in the reflection.

"I feel like one of those shallow bimbos you see in shampoo commercials," she grumbled, "but it's gotten so bad that it's starting to droop down into my eyes!"

"Not to worry," said Hess as he and Franklin came up behind the pair. "There's a fully equipped washroom aboard the Noah. We'll be back in the cradling arms of technology in no time."

"Yeah, yeah. Don't baby me," she huffed. "I already feel girly enough as it is. Don't make it any worse."

Leaving the garden, which Joey was loath to do, the four strode off towards the open gate where Jamjar was waiting with a gap toothed grin spread across his ruddy face.

"Ahoy!" he called. "I hear-ee've big plans today with the bicker brothers! Ready to wallop some Mites till they squeal? Ain't nothin' quite so fine as the sound of a frightened little demon yelpin' in the morning."

"That we are, Jamjar," replied Hess. "Any tips for a couple of rookies?"

"Tips? From little ole' me? I should think not, strange-ee! I ain't the one-ee want to be learning from about such things." He stuck his head briefly out the porthole and then retracted it. "In fact, the two-eel be wanting to learn from are a-comin' up the road right this very moment. Look! Yonder approaches our finest youths and bravest of warriors: Stingwhit and Fluthers!"

The two hunters trudged wearily into the open gate, wiping away the sweat which cascaded off their brows. It looked as if they had been busily at work all the morning, and their expressions were far from pleasant. But their eyes lit up at the sight of the children, their newfound charges, and they smiled broadly.

"Hail, strange-ees, and well met!" greeted Stingwhit, sweeping his hat off his head and placing his hand over his heart. "Are-ee ready, then, to learn the rules of the oldest practice on this planet? Are-ee ready to learn how to fight?"

"Ready as we'll ever be," replied Ellie, cutting off Hess who was about to offer an overly enthusiastic response. She looked at Franklin sympathetically and then back to the warriors. "We'd rather not kill anything today, if it's all the same."

"Why ever not?" demanded Fluthers. "Killin' Mites don't

count, so far as the Lonies see it."

"All the same." The girl offered up a stern scowl. "We'll gladly learn your ways and use them if the urgent need arises, but till then we'd like to keep our hands free from any unnecessary bloodshed."

"Mite blood don't stain so bad!" Stingwhit raised his palms, which, while caked with muck and filth, appeared to be quite blood free.

"Now see here!" called Jamjar down from his rampart. "If'n the angels don't want to kill, ee-musn't make 'em! Certainly teach 'em how to wallop and how to spar, teach 'em how to run and how to parry, even teach 'em how to slit a dirty Mite throat, but don't make 'em do it if'n they'd rather not. We's to treat these strange-ees well and with respect: orders from Ole' Sacks himself." The children were quite surprised; they hadn't been aware Old Sacks had issued any such generous commands on their behalf.

Stingwhit sighed and relented, pulling his cap firmly back down over his brow and scowling. "Very well! Makes no difference up here whether they do or don't; but down in the Well, it'll be them or the Mites."

"We're aware of the circumstances," Hess assured him. "Now then, shall we be off? We don't want to waste any more of your time than we have to. We know you're a busy pair."

Fluthers laughed heartily. "Waste of time? Never! We've been blessin Old Bess all the morning for the chance to have a bit of fun with-ee all. Come on then, we've work to be doin'! Though we take many patrol routes every week, the one which we'll be followin' this morning is our purr-tick-yew-lur favorite on account of we always finds us a bit of fighting. We calls it the Hollow Hunt, we do!"

At once, the group set off into New Hollow, leaving the safety of the Lonie sanctuary behind them. The city was just as the children had left it nearly two days prior; dismal and desolate as ancient ruin. This was the first time they had seen sunlight in earnest for several hours, but the milky and lackluster rays that dribbled out from the sky were easy on their eyes. Even though the city stank of decay and hopelessness, Franklin had to admit it was good to be outdoors again, no matter how bleak those outdoors seemed.

They wound their way through the streets and back alleys, Stingwhit and Fluthers taking care to point out landmarks and the sites of battles fought long ago. "There was The Siege of Richlin's Pharmaceuticals! We barely made it out of that one! And here the great Oldman's Podiatry Massacre. This place is wrought with the sick and sweet smell of long faded battle cries and the scent of Mite blood! Each storefront, each office, each playground holds a more grisly memory of combat than the last. All these areas are under Lonie control now, of course, but they are the few that remain protected by us. Much of the city belongs now to the Mites, like you will soon see. However, some of the bolder among them foray into our territory from time to time. Hopefully we will be so lucky today and catch one of them loping across our borders."

Suddenly, a sound echoed through the street and the companions froze in their tracks. The noise was not unlike the call a loon might have made back in the marsh at Stony Creek, and it took the children off guard; they had thought all such animal life vanished from the planet.

"That'll be Nimrod," murmured Fluthers. "Makin' his secret calls, he is. He's waiting for us up ahead. He'll be helping with er training today, ee-see."

Stingwhit cupped his hands around his mouth and returned the call into the open air, though with several more notes and variations to it. A moment later, a response sounded.

"He says to proceed with caution," said Stingwhit. "Mayhap he's cornered a beast! How lucky we should be! But I suppose the training begins now." Nodding grimly, he opened up a dirty satchel slung over his shoulder and produced from it four small clubs (though they really looked like scavenged legs from the wooden chairs upon which the Lonies sat). He quickly distributed these rudimentary weapons to the children, but Hess politely declined the offer, indicating that he would utilize the several impressive weapons locked onto his arms instead.

"I know they are only stout, blunt objects," explained Stingwhit. "But for a lot of-er stature they're near perfect in a pinch: light enough to not load-ee down and strong enough to beat off even the nastiest of brutes."

Franklin hefted the club and then stuck it into his belt; imagining himself for a moment like a gallant knight of old, a majestic sword strapped to his side. Joey and Ellie were less romantic with their weapons and simply carried them over their shoulders; ready to play whack-a-mole with whatever Mites came crawling out of the woodwork.

"A club or a knife is good medicine indeed against the plague that is Bhasmites," said Fluthers, tapping the machete on his back. "But it is not the first step to defeating them. No, the first step to properly besting an enemy lies not in the weapon but in the wielder. And not within his martial skill, either - it is the face of the warrior that does a Mite in real nice like."

"What do you mean?" asked Franklin. In his head he pictured the Maori peoples of New Zealand he had read about in one of his books; to intimidate their enemies, they had marked their faces with war paint and stuck their tongues out when charging into battle. "You mean like a battle cry or something?"

"Nay!" Fluthers shook his head vigorously. "Battle cries certainly have their place in wars betwixt hundreds of souls, but they will do-ee no good here when the conflict is small. In fact, they will do-ee more harm than anything else!"

"Why's that?" asked Joey.

"The Mites feed off of chaos," said Fluthers. "Each night they make a ruckus like no other and fill the air with their dreadful chanting and howling. They are most at home in the noisy tumult, ee-see, and to utter a battle cry or make much sound at all would only stoke their insatiable appetite for maelstrom and push them further into violence."

Fluthers now pointed to his face over which a stern, unflinching scowl was spread. "Here is what scares the demons right. To show them-ee are unafraid and unmoved by their hateful chattering and screaming is the greatest offense and injury-ee can deliver them, greater than even a thwack from one of them clubs." He indicated the weapons, which the children had begun to grip so tightly.

"Aye," Stingwhit nodded and assumed a rock-like expression as well. "Mites are a single minded lot, each of them instructed by the same horrible hive mind, and they live in chaos. They live in the storm. When faced with those who eke out their lives in a more stalwart fashion, that is to say, those who do not elect the savage way and perform with grace under pressure instead of snarling and yelping, the Mites are sorely hurt indeed."

"So we just have to make stern faces like your and they'll go away?" said Ellie, mimicking the warriors' expressions, and mimicking them quite well, too.

"Yes," replied Fluthers. "But this is a simple task indeed when none of the jaw-snapping little buggers is gnawing at-er flesh or charging-ee from across a battlefield. And do not think simply showing them-ee are unafraid will be enough to defeat them, neither! It will confuse them and make them hesitate, certainly, but eventually they will attack no matter how stony-er face is. The second step to defeating a Mite is much more self explanatory!" He patted his machete. "And we'll teach it-ee shortly!"

Quickly arraying themselves into single file, the warriors at the front, followed by Hess and then the children in the rear, the group marched quietly down a side street and emerged onto what looked like a wide set of steps, similar to ones Franklin had often seen at the base of public libraries. At the top of these steps, hunkered safely away from the sun in the shade and bent over some unseen object with their backs to the group, were four especially ugly Mites. Franklin nearly yelped at the sight of them but Fluthers clapped his grimy hand over the boy's mouth.

"Remember," he whispered softly. "The din of an angry mob is what these creatures are used to. Crying out in fear will only fuel their appetites to cause-ee more of it. Silence is unheard of when it comes to the Mites, and their ears are quite dulled and desensitized; if-ees move softly without much sound, they will never hear-ee coming. This knowledge will serve-ee mightily while-er down in the Well where they swarm out of every nook and cranny. Remember, soft steps have Lonies safely kept. More than once a time."

Franklin nodded and Fluthers removed his hand, allowing the boy to breathe and practice his sternest gaze. "Now, you just let us handle this bunch and watch from afar," the Lonie warriors whispered to them. "Watch how it is our arms move and where we keep our feet; these are the most important actions to take note of."

The two hunters left the companions behind and plodded softly up the steps, stooping low so that the creatures might not see them coming. Franklin watched in awe as the pair drew within almost a breath's distance of the Mites hairy backs. Truly, he thought, these two had learned how to move without making a sound, to glide across the ground like ghosts.

Stingwhit, who was so still and balanced that it didn't even look like he was breathing, unhitched a small club like the ones the children carried from the back of his belt. In one fluid, noiseless motion, he raised it over his head as if he were about to behead one of the sorry creatures. Fluthers did the same. The two warriors glanced back at the children, winked with sly little grins, then brought their clubs crashing suddenly down upon two of the wretched creatures' skulls.

At once, the Mites who had not been stung by the warriors began yelping and snarling, leaping from side to side and howling like angry chimpanzees. The two creatures on the receiving end of the blows, however, tumbled down the steps, quite dazed, and crumpled in a heap on the pavement below. Stingwhit and Fluthers turned their stony gazes to the remaining monsters who complained and snarled so angrily. It was time now to strike these ones down as well.

Suddenly, and without warning, the two Mites ceased their vicious chattering and launched themselves at the warriors, clawing at their legs and torsos in a desperate attempt to latch onto the pair and grapple them to the ground. But Fluthers would have none of this and swung his club out in a wide arc, catching both Mites by their faces and sending them bouncing down the steps as well to join there already grounded brethren

"See that?" called Stingwhit. "Nothing to it when there's only a couple of the buggers!" With that, the two Lonies chased the tumbling Mites down the steps. The creatures had regrouped with their dazed companions at the bottom. Chattering and cackling, undeterred by their initial failures against the Lonie brothers, the beasts charged up the stairs to face their assailants but were sent reeling again by the whirling clubs and kicking feet of the brave hunters.

Stingwhit and Fluthers threw their heads back and laughed quietly at their success. But the Mites took note of their momentary distraction and quickly decided it was time for a change in tactics. They spun about on their clawed feet and now charged for the children, gnashing their teeth and screeching in delight; they had found new, smaller prey who would not so easily resist them. "Bhasma! Bhasma!" they howled.

Panic seized the companions and Franklin drew his club out from his belt, hands trembling like they never had before. Joey, too, had wild eyes and fumbled to brandish his weapon before him, his palms sweating so profusely that the club nearly slipped from his grasp. But Hess and Ellie were undeterred; they stood stalwart as a phalanx, ready to repel whatever assault the Mites brought upon them.

Suddenly, as the beasts scrambled towards them, one of the Mites crumpled to the ground with an arrow in his back, shot from some unseen location. So far as Franklin could see, Stingwhit and Fluthers (who were rushing to aid the children) had brought no bows that day and therefore could not have fired the projectile.

The three other beasts ignored their fallen ally and came upon the children like a tidal wave brimming with claws, teeth, and angry red eyes. Hess dispatched one with ease, belting it across the snout with a heavy metal hand, and Stingwhit and

Fluthers (who had caught up with the Mites) pounced on the other two remaining creatures and beat them into submission, leaving Franklin and Joey quite relieved and Ellie angry, disappointed she hadn't been able to join the fight.

Soon, the Mites broke free of their Lonie captors and scampered off down an alleyway, defeated. They were quickly joined by the beast Hess had struck, who was barely able to keep his balance as he scurried away; never had a Mite been punched by a force so tremendous as the one delivered by the Burke brand **H**ydraulic **E**xoskeleton **S**urvival **S**uit.

"That'll do it," sighed Stingwhit, dusting off his hands and wiping his brow. "Three routed and one kilt, though not by any of our hands." He pointed to the Mite who lay slain with the arrow in its back. "That'd be one of Nimrod's arrows, it will. Seems to me that the old coot is watching out for-ee lot from the rooftops above. I'm sure he'll show his wrinkly old face sooner or later today. But, for now, he'll remain well hidden so as to not give away his location."

"Aye," agreed Fluthers. "Pardon us, strange-ees! We hadn't realized the Mites had spotted-ees till it was nearly too late! But-er metal guardian here proved more than a formidable match for them." The two warriors bowed to Hess. "Never have we seen so spectacular a wallop! We applaud-er efforts, metal man." Hess bowed back, blushing beneath his visor.

"Of course," muttered Ellie angrily under her breath. "Hess gets all the glory."

Franklin had nothing to say; he and Joey were just relieved none of the creatures had made it near enough to accost them.

"Worry not," declared Fluthers, who had noticed Ellie's disappointed face. "There are more than enough Bhasmites to go around! Would that more folks were like you and wished to whack 'em so heartily!"

Another loon call echoed out from above, to which Stingwhit responded in turn. "Nimrod says there're more Mites a come!" he declared. "Our escaped enemies have summoned up reinforcements! We had better make ourselves scarce. Bother! And I was having such a nice time!"

Hurriedly, the group abandoned the Mite corpse with the arrow still sticking awkwardly up out of its back and followed the two warriors up a side street than ran away from the steps to the north. They were quiet as church mice as they went and, whenever one of the children stumbled and caused a noise (no matter how small) Stingwhit would shoot them a look of disapproval and hurry them forwards. More loon calls from above came and went, all of which Fluthers kept track of and interpreted quietly to himself, breathlessly muttering whatever it was they meant. Suddenly, after a particularly long call, he stopped and began to laugh.

"Oh my! It seems Nimrod has been in error, or at least so he thinks. He says he was mistaken, and that the reinforcements coming are not so mighty as he thought; only a small war party, really, and nothing we can't handle. Armies of Mites are ferocious indeed and can never be contended with, only run from; but when in small groups they are simple enough to defeat. If anything, this should prove to be good practice for-ee, strange-ees!" He gestured now to a crumbling stonewall which stood about chest high and beckoned them towards it. "Come, they are sure to be on our heels and will enclose any moment. Let us have the upper hand and spring an ambush upon the damned bastards."

The companions hunkered into a low crouch and shuffled up against the back of the wall where they would not be seen. A minute passed in silence, then the quiet was broken by the sound of a mob of at least ten beasts.

"Bhasma! Bhasma! Bhasma!" they chanted and howled as they scurried down the street like a pack of hungry rats, their claws clicking against the ground and scraping like fingernails on a chalkboard.

Stingwhit held his finger up to his lips, silently counted to three and, when it seemed the Mites were passing just over their heads, sprang up and dove into their ranks, his club whirling and smacking the brutes like a stick to a snare drum. The children, following in his lead, issued forth from behind the wall and charged into battle.

Hess delved straight into the thick of things, pounding Mites left and right with his hammer-like hands. Ellie followed close behind, protecting his flank and finishing off any sly creatures lucky enough to evade her companion's metal limbs.

Franklin and Joey hung back at first, still afraid to take any lives, but quickly realized in their observance of the battle that no Mites were being smote to death; instead, after they had been walloped two or three times, the little beasts would simply scurry away, sucking at their smarting wounds or chattering angrily to themselves.

The two boys shrugged and charged in, following in Hess and Ellie's wake, beating their own swath through the demon mob. Left and right Franklin swung the little club, pounding and hammering away at all the ugly blue faces that saw fit to rear at him. Joey was having similar luck, and finding the combat more enjoyable than he had anticipated. But the both of them knew better than to smile or growl, and instead kept their faces clenched in that stern sort of expression which the Lonie warriors had been so diligent as to demonstrate for them.

Franklin looked up for a moment from his busy work to see how the others were faring. Ahead of he and Joey, Hess had begun to scoop the brutes up by their scruffs, one in each hand, and using his great strength, fling them all the way to the end of the alleyway. Ellie, too, was darting back and forth; thumping most anything she could lay her club on. But most impressive were Stingwhit and Fluthers. Their fighting seemed less like a game of whack-a-mole and more like a carefully choreographed dance. They tangoed in the center of the mob, rolling over one another and trading off opponents as naturally as any waltzing pair Franklin had ever seen.

"Franny!" Joey yelped suddenly, trying to get the boys attention, but it was too late. A mite, who had been smacked down onto the ground only moments prior, sprang up and latched onto Franklin's back, digging its claws into his chest. The pain was excruciating and, forgetting his composure, Franklin cried out in pain and began to stumble about, desperately trying to wrench the stubborn beast off of him. But it was no good, he could not manage to pry the brute off with only one hand; his other hand was quite busy shoving his club again and again into the Mite's mouth so that it wouldn't sink its long fangs into his soft, fleshy neck and kill the boy.

Suddenly, before any of Franklin's companions could rush to his aid, a voice called out from the rooftops. "You there! Strange-ee with the bugger on-er back! Hold still! I can't get a clear shot if-ee keep stumbling around like that."

Franklin's eyes grew wide and his face went pale. He shook his head vigorously and continued to stumble about with renewed ardor; he did not want the arrow to miss and catch him in the head instead of the Mite.

"Have it-er way!" cried the voice, annoyed. "My back is too rickety for such antics as this, but if the strange-ee will not stop squirming, then I'll have to try my luck down below."

Like Tarzan, Nimrod appeared overhead on one of the rooftops above and swung down into the alleyway on a rope tied to the building's ledge. As he reached the lowest point of his swinging arch, he snatched up the Mite that clung to Franklin's back and threw it by its scruff into a nearby building's wall. The creature fell some ten feet and crumpled onto the ground below.

As gracefully as a ballerina, Nimrod dropped off the rope, landing on his toes. He nodded politely to Franklin and joined the fray, producing a club of his own in favor of the composite bow slung across his back. Franklin was left quite unnerved and, seeking safety at his friend's side, put his back against Joey's so neither could be snuck up upon.

After what seemed like hours, but in reality was only a few minutes, the battle ended and what few creatures remained of the straggling Mite forces either scampered away or lay moaning on the ground.

"You idiots!" bellowed Nimrod, boxing Stingwhit and Fluthers over their heads. "Bless Ole' Bess no one was hurt! When I told-ees the war party wasn't as big as I thought, I didn't mean-ee should go and try to fight 'em! Old Sacks would have-er heads if he knew about this reckless display." He scratched his beard. "I might just have-er heads anyway. They'd look mighty nice above my fire, they would."

"What a fight!" declared Ellie happily, smacking her club into her palms. "Did you see me and Hess? They were afraid of us by the end of all of that! They really were!"

Hess nodded in agreement as he picked up one of the straggling Mites by the ankle, whirled it above his head, and sent it sailing down the alleyway. "I'm impressed, Ellie. I think you got more than me and you're not even wearing a suit."

Stingwhit and Fluthers, who were still getting their ears tugged by the elder Nimrod, grimaced and broke away from the punishment. "Come, old man!" pleaded Stingwhit. "We've sent a whole mob of 'em packing and the strange-ees have learned a thing or two to boot! No harm done."

Suddenly, Joey's eyes became wide and he stared at Franklin, horrified, and pointed a quivering finger at they boy's torso. "Franny! Your chest!"

In the commotion, Franklin had all but forgotten about his struggle with the Mite as he desperately fought so that it wouldn't happen again. Now he looked down to inspect the damage and nearly fainted. Scarlet blood was leaking down the front of his shirt as if someone had thrown a bucket of it at him, soaking through the cotton of the garment out of several long gashes which were torn across it, made by the Mite's rending claws. Franklin's head began to spin and his knees to buckle, though he still didn't feel much pain to speak of.

"No one hurt, eh?" bellowed Nimrod and whacked the two warriors again. "An angel comes to New Hollow and the first thing-ees do is to make'em bleed? Typical!" Nimrod's face became softer now and he drew Franklin close to inspect the boy's wounds. "Well now, lad. Let's hope whatever injury lies beneath these strange clothes of-ers has more bark than it does bite. Remember, tis often the smallest scrapes what bleed the worst! Off with-er shirt, then!"

Suddenly, Franklin snapped out of his blood-induced wooziness. The shirt would simply have to stay, there was no way it could go, not with Ellie standing by and watching. Franklin got nervous to take his shirt off in front of girls at the beach and by the public swimming pool, there wasn't any way he could disrobe in front of Ellie for the first time with blood oozing out of him in the middle of a post apocalyptic city. He hadn't really a muscle to speak of and had often been compared to a beansprout instead of a beefsteak. He was skinny in places that should have been muscles, and flabby in places that ought to have been skinny! How humiliating.

"That's alright, I'm alright. Nothing to worry about," he murmured, doing his best to smile.

"Nonsense!" exclaimed Nimrod. "Ee may not feel it now with the heat of battle still a-coursing through-er veins, but things could be bad 'neath that shirt!"

"Really, it's okay!" insisted the boy.

Ellie looked at him with warm, worried eyes. "Don't be silly, Franklin. What if you're seriously hurt?" Those eyes, they made him want to bundle up under at least another three layers, not shed the only one he had. Franklin sighed and pulled the shirt off. Nimrod stooped to investigate.

"Now, now," he murmured to himself. "Not all that bad! Seen worse." It was true. Even Franklin, who was the least seasoned warrior in the world at that moment, had seen worse injuries than the ones rent into his chest. The scratches were long and scattered across his torso and arms, but they weren't too deep. The bleeding had stopped for the most part now, and Nimrod produced a dirty handkerchief, which he dabbed at the gashes with.

"All the same. We had better get-ee back to the sanctuary right quick. Mite cuts, even small'ns, can infect speedily out here. Wouldn't want that, now would we?" The grizzly old warrior smiled at Franklin. "I saw-ee fighting out there, even offered to pluck the bugger off with an arrow, but methinks-ee were wise to refuse. Ee've got a bit of the fighting spirit in-ee yet, lad! With a bit of training-eed make a fine warrior indeed, not like these dimwits." He scowled at Stingwhit and Fluthers

Red in the face and still quite red in the chest, Franklin

donned his tattered shirt and the group set off, back towards the sanctuary. Ellie and Joey doted on him as they went, worrying and cooing to him that the cuts weren't so bad, and wetting their thumbs to wipe away blood on his neck and ears. Even Hess, who was so often rather cold and distant in sentimental matters, brought out a medical cloth from his sack and dabbed at the cuts visible just above Franklin's collarbone.

As the crew of the Noah fussed over their injured companion, Nimrod further chided his two young charges. "Foolish indeed!" he hollered. "Challenging the four Mites on the steps was no beginner's game, though I will not begrudge-ee it, for-ees did most of the fighting. But to spring an ambush on an entire party of the demons with ill seasoned warriors in tow? Never has Nimrod seen such foolishness from Stingwhit and Fluthers! Is this what awaits in the future generations of the Lonies? Rash decisions? Bold and needless endangerment? Me oh my! Wait 'till Ole' Sacks finds out about this!"

"If-ee saw so much danger, why didn't-ee shoot a few more arrows of-ers at it?" retorted Fluthers who was still sore from having his ears boxed so much.

"Unlike-ee lot who have been on that lazy route-ees call patrol all morning, I have been hunting all the day and my quiver is nearly spent!" Nimrod indicated his sparse stock of arrows. "Each day many Mites fall to the bow of Nimrod, but each night more of 'em spring up to replace their dead. A losing fight, if I ever saw one."

"Don't say such things!" cried Stingwhit. "We must keep our heads high, despite the sludge which creeps up to our necks."

Nimrod sighed sadly at this and could offer no response. He walked silently on as the two warriors began to bicker behind him as to who had walloped more beasts that day.

The last leg of their journey became a hurried one as they noticed the sun was sliding quickly out of the sky. Though they reached the gate well before dusk, Franklin had begun to notice those hateful red eyes peering out of every hole they passed in their rush towards the sanctuary. When they arrived, the gate was tightly shut and the air, quiet. Nimrod rapped on the door, glancing worriedly about, spotting those same red eyes which had been troubling Franklin.

"Jamjar!" he called out. "Jamjar! Open up! Jamjar! Jamjar Brickbeard-ee open this gate this very instant!" He was bellowing now. But the gate did not open, nor did the ruddy-faced little man pop his head out of the peephole above. "Bother!" cursed Nimrod under his breath.

The sounds of Bhasmites all around them began to drone now as the demons chanted and snickered from the safety of their shadowy hiding spots. They jeered and shrieked in delight as they watched the lonely group of veterans and rookies stranded outside of their own home, eyeing Franklin in particular, for he was the wounded lamb of the flock and would make an easy prospect indeed; they could do nothing but lick their lips at the malevolent thought. Darkness would soon close upon the city and even the Lonies' prowess in battle would not be able to save them this time, not from the near thousand Mites who crowded around the sanctuary like a hornet's nest ready to explode at any moment.

As if sent by some divine providence, a young Lonie face popped out of the hole above the gate and looked down on the sorry bunch. "Beg-er pardon!" the little boy squeaked. "Mr. Jamjar's in meeting with the council. I've been mindin' the gate, but it took me a while to climb up the ladder with these short legs of mine. Beg-er pardon."

"In council?" demanded Nimrod as he, Stingwhit, and Fluthers peered up at the tot indignantly. "How could a council be called without three of its most important members? Why have me and the boys here been forgotten?" Hess nudged the hunter, jerking his thumb at the swarm of red eyes that grew larger around them. "Pah," the old Lonie scoffed. "Never mind! Just open the gate and let us in, that we might repair this incomplete council!"

"Right away, surah!" The boy saluted and disappeared back into the sanctuary. After a few uneventful moments his head popped back out again. "Beg-er pardon, surah!" he called down. "But I've forgotten what old Mr. Jamjar said concerning' how to open this here gate! I knows it were important, but I were daydreaming when he 'splained how to do it, I'm sorry to confess."

Nimrod looked furious and his hands were beginning to shake. "Can't-ee see we've got wounded soldier here? To open the gate is simple! Just... Just give it a... Well, Bless Ole' Bess: I haven't the foggiest clue as to how to open this beast of a door either." He turned helplessly to Stingwhit and Fluthers, who merely shrugged.

"Don't look at us! Jamjar offers to teach everyone who comes his way how to open it, but we declined just like-ee did and every other Lonie in the sanctuary!" they spat defensively.

Franklin and Joey sighed, stepped forward, and recounted to the boy what steps they could remember from Jamjar's complicated lesson. The boy seemed still to be daydreaming, though, and asked for many things to be repeated. Joey and Franklin began to holler in frustration as the befuddled boy continued to ask questions whilst the Mites, who had fallen into an uproar of nefarious laughter, drew nearer as the last rays of the setting sun began to fade.

"And a flick of the wrist?" he echoed.

"And a flick of the wrist," they replied, voices all but spent. The boy nodded, saluted again, and vanished. One minute passed. Two. Three. Nearly four. Franklin could hear Mite lips smacking and the click of claws against stone. "Bhasma! Bhasma! Bhasma!"

Finally, the creatures were silenced when the gate creaked and then groaned. The noise rang out over the area, and the monsters loped off dejectedly; they knew their prey had escaped for the time being.

The companions hurried inside and Nimrod proceeded to give the frustrating lad the worst and most vicious spanking Franklin had ever seen. It made the wounds on his chest look like cat scratches. After the punishment, the boy stood to wipe at his wet eyes and rub his sore behind.

Nimrod, whose face had cooled and lost its crimson hue,

stooped and patted the boy on the head. "Despite all the trouble-ee've caused, ee've saved us all a great deal of hurt tonight. In the future, I should hope-ee be more expedient with-er heroics, but remember this evening and the lives-ee saved upon it." He reached back to his quiver, removed one of his last arrows, and gave it to the boy, who beamed at the gift. "Take-ee this arrow so one day-ee might grow to fight the Mite menace when we are dead and gone. Run along now."

Bowing and thanking the old man profusely, the lad galloped off to show his friends the prize, having all but forgotten his smarting rear.

"Now then," said Nimrod, turning back to the children who were half horrified, half delighted with his treatment of the boy, "the lads and I best be visiting this council meeting they've been so polite to call without us! You lot go and seek Lazlo, he'll be sure to treat-er wounds well, boy." Nimrod tipped his hat to Franklin and, with a flourish of his warn out coat, marched off towards the council chambers, flanked by Stingwhit and Fluthers on either side.

The Barren Earth

CHAPTER SIXTEEN

STARLIGHT FORGOTTEN

Lazlo was waiting for them with dinner on the table when they arrived at his apartment. Immediately, his emerald eyes lit up with alarm and he rushed to Franklin.

"Oh my!" he cried. "Oh my! You've been hurt! Poor child! I bring you to my home, encourage you into danger, and now look what has befallen you! It was never my intention! Oh my!"

"It's only a couple scratches," said Franklin to Lazlo's back as the robot rooted around in some cabinets, searching for his first aid kit. "It doesn't even hurt." This was a lie; Franklin had begun to wince on the walk home and each step had become laborious, but he dared not show it in front of Ellie.

Suddenly, the troublesome girl was in front of him and pulling his shirt off. "Ellie!" he cried out, tugging the shirt back down over his head.

"Don't be an idiot, Franklin!" she growled. "Lazlo's got to bandage you up. Why are you so attached to this ratty old shirt, anyway? It's practically torn to pieces! Plus, it's all stained with dry blood; and if they haven't got water for me to wash my hair, they certainly haven't got it to wash your clothes with. Off with it!" she demanded. Franklin was growing tired of being ordered to disrobe so hastily that day, but he submitted anyway.

Lazlo bustled up to the injured boy and, with the precision of a neurosurgeon, began to patch Franklin up with all manner of fancy bandages, the likes of which the boy had never seen before. "Unfortunately," said the robot, "the antiseptic reserves ran dry nearly a century ago, so we will have to clean the wounds with some water as best we may. If you could-"

"Here," Hess interrupted him and held out a little tube of antiseptic he had taken from one of the many utility slots that studded his armor.

"Such treasures have you!" exclaimed the robot, taking the

medicine and cradling it in his hands. "Don't let the other Lonies see you with this; they'd sooner roast themselves alive than see it go unused."

Lazlo plastered the stuff all over Franklin's chest. Unlike the iodine of his time, noted the boy, this substance hardly stung at all and the wounds seemed to dissipate almost to nothing before his very eyes. The motherly robot finished the procedure and wrapped Franklin so thoroughly in bandages that the boy looked like a mummy from waist to neck; at least he didn't feel quite so shirtless now.

"Now that we've seen to that, I'm sure you're all hungry, so help yourselves to what I've prepared for supper," offered Lazlo. "It's no different than usual, I'm afraid, but it is a well deserved meal by you lot after such a hard day of fighting Mites and showing the Lonies just what stern stuff you are made of."

Just as the children and Hess had nearly finished polishing away the dry Burke bars, which even they ate greedily in their hunger, Mia bustled into Lazlo's apartment, out of breath. She had been running. "Please," she panted. "Please, master angels, er-presence has been requested at once in the Lonie council chamber, and urgently so. There is no time to dawdle, hurry now!"

Abandoning their cutlery along with their meager dinner, Lazlo and Mia escorted the companions back into the forum where once they had been tried as spies for the Mites. The tribunal was of a warmer sort now, though, and the faces, which lined the amphitheater benches were friendly and familiar. Stingwhit and Fluthers, who sat eagerly in the front row, looked particularly happy and excited.

Old Sacks stood before the audience, banging his staff for quiet. "Here they come now," he hollered, and the room became silent. The old man greeted them, his face just as grave and serious as ever. "Well met, Strange-ees. I take it it-er day has been an exciting one, and-ee have become familiar with the wiles, trickery, and cunning of the Bhasmite hordes?"

"Indeed we have," replied Hess. "But we have been well

taught by your finest warriors, and are fully equipped to deal with the beasts should we encounter them again."

"And encounter them you may, most likely, for they outnumber the Lonies upon this planet ten-million to one." Old Sacks turned his gaze now to Franklin. "Angels are fine soldiers, it seems, but I hear even angels bleed red like the Lonies do." He winked at the boy and his lips, parched and dusty as they were, cracked into a wry smile. "How fares the wounded warrior?"

"Not bad at all," admitted Franklin, picking at the scrapes. "Thanks to mister Lazlo here, I'm as good as new."

Lazlo waved his hands, deflecting the approving gazes, which fell upon him from the council ranks. "Not at all, not at all. The wounds were not serious, for the lad protected himself well and his instinct warded off the worst of the Mite's ferocity. And safe was he in the care of the captains Stingwhit and Fluthers, we must not forget that. But it was Nimrod who saved the boy in the end."

"Indeed." Old Sacks nodded and stroked his beard. "Though I am disturbed that even a single hair on the strange-ee's head should have been harmed at all, I am grateful for his safe return anyway. And Mr. Lazlo has tender, gentle hands that mend the body nicely. That more of our fleshy hands could be so loving as his metal ones, but ah well."

The crowd began to applaud. "To the captains, Stingwhit and Fluthers! To Nimrod! To Lazlo, who is generous above any other!" they cheered.

Old Sacks banged his staff again. "Order! Order! Now, strange-ees, I'm sure you are wondering why it is I've summoned you here so suddenly, though perhaps in your minds you already know! The council has been deliberating the entire daylong upon your proposition, that is to say, the opening of the Well so that you might venture into it. Votes have been cast and re-cast for hours, and finally our three warriors here arrived to cast theirs. And they proved the tie-breaker, I might add."

Old Sacks now stood tall, puffed out his chest beneath his

burlap tunic, and declared in his most authoritative voice, "The council has decided the strange-ees **may** enter the Well upon a teetering vote which was just barely tipped in your favor."

With this, the chamber burst into vigorous applause, and several familiar Lonie faces beamed down onto the companions; the children were sure in that moment that those friendly souls whom they had encountered the past few days were the same ones who has voted in their favor: Suds, Chunk, Stingwhit, Fluthers, Nimrod, Mia, Zaki, Jamjar, surely Lazlo, and perhaps even Old Sacks himself. The moment was a bittersweet one for Franklin, though; while he was thrilled they had moved a step closer towards the completion of their mission and therefore a step closer to home, the prospect of descending into a veritable wasp's nest full of all sorts of monsters was none too appetizing to his already aching person.

"Thank you, Lonies! How can I ever thank you all properly?" exclaimed Hess. "You have no idea what a great aid you have just given us! If only I could-"

"Hold, strange-ee." Old Sacks cut him off. "My proclamation is not yet complete. There are conditions and rules to this endeavor, you see. Opening the Well, even for a short while, is a terrible threat to the Lonies and to our survival here in the sanctuary. It makes plain a hole in our defenses for the Mites to abuse. To do so out of the goodness of our hearts is a tempting prospect, but even you must admit that should we risk our lives and well beings, we ought to profit at least a little. Is this not reasonable?"

"I suppose so," replied Hess, but he was worried more complications would ensue. "What is it you want of us in exchange?"

"It is a simple request, really," said Old Sacks. "And it should not take you far from your intended course. All we ask is as follows: Old Bess long ago disappeared into that Well, and our leader is sorely missed by us. Though she vanished into that place nearly two centuries ago, not long after the Bhasma Cloud struck, and she is most likely dead, we would like at least come clue as to her fate. Please, while you search in the Well for whatever treasure eludes you, keep your eyes peeled for signs of our Old Bess and then, should you find any, report them to us on your return, now matter how small they be."

Hess turned to the children who shrugged and smiled; the request sounded reasonable enough. "Certainly we will do that for you!" replied Hess to the council. "It is the least we can do in gratitude for your kindness."

"Excellent," exclaimed Old Sacks, and managed yet another smile. "Now there comes the business of planning. We only have but a small window of time to offer you. Because the Mites beneath the earth sleep during the daylight hours and rise as the sun sets, we insist that you descend in the morning and come back up before dusk, otherwise we will shut the gate and you will have to find some other escape route from that wretched dungeon. If you leave early enough, this offers about twelve hours for the Well's exploration; surely enough time for such seasoned angelic warriors as you are." Another grin to Franklin (who was beginning to feel a bit made fun of.)

"Mozi Box," Hess called to his long dormant computer assistant. "Do you think we'll be able to locate the thruster core in the time that's been allotted to us?"

"Mozi Box calculates the Thruster Core will be located and safely obtained in much less than twelve hours. How exciting! How fun!" squealed the AI from Hess's chest.

"Very well," said the armored boy, nodding. "I think that's more than enough time."

"Will we send someone to go with them? To protect them?" demanded Jamjar, who had grown fond of the Strange-ees and didn't want to see them butchered like game.

"Jamjar!" snapped Old Sacks angrily. "You know well it was said long ago that whomsoever should enter the Well shall be expelled from the Lonie creed. Old Bess herself said this when she vanished into it. To go into the Well is to be exiled from New Hollow and never return; this is our most ancient, sacred law! Though protection would be a boon on their journey, Stingwhit, Fluthers, and Nimrod have trained them up for that very purpose: their own protection."

"Of course, sir," muttered Jamjar meekly, and then sat down to twiddle his thumbs.

"You needn't worry so much!" said Hess to the crowd. "Only I will be going into the Well. My friends here will be staying up here on the surface with you, if that's alright."

"Excuse me?" Ellie nearly exploded on the armored boy. "What on earth do you think you're talking about? I know I told you we didn't want to go the other day, but I was only giving you a hard time! We've come this far, all the way from Stony Creek, across the wasteland, and through the city. We've been chased by the Stalo, Mites, and God knows what else! We've eaten nothing but sandy meal supplements for days! We've left our homes entirely and learned how to go toe to toe with monsters! And for what? To sit around, while you have all the fun? I don't think so you great, bumbling bucket of bolts! You'd better believe we'd be coming with you! In fact, I'll be two steps ahead of you the whole time! Isn't that right, boys?" She swiveled and glared at the two.

Franklin had expected to see anger in her expression, outrage at her exclusion, but instead he only found courage; those same, brilliant and shimmering eyes which had coerced him into taking that first leap into the crater all those days ago, back in 2012. At first he faltered, hesitated, bit his lip, shuffled his feet, and coughed once or twice, but he could not escape the piercing gaze of Ellie Mars; it was too vivacious and sought him like the hawk does the field mouse. He never stood a chance.

Sighing, he glanced at Joey who was under a similar spell of persuasion. 'How many times will we fall for this?' his pleading eyes seemed to say, but Franklin could offer no coherent reply. Instead, the two simply shrugged and nodded. "We want to go as well, Hess."

Old Sacks began to laugh like an asthmatic barking dog. "It seems you have not a choice in the matter, metal man! Har har har! Me oh my! What a bold bunch! I have not seen the likes of them since the earliest days of my youth!"

Hess, at once unhappy to have the burden of the children

but at the same time pleased he would not be going it alone, folded his arms and relented.

"Fine," he said. "We'll all go together."

"Then make your preparations right quick!" Old Sacks declared, stamping his feet and brandishing his staff. "For you leave tomorrow morning, at dawn! Council dismissed!"

Quickly, the chamber emptied as its cheerful inhabitants shuffled away, chatting excitedly about the momentous day to come. Before Franklin could make his leave, however, Old Sacks plucked him by the wrist and indicated for the boy to stay behind.

Once all the council had departed, and even the other children and Hess, who Franklin told to, "Go on ahead without me," Old Sacks swept across the room like an aggravated poltergeist, dragging his jacket of burlap sacks over the dirty floor.

"I am exhausted by such public forums," he grumbled. "Sometimes, I wish I could simply command the Lonies and they would obey without quarrel or democracy! They probably would, at that, but it is not our way; Old Bess instructed us to vote on all matters of great importance, and to defer to our better judgment for those of less gravity. And that, strange-ee, is why I have asked you to stay behind and chat with me. Tomorrow, when you depart, there will be great fanfare and fuss. It was my intent to let you slip quietly away while all the rest slept, but the Lonies would have none of it; they wish to see you and your companions off, Old Bess knows why. In any case, with all this ruckus that is sure to come, I would not be able to make this final request of you."

"And what is that?" asked Franklin, worried he might be asked to ambush another troop of unruly Mites; an idea which his aching chest disagreed with.

"I see your garments are tattered and in ruin! Hardly worthy dress for an angel, especially one about to embark upon a dangerous, heroic journey," Sacks pointed out. Franklin cringed in his mind as he figured the old man might be lending him one of his dirty sacks to wear. But this was not to be.

Instead, Old Sacks snatched something from behind the council podium and held it up for the boy to see.

It was a cloak of sorts that would hang draped about the wearer's shoulders and down unto his waist, much like a poncho or a shawl. Where one side of the cape met the other about the neck hole was a golden brooch, which functioned as a clasp, holding the two sides of the cloak together. The brooch was shaped like a many-pointed star. Franklin had seen the design somewhere before, and recently too, but his mind could not place the symbol.

"Besides the garden, this is all the Lonies have left of Old Bess," the ancient Lonie told him. "It was her favorite shawl and rarely left her shoulders, but for some peculiar reason it was left behind when she descended into the Well. I would like you to have it and keep it well! It has been passed down from Lonie leader to Lonie leader for over a hundred sun cycles!"

Franklin was flattered and a bit confused. "That's very nice of you, Mr. Sacks, but you don't have to go giving me one of your sacred treasures to wear just because my shirt's beat up. I can make due. I'm sure Jamjar or somebody can loan me something to wear. Don't get me wrong, that's very generous of you, but it isn't necessary. I'd rather you keep it."

"Boy," said Old Sacks, rolling his aging eyes about in their wrinkly sockets, "I do not give you this cloak out of charity! You are the first mortal souls to descend into the well since Old Bess, and likely the last, I would venture to guess. She is almost certainly dead after so long. But it gives me hope to think that, using her magic... Her 'science', as you called it, she prolonged her mortality and yet lives on today! Perhaps, if indeed she does still wander the depths of the Well, she will see the cloak about your shoulders and recognize you as friend. Or perhaps it will cheer her lonely and wandering spirit, should she now be nothing more but a ghost. I ask you wear this cape catch the eye of Old Bess if she still be alive, lad. It will be familiar to her. It will distinguish you as a friend. If this be the case, perhaps you could convince her to return here and lead her peoples once again. I am a sorry excuse in her absence!"

The old man was beginning to sound crazy; how could a woman still be alive after two centuries, not to mention wandering alone around a monster-infested hole all the while? His eyes shone with a genuine spark of hope, though, and Franklin could not refuse the codger such a wish, even one so foolhardy.

"Of course," said the boy and graciously accepted the cape. The cloth felt incomparably fine between his fingers, and strong too; in superb condition considering it had been lying around for two hundred years. "I'll wear it for you, Mr. Sacks. Who knows, maybe she will notice!" Franklin smiled at the Lonie who watched the garment leave his withered hands with sad eyes.

"I ask this of you in particular because you remind me of her, lad," admitted Old Sacks. "You remind me of Old Bess, at least what images I have seen of her and stories I have heard, too. They say her hair was the color of yours and that her eyes shone brightly like your'n do. Let me see it about your shoulders."

In one motion, Franklin brought the cloak up over his head and it seemed almost to fall perfectly about his shoulders, reaching all the way down to his wrists.

"You do remind me of her, indeed!" cried Old Sacks. "How strange! That cloak'll keep you warm in the cold and cool in the heat. It is light, no?" It was, as a feather. "But it feels as if it could repel even the sharpest of Mite claws at the same time, aye?" It did. It felt like weightless Kevlar.

For a moment, Old Sacks' eyes began to water as he looked the boy up and down wrapped snugly Ole' Bess' shawl. " It is a strange garment with mysterious powers, to say the least. She was particularly fond of that brooch there, that many pointed star below your neck. The Lonies do not know why. See that you treat it well and polish it to make it shine out in the darkness."

"I will," said Franklin. He would. "Is that all? I should probably get to bed soon. Early morning, you know?"

"Of course, lad!" Old Sacks sniffed and dabbed at his eyes,

turning suddenly away from the boy to hide his emotion. "Be gone with you! Let me not see your face again till the morn!"

Franklin found his friends bustling about Lazlo's apartment, preparing for the journey to come. Hess in particular was very busy, arranging various tools he had brought out from his sack onto the floor and scrutinizing each one to see that it was in proper working order. Joey and Ellie had set about wiping off their clubs and rummaging through Lazlo's cupboards for anything else they might need. The robot, however, was sitting quietly in the corner and watching the commotion sweep through his little home.

"Lazlo?" asked Franklin as he entered the apartment. "Are you alright?"

The android's eyes lit up suddenly, as if they had been glazed over with computerized thought. He looked Franklin up and down. "Why, yes Master Freeman! I was only mulling a few things over in my processors is all. My goodness! How ever did you come by that fine cloak? I remember it was a favorite of Madame Bess while I knew her. I have not laid eyes upon it for some time."

"Old Sacks gave it to me. He figured it might come in handy down in the well."

"How so?"

"To be honest, he hopes that her ghost will see it and recognize us, or better yet that she's still alive." Franklin scratched the back of his head awkwardly.

"You must forgive our leader!" laughed Lazlo. "He has very little to hope for. Though this request may seem bizarre, I'm sure it will grant him some pleasant dreams to fill his sleepless hours."

Franklin nodded; Lazlo was right, of course. Soon, his friends also inquired about the burgundy cape that hung about his shoulders, taking special notice its golden clasp. Franklin recounted his exchange Old Sacks to them.

"It is familiar, that brooch," said Ellie. "But I can't reckon from where. Maybe it's on a flag back home or something."

"I recognize it too," said Hess. "Oh well, we haven't got any time to worry about things like that. Franklin, go help Joey and Ellie with the cupboards; we've only got one light so far and it's attached to my wrist."

After several more minutes of rummaging through various dusty odds and ends the robot had collected over the years, Joey finally exclaimed "Ah!" and pulled out three glass lanterns with little handles on top of them.

"Well, I'll be!" said Lazlo, coming over and delicately scooping up one of the lamps. "The last time the Lonies used these was in the days of my youth, when the sanctuary was not so fully lit as it is now."

"How do we work them?" asked Joey. "I haven't found any oil or anything."

Lazlo took the lamp and disappeared from the apartment for a moment. He returned, his lantern glowing with a turquoise light. Inside the glass lamp was one of the many fluorescent mushrooms which lined the inside of the Lonie compound.

"Once picked, they last for several hours, you see," he said. "And to extinguish them, one only has to cover up the lantern with a black handkerchief. You'll find several of them inside the cupboard, Master Jensen, and enough lanterns for all of you."

So, having solved their lighting issues and carefully prepared their weapons for any further battle, the children, Hess, and Lazlo all hunkered down for the evening, intent on finding an early sleep to fuel them through what was to be a trying affair the next morning. A half-hour full of hushed murmurs and giggles passed, and then another, and soon, the apartment quieted down to only the sounds of their breath, but there was still a buzz of energy that shivered through them. Joey coughed, Franklin restlessly shifted about, Ellie sighed, and even Hess drummed his fingers on his metal chest.

At least another fitful hour passed like this, and the children began to curse their useless bodies; when they needed rest, it would not come, but when they didn't, it seemed as abundant as apples in an orchard.

"Is everyone else awake too?" asked Joey, his voice cutting through the quiet.

"I'm not particularly nervous," said Ellie, "just excited. I wonder what it'll be like down there."

"I imagine you **should** be nervous," murmured Hess. "From what the Lonies say, it's like a living hell down there. At least the Mites will be sleeping while we're around. I hope."

"What do the Lonies know?" demanded the impertinent girl. "None of them have ever been down there! It could be nothing but a Mite graveyard by this point!"

"I don't think so," said Franklin, wincing as he remembered the haunting songs which had issued forth from the Well and Old Sack's story about the most awful Bhasmite of them all: Cherophobe.

"Imagine the species!" whispered Joey wistfully. "A manmade series of caverns where hardly any light gets in, left untouched for two centuries! Just imagine!" Franklin was trying his best not to.

Hess stirred again and jolted up, agitated. "This isn't any good! We've got to get to sleep! We'll be a wreck tomorrow morning if we don't get some rest soon, and a Mite infested cave isn't a good place to not be on the top of your game."

"Excuse me," Lazlo said from the corner. Franklin thought he had gone to sleep hours ago, or whatever it is robots do during the night. "I couldn't help but overhear. If I might make a suggestion: sometimes, when I have trouble defragmenting my hard drive and going into sleep mode, I visit a special place here in the sanctuary. It is a soothing sort of spot, and I believe I am one of the few who knows about it."

"That sounds perfect," said Ellie. "Back in Maine, I would take a walk around my house and look at the woods by night when I couldn't sleep."

Franklin and Joey nodded. Even Hess, hell-bent on getting

a proper rest, figured a little walk might be helpful.

"Very well," said Lazlo. "Follow me. And do keep your voices down; insomnia is not commonplace among the Lonies and they would be disturbed indeed to find us skulking noisily about while they slumber."

The robots tiptoed out of the apartment and lead them through the residence corridors in the dark. When they came to the main chamber, where Jamjar was snoozing nosily by his gate, Lazlo beckoned them up onto the rickety wooden walkways which led up towards the rafters above. Quiet as church mice scurrying through a chapel, they ascended toward the ceiling, winding their way higher and higher on the crisscrossing ramparts.

Eventually, they came to the highest spot in the sanctuary, where Hess had been trying to contact Mozi some days before, but this was not Lazlo's destination. The robot reached up with one long, aluminum arm and grabbed onto a handle of sorts situated on the ceiling. He yanked on it and, much like the Freeman's attic hatch back home, a little trapdoor opened up and a ladder slid down onto the platform on which they stood. The night sky, brimming and luminous, streamed in through the opening and lit their faces with a pale glow.

"You mustn't speak a word of this to anyone," whispered Lazlo, clambering onto the base of the ladder. "I believe only Old Sacks and myself know of its existence; but he regards it as a dangerous spot and a weakness in the sanctuary's defenses."

"Wait, Lazlo!" hissed Franklin. "Maybe this is dangerous! I thought we weren't supposed to go outside at night because of the Mites. What if they spot us?"

"Spot us?" the robot scoffed. "Even if they manage to spy us, I challenge them to do anything about it. Up so high, they have little chance of seeing us, much less harming us! Come!" Lazlo climbed up the rest of the ladder and scrambled up into the hatch, vanishing. Hess looked at the children, shrugged, and followed the robot. Joey and Ellie were quick to ascend as well.

Franklin was last to climb the ladder, and he nearly went

dizzy as his head emerged from the trapdoor and out into the cool, night air. The city of New Hollow sprawled all around him, etched against the background of the sloping, earthen walls of the crater. Decrepit and miserable as New Hollow was, when speckled with starlight and colored silver in the dim, blue night, it appeared more like an ancient Roman ruin than a wasteland; full of history, wisdom, and secrets.

They were on the very top of the Lonie sanctuary, the highest point on that large, silver egg. A small, ramshackle balcony, much like a widow's watch, had been constructed beneath the hatch door, which Franklin dropped down onto to join his friends. Twinkling above New Hollow was the same tremendous and brilliant star-scape they had gazed at while camping in the desert. Though they were quite high up, the rim of the crater was higher still about them, and it seemed as if they were looking up at the sky from the bottom of a shallow hole. The rocky, dirt lips of the New Hollow crater, almost like a painting frame, outlined the cosmos. Franklin felt as if he was viewing a great ocean through a tiny porthole. Still, the starlight would not be denied and came down in misty beams all around them.

Hess had scooted forward on the balcony to dangle his legs over its edge; he seemed quite taken with the view and reclined his great, metal body so that the evening's light made him shine. Lazlo was leaning against the sanctuary wall, just next to the trapdoor, and Joey with him. But Ellie sat on the edge of the porch, away from Hess, all on her own. When Franklin approached, she looked up at him with worried eyes and gestured for the boy to sit.

They were quiet, overwhelmed not only by the enormity of the night sky that drifted overhead but also by the daunting task that faced them. The fire, which had urged Ellie to boldly deny any notion of nervousness, seemed gone from her now. Franklin couldn't be sure, but to him it seemed her expression was tinged with the lightest trace of fear.

He sat down next to the girl, much closer than he would have ever dared during daylight hours, and dangled his legs over the edge of the balcony, kicking them silently into open air.

He kept his eyes locked forward where they would not be tempted to wander and glance at Ellie, whose skin was silver and pale in the night light and whose eyes shimmered just as brightly as the stars which shone above them. Those eyes were occupied, searching the sky for some sort of answer, some sort of courage which Franklin wished he could offer the girl, but he felt just as lost as she did.

Now, she turned her head and looked at him. He was forced to return the gaze and quickly found himself beginning to tremble as her glimmering eyes searched his own, which were rather brown and boring, he thought.

That look. That look. Oh, that look. It was different from the blazing flames of challenge that had ignited courage in him on Sachem's Head Peak. It was pleading, now, and full of uncertainty. Unable to bear her gaze any longer, and unable to tear himself away, Franklin began to sweat. At last, without a word, Ellie turned her attention back towards the sky above.

The balcony remained quiet; nobody had much to say. Franklin, still reeling from Ellie's glance, looked to Joey in a desperate attempt to steady his dizzy head. His friend was letting his eyes wander the cosmos above, silently mouthing to himself whatever constellations he could pick out.

Suddenly, Franklin's attention was drawn with all due haste back to his own situation. Ellie had reached up, scratched behind her ear thoughtfully, and placed her hand back down onto the ledge, right next to Franklin's. They were touching now. The hand of Ellie Mars, with its soft skin and delicate fingers, was touching the hand of Franklin Freeman.

Butterflies.

This was only a small instance of touching, of course, and Franklin quickly chided himself for making anything of it. Only their pinky fingers were touching, really, and only just barely.

But what if that wasn't all it was? What if it was an

invitation? The timid boy's heart began to race and he was sure even Lazlo, who stood all the way at the other end of the balcony, could hear his palpitations. Was he supposed to reach out and grab the girl's hand, look her in the eyes and tell her it was okay? Was this his lot in life: to constantly be guessing what it was Ellie was thinking or what she wanted him to do? Bother. Rats. Damn. Franklin's sweat returned, and he could do nothing but pray his clamminess stayed above his wrists where it wouldn't infect the girl's hand.

The easiest thing to do would be to simply take his hand away and scratch the back of his head, or something like that. Play it casual, aloof. Yes, that's what he, Franklin Freeman, hard-to-get tough guy, would do. He'd lift his hand up and look at his fingernails or something. What did he care about some silly girl's stupid pinky finger? She probably didn't even realize she was doing it! She certainly hadn't looked down.

What was he **thinking**? Not for all the gold in El Dorado, not for all the tea in China would he move his pinky away from hers. What to do? What to do? Would moving in closer be the bold thing? Would it show her just how brave he was? Or maybe things were just right the way they were and advancing any nearer would simply make things awkward. Bother! Bother! Franklin felt like his head was about to explode.

With a yawn, and in one fluid motion, Ellie Mars nestled closer to Franklin Freeman and took his hand in hers, caressing it gently with her thumb.

Bells.

Bells on the hills. Somehow, even though the New Hollow church had long ago been destroyed by a dismal apocalypse, Franklin heard bells, and they were ringing like angelic songs. Birds he heard, too, and choruses of hallelujah. There was even a fanfare of trumpets that sounded as if it was heralding the return of some brave knights, finally come home from a far off war.

The butterflies in his stomach had all but burst out of his

intestines and fluttered rapidly to every corner of his poor, trembling body. Each time that thumb of hers glided slowly across the back of his hand, the butterflies leapt and sang. He was beginning to feel queasy. But who cared? Who cared what Franklin Freeman's easily upset stomach was feeling? The girl's palm was warm and soft, and her fingers as light and delicate as a freshly fallen snow.

Though he was dumbfounded and felt as if he was groping about in a dark haystack looking for a black needle, Franklin began to return the girl's affectionate caress and brushed his thumb against her palm.

What a feeling. Like no other. Now, she turned to him and looked him in the eye. Though worry and doubt still played across her features, her eyes were certain now and determined; they shone not with starlight but with that charismatic fire, for the flame had returned and burned brighter than ever. It was an infectious inferno and danced out across the air between them, setting Franklin's courage alight as well. There seemed to be an electrical current passing between the two, now, and not just through their interlocked hands but through their gazes, too.

Though his mind still raced with confusion and emotion at a mile a minute, and though his hand still trembled, even in her grasp, Franklin Freeman could not help but smile. And Ellie smiled back. Despite all the chaos which now threatened to push into their lives, these two souls had become suddenly entangled and intertwined with each other. And they were glad for it.

Quite removed from all of this, and unaware to boot, was Lazlo. Hess had joined the robot and Joey, leaning against the sanctuary wall. Lazlo's emerald eyes were particularly bright in the dark blue of the night.

"Are you alright, Lazlo?" asked Joey.

"Don't tell me you're sorry to see us go," said Hess jokingly.

"You haven't the foggiest idea," laughed Lazlo, suddenly snapping out of his grim demeanor. "You really haven't. In any case, I think we've had enough night air for now. But I can hardly tear my gaze away from these stars. I wonder what exactly happens to them when the sun rises. I know, of course, they remain where they are, but we forget about them during daylight, don't we? We forget what a vast place we live in and instead focus on our tiny lives inside of it. When the sun sinks and the sky begins to twinkle, once again we are overwhelmed by the immensity that lies above. Come, let's retire before it gets any later."

Silently, they returned to the apartment and crawled into their bedrolls. Though his friends quickly began to snore, Franklin's sleep evaded him more than ever. How could he possibly shut his eyes and keep them that way when the girl, with whom he had just entwined his fingers and his spirit, breathed softly behind him? And what did it mean for the both of them now? Were they something that they had not been before? Or perhaps that was overthinking it.

At one point, as Franklin rustled restlessly about in his bedroll, Joey turned over and pinched the fretful boy.

"Franny!" he hissed. "Would you stop freaking out and tossing and turning? Get some sleep! Just shut your brain off! Is this Well worrying you so much? My gosh."

If only Joey knew, Franklin wished, but he couldn't tell him. Not yet, anyway; not with Ellie so nearby.

But the fitful lad did as he was told and begged his brain to shut off which, being weary and open to persuasion, it did.

The fog of sleep soon claimed him and drifted lazily before his eyes. But it was a thin fog, and through it he could see a shape moving; a small, white object that seemed to flit about like a bird. In fact, it was a bird! It was a white dove, the same that had visited him in his dreams aboard the Noah. Gracefully, it fluttered up to his face and hovered there, cooing softly.

"Not you again!" he groaned. "Listen, I don't know what

you want from me, you dream-bird-girl-crackpot-thing! Can't you see I've already got enough on my plate without all of this Freudian nonsense?"

The dove giggled a few melodic notes. "Franklin Freeman," it whispered with that girl's voice, the same voice which had spoken to him twice before. "You're all bothered. Be at peace, my love, for there is little need to worry in a dream, especially one so pleasant as this."

"But I've only got a couple hours to sleep!" he protested. "Can't I just be one of those people who never remembers their dreams and has a good night's rest every single evening?"

Suddenly, the dove shimmered before his eyes and seemed to stretch out in every direction. In an instant, it had transformed into that same girl who had kissed him on the dream stage, shoved a ticket into his pocket, and pushed him into a hole. Again, he was forced to hide his eyes away from her face for it was blinding in its white-hot radiance, as brilliant as a small star, and its blazing light threatened to blind him. How many times would he encounter this strange girl only to never see her features or look into her eyes? He imagined her face must be quite beautiful; if only he could look into it.

Where the dove's feathers had been, there now hung a white, silken dress which clung to her nimble frame. Down onto it fell her long locks of hair, hair the color of silver starlight, unlike any head of hair Franklin had ever seen. She placed a long, delicate finger to his lips and shushed him softly.

"I will allow you your regularly scheduled dreams and sheep counting soon enough," she whispered. "Now hear me, and do not protest! What I am about to tell you is invaluable information indeed. Should you become hopeless and lost upon your way, do not hesitate to call on that gift with which I presented you. You must not think it foolish or silly, for it may yet save your entire mission, not to mention your life."

"What gift? You've given me nothing but stress in the only place I'm not supposed to have it!"

"Quiet, love," she said, and sank into him, coiling her arms about his neck and whispering softly into his ear. His knees began to feel weak, even though they were only dream knees.

"Peril will plague your every turn tomorrow when you venture forth into hell. I imagine your courage and your tremendous faith in your friends will see you through most of it; but if all should go black and your path disappears, call on me, for I will answer you, my love." Gently, she kissed his cheek and pulled away from him.

In an instant, she was a dove once more and flitted back into the mist, leaving him to ponder his strange subconscious for the rest of the night.

CHAPTER SEVENTEEN

THE BOTTOM OF THE WELL

"**G**ood morning, Noah-nauts!" squealed Mozi box and jarred the children from their sleep. He was only performing the wakeup call requested of him by Hess, of course, but still, he was louder than any alarm clock and at least ten times more frustrating. Persistent as ever, the little computer continued to chime his waking bells as loudly as he could till Hess grumbled and slammed an agitated hand down onto Mozi Box's pixelated face.

"That's enough!" he groaned. "I'm awake. For God's sake, I'm awake!"

Aching, the children rose and stretched. Franklin was in a daze; he wasn't particularly sure where he was, or why he was there. Eventually, vague memories drifted back into his groggy mind. Ellie had held his hand the night before - that was nice. It wasn't till he remembered the tremendous task which now loomed closer than ever that that his grin shrank and his demeanor grew somber. Apparently, Joey faced no such worries, for seemed to be all smiles.

"Why are you so happy?" Franklin asked.

"I already told you! This is a dream come true. Maybe I'll be able to collect some new fungus samples for my terrarium back home. I'll bet they're really wild with all the Bhasma radiation floating around."

"Please," Hess turned around and begged him wearily, as if he was barely awake enough to deal with such nonsense. "Please don't take anything out of that hole. That's the kind of thing we really don't want to infect the past with. God. I can't even imagine."

Joey shrugged and winked at Franklin. Ellie hadn't said a word yet; she was busy double and triple checking all of their packs. Franklin worried she regretted what she had done the night before by holding his hand; certainly she must have felt silly showing such affection to a goofy boy like him. But he pushed the thought out of his head. It was simply not the time to worry. He could worry when he was safely back aboard the Noah or, better yet, back home in 2012. More pressing matters required his attention. Soon, Lazlo rose from out of the corner and unplugged his rear end.

"Are you all ready, then?" he asked, coming towards them.

"As ready as we're ever going to be," murmured Ellie. She stood and strode over to the robot, the top of her head only coming up to the base of his artificial neck. "Lazlo," she said, "how can we ever thank you for everything that you've done for us? You've been our guide and counselor, given us a roof overhead and supper every night, not to mention all the arguing you did on our behalf. How can we ever thank you for all of that? You're a wonder, Lazlo, a real wonder. It kills me that we have to leave you behind, but you've finally come home again and I wouldn't want to take you away from all of that. Oh, Lazlo!"

She wrapped her arms around his metal torso and buried her face into his chest. Taken aback by her sweetness, the robot gently patted her shoulder. If Lazlo could have wept, he would have burst into tears that very moment.

"Why, Miss Mars," he stammered. "If only you knew... You have nothing to repay... It is I... It is I who owes..." His robot voice croaked and went silent. He could say no more, his processors were choked up, Franklin imagined. The girl broke away from the embrace and looked up into his dazzling, green eyes.

"I'll never forget you, Lazlo!" she cried out, and hugged him again. Even though he was an artificial being and not really subject to such tremors, Franklin could swear he saw Lazlo shudder with a sob.

Soon, after all their lanterns and clubs had been hung on their belts and all their unnecessary provisions stored in Lazlo's apartment where they would retrieve them later, the companions arrived in front of the sacred garden where a massive Lonie crowd had gathered. The throngs of people were bleary eyed and sleepy, having risen quite early, but there was a buzz of excitement and nervousness about them nonetheless. Old Sacks stood at the head of the crowd, leaning on his staff and flanked by Stingwhit and Fluthers on one side, Jamjar and Nimrod on the other.

Hovering close by Nimrod's shins was the boy from the previous day, the one who had nearly locked them out of the sanctuary for the night. He was cradling his arrow and beaming up at the wizened old hunter who had given it him.

The moment the children entered the chamber, the crowd became hushed immediately and ceased all their gossip and chatter. Old Sacks watched them come with troubled, bloodshot eyes. It appeared he had not slept either. But when his gaze fell upon Franklin, and upon the burgundy cloak hanging around the boy's shoulders, a touch of levity crossed the old man's face and his smile brightened a bit. "Good morning," he croaked, his voice hoarse and raspy.

"Good morning," replied Hess. "Is everything ready?"

"We shall soon see. And of the strange-ees? Have they all their sundry weapons and tricks?"

"We have," replied Ellie, patting the club which hung from one of her belt loops. "We're ready for anything, I think."

"And well you should be ready," said Old Sacks gravely. "For methinks you will encounter much worse than anything you can imagine, as you say. But let me not deter your hearts. Come, now, and stand before the Lonies. There are words to be spake before such an undertaking!"

The companions shuffled over to Old Sacks and turned toward the crowd. Lazlo bowed his head and joined the throngs of Lonies. Suddenly, Franklin felt a twinge of sadness to see the robot leave their side after so many days, only to become another face in the crowd.

"Now hear this!" exclaimed Old Sacks as he addressed his people. "These bold strange-ees have to come to us from a far-off land. Wherever that land is you may decide for yourselves! But regardless, they have come seeking a treasure that is dear to them, and to reclaim it they must enter that most despicable and hated of all holes. They must descend into the Well."

Some Lonies, the ones who had not heard the council's news, Franklin guessed, gasped and shrank back. "But fear not!" their leader went on. "Though we Lonies be good natured, and the strange-ees prove kind as well, we have come to a bargain. In a few moments, when the sun rises and brings light to the earth, we will open this gate here for the first time since dear Old Bess closed it behind her. But when dusk comes and the Mites awaken and clamber for blood, the gate will close and never open thereafter. It will be boarded up and sealed permanently this time. This morning is the second and last time this door will be used in earnest, for it is a gateway that many hellish things and demons might use against us in the future. Such a plight I seek to avoid at all costs."

"What if'n the strange-ees don't make it back in time?" cried the little boy, clutching his arrow tightly.

"Then they will be trapped at the bottom of the Well with all the horrors therein." The crowd gasped again. "But fear you none! The strange-ees understand the risk they take, for it is one they have themselves requested! And if they are to be trapped, I'm sure they shall find some other means of escape, for they are a resourceful lot. The Mites manage to find holes to crawl out of on to the surface, I'm sure the Strange-ee will be able to as well." Somehow, Franklin doubted that Old Sacks meant what he said. If that door closed on them, they were doomed, so far as he was concerned.

"Excuser me surrah," called Suds, "but why is the strange-ee Frodeman Freakman wearing Old Bess's shawl? Is that not one the few remaining artifacts we have left to remember her by? The burgundy poncho of Ole' Bess is sacred indeed!"

"Ah." Old Sacks touched a bony finger to an equally bony nose. "This is another boon to us granted by the strange-ees! Master Freeman has accepted this cloak as a parting gift with the intent to use it!"

"How?" demanded Suds.

"To attract the spirit of Ole' Bess! Or better yet, her living being!" declared Old Sacks, and the Lonies' eyes went wide. Suddenly, they burst into uproarious cheers and applause. In an instant, Franklin had skyrocketed from suspicious strange-ee to celebrity status. The Lonies could think of no greater gift than the return of Old Bess, besides the opening of the garden dome, perhaps.

Now, Jamjar came forward. "Old Sacks, sir. The sun has just about risen by now. It's time. Shall I do-ee the honors?"

"With Old Bess guiding your hands! Perform this ceremony cautiously, Jamjar!" warned the elder.

The bearded doorman nodded gravely and proceeded to the tremendous gate, running his hands across its ancient, rusted surface. Franklin could still make out the hole through which the thruster core had apparently punctured the gate and fallen into the Well behind it. Jamjar opened up a little electrical box beside the gate and fiddled with it. After a few minutes, a loud creak swept across the chamber.

The gate moaned and trembled but it began to open, ever so slowly. Beyond was blackness, pure and dark. A rope hung just past the gate, a basket suspended from it, much like the kind one finds on a hot air balloon.

When the door had creaked up as high as it was going to go, it groaned and settled. "There we are," said Jamjar, dusting off his hands. "Good as new. Now, see-ee here, strange-ees! This basket is an elevatin'omator of sorts and will take-ees all the way down to the bottom of the well. It'll be slow goin', but it's the only way down besides scaling the walls of the pit, which ain't possible for anything but one of them scaly Mite buggers. Once-ee's are ready to come back up with-er treasure, and maybe Ole' Bess safely at hand, all-ee must do is give the rope three solid tugs and we'll haul-ee back up right quick. Savvy?"

"Sounds reasonable," admitted Hess, who was rather relieved they wouldn't be walking nearly a mile into the earth. The armored amnesiac turned to his companions. "Are you all ready?" They nodded grimly.

"As am I!" a voice suddenly called out. It was Lazlo. He rushed forward to join them. "Allow me to accompany you!"

"Lazlo!" hissed Old Sacks. "Don't be foolish! Lonies are

forbidden to enter the Well. This is our most ancient and sacred law! To descend that pit is to be banished for all time from our creed. If you should enter, I cannot allow you to return and live with us. My apologies, dear friend, but the law has no favorites, even concerning such a charitable fellow as yourself."

"It pains me to speak such treason," said Lazlo, "but if that is to be the case, you must banish me, sir, for I intend to break our most sacred covenant. To these people, particularly to this angelic girl whom you see now, I owe a greater debt than I can ever hope to repay. They gave me life and love when all other hope was lost to me. They resurrected me from the land of the dead and offered me one last chance at life. To allow them to go unprotected and risk my Mistress Mars's wellbeing in that dreadful hole... I simply would never be able to live with myself if anything were to happen to them. If one sweet hair upon her head were to be harmed... Please, Old Sacks, forgive me, but theirs is a journey more important than any of us can imagine, I think, and now I must join them upon it." He turned to the children. "If they will have me, that is."

Ellie's eyes lit up and she sprang at the robot, clapping him in another hug. "Of course we'll have you, Lazlo! Of course!"

Hess was not so sure about all of this; was there room on board the Noah for yet another hulking, metal man? But he kept his concerns to himself.

"Won't you miss all your friends and family here, though?" asked the girl.

"Indeed, I shall," said Lazlo and looked to Jamjar, who had removed his hat and begun to dab at his eyes with it. "But these kindly folk understand. The duty of the Lonie is to his mission, and now yours is become mine, now. Wherever it is you will go, I will go also and protect you with every fiber, or rather filament, of my being."

Old Sacks bent his head and sighed. "Very well, Lazlo. Eee will be sorely missed, and I am loath to see-ee go when only you have just been received again. But let us not talk about such sad things until your triumphant return from the Well.

Then and only then will we discuss the details of your eternal departure."

Lazlo nodded and bowed before the ancient man. "Of course, sir. I will not forget you, Adam Sacks. Remember, I watched you play when you were only a boy nearly a century ago. But you have made a fine king, yet, and the Lonies could not ask for a kinder shepherd to guide their flock. Hail, Old Sacks!" He saluted his leader.

"Hail, Lazlo!" Sacks returned the gesture. "Come now, strange-ees!" he declared. "The sun rises higher with every word we speak. The time for your descent is nigh. If any of you should wish to stay behind, speak the wish now or forever hold it."

The children and Lazlo shuffled towards the basket, which Jamjar had drawn close to the ledge for them. Gulping, Franklin peered down over the precipice and into the abyss below. He beheld a pit of black and nothingness, so hollow and deep it could have very well travelled to the other side of the earth. A fowl stench rank with garbage and death wafted up and stung his nose. He winced.

One by one, Hess, Ellie, and Lazlo all piled into the basket. Joey, after some coaxing and wincing, ignored the dizzying height and joined them. Franklin remained on the edge. Joey and Ellie, his most familiar friends in the little fellowship, stretched out their hands for him to take, much like he had done for Joey all the way back on Sachem's Head Peak.

He gulped. This, he supposed, was where his true battle was to be fought. All that really mattered lay in the momentous step ahead; anything that came afterwards was nothing.

You can still go back, he reminded himself, glancing over his shoulder to where the Lonie crowd watched with baited breath. But to step forward and into that basket which dangled so precariously over a pit of despair and gloom; surely that would be the bravest step he could ever muster up enough courage to take. Whatever trials awaited him below were nothing compared to that one tremendous step. And so, taking a deep breath and closing his eyes, he took it.

At Hess's signal, Jamjar slackened his grip on the cord he had used to draw the basket towards the ledge. Slowly, it swung out into the middle of the pit and the companions along with it. The hole was some fifty feet wide, and god knew how many deep. However far down it went, the descent was sure to be a long one, Franklin was sure. The walls about them were of stone and brick, manmade but at the same time lost to the wear of centuries and the decay of dark places. They were damp and the pit was cold. Franklin pulled his cloak tighter about him.

"Ready, then?" hollered Jamjar across the pit from where he stood. Hess gave another signal and Jamjar began to rotate a crank lever. Slowly, the basket started to lower into the pit.

"Remember what we taught-ees!" called Stingwhit and Fluthers.

"And beware those creatures more dangerous than mere Mites, for you are sure to enter into their homes!" Old Sacks reminded them.

Eventually, the curious Lonie crowd slipped out of sight. The further the basket lowered, the open gate above them seemed more and more to be only a speck of light in the distance. After what felt like an hour, it disappeared entirely and darkness washed over them. Only Lazlo's eyes cast a dim light across the children's faces and reassured them they had not dropped out of existence entirely.

Joey quickly pulled the black handkerchief off of his mushroom lantern and a florescent glow filled the basket. He and Franklin moved to the rim of the makeshift elevator and peered cautiously down into the well. Nothing. No bottom in sight. Joey produced a pebble from out of his shoe and cast it into the pit. They counted the seconds, ears pricked, but they never heard from that poor, little rock again; it had been swallowed up forever by the abyss.

No one talked. The children had been warned time and time again to keep their noisemaking down to a minimum. The less warning they could give the Mites as to their approach, the better.

Minutes turned into hours, and Franklin began to doze on his feet. In the middle of a particularly pleasant dream about trees and freshly baked pies, Joey nudged him and gestured to his ear. Franklin listened intently. Though at first he swore the pit was just as silent as it had always been, eventually the din of running water reached his ears, growing louder the further down they dropped. It was not the thunder of a mighty river, to be sure, but Franklin guessed a small stream trickled somewhere beneath their feet.

"You must remember," whispered Lazlo, "the caverns below are what remains of an ancient sewer system. Though they may appear to be tame and uniform, make no mistake, they have been rerouted and mutated by the Mites into some manner of hideous, maddening labyrinth, I am sure. Do not trust whatever signs you might see and, above all, do not drink from any water that runs beneath us. It is sure to be tainted with the wickedness of Bhasma."

"Bhasma this and Bhasma that," mused Ellie. "I wish I knew what the damn name meant. Where did all these monsters and Lonies get a name like Bhasma from?"

"I wish I could tell you, Miss Mars, but I was only activated after the cloud's assault. It is something of a taboo to the Lonies, the Bhasma Cloud is, and its name uttered sparingly. I suppose I never thought to ask about its nomenclature."

"I'll admit, it's got a frightful ring to it," said Hess. "Burke was always certain the apocalypse was the work of some sort of living being and not just a natural catastrophe. I suppose this whole Bhasma affair, along with the presence of the Mites, confirms that hypothesis in one way or another."

"Whatever ancient civilization beat this cloud," said Joey, picking at his fingernails absent mindedly, "it must have had some miraculous kind of weapon - something really out of this world. All the defenses of the year 3012 got snuffed out like they were nothing. God knows how a bunch of Egyptians or Babylonians or whoever they were fought the damn thing."

"That remains to be seen," said Hess. "I only hope I can get whatever it is back to the future so Burke can make use of it. I don't think my heart was ever really in the mission till I saw just how bad things got here in the wasteland. No offense, Lazlo. The Lonies are nice and all, but this is no way for mankind to be living in such a late day and age."

"None taken," replied the robot. "I take it, then, that you have just revealed to me some of the secrets of your mission which you have all kept veiled in so much secrecy. Is it your intention to ensure the Bhasma Cloud never completes its assault and turn it away before the earth is ravaged by its misery by travelling through time?"

"Something along those lines," said Hess.

"Then the Lonies are never to be? By whatever sorcery you possess, you plan on altering the very fabric of the timeline itself so that this apocalyptic realm will never come to fruition, remaining naught but a dream in your minds?"

"I know it sounds harsh, Lazlo," said Hess. "And I know it's upsetting to think that the Lonies will be... erased, so to speak. But it really is for the best."

"I would give each of my limbs and half of my circuit boards to know the Lonies will never have to exist upon this planet," exclaimed Lazlo indignantly. "I would much prefer the earth simply remained its verdant self. I'm sure my brethren above would agree with me! Believe you me; I am neither hurt nor perplexed by your objective. Rather, it in inspires within me the further need to come you your aid! Lazlo will see this terrible present undone, even if it means he should disappear along with it!"

Though the children were pleased to see Lazlo excited instead of disappointed, his words sobered them; not one among them could equal his passion, not one among them could imagine destroying themselves in order to complete a quest. Not one, save perhaps Hess, who had very little stake in any sort of life to speak of.

At last, the basket came to rest and the creaking of the rope ceased. They had touched down at the bottom of the Well. Joey held his lantern aloft and cast its light about the pit. The narrowness of the hole had widened considerably since the beginning of their descent and the walls were no longer visible from where they stood. It was a vast place indeed and each step taken echoed a thousand times over. Silence would be impossible. Taking great care, each of them dropped quietly out of the basket and onto the ground below, leaving the makeshift elevator hanging a few feet above the floor.

What appeared at first to be water snaked around their feet, flowing at least a few inches over their shoes; but when Joey stooped and shone the lantern's light over the running liquid, the companions quickly discovered it was no typical river water. Instead, a sort of impenetrably black sludge oozed sluggishly over their feet, like mud rolling down a hill.

"I've never seen anything like this before," whispered Joey. "Its consistency and color are too uniform, there's not enough variation in it! Whatever this is, it isn't natural. It isn't even unnatural, like some pollution is... It's entirely..." At a loss for words, Joey stretched out his hand to touch the stuff. Lazlo's arm flashed out and caught the boy before his fingers reached their destination.

"You are correct indeed, Master Jensen," warned the robot. "This substance is as far from natural as most anything can be. It was water or mud once, perhaps, but now it has been infected by the black taint of Bhasma and runs not merrily like a stream but slowly and wickedly, like some great, lumbering glutton intent on devouring all that is fair. You mustn't touch it, lest you would risk your standing as a human being; that terrible sludge could very well transform you into one of them, into one of the Bhasmites."

While Joey seemed quite intrigued and fascinated by Lazlo's words, Franklin had already begun wishing he weren't ankle deep in the malevolent goo.

"It may be running slowly," said Hess. "But not that slowly. It seems that when the thruster core fell down here, it was carried off by this stream to God knows where." He held up the Rok counter and examined it. "It's still pretty far off. Blast, I was hoping it'd be smack-dab at the center of the bottom and we could just call it an early day. Oh well." He sighed. "Never quite so lucky, huh? The Rok Counter says it's off in this direction. Remember to keep quiet! It seems like we've entered the Well undetected and I'd rather we kept it that way."

Splashing softly out of the stream and onto its rocky bank, the companions continued along, following its current and the steady compass hands of the Rok Counter toward where they hoped the thruster core, their only means of escape, was waiting for them. As they tiptoed on, the cavernous pit bottom began to close about them and they soon found themselves meandering into a narrow tunnel. Its ceiling was so low that Lazlo and Hess had to stoop and proceed through it hunched over.

The bioluminescent light from Joey's lantern filled the little passageway and played down onto the ground. The walls of the tunnel grew tighter about them and, begrudgingly, they were forced again to step into the stream of black sludge. The bricks, which had once composed the walls on either side of them, had melded into one another with years of age and corrosion. Little by little, the narrow tunnel began to look less like a creation of man and more like a natural cave, hollow and quietly menacing. Their footsteps grew louder and louder as they splashed and there didn't seem to be any end to the corridor in sight.

"So far, there doesn't seem to be any life down here at all," hissed Ellie. "I guess all that training was kind of pointless."

"You must not forget, my sweet Mistress Mars, that this miniscule stream is likely only a tributary to some vast body of the sludge," said Lazlo. "The sewers beneath New Hollow are immense. I surmise the Mites make their home in the grandest sections therein. Do not be so hasty as to let your guard down already for this is only the first leg of our journey. This is but a small passageway to the bottom of the Well, though I am sure there are larger ones hollowed out by the tremendous and terrible Cherophobe himself."

"Agreed," added Hess. "Stay on your toes. I'm almost certain the thruster core floated down this way, but that doesn't mean it's a safe path to take. We could be walking into an ambush for all we know. Keep your weap-"

"Look," hissed Joey, interrupting him. "Look!" He held up the lantern and pointed. There, far away at the end of the tunnel, was the faintest outline of an opening. Keeping their mouths shut, they hurried along through the stream towards it, lifting their feet higher and higher out of the sludge as it grew deeper and more hindering with each step.

Now, they stumbled out of the opening and Joey, who was in front with the lantern, was nearly pushed to his death by his companions jostling out of the tunnel behind him, for the passageway let out onto a narrow ledge which ran perpendicular to the tunnel's exit. He staggered, waved his arms about, and was caught about the waist just in time by Hess.

"Gotcha," snapped Hess, hauling Joey back onto the ledge and pinning him against the wall. The ledge was frightfully narrow, only a little longer than Franklin's feet, and each of them were forced to sidle carefully out onto it. There they stood, pressed against the stone wall behind them, barely daring to breathe for fear it would push their torsos out too far and demolish their balance, sending them tumbling into the chasm below. His hands shaking, Joey held the lantern out over the ledge and he and Franklin peered cautiously down over it.

About thirty feet below them, a tremendous river of the black sludge rolled slowly on. The river was vast and wide, for they could not spy the bank on the other side of the gorge from where they stood.

"You weren't kidding, Lazlo," said Franklin, pushing back up against the wall to steady his vertigo.

"Indeed," replied the robot. "See how the stream through which we have trodden runs over the side of this ledge and into the filth below? It is one of thousands, I guess, that pour from all over this subterranean kingdom and into the river rank with malice. A sludgefall, if you will."

"What is this stuff anyway?" demanded Ellie, scrunching her nose. "It's smells awful." Franklin agreed; though he hadn't noticed it before, now that an entire river of the ooze ran beneath their feet, its unnatural stench wafted sharply into his nostrils.

"I surmise it is the food source of the Mites and that which gives them all their power," conjectured Lazlo. "But I cannot be positive. Surely, they do not slay nearly enough Lonies to feed such a tremendous population as theirs, and there is precious little else to feed on."

Hess pounded a metal fist into his palm. "Damn," he cursed. "Well, whatever it is, the thruster core must've been carried right off the ledge and down into the river by this stream. It's much too high to jump. What on earth am I supposed to do?"

"We'll have to find another way down," said Franklin. "It looks like this ledge runs off to the right for quite a while. Maybe we can continue along it and see where it takes us."

"Indeed," agreed Lazlo. "While this place has been long controlled by Mites, it was designed for men to travel through, originally. Surely there will be a staircase or a ladder further along the ledge, or at least a point of crossing- perhaps a bridge. Do not give up hope yet, Mr. Hess."

At once, not wanting to waste any of their precious time bogged down in decision-making, the companions began to sidle along the ledge in single file. Taking care to stay pressed firmly against the wall, their going was slow and their footing unsure. Several times Franklin nearly stumbled off the ledge and into the chasm below, but he was luckily saved by one of his friends each of these nearly deadly moments. At one point, they happily came upon another tunnel opening in the wall behind him, but the foul and ominous sound of cackling Mites echoed from within it, so they continued to sidle on.

Finally, after what seemed like hours, a shape loomed up out of the darkness in front of them. It was an ancient, stone bridge that ran out across the chasm further than their eyes could comprehend. The crossing would have appeared sound enough were it not for the fact that they could see nary a beam to support the bottom side of it; the bridge seemed almost to be suspended in mid air, anchored only by each bank to which it clung. For a walkway nearly thirty feet above a sheer drop into a river of toxic sludge, the idea of its fragility was none too appetizing. But, after Hess weighed both the odds of their survival and the time remaining in the day, he resolved its crossing could be their only option at that present moment, no matter how precarious the action seemed.

Joey vehemently rejected this course of action again and again, his head spinning at the mere prospect of crossing such a narrow walkway and so high up. But Lazlo, kind robotic soul that he was, quickly hoisted the worrisome boy up onto his back and spoke softly to him.

"Be at ease now, Master Jensen! Hush! Do not squirm. Lazlo will bear you over these troubles. You need not be afraid, for Lazlo's footing is always sure thanks to the gyroscopes in his ankles. And his grip is strong, too. Not even the mightiest of falls could part us, I guarantee you."

"I don't care! Put me down! I'll just go get back in the basket and go back up! Put me down, will you?" protested the boy, wriggling on Lazlo's back and kicking his feet.

"Man up, Joey!" demanded Ellie, shooting him a stern glance. Now, he turned to Franklin and looked his friend deep in the eye.

"Trust me, Joey," Franklin whispered, peering into the frightened boy's face. "It'll all be fine. We'll all be fine. You trusted me in Cankerwood, now you have to trust me again; Lazlo won't drop you and the bridge will hold." Joey's eyes watered for a moment, locked with Franklin's, then steeled and gleamed in the darkness.

"Okay," he sniffled. "Okay let's go. I'm just going to close my eyes. Tell me when we get to the other side."

"I will do that, Master Jensen!" declared Lazlo cheerily and adjusted the boy to a more comfortable position on his back. "In fact, it is maybe best you all hold on to one another and onto me, transitively. Should someone slip, perhaps we can form a human chain between Hess and myself; I'm sure our strength combined will hold us all secure." And so they proceeded out onto the bridge, Lazlo with Joey (eyes squeezed shut) in the front, Franklin then Ellie in the middle, and Hess bringing up the rear, all their hands interlocked.

Though the bridge was frightfully thin in width, only affording enough room to shuffle awkwardly forward at a snail's pace, and any glance over the edge into the chasm below induced waves of vertigo in Franklin's head, his mind was quite occupied with the soft, girlish hand which gripped his behind him. Each time she touched him, those same butterflies from the night before returned and pillaged through his body. It was a wonder, he remarked to himself, the fluttering beasts hadn't knocked him off his feet and into the chasm yet, so vivacious were they in their cheer.

It was Ellie, as a matter of fact, who did the stumbling. Slipping on a particularly damp patch of the bridge's slick, stone surface, she reeled to the side and began to drop off the walkway, screeching as she went. Hess and Franklin's grips remained steadfast, however, and she was saved the lethal plummet. Franklin could not help but wonder selfishly to himself, as he and Hess pulled the trembling girl back onto the bridge, if Ellie had a flock of butterflies to call her own, and it was her mischievous urchins, not his, which had caused the misstep.

"I'm okay," she panted. "I'm okay. I'm fine." She stooped over and breathed deeply. "I'm sorry for screaming... It just came out."

"That's alright," Hess reassured her. "All seems still. I doubt anything heard you. We're fine. We're completely fi-"

He was cut off by a far-off howl which sent chills up and down the children's' spines. Ellie winced and kicked herself quietly, cursing the outburst which had alerted whatever beast made such a racket. Soon the howl was joined by others, and seemed to intensify in its horror, tenfold. The cacophony escalated till tumultuous cackles, snarls, barks, and chants could be heard echoing all around them. It was deafening. "Bhasma! Bhasma! Bhasma!"

Joey, whose eyes were still squeezed tightly shut, began to

squirm again and begrudgingly peeled open one eye. He swiveled on Lazlo's back and peered over the bridge and out into the darkness from where they had come. Immediately, his eyes snapped shut again and his face contorted into an awful grimace. "I hate to say it given how high up we are, but we have to move. Now!" he hissed. "I can see their terrible red eyes coming towards us through the gloom. They'll be on the bridge any moment. Go! **GO**!" He kicked at Lazlo's iron ribs as if he had his feet in invisible stirrups.

Needing no further convincing, the companions forewent their caution and raced across the bridge as the bloodthirsty racket drew nearer their backs. Though each of them, save Lazlo, stumbled and slipped plenty of times, they simply relied on the fortitude of the human chain to which they were all bound to keep them from falling. And the chain held soundly, despite their panic.

Franklin hadn't dared to look back over his shoulder, but as the sound of the rabble grew more and more cacophonous behind them, he sneaked small peeks in between steps. Far off in the distance, he could see a swarm of angry red eyes clambering across the same ledge they had sidled along. They were beginning to pile onto the bridge, charging forward like a pack of hungry wolves.

"Hess," he shouted. "We've got company!"

"I think it's just about time I show you all what this suit can really do," muttered the armored boy, spinning on his heels and aiming his wrist back at the encroaching mob. With a flash and a shower of sparks, a tiny rocket whizzed out of Hess's arm-mounted cannon and zipped across the bridge. There was a sudden screech of pain as the projectile found its way into the Mite horde, and then a moment of silence. Suddenly, with a tremendous hiss, then a boom, the rabble of creatures was lit up bright orange as they were engulfed in an explosive inferno.

Even from so far off, Franklin could see the beasts as they tumbled off the bridge into the abyss below, roaring and bellowing all manner of curses. The mass of red eyes had dimmed considerably now, the Mite ranks culled by Hess's rocket attack, but still they advanced on, largely undeterred. Some of the monsters seemed jovial at the wanton destruction, and they cackled, mocking their unlucky comrades.

"Not satisfied, eh?" muttered Hess, adjusting a few dials and knobs on his chest. "Mozi Box, double the power!"

"Roger, Mister Hess! Copy, copy! Mozi Box will thrash 'em!" exclaimed the little computer, taken with the fervor of battle.

At Hess's command, another rocket spun out through the air across the bridge and collided with what remained of the Bhasmite forces. Another terrible explosion ensued, and Franklin swore he could feel the walkway tremble beneath his feet. While there had been several more casualties within the enemy war band, the Mites still pressed on.

"Master Hess, I'd advise we abandon this fighting stand and continue on," suggested Lazlo. "I do not believe this bridge can endure much more stress; if we're not careful, those fireballs leaping out of your wrist will bring us and the bridge crashing to our dooms!"

"Right!" hollered Hess over the Mites' chanting and howling. "I think I've shown them just what they're up against, anyway. I told you all I didn't need a club! Come on, quickly, before they gain any more ground."

The companions nodded and, after Lazlo had hoisted Joey up further onto his shoulders, they took off once again across the bridge. Soon, they came to its end, but the Mites had drawn frightfully close and were nearly nipping at their heels. The bridge ended in a small opening, another tunnel, carved into an immense wall opposite the one they had travelled from.

"Quickly! Quickly!" hollered Lazlo as he tossed Joey off his back and into the passageway, ushering the others in as well. "Though perhaps we could best what remains of this obstreperous lot, it would matter little; more and more would rise up to replace them! Soon enough, all the legions of the Well will be upon us if we do not find some place to hide and wait for them to return to their sleep!"

Not missing a beat, the companions squeezed into the

tunnel and hurried on, their shoulders scraping up against the narrow walls on either side of them. Franklin's feet began to pump faster than they ever had before as he heard the Mites enter the corridor behind them, their cackles echoing like bats. Silently, he cursed all his gym teachers for making him play dodge ball instead of teaching his class how to run properly; how on earth was dodge ball supposed to help him while he was being chased by a pack of bloodthirsty brutes? He did concede that, perhaps, he could turn and hock a rock at one of the beasts and utilize some of those dodge ball skills, but that was beside the point.

"Bhasma! Bhasma! Bhasma!" shrieked the monsters as they clambered over one another in the tight passageway, scuttling forward to pounce on the companions. Even Hess had begun to sweat inside of his survival suit.

"We'll never outrun them!" panted Ellie. "We don't stand a chance like this! We've got to change tactics." The children had begun to stagger with exhaustion.

"You're right," agreed Hess. "You all keep running. I think I can buy us a bit of time. Just keep going! I'll be along shortly." For the second time that day, Hess turned to face the oncoming horde alone. Over his shoulder, Franklin watched his armored friend extend his wrist and plant his heels. But this time, no rocket emerged. No, this time a plume of flame issued fourth from the Hess suit and filled up the tunnel behind the companions with a column of fire.

"A flamethrower!" cheered Franklin. "He's got a flamethrower!" Hess paid him no heed, however, and continued his fiery barrage against the Mites. Above the roar and crackle of flame, they could just barely hear the creatures yelping as they were consumed by the inferno and reduced to nothing but smoldering, hairless weasels, whimpering in their retreat. Hess lowered his wrist, pumped his arm triumphantly, and raced forward to join his friends. "That'll give us at least a minute's advantage!" he cried.

"And well we shall need it, too!" barked Lazlo, gesturing wildly forward. "For behold, the tunnel opens up again not a hundred feet ahead of us! Who knows what new challenge awaits us there? Pray reinforcements do not lie in wait to ambush us!"

The companions staggered out of the passage and into a rather small, dark chamber. It was featureless and there didn't appear to be another way out.

They were trapped. As Lazlo and Hess began to scour the walls, looking for another tunnel opening they reckoned might have eluded their eyes on first inspection, Franklin peered back into the passageway. The smell of burnt flesh and hair wafted unpleasantly out of it, and he could make out several Mite bodies strewn across the floor, behind which were glaring, red eyes, surging forward like water through a pipe towards the helpless children. "They're charging again!" he bellowed.

"Blast!" cursed Hess, redoubling the efforts of his search. "I don't think there's any other way out of this room! We're trapped! We've got to fight our way back out through the tunnel!"

"Preposterous!" protested Lazlo. "Not even your advanced weaponry could stand against the multitude of evil that threatens to assault us now. Continue the search! Surely this chamber is not entirely bare."

Sweating out of every pore, Franklin joined Joey and Ellie as they ran their hands across the smooth, rock walls all around them. Again and again they swept the chamber, but to no avail; and the Mites were growing louder with every minute.

"Look here," exclaimed Joey suddenly. Wildly, he smacked a patch of wall in front of him. There, on its smooth surface, was a symbol etched into the rock. It was the same many-pointed star that Franklin wore as a brooch on his cloak. It had been encrusted into the wall with gold, like gems laid into a ring. Franklin drew near to it and, as if in greeting, the symbol lit up and began to pulsate with a whitish glow. A beam of light shot out from it and landed on Franklin's brooch, as if in recognition of its similarity. At once, the whitish light died and the wall before him began to shake and tremble as if the chamber were about to crumble all around them.

Slowly, the section of the wall inlaid with the symbol seemed to slide backwards, as if on some sort of track, revealing a human sized hole: a door.

"Should we go in?" asked Franklin in a panic; the Mites sounded closer than ever.

"There's no time to reason!" cried Lazlo! "Quickly! Inside!" The companions piled through the opening and, just as Franklin cast a frightened glance back to see the Mites surge forth, their slimy jaws snapping and their red eyes wild with bloodlust, the wall slid shut again and blocked out the worrisome sight. At once, Lazlo and Hess braced themselves against the wall where the opening had been (it had all but vanished now) and waited silently, certain the Mites would begin battering the barrier at any moment. But the onslaught never came. In fact, as they waited in silence, trying to keep their ragged breath quiet as their chests heaved, they realized they could no longer hear the beasts chattering and howling on the other side of the door. Either the creatures had given up the chase or the stone slab was too thick for even sound to penetrate through.

Children of the Noah

CHAPTER EIGHTEEN

THE LEGACY OF DOCTOR SPERO

Finally, Hess and Lazlo turned and sank back against the wall in relief. "I think we're safe- for now, anyway," muttered Hess. Franklin placed his ear against the wall and listened intently: nothing.

"Yes." He nodded in agreement. "I think we are. It seems like they've given up on chasing us. I don't think they saw us slip into this room; they probably figured we just vanished into thin air."

"What is this place, anyway?" asked Joey raising his lantern high.

"And how did we get in?" added Ellie, bewildered. "It seemed like that symbol recognized your brooch, Franklin."

Joey stepped forward into the darkness, the light from his lantern streaming across a small chamber which appeared to have not seen illumination in ages. There was an iron door laid into the wall on the left, hanging off its hinges as if it had been broken down long ago, and what appeared to be some sort of machine in the center of the chamber. But save these things the place was bare and plagued with cobwebs.

"Well, at least we know we've got a way out," said Lazlo, indicating the broken door. "But what have we stumbled onto here?" He pointed to the machine in the center of the room.

"I'd like to know, I really would," said Hess. "But we just haven't got any time! Whatever it is, we'll just have to leave it and let our imaginations fill in the blanks."

Sighing in disappointment, the companions shuffled past the apparatus, but were arrested when it began to suddenly glow. A beam of light shot out from within it and again landed on the clasp on Franklin's cloak. The light lingered and the machine began to purr, as if starting up from a very long period of dormancy. The air above the device began to shimmer. Like a fog rolling in, the light became misty and took on a ghostly, smoky shape. A woman seemed to materialize out of it; tall and thin, with her raven black hair pulled tightly into a bun. She wore a stern expression and was silent.

"Impossible!" exclaimed Lazlo. "Impossible! No! It cannot be! This means Old Sacks was not so wistful in his prophesizing! Why, it is Old Bess herself! It is the phantom of Old Bess! Have mercy, oh wandering spirit! Do you not remember your faithful servant Lazlo, the utility bot? Oh spare my friends and I your ghostly wrath, please?" The robot threw himself on the floor and hid his eyes from the apparition. Franklin had never seen Lazlo so affected. Then again, he noted, he'd be startled too if he saw a woman he had supposed to be dead for two centuries.

"Calm down, Lazlo!" murmured Hess, patting the robot's back. "It's not a ghost. It's a hologram, a projection, a video recording. There's nothing to be frightened of, it's only an illusion. See, the light is being projected out of that machine below the apparition. Nothing to worry about." Lazlo raised his head, but he still seemed ill at ease.

Now the hologram spoke. Its voice was not womanly or girlish; rather, it had a grave, deep tone that made the listener clench his muscles and stand at attention. It was the same voice that had played in the goggle projections, only much less pleasant in tone.

"Greetings, you brave souls who have so foolishly wandered into this hell-hole," she said. "I suppose you have discovered now that the medallion attached to the cloak I left behind is the secret key into this, my makeshift lair. And because you bear it, I assume you must be allies of the Lonies in one regard or another." She offered up a sad, little smile. How lonely she looked, a figure of light shrouded by all the dust and darkness of her forgotten chamber around her. "My name is Bess, Bess Spero."

"It is Old Bess! My goodness!" exclaimed Lazlo, bowing again.

"Wait a minute..." breathed Hess. "Wait a minute... No one told me her last name was Spero! No one told me that Old Bess was really Bess Spero! My God!"

"Why?" asked Franklin. "Who's Bess Spero? How do you know her?"

"Dr. Bess Spero was Hodel Burke's last ex-wife, I'm sorry to say," replied Hess, disbelief still palpable in his voice. "And not just any ex-wife either. She was the one he really loved, at least that's what he told me. She was the 'one that got away'. He'd often go on and on about how much of a genius she was, smarter than him, even."

"No way," whispered the children.

Now, the apparition spoke again. "Worry not, friends, for I am indeed gone from this place; the figure you look upon now is but a recording of my last living moments in this, the year 3,025. I suppose I ought to explain, and to apologize as well, if you are Lonies. Before the apocalypse, before the Bhasma

Cloud arrived and ravaged this planet to near extinction, I was a scientist. I studied with the finest minds, learning all that I could about the secrets of the universe, space, and time. In fact, I fell in love with one of these minds: the brilliant Dr. Hodel Burke. While our romance did not last, and ended in a way I'd rather not describe here, I will not let any of that stop me from admitting to you his genius. Though few believed him, he predicted the apocalypse and tried to warn the peoples of this ignorant planet about it. I am ashamed to admit that even I, a scientific peer of his despite our ill standing, would not believe his wild claims at first. But as the cloud drew nearer, he and I commiserated and I relented. Armageddon was certain!

"But Burke, like always, had a plan. I kick myself now for calling him a fool and condemning his scheme, no matter how bizarre it seemed. It was his intent to utilize an artifact that had been in my family's possession for as long as anyone can remember. He intended to use this artifact to send his lab assistant back in time. Of all the people he could have chosen, God knows why he chose that strange young boy. While the time travel aspect of this plan seemed farfetched enough, its second stage was even more foolhardy. It was Burke's idea to have the boy retrieve some manner of weapon from a strange, nameless civilization of that past that had gone extinct millennia ago. For whatever reason, Burke believed this weapon was the one and only key to defeating the Bhasma Cloud. I suppose he reckoned the boy would bring it back to him, and he'd single handedly save the world with it. Despite how pressing the situation was, I'm ashamed to say I laughed in his face and called him a crackpot, chiding him for such silly, impossible notions.

"Leaving Burke to his schemes and abandoning the poor man, I set out to provide another solution for the human population; one that looked not to the past for help, but to the future. Utilizing an alchemical recipe, one that had been passed down through my family (along with the artifact Burke borrowed) for centuries, I manufactured a material that I thought would be able to withstand the Bhasma Cloud's wrath, the first of its kind, and used it to construct a sanctuary, the fortress of the Lonies, where some souls would be safe, spared Armageddon. I would have made more, but manufacturing the material drained my finances and at that point, as the Bhasma Cloud loomed just above the atmosphere, the industrial world was in too much of a panic to construct anything useful. And so it was only a handful of souls were saved, sequestered away inside my sanctuary here in New Hollow. Just as I was about to seal the gates shut and wait out the storm, I managed to record this footage of the dread cloud as it approached the city."

Now, the image of Spero wavered and began to change. In her place appeared a city, gleaming and tall in the sunlight. Though it was strange and futuristic in its appearance, Franklin was sure it was New Hollow. The image was trembling and quaking as a rumbling noise played out, the sound of the sewer systems collapsing beneath the urban sprawl as earth tremors shook the ground.

Like an angry specter, a black cloud loomed up on the horizon. It was immense and formless, billowing out in every direction with dark plumes of smoke. It rolled across the land like a steamroller, obliterating whatever stood in its way. Franklin was immediately reminded of those pictures he had seen of the dust cloud on Black Sunday in his history textbooks, the same dust cloud which had nearly wiped away Middle America in the 1930s. The storm thundered on, drawing nearer the city, blasts of crimson lightning crackling down from inside of it and ravaging the country below.

The cloud began to boom with a hateful voice, one that belched out with hatred and terror. "Bhasma! Bhasma!" it seemed to screech, drowning out the blood curdling screams of the people below it. So that was how it had come by its name. Bhasma was no nonsensical moniker invented by the Mites. Not only had the dread storm thundered down onto the planet, it had announced its presence as it came! Now, the image was consumed by the cloud and suffocated in its unbreakable blackness. With a hiss of static, the terrible scene fizzled away and Bess Spero reappeared in its place.

Franklin realized his eyes had begun to water; though he had already viewed the aftermath of the cloud's devastation in several forms, this was the first time he had laid eyes on the immensity of its terror and hatred as it had come to earth. He was afraid. He was angry. And above all, his heart was sick and sad; those millions of screams had been snuffed out as suddenly as candles left open to a wind. Tears began to roll down his cheeks. He glanced at Joey, who looked equally disturbed, but when he glanced to Ellie, all he beheld in her expression was anger, and a sort of grim determination. She clenched her fists and gritted her teeth; some sort of invisible switch had been flipped in her mind.

"As you can see," continued the holographic doctor, "this calamity came on the world like nothing anyone could have imagined, save my former husband- poor man. This can be no work of God, but a cosmic evil so far gone from human imagining that it makes my head reel even to think about it. How could humanity possibly hope to stand against such chaos, such maelstrom, such arbitrary and wanton hate and destruction? How? Though I may have thought Burke's plan ridiculous when he told it to me, as that cloud rampaged across the horizon, any alternative, even Burke's, seemed a paradise when compared to such hell on earth. As the doors of the sanctuary slid shut in front of me and I waited with the group of people who would become the Lonies for the cloud's onslaught to pass, I cursed my narrow mindedness and wept for Burke. To this day, I am uncertain whether or not his plan was successful; but, given these bleak and weary surroundings, I am afraid the poor man failed."

Hess could not help but smile beneath his visor; though Spero didn't know it, Burke's plan was running its course right before her long dead eyes. He found a certain comfort in this thought.

"But I had to move on, had to move forward," said Old Bess's apparition. "Burke had chosen his path just as I had chosen mine. These people, these lonely, frightened people, were to be my responsibility now. Together we formed a tribe, a sort of coalition that we hoped could rekindle the flame of life and civilization in the world. I had planted a garden, a project I called the Eden Initiative, which everyday we nurtured. Things seemed happy and prosperous; we even stood against those awful creatures that emerged from holes in the ground, chanting the storm's name. They have come to be known as the Bhasmites. While I am still not sure what they are, I am certain they are a wicked, heartless lot and will never prove good to the restoration of this earth. The Lonies seemed to have a chance at our hopeless mission, at least for a little while. But as the years drew on and water and food became scarce, the Lonies began to battle amongst themselves, splitting into factions and roping off territory to call 'their own'. When we were united, the Mites had not troubled us much. Recently, however, in our division, the creatures nearly overwhelmed our meager forces time and time again. No matter how much the council and I pleaded with the people, they would not come together again. I realize, now, this is the same trouble Burke had all those years ago. He begged the planet to unite under one banner and counter an evil which could only possibly be opposed by the might of all the human peoples combined, but he was ignored.

"I decided that it was time for the most drastic of measures. Mankind had to be tested! Whereas my ex-husband had to contend with the population of the entire world, a number in the billions, I had a much smaller community to deal with. And it is easy to make powerful statements when everyone knows who you are. If they proved unworthy to inherit the earth and simply continued to dole out the sins of their fathers, I decided the planet was better off without them. I sealed away the garden, I sealed away my Eden Initiative and with it, the Lonies' only chance at repopulation. I promised them the seal would remain tightly shut for three hundred years, and so it will! When that time has passed, the garden will open up again. If there are Lonies still living, if there are human beings to greet it, then man will walk the earth once more and thrive. If not, if they end up killing off one another like they have been recently, then the garden's seeds will have to spread by the wind alone and give life to the planet as it had been given the first time: by the hand of God and not man. This was my decision, and still I stand by it. I wonder how the planet will fare.

"In any case, I sequestered myself away from my former tribe, down here where the Mites live. I have come here in my self-exile to study the past and contemplate Burke's plans whilst seeking a way to perhaps cure these strange Bhasmites of their terrible affliction. Though Burke left me few resources to work with, and the cloud destroyed many of them, I still have managed to maintain enough of his papers and files to better understand his scheme. It seems plausible, now after I have poured over his musings again and again, that an ancient civilization did indeed do battle with the Bhasma Cloud 6,000 years ago! In fact, I remember my great grandmother telling me similar legends. She said a malevolent demon that had come from the skies had plagued our ancestors, a people long swallowed up by the seas of time. At first, I thought her tales simply myths, the rants of an old woman nostalgic for her ancestry. But the more I recalled them, and the more I compared them to Burke's notes, I began to realize perhaps my old Great Grandmother, God rest her soul, had not been so imaginative as I thought.

"My ancestry, my long reaching lineage, is well recorded and easily readable. With the technology of our time, families have traced their genealogy back to ancient Egypt and even Mesopotamia without issue. But the Spero history suddenly becomes misty and difficult to read when I trace it too far back, to around the epoch Burke was so fixated upon. Though I know I sound foolish, insane even, I am convinced my ancestors are those same people who did battle with the Bhasma Cloud all those many thousands of years ago. What few things my Great Grandmother left me, she informed me were the treasures of our ancestors, and the cloak which I am sure my viewer now wears is among them."

Franklin looked down at the garment, suddenly nervous to be wearing something so important and so ancient.

"Alas, it can do me no good now!" she lamented. "But I have left it to the Lonies to keep safe in the hopes that someday perhaps someone will find a better use for it. Perhaps it can aid in completing Burke's plan; surely it has some relation to those long forgotten people who mastered the secret to defeating Armageddon! Though I have abandoned them in the hopes it would force them to unite under the common banner of humanity, I believe there is a great deal of hope for the Lonies yet! If they can preserve that garden and peace amongst themselves along with it, perhaps the planet has a chance too. Who knows? You, my visitors, are the new hope for the world; whatever era you might belong to. Remember well the responsibility that man has to the soil- that is, to plant seeds in it so that flowers will continue to blossom and trees to grow tall.

"Now, I suppose you are wondering what is to become of me! Or perhaps that is a selfish thought." Spero smiled sadly. "I have forsaken the Lonies and cannot return to them. Therefore, I have come down here, to the place known as the Well. Though I've lived with caution as quietly as I could, my presence has not gone unnoticed by the Mites. Eventually, they discovered my lair and just yesterday they began to batter down the my iron door, here." She indicated the solitary door in the left of the chamber. "I hear its hinges creaking, and soon they will be upon me. The typical Mite is much too small to do much damage to this iron door, but I hear thunderous steps booming through the tunnels. I believe Cherophobe himself comes here to challenge me. I have vaporized all my possessions so the Mites will not abuse them; luckily, the cloak and brooch are still secure on the surface with my people.

"I have one last statement to make. In fact, it is the real reason I have left behind this recording." The holographic woman undid her hair and it fell about her shoulders. She smiled sadly. "I have spoken to you of my family, of my heritage. I have told you that I believe my genealogy to be intertwined with that lost civilization which fascinated Burke so. I have told you I inherited a chemical recipe from my ancestors with which I constructed the sanctuary above and spared the Lonies from Armageddon. I have told you of the cloak and brooch passed down from one generation to the next, the same cloak and brooch which acted as a key and allowed you into my chamber here. But there is one thing that has always been kept secret by my family. It is a phrase only uttered by those individuals of the Spero bloodline, and only uttered in secret, quiet places. I have never really known what it means, but I've kept it a closely guarded secret just like generations of Speros me did before me. When I was small, my Great Grandmother used to whisper it to me each night before I went to sleep. '**There is another**,' she would say. I often asked her what it meant, but every time she said she did not know, only that she knew I ought to keep it secret just like my ancestors had for millennia. '**There is another**.' Those words echo with me, even now. Perhaps they are just nonsense, the verse of a long forgotten nursery rhyme, but they are all that remains of my family, of my heritage. I tell you this because I suppose there is no longer any reason for keeping it a secret. "

Now, the recorded sounds of the door being hammered against grew louder. Spero looked back towards it and sighed. "My time has come. Would that I could see the light of day and the green of trees one more time. We must hope for everything. Farewell, my visitors, and goodbye. Forever." The sound of the door breaking in penetrated the projection, Spero closed her eyes, and the image fizzled away.

The companions were left in stunned silence, their mouths agape, hardly daring to breathe. In an instant, Bess Spero, that legendary figure the Lonies held so dear, had come into their lives and then exited out of them, like a ghost.

Lazlo held his head in his hands. "To think poor Old Bess met her fate at the hands of those brutes! Oh, it is a tragedy too terrible to imagine. But I suppose most Lonies have died that way. How pitiable. How sad."

"Franklin," said Hess suddenly. "Hold still a second, will

you?" Hess held the Rok Counter up to Franklin's cloak, hovering it over the brooch. "Dr. Spero said she believed this cloak to have been passed down from that same civilization in 3,000 BC that we're supposed to be locating." The Rok Counter beeped. "And I think she's right. It seems this cape has the same traces of radiation on it that the artifact powering the Noah does. My God. Bess Spero is just as mixed up in this whole mess as we are."

"Well, not anymore. She's dead," said Joey somewhat bluntly.

"She faced her death with such calm, so far as I could see," added Ellie. "She didn't even flinch! Imagine knowing you're about to be torn to shreds by monsters and still keeping your voice so steady and your eyes so dry."

"But why?" asked Lazlo, still kneeling on the floor. "Why did she record all of this just before her death."

Hess scratched at his helmet. "I reckon she recorded it to explain why she did what she did, leaving the Lonies and all. And she wanted to tell the world in some way or another about her discovery regarding the ancient civilization and how it correlated to Burke's work. I guess she wanted future generations to be able to use that information in whatever way they could. And now we've got the cloak! Another artifact of those lost people. Hey, who knows, if we ever get where we're going, that cape might just come in handy someday."

"Old Bess would have wanted it that way," said Lazlo. "I am sure she wouldn't have wanted such a treasure to be wasted away, let us see that it serves this journey well." He paused, then. "I should like to give my old master a proper farewell, a proper funeral and burial rights, you know? But I'm afraid there's not a trace of the poor woman to be found in this dismal hole. How on earth did she live so long in an empty place like this, I wonder."

"She said she burned what remained of her possessions," recalled Hess. "I don't think there's really anything left to bury. And I hate to be so pushy, Lazlo, but the clock is ticking and we've still got to find the thruster core. We should keep moving."

"Of course," replied Lazlo. "Sentimentality is a machine's greatest flaw, I'm sorry to say, and I am cursed with it. My design intends for my being to be the picture of efficiency, but sometimes these bothersome emotions plague my mind and trouble my feet to cease their forward movement. Forgive me."

"Wait!" said Joey. "We can't be going out through that door! No way!"

"Why not?" asked Ellie.

"You heard Spero! That's where the Mites came through when they broke in. We can't go that way."

"That was almost two hundred years ago, Joseph," said Franklin, patting his friend on the back. "I'm sure the Mites have forgotten about it by now. This room looks like it's gone untouched for ages."

"Yes," agreed Hess. "And we're certainly not going out the way we came. We know for a fact that direction is crawling with monsters. Come on!" He set off at trot towards the door. "We're wasting precious time!"

Not so eagerly, the companions filed out of the lonely room and into another passageway, much like the ones they had passed through before; Lazlo was last in line. The robot stopped and turned his head, casting a backward glance at the room where Bess Spero had taken her last few breaths. "Goodbye, Miss Bess," he said sadly, if a robot can sound sad at all. His emerald eyes glittered in the darkness like two far-off, green stars. "I must go towards the future now, as you once did - and perhaps towards the past. Who knows? I hope that one day you and I shall meet once again and I will know you as you were: a brave, strong woman determined not only to lead humanity, but to better it in the process. Worry not, my dear leader, for I will keep the details of your end from the Lonies. I will tell them I have met with the spirit of Old Bess, a spirit who shines like the sun, even in the midst of all this gloom. I will tell them you died a peaceful death, but that your soul has become eternal and always it will guide them through the night. This will give the Lonies hope, for they need it now more than ever. Would you have wanted them to hope? Would you have wanted them to prevail, my master?"

His eyes began to dim now. "Farewell, Old Bess. Goodbye, my mother. It's time to go." Lazlo turned to face the machine where Spero had appeared to them. He bowed low, and remained bent for some time. Clenching his fists and turning his head forward, the robot marched on and rejoined the group. Franklin felt as if his heart was about to break; he could hardly imagine saying such a goodbye to his mother, and pushed the thought out of his head at once. He glanced at Ellie. While her teeth were still gritted in grim determination, her eyes had gone soft. She reached and out squeezed Franklin's hand for a brief moment, then proceeded to the back of the line where she hugged Lazlo. Though at first the robot's arms remained stationary at his sides, Ellie's embrace persisted and he eventually wrapped his arms around her in return.

"Thank you, Miss Mars," he barely managed to utter as his voice seemed to crack. "I can never thank you enough for all you've done. You are truly my angel."

Franklin could not help but to think to himself of Bess Spero's last words. Certainly all that she had said about the Lonies and Dr. Burke was important, but he felt something else she had mentioned was more crucial than anything, though he did not know why. **'There is another,'** he thought to himself, her soft words ringing in his head. What on earth could she have meant? It was, apparently, something her family had been saying in secret for thousands and thousands of years. But what did it mean? He shrugged silently to himself. Perhaps he would never find out.

The companions marched on and left the lonely place of dying behind them.

Children of the Noah

CHAPTER NINETEEN

HIRUDO MEDICINALIS

The friends meandered further into the tunnel as it wound through the black, wet rock. This passage was not so straight and it curved and twisted like an aggravated snake.

Time was wearing on and Franklin was sure at least half of the day had passed. His heart began to beat a bit faster as he imagined returning to a closed gate and being trapped in the Well forever, like Old Bess Spero had been. "We should pick up the pace," he stammered nervously. "I don't think we've got that much time left, and there's still the return trip to think of."

At his request, their step quickened and they began to jog through the stony corridor. As they went on, a truly foul stench began to pervade the passageway, smothering them till at last Joey, who had a slight case of asthma, began to croak and cough. Soon, Franklin joined him and even Ellie gagged once or twice. Hess and Lazlo, one being quite snug inside a suit of armor and the other not really needing oxygen in the first place, didn't much notice.

They soon stumbled upon the source of the miserable

odor. Exiting out of the tunnel they came into an open space. Franklin could just barely spy another passageway set into the wall opposite the one they had emerged out of, but it was hundreds of feet away and only just dimly visible in the gloom. It was not their destination, however, that drew his wandering eye.

In front of them, not ten feet away, was a mire of the black ooze, a stagnant swamp of the stuff that covered every inch of ground they could see. Every so often, a bubble would rise up out of the sludge, hover a few feet into the air, and burst with a resounding 'plop' that punctured the silence of the cavern. The area was positively drenched with the hideous stench; Franklin could hardly breathe.

"It's pooled!" declared Joey. He had raced up to the bog's edge, intrigued as always. "Its source must have been cut off a while ago, because it's completely still now. Stagnant bodies of liquid like this are a perfect breeding ground for all sorts of microbes and fungi; real strange sorts of life that can live without air or light. The kind of stuff you find way down at the bottom of an ocean or in a real muddy swamp. I was hoping we'd see something like this!"

"Be careful, Joseph! Get away from there!" called Franklin as the curious boy reached down to dip his finger into the mud.

"Why, Franny? Whatsamatter?" His hand had stopped mid reach, quivering with excitement.

"Just get away from the edge, okay? I'm not sure what it is, but this place gives me a rotten feeling." The hairs on the back of Franklin's neck were standing at attention.

"Franklin's right. Just get back for a moment, Joey," ordered Hess. "Now let me see." He switched on the flashlight fixed to his wrist and cast its beam up and down the bank of the mire. It seemed to travel on indefinitely in either direction and they could make out no bridges or dry spots to cross. Now, Hess fixed the beam of light on the opposite bank and peered at the passageway which awaited them on the other side of the bog. "Well," he muttered. "There doesn't seem to be any way across or over the swamp, so that leaves only one option-" Franklin cringed and moaned silently in his head as Hess finished his sentence, "we've got to go through it."

Ellie wrinkled her nose. "I thought Lazlo said we shouldn't be touching this stuff."

"I suppose it is a risk we will have to accept if Mr. Hess thinks this is the only way," said Lazlo.

Joey looked up at Franklin and frowned. "You're as white as a sheet, Franklin. Oh God, you're not going to pull this again, are you?"

Franklin didn't answer.

"Pull what?" asked Ellie, glancing at Franklin and chuckling, amused at his ghastly expression.

Joey sighed. "Franny's always had a thing about deep water. He'd never go very far out when we went swimming in the ocean. He even stays in the shallow ends of swimming pools when he can."

"Why's that?" The girl was intrigued.

"We don't really know," admitted Joey. "We tried to psycho-analyze him once, but it didn't really work. We think it might be because he accidentally watched one of those shark movies when he was a little kid. But it's not just sharks. He's afraid of whales, dolphins, even some big fish we pull out of the marsh give him the heebie-jeebies."

Ellie began to giggle. Now Franklin's cheeks began to complement his white face as they began to blush a deep, scarlet red. His eyes were still transfixed on the swamp.

"But this doesn't look that deep!" laughed the girl. "Your feet will be touching the bottom the whole time, Franklin. Come on, don't be such a baby!"

With that, she marched forward and stepped into the bog, splashing into the thick sludge and trudging sternly forward. Reluctantly, the rest followed, and soon they were wading knee deep. Whereas Franklin had expected the muck to be clammy and cool, it was surprisingly warm, a fact that disturbed him more than pleasantly surprised him; there was something very alive about this sludge and he didn't like it.

Step by step it came up to his ankles, his knees, and finally all the way up to his waist. Silently, he swore to himself that he would burn his trousers when he got the chance; surely, they would never smell right again. His heart sank as he looked forward to see the others up to their chests in the stuff, their arms outstretched and slogging forward as slowly as if they were wading through custard. He stopped then and stood still, unwilling to go any further.

Joey turned and scowled. "C'mon Franny!" he pleaded. "It's just like the marsh mud! We're nearly there."

"It isn't like marsh mud and you know it, Joseph!" exclaimed Franklin. "Something isn't right about this stuff. I've got a very bad feeling, I'm shaking all over."

Now it was Hess's turn to chide the boy. "Of all the things we've encountered down here, I think this is the least of our worries. I know it doesn't smell very good, and maybe you've got a thing about deep water-- but come on! Time's a wasting! Do you need Lazlo to carry you or somethi-" Hess couldn't finish, his attention had been drawn to a ripple in the ooze a few feet away from him. He stared at it intently for a moment, and then sighed in relief. "Just a bubble," he muttered.

Without warning, he yelped suddenly and disappeared beneath the surface of the sludge, as if sucked under by an unseen riptide. At once, the muck above where he had vanished into returned to its placid state, as if no one had been standing there in the first place.

The children and Lazlo stared, dumbfounded. "Hess?" demanded Ellie into the empty air. "Hess?"

"A sinkhole, I'd guess!" declared Lazlo! "I'd best fetch him out of it"

As the robot was about to dive into the sludge after their lost companion, Hess popped back up like a bobber a few yards from where he had vanished. He clawed at the air as again he was dragged down into the swamp, but slowly this time. He was struggling against something just beneath the surface; and it was something strong too (strong enough to contend even with the Hess suit's nearly superhuman strength.)

"Run!" he managed to bellow. Suddenly, a lithe black form shot up out of the liquid beneath him, wriggled in the air like a gigantic earthworm for a moment, and then tackled him, knocking him back under the ooze.

"What in the hell was that?" cried Ellie.

"There is no time!" barked Lazlo! "You heard him, children: run! I will aid him, you all escape to the other bank!"

Though Franklin was shaking badly now and would rather have turned back and raced to the bank from where they had come, Joey and Ellie seized him by his shoulders and dragged him forward.

Lazlo began to wade out, now, casting his arms from side to side in a blind attempt to locate Hess, but it wasn't long before the armored boy resurfaced again, thrashing violently. The black form, which was about as wide as Franklin was, and at least as long as a canoe from end to end, was coiled around Hess like a snake. It slammed its head, which was black and featureless, against his helmet again and again, as if trying to puncture through his armor, but to no avail.

"I know what that is!" shouted Joey as they trudged forward at a sickeningly slow pace. "Hirudo medicinalis!"

"Hirudo what?" demanded Franklin, not daring to look over his shoulder at the commotion behind them.

"A leech! It's a leech!" Joey shrieked. Franklin's stomach nearly dropped down out of his body and into the ooze.

"That's no leech!" argued the girl as both of them dragged Franklin on. "Leeches are barely bigger than my finger!"

"It is too a leech," protested Joey. "Look at it. It's long and black, featureless, and it's got some sort sucker it keeps trying to stick into Hess, but it's not working thanks to his armor, luckily! No eyes, no nothing! Like a snake without the charm! A gigantic leech."

Franklin was about to be sick. A leech as long and big as a porpoise? No thank you, he thought, and quickened his pace through the dense mud.

Lazlo reached out and grabbed at the creature with the intent to pull it off of the struggling Hess, but his metal hands slipped right off the beast's slick and oily body as it convulsed and writhed in his feeble grasp. Lazlo shrugged and instead seized the worm by its narrower end, the end accosting Hess, and began to strike it again and again with a fist that could shatter bricks. With a hideous hiss and a shriek, the creature slithered back into the ooze and disappeared, abandoning its metal and unappetizing prey. Lazlo helped Hess up out of the sludge and to his feet, though he was still chest deep in the stuff.

"Thank God for this suit," the boy panted. "I'd have drowned, or worse, been sucked dry without it."

Lazlo did not share his relieved tone. "Quickly, Master Hess!" he cried out. "This monster has fled us metal fellows and gone to seek out more fleshy folk!" As if cued by the robot's warning, something wet and smooth grazed Franklin's leg as it slithered by him deep beneath the surface.

"Oh God," he gasped. "Why the hell did I ever agree to any of this nonsense? It's got me! It's got me!" The supersized leech wrapped around his leg now and began to squeeze, constricting his blood flow and sending shivers up and down his spine. He stumbled and fell forward, out of Joey and Ellie's grasp. His face slammed straight into the slime and he recoiled up out of it, coughing and sputtering.

As he knelt there in the muck, eyes level with its surface, the sludge in front of his nose rippled and the leech's featureless, black head rose slowly out of it, twisting and writhing in the air like something out of a nightmare.

It paused and bobbed back and forth for a moment; if it had any eyes, Franklin would have been certain it was inspecting him with them. It hissed slowly, as if scenting the air, and then its face changed. Where there had been naught but slimy, inky blackness, there opened up a hole and a long, grey proboscis slithered out of it, coming very near Franklin's face. At the end of the awful appendage were dozens of rows of triangular fangs; all-facing inward towards what Franklin was sure was the creature's gaping, hungry gullet.

It hissed again and screeched, diving forward and drawing

Franklin toward it simultaneously with its tail still wrapped tightly around his leg. Had he not ducked and wriggled under the creature's lunging, serpentine form, Franklin was quite sure the creature would have taken his entire head into its mouth and sunk its immense teeth deep into his fleshy neck. But he just barely avoided the attack and soon found himself entangled with the worm.

It lunged again, but this time Ellie brought her club smashing down onto its head and drove it deep into the sludge. Its grip on Franklin's leg slackened, suddenly, and it slithered away into the dank muck, vanishing again.

As Joey helped Franklin to his feet and began to wipe the ooze from his hair and face, Ellie chuckled victoriously. "I guess the fleshy folk are just as difficult to suck dry as the metal ones! We certainly showed that slug that we're filled with tougher stuff than blood."

By this time, Hess and Lazlo had made their way back to the children and they all regrouped. "You all right, Franklin?" asked Hess. Though he was pale as a ghost and couldn't keep his hands from shaking madly, the boy nodded; he had avoided any serious harm. "Good," said Hess. "Now I think that thing's retreated. Let's get to the other bank. Pronto."

As they began to trudge again, something popped into Joey's head, something he had read once in a nature magazine. "Did you say it retreated, Hess?" The armored boy nodded. "I wouldn't be so sure. Maybe it's retreated for now, but it might be back. I guess we should be glad there's not more than one. Leeches have chemosensory organs and they can detect blood in the water. But then again, no one's bleeding so-"

"Uh, Joey," said Ellie nervously, tugging at his arm and gesturing to Franklin. There, under the boy's burgundy cloak Franklin's shirt was wet with a crimson stain. Franklin looked down and groaned.

"The cuts from yesterday must have opened up again with all the commotion!" he whimpered. "Oh God!"

"There's no need to fret!" declared Lazlo. "Come, we're still nearly neck deep in this filth. Let's hurry on and be done with it!" And so they did, rushing forward through the dense sludge as fast as they could push their weary legs. And they came very near the bank too, the filth receding so that it was only about waist deep now, but the rest of the crossing was not to be any easier.

Like a many-headed hydra, several more leeches now rose up out of the sludge in front of them, their mucus coated forms gleaming. They thrashed and squirmed in the air, wavering before their assault, and then lunged forward all at once. The children were better prepared this time, however, and beat the slugs back with their clubs, raining blow after blow down upon the hideous worms. But to their horror, several more of the slimy creatures slithered in between their legs and began to constrict them, dragging them towards the gaping jowls of their lunging, surface faring cousins. They were overwhelmed.

Franklin took a deep and desperate gulp of air as he felt the leech beneath him tighten its grip about his leg and jerk violently, dragging him beneath the surface as suddenly as a fish devours an unsuspecting mosquito.

Everything went black. His nose, mouth, and ears were immediately clogged with the muck and he began to choke, though he couldn't even hear his own helpless coughs. Despite the flurry of activity all around him, it was silent and still below the surface of the slime. Though he struggled and writhed in the beast's awful grip, it simply wound its way further up his body, slithering ever nearer his neck.

Like a boa constrictor, the leech had clamped his arms to his sides and squeezed his legs so tightly together he felt as if they were going to snap. His chest began to heave; though there wasn't any air to breathe suspended in the mud like he was, the creature had wound about his torso so tightly he felt his ribs beginning to tremble under the pressure.

'So this is how you die, Franklin Freeman?' he thought in a panic. 'Trapped three feet under the mud, squeezed and suffocated slowly to death by a gigantic leech straight out of hell? Sounds more like something Joey would've gotten himself into one day, not you! I always imagined you just falling off a ladder or something boring like that. Oh well, if this really is the end, might as well give it another go, just so you can say you did.'

Unwilling to resign and accept his death just yet, Franklin began to struggle and wriggle violently in the worm's hold, kicking and striking out with all his might. But the leech's grip was not to be undone. Now, the helpless boy felt the life draining out of him; he was slowly being crushed to death, he knew. But the wicked slug had a less merciful plan in mind and slithered its head up his chest, its fangs protruding. Just as it was about to sink its vampire-like teeth into Franklin's neck and suck every last drop of blood out of him, a great metal hand punctured the surface of the swamp above and dove down, strangling the leech by the neck and yanking it off the dying boy. Another metal hand shot down and dragged Franklin back up to air.

Coughing and sputtering, Franklin began to hack up all the sludge that had been clogging his throat, allowing himself deep and rasping breaths into his finally unrestricted chest. His eyes fluttered open, though they were still caked with muck. There he beheld Lazlo, standing like Heracles with the leech that had accosted him strangled in his metal grip.

Without missing a beat, the robot began to squeeze the worm till at last it squealed and emptied fourth all its innards out of its mouth and into the sludge like a tube of toothpaste squeezed too hard near the cap. It was utterly beaten and hung loose now in the automaton's grasp like a deflated balloon. Lazlo's emerald eyes burned now with fierceness Franklin had never seen before.

"Are you alright, my child?" asked Lazlo with a voice that belied his smoldering rage. "You were under for some time; I feared the worst!"

"You saved me," Franklin managed to sputter in between ragged gasps. "You saved me. Thank you. Thank you. I was almost a goner.

"As I have said before, I am only returning the favor!"

exclaimed Lazlo. "Come now and stay close to me! More of the serpents have swum up from their deep lairs to join their compatriots in your absence. The battle rages on."

Lazlo was right: Joey and Ellie were hunkered beneath Hess, clinging to his metal torso and striking out with their clubs as an umbrella of slimy, tendril-like leeches descended on the armored boy. Though he had one in each hand, there were simply too many and they were rapidly wriggling their way down his armor, ignoring him entirely, toward where the blood filled children waited.

Franklin tried to step forward but his chest seized up and pain shot into his back and throat. "Lazlo," he barely managed to say, wincing and doubling over. "I... I can't... Don't leave me..." Like a protective mother ape, the mighty robot swung Franklin up onto his back where the boy clung on for dear life.

"Stay there, where I can keep an eye on you, Master Freeman!" cried Lazlo, rushing forward to rejoin the fray. "Keep your club at hand; these beasties leap up out of the mud! One could very well come straight for you!" And so the leeches did, propelling up out of the slime like Franklin had seen great white sharks do in a documentary about South African oceans he had been forced to watch for a science project; an entirely unpleasant motion picture. But, waving his club out like there was no tomorrow, Franklin managed to beat them away as Lazlo hammered a path back to their companions.

Finally, all five of them were reunited and, still waist deep in the muck, they formed a sort of chain (the children in between Hess and Lazlo) and faced the vampire worms together, But it was no use: for each slug they smote, at least two more writhed up to take its place. They could no longer see the sludge's surface around them; instead only a mass of wriggling, mucus covered leeches thrashing about, lunging for any inch of flesh they could locate.

"This is bad!" screamed Ellie. "Any bright ideas, Hess?"

She's asking the wrong person, Franklin thought. "Joey!" he cried out. "What do we do?"

"Let me think! Let me think!" barked the boy, wiping filth away from his forehead with one hand and walloping a leech with his club in the other. "Wait a second! I've got it! I've got it! In the old days, when doctors used to use to have leeches suck onto people to let their blood or whatever, sometimes the leeches would bury their heads too deep into the skin and they couldn't pull them off using just their hands!"

"So?" demanded Ellie. "These things haven't gotten that far... yet!" She swatted one away, smashing its three fangs into bits with her club.

"So-" continued Joey, "-instead of using their fingers to pry the leeches off, doctors used to just light a match right near the little buggers' heads. They'd pop right off; leeches hate flames, I guess. Now if only we had a match! I might have an old lighter down in my pocket somewhere from when we built that model rocket... Franny, hold my club while I look!"

"Joey!" barked Hess. "I think I've got this one. I don't know why I didn't try this earlier! Mozi Box, can you hear me?"

Even through the wriggling mass of tendrils laced across Hess's chest, Franklin could see the cheerful computer screen light up in response. "Shall we give it to them, Mr. Hess?" squealed the computer.

"Everything we've got!" growled the boy from beneath his helmet. "Everyone! Duck!" Lazlo flung himself over the children and hunkered down with them as flames erupted from Hess's wrists and roared out across the surface of the muck, incinerating the thrashing beasts like they were kindling at a bonfire. They began to hiss and shriek, fleeing before the inferno, but the majority of them could not escape Hess's fiery wrath. They were engulfed with flames and plunged deep into the muck, writhing as they burned.

"Quickly!" yelled the armored boy. "While we've got them on the run, now! Quickly!" They scrambled forward and after what seemed like an eternity of trudging nervously on, they clambered up onto the bank and dragged themselves onto dry land, panting. Glancing back, Franklin could see the battleground they had emerged from: the surface of the slime was charred and some of it still burning, dotted with the corpses of burnt leeches floating slowly to the surface from the bottom where they had died. Apparently, the flame had not been extinguished beneath the muck and had only burned on. Fitting, thought Franklin, for such a terrible bunch of beasts.

"Whatever creatures are these," muttered Lazlo grimly, "they are born out of Bhasma's malignance, I am sure, like the Mites. It appears their bloodlust knows no bounds: behold!" He pointed into the swamp where the surviving leeches had begun to feed on their dead and injured compatriots. Those unlucky worms which had not yet died but now were slowly being sucked to death by their former allies let out the most bloodcurdling and pitiable screams one could imagine; Franklin was glad his ears were still mostly clogged with mud.

When Ellie and Joey had regained their breath, they knelt by Franklin. "You're a mess, Franny," said Joey.

"Yes, you certainly are. Are you alright?" asked Ellie, wiping mud away from his forehead and eyelashes.

"I guess so. The cuts opened back up and that thing squeezed me pretty tight, though; I thought I was going to die!" Franklin heaved a heavy sigh, reveling in his freedom from both the sludge and the leeches, too. "Why is it me who always gets whacked around so bad?"

"Because if it wasn't you it would be Joey or me," laughed Ellie. "Hess and Lazlo certainly aren't going to get hurt with their three-inch-thick metal skins."

Joey nodded. "I'm beginning to realize they've been acting as our babysitters. Maybe we shouldn't have come down here at all! We're just too fragile for a place like this. Maybe we should've never left the Noah in the first place!"

"Master Jensen!" exclaimed Lazlo, who had been listening. "Pardon me, but that's nonsense! It was you, not Mr. Hess or I, who gave us a method to defeat those malicious beasts! I certainly would have never thought to use fire against such wet creatures, but your brilliant mind managed to manufacture a brilliant solution to use against them. You have saved me again, I think, and I thank you for it."

"Yeah, Joey. That was some quick thinking. You saved our hides," admitted Hess. "How can we repay you?"

Joey was not one to turn down offers like that. "Well, if you really feel that indebted... You could wade back out there and snag one of those leech corpses for me; I'd like to take a closer look at it."

"Forget it," mumbled Hess, and returned to wiping mud from his suit.

"Can you stand, Franklin?" Ellie slid her arm under his head and propped it up. He coughed, hacking out another glob of the ooze.

"Yes," he sputtered. "I think I can." Though his knees knocked and his ankles felt like jelly, with the help of his friends, Franklin dragged himself to his feet and took in a great breath of air, simply happy to be alive.

"Your wounds have closed back up, Franny," said Joey. "I'd offer to help clean you up some more, but I think you got it worst than the rest of us. It'll take quite a few showers to get you good and truly clean." Joey was right: whereas the rest of them were only drenched with slime from the waist down, Franklin was positively caked with it, his skin dyed nearly grey by the stuff. It had already crusted over in his hair and eyelashes, and some of it even squelched around in his trousers (not a pleasant feeling). The only part of him that had remained clean was the cloak, which was entirely muck-free and still looked brand new.

Franklin shrugged and shook his head: only a few days ago he had been sitting in his Algebra final and wondering why nothing exciting ever happened.

CHAPTER TWENTY

A DOVE IN THE DARK

"If everyone's okay, I think we should keep moving," said Hess, straightening and heading for the tunnel entrance. "It's a miracle the Mites didn't hear us with all that screaming and commotion, and if they did I'd rather not give them the chance to find us here. Being trapped between a lake full of leeches and a horde of angry Mites does not sound like the ideal situation to be in when you're on the clock."

"Or...like...ever," mused Ellie and followed him, helping Franklin along.

The companions filed one by one into this new tunnel and followed along its meandering path for some time, their wet feet and pants sloshing noisily, till at last they came to a spot where the tunnel split into three separate passageways. Hess held up the Rok counter, but it could not seem to decide which direction they ought to head in and simply beeped on and off for a while.

"Well, the thruster core is definitely down one of these ways," he murmured. "The question is, which one?"

"I'm afraid we haven't got time to try them all!" exclaimed Lazlo. "In fact, it's nearly time we began our return journey, which will not be an inconsiderable one given all the obstacles we've encountered thus far. That is unless we can find a more facile route back, of course."

"So, Hess?" asked Franklin. "Which will it be? Is the thruster core behind door number one, door number two, or door number three?"

"Wait a minute!" said Ellie after Hess had thought for a few moments. "We don't have to pick just one. If we split up, we can explore all three. We'll meet back here in a few minutes and report our findings. Hess and Lazlo, you take the tunnel on the right. Joey and Franklin, you guys take the one on the left. I'll go down the middle."

"This is a sound plan, I think," said Lazlo. "Except for one thing: Mr. Hess and I are quite capable without each other's help. I think it would be best if I joined you, Mistress Mars; I should very much like to see my guardian angel guarded well herself." Ellie shrugged and nodded.

"Fine," muttered Hess. "While I don't like the idea of splitting up, I guess it's our only choice. Besides, I can handle myself, Lazlo will protect Ellie, and Franklin and Joey can be a formidable pair when left to their own devices, I'd imagine. Just remember all of you: we meet back here in twenty minutes! We haven't got time for any search and rescue missions!"

"All right, then let's stop wasting it!" exclaimed Ellie and, taking Lazlo's hand, she marched off down the central corridor and disappeared into the darkness.

"I swear... Sometimes I want to kill that girl," grumbled Hess. "Do you two think you'll be alright on your own? So long as you both stay quiet and keep that lantern as dim as possible, you ought to be fine; just don't step into any more bogs or anything like that."

Joey looked to Franklin, who sighed and nodded. "We'll be

fine." He wasn't thrilled about dividing the group and he was particularly worried about being away from his mighty, metal companions and at the mercy of the Mites; but he and Joey had been through more pickles together than he could count and he reckoned they ought to be safe enough so long as they stuck with one another. Hess nodded, gave a little salute, then clanked off down the passageway to the right.

"Well, Franny, it's you and me- just like the good old days!" said Joey, dusting off his mushroom lantern.

"Good old days? Do you mean, like, a week ago?" laughed Franklin; he realized Joey and he had not had a moment between the two of them in a while with all the commotion. His friend returned the chuckle.

"Come on, Franny, let's get a move on." With quiet steps, they set off down the tunnel and into the blackness. "Do you think Mr. Whiffin would ever believe any of this?"

"We're not supposed to tell people about it when we get back, Joseph. Remember what Hess said?"

"Yeah, but hypothetically- what if we told him. You think he'd buy it?"

"I love Mr. Whiffin as much as the next guy, and he sure as hell is imaginative and open minded but-- not a chance," admitted Franklin, snickering at the absolute ridiculousness of their predicament. Joey laughed as well. Soon, they found themselves stifling great guffaws and choking back hysterical outbursts as they reminisced and made commentary on the strangest week of their lives.

"I'll bet Ellie's really kicking herself for ever coming to dinner that night!" Joey chortled.

"And I bet Hess wishes the Stalo had just vaporized us and saved him all the trouble," added Franklin. For a boy who had nearly just been constricted to death by a mutant leech in a post apocalyptic sewer, he was surprisingly cheery; being able to laugh and joke with his best friend had lifted his spirits, and he felt like sharing a secret.

"Ellie held my hand the other night, you know."

"Did she?" Joey seemed uninterested. His mind was still

completely absorbed with the 'fascinating' leeches.

"Yeah, when we were on top of the sanctuary."

"I figured you two were up to something over there, that's why I stayed out of your hair. What was it like?"

"I don't know. We were supposed to get the whole handholding thing out of the way years ago, Joseph, in middle school at the very least; but we're late to the game." Franklin shrugged. "I guess to someone more experienced it would have been fine, but to me... To me it was out of this world! I can't even describe it." He could, of course, describe the entire event and include every minute detail, but he didn't want to appear to Joey quite so pathetic as he appeared to himself.

"Someone more experienced?" echoed his friend. "Do you think she's more experienced?"

Franklin hadn't even considered that notion and he began to get nervous at the prospect. What if he hadn't delivered what she was used to? What if there was some hunk of a man up in Maine she was missing and Franklin was only her wimpy substitute. "I... I don't know. I never asked," he stammered.

"I'll bet you wish she could've just held your hand back in Stony Creek without all of this other crazy stuff going on, don't you?"

"I guess so. But something tells me it would've never even come near to happening back home. I guess I'm lucky - or maybe not. Who knows? We have been through hell and back, but that one little moment last night made it all worth it, if just for a little while." He sighed. "Pendel Circle seems a long way off now, doesn't it?"

"Sure does." Joey nodded. "Feels like it's million years and a million miles since then."

"Maybe not a million, but a thousand for sure," said Franklin smiling. "Some summer break, huh?"

"Not what you were expecting on the first day of summer, Franny?"

"Not even close. We only got to go fishing once!"

"Hey now!" Joey smirked. "I think we just got the best fishing story we're ever going to be able to tell back there in that bog. But you're right: this has been a helluva summer break. And only a week in, too! Can you imagine what will happen if we're out here all the way to August? Why, we'll-"

"Joey, quiet!" Franklin hissed, cutting him off. "Look!" There, at the end of the passageway, was a faint, greenish glow. The two boys slipped quietly towards it and, crouching low, peered into the chamber that lay beyond.

"Oh no," gasped Joey in a whisper. The room into which they spied was vast indeed and cavernous as an ancient cathedral. The same mushrooms as the kind in their lantern lined the walls and illuminated the space. But it was the cave's inhabitants which disturbed them more than anything. Covering every inch of floor they could make out were heaps upon heaps of grimy Bhasmites, slumbering one on top of the other in piles that climbed nearly as high as the ceiling.

The cavern was quiet save the occasional growl or burp of a sleeping Mite when it shifted against its companions. But another peculiar noise pervaded the area, too, one much louder than the others. It sounded like a slow intake of breath, rattling and deep, followed by its inevitable exhale, and the whole cavern shook each time it sounded out.

"Where's that noise coming from?" whispered Franklin, deathly afraid to stir any of the thousands of creatures from their slumber.

"I think it's coming from... that." Joey pointed a trembling finger toward one of the piles of Mites. Or at least at what Franklin had at first thought was a pile of Mites. He squinted and then recoiled in silent horror. This mass of black fur and blue, scaly skin was not, in fact, a heap of the monsters, but one truly tremendous and terrible one. It lay on its side and was at least twenty or so feet tall from head to foot. Each time its immense chest drew in, the cavern about them trembled, and each time it exhaled, a foul wind of horrific halitosis rolled out of it like a tropical storm, nearly knocking the boys from their feet.

Franklin could hardly bring himself to utter the name. "Cherophobe," he breathed. "I hardly believed Old Sacks when he told me how big he was, but this..." The monstrosity nearly filled up the entire chamber.

"So this is the legendary Cherophobe?" whispered Joey. "He doesn't look different from any of the other Mites, except for the fact that he's fifteen feet taller of course. And then there's the matter of the fire." He pointed to the beast's humongous jaw. Each time the giant breathed out, small blue flames flickered on his lips and tongue (which was as big as a crocodile itself.)

"That can't be good," muttered Franklin, picturing all the fire-breathing dragons he had read about in storybooks when he was little. "Come on, Joseph. Let's get out of here and report back to the others. There's no way this is the passage we're going to end up heading down with all these Bhasmites inside."

"But Franklin," hissed Joey back. "This is **exactly** the way we have to go! Look!" He gestured out into the center of the Mite hive. There, resting on a stony dais in between all the piles of creatures and right in front of Cherophobe himself, was a small, circular piece of machinery with the white letters 'NOAH' emblazoned across it.

"No way," Franklin nearly cried out, but Joey shoved his hands over his mouth and stifled the boy's outburst.

"Yes way," Joey whispered. "They must have found it floating along the sludge river and fished it out. I don't know why they didn't destroy it or something. Maybe they just like shiny things like crows do." He turned. "Come on, Franny, Let's go wait for the others and tell them we've found it."

"Hang on, Joseph!" Franklin plucked him by the arm and drew him back. "Who knows how long it'll take the others to get back? And besides, if Hess comes clanking in here (like I'm sure he'll insist on doing) he'll just wake up all the Mites with the racket his metal boots always make. Then we'll really be sunk; his rockets might work well against a few, but against an army? I don't think so. And then there's Cherophobe to worry about, too, and we don't even know what he's capable of. I'd venture to say he's not any more friendly than the other

Bhasmites, though."

"What are you suggesting?" Joey arched an eyebrow in disbelief at his timid friend's sudden audacity.

"All I'm saying is this: if we let Hess or Lazlo march in here, they'll wake all these buggers up. And even if we don't, how long will they stay asleep? It's got to be nearly sundown by now! We can't afford to waste another minute. So let's just grab the thing and go!"

Joey shrugged. "Alright. I guess you're right, we can move a lot more quietly than the others. Let's just make this quick."

Like mice, they slipped silently into the hive and began to carefully tiptoe their way around the sprawled and slumbering Mite forms which littered the floor. There were a few close calls, of course; one of the creatures even rolled over in its sleep and clung suddenly onto Franklin's ankle like a teddy bear. Though he was about to scream, he remembered his calm and carefully extracted his limb from the beast's grasp.

Now, they clambered quietly up onto the stone dais and came face to face with the colossal head of Cherophobe. His breath was unbearable and several times nearly knocked them from the platform with its gale-force power. But the boys wrinkled their noses and knelt beside the lost thruster core. All this trouble for this little thing, thought Franklin, but he knew better: even in his day and age the most complex technologies came in small packages.

Joey handed him the lantern and gathered the device up into his own arms. It was surprisingly light. They nodded to one another, hopped nimbly down off the dais, and made a silent dash for the exit. Of course, the silence of their swift departure was utterly and completely eradicated when Joey, having slipped on a puddle of Mite drool, stumbled forward and lost his grip on the thruster core. It sailed through the air as the boys looked on in horror and fell to the ground, bouncing several times and emitting a series of loud 'clangs' before it at last came to rest. They winced and their spines straightened as the metallic racket echoed off the walls.

In a flash, a sea of blinking, red eyes surrounded them.

Worst of all were the basketball-sized eyes which opened up behind them and began to seethe with a crimson hatred.

Cherophobe let out a roar which rattled the walls so badly Franklin was sure the Well would come crashing down around them at any moment. At once, the Mite hordes sprung into a flurry of action like an angry wasp's nest. Their hungry gazes were fixated on the two meaty boys who had dared to enter their den and steal their treasure. Franklin felt the giant behind them begin to struggle to his feet, wincing as he roared again.

The two boys didn't think, didn't talk, and didn't even look at each other. They leapt forward, Joey snatched up the thruster core, and then they bolted into the passageway they had come out of, not daring to look back over their shoulders; the cacophony of whoops and snarls told them quite enough: the Mites were in hot pursuit

They raced down the corridor, pumping their short and muddy legs as fast as their feet would carry them. The ground trembled and shook with a tremendous 'pound pound pound' as they felt Cherophobe striding behind them, his monster hordes swarming around his mini-van sized feet. Of course, he had to stoop to fit into the passageway, but this did not deter him. He cackled and laughed like claps of booming thunder. Franklin shivered all over.

Now, the two boys rounded a bend out of breath and nearly collided with Lazlo, Hess, and Ellie who were all waiting at the intersection of the three tunnels where they had agreed to meet.

"No time... to explain!" panted Franklin.

"The Mites! Cherophobe!" managed Joey in between ragged breaths. "We've got the thruster core! We have to run!"

Hess darted around the corner in alarm and gazed upon the rapidly approaching army of hungry teeth, glowing eyes, and legs the size of tree trunks. "We can't go the way we came!" he bellowed. "Between the leeches and them, we'll never make it! Come on! The passageway I went down splits into a bunch more. One of them has got to lead out of here! Follow me!" Hess snatched the thruster core from Joey and charged off down the tunnel he had indicated. The rest followed at a sprint.

Ellie glared at Franklin and Joey as they all ran, side-by-side. "What in the hell did you two clowns do now? You've got the whole population of Well on our heels!"

"At least we got the thruster core!" retorted Joey as he raced. "What did you find?"

"Our tunnel ended in a dead end, Master Jensen!" exclaimed Lazlo, throwing a worried glance behind them. "It seems we've put some distance between us and the Mites, but the gap will soon close! Hurry! Hurry! Before you are made into flank steaks and me into a pile of scrap metal!"

They hustled down the passageway, close at Hess' heels, wincing with every quaking step the gargantuan Cherophobe pounded into the earth behind them. Every few seconds, he would join into his underling's jeering chorus. "Bhasma! Bhasma!" he boomed and blue sparks along with bursts of flame spat out of his gaping maw, showering the children's backs and stinging their necks. But they sped on and eventually outran even the smaller Mites, who scrambled quite quickly. Hess slowed to a halt in front of another spot where the tunnel snaked off in several directions.

"We've got about a minute on them!" he hollered.

"Which way?" Ellie demanded.

"I don't know! I don't know! Just let me think!" barked the armored boy, burying his head into his palms. Each of the paths looked just as daunting as the other, and none of them offered up any clues as to which was the way out. Franklin's blood began to pump and his forehead to sweat as he listened to the Mites drawing nearer and nearer. But the companions remained still, and it was beginning to drive him mad. His hands began to quiver.

"We've really got to move!" he said shakily.

"I know!" snapped Hess, who felt like his head was just about to explode inside his helmet. "By my clock, we've only got a little time left before the gate shuts. And if we take a wrong turn we could get locked out forever, and if we hit a

dead end, the Mites will overtake us and we'll be dead meat."
He shook his head wildly back and fourth. "Damn, damn,
damn! Mozi Box, can you give me anything!"

"I'm sorry Mr. Hess but-"

"Lazlo? Joey? Ellie? Franklin? Anyone?!" Hess was frantic,
and his voice was beginning to crack.

Ellie opened her mouth to say something, but only a weak
little gasp came out. Joey scratched his head wildly, but nothing
seemed to come to him. Franklin racked his brain again and
again for anything- ANYTHING- he could possibly think of.

"Bhasma! Bhasma!" chanted the monsters, conducted by
their enormous, fiery chorus leader. They were closer now,
almost upon the companions. Franklin could hear their
horrible fangs slashing against each other, could hear their
claws scraping against the ground, and of course their long,
black tongues sliding over slobbering lips. Joey's lantern was
only faint in such a long and dismal cavern. It had become
impossibly dark. All that remained to be seen was the tidal
wave of glowing, red eyes.

Then it came to him. With a trembling hand, Franklin
reached deep down into his pocket and groped blindly amidst
the lint and muck that had gathered therein. Nothing. He
squeezed his eyes tightly shut and concentrated.

'Please,' he prayed silently. 'Please. I know you're just a
dream girl dove thing. I know you're just a stupid, silly fantasy
and I shouldn't even be thinking about you at a time like this;
but you always show up when I'm not looking for you so
please, just this once, make an invited appearance.' Nothing.
He prayed even harder, blocking out the maelstrom of
howling, cackling creatures behind him. 'Please! Please! Guide
me! Help us! Whoever you are, whatever you are, help us!'

Suddenly, his hand closed around the little ticket stub that
the girl had given him in the burning dream theater, right
before she pushed him into the open trapdoor. He yanked the
stub out of his pocket and held it out in his palm, staring at it
dumbly. Upon it was that same symbol, the many-pointed star
that hung about the neck of his cloak. Without warning, one of

Cherophobe's fiery gusts of breath blew the ticket out of his hand and up into the air where it fluttered, caught on the wind, for a few moments. None of the others seemed to notice it, even as it began to transform right before their very eyes into a shimmering, white dove. Without a word, the brilliant bird took off down one of the corridors, gliding gracefully into the darkness and illuminating a path. Franklin bolted after it.

"Franklin!" screamed Ellie to his back, still in a panic and completely unaware of the dove, just like the rest of them. "Where are you going?"

"It's this way! It's this way! I'm sure of it!" he screamed back. The companions didn't argue and sprinted after him, following him even though they didn't know **he** was secretly following some sort of invisible, ethereal pigeon.

"How do you know?" demanded Hess, still unsure they had made the right decision- although there was little they could do to change it now.

"I've just got a feeling! Trust me! If I'm wrong, you can feed me to the Mites first and escape while they're devouring me!" cried Franklin, leaping after the dove. It shot around corners and turns, and it seemed to his friends that Franklin was selecting pathways at random, picking his way through the labyrinth of tunnels at a whim, but they hurried after him nevertheless. The Mites followed too, and the distance between the groups was closing rapidly.

Now, the dove began to speak softly to Franklin, and he could hear its soft feminine voice well, even over his ragged panting and the sound of his heart pumping in his ears, for the dove seemed to talk to him directly from the center of his mind.

"Seek me out, Franklin Freeman," she instructed. "Of course, I will not recognize and perhaps you will not see me for the woman I am immediately, but you must seek me out nonetheless! Our fates rest upon it!"

"Whatever you say, bird chick!" he declared happily, completely agreeable where he was normally stubborn with the apparition; he was simply elated that they had gotten moving again instead of waiting for the Mites to pounce on them. And for once, he noted, he was leading the party on! Well, sort of...

"You are a kindly boy. If only fate had not been quite so cruel to us, perhaps..." The dove sniffed, as if holding back a sob. "How lucky you are, my handsome love, to relive our first meeting all over again and in the flesh. Certainly, I will be perched secretly on your shoulder to observe the encounter. Oh my! I think it might best if I refrained, actually; I wouldn't want my heart to burst all over again."

"I have no idea what you're talking about, lady!" said Franklin. "But you can say as much of it as you want. Hell, you can even sing it!"

"Franklin!" snapped Ellie, bewildered. "Who the hell are you talking to?" Franklin ignored her.

'Are you're sure you're taking us the right way?' he thought in his head.

"Quite sure, dear boy," cooed the strange, ghostly dove in reply. "Birds have a special sense about this sort of thing. It's the lodestones, I'm sure you know; they keep us quite well oriented, even in the dark like this."

"Look!" exclaimed Lazlo, gesturing as wildly as a robot can. There, though it was only a faraway speck of color in the inky black, they could see the basket elevator resting on the floor, still waiting for them. Only a little further.

"Uh guys," yelped Joey, stumbling a bit as he cast a nervous glance over his shoulder. They looked back at him. "Duck!" he just barely managed to scream. Spinning on their heels, they saw Cherophobe reel backwards and open his cavernous maw. A pillar of blue flames spewed fourth from the depths of his fiery innards, out his gaping mouth, and towards the children who dove to the ground just in time to avoid being completely immolated (though Franklin could feel the tips of his hairs singe a bit.)

"Keep going! Keep going!" urged Hess. "He's nothing special! I can do that too! Come on!" Without missing a beat, they staggered to their feet and carried on toward the basket, ignoring the chattering and howling mob, which pressed ever nearer.

The dove, Franklin observed, had vanished in the commotion; but it had led them well. He said a little prayer of thanks in his head, but it was interrupted by another belch of flame which nearly caught him on the arm.

Finally, they reached the basket and unceremoniously clambered into it, all at once, Hess still clutching the thruster core to his chest. Lazlo began to tug ferociously on the rope and, after a painfully uneventful moment, the basket started to rise, but at a sickeningly slow pace.

"Curses, Jamjar Brickbeard!" exclaimed the robot. "You are a gatekeeper by trade and not cut out for the raising and lowering of elevators such as this. Again, you pass your job off to Lazlo! Lazy old fellow! A man should never do a robot's work." He seized the rope in both his hands, wriggled his feet into notches carved into the sides of the basket, and began to pull the elevator up, hand over hand, at an alarmingly speedy rate. With Lazlo as their motor, they shot up by at least ten times faster than they had come down, if not more.

"Thank God for Lazlo!" breathed Franklin.

"And thank God for you, Franklin!" exclaimed Hess, slapping him heartily on the back. "How on earth did you know which tunnels would lead us back to the basket? Surely you weren't just guessing!"

"Pure luck and intuition, I suppose!" he lied.

"We're not out of trouble yet," gulped Ellie, peering down over the basket's edge. Franklin and Joey joined her. At the bottom of the Well some hundred feet below them, where they had expected to see a group of dejected creatures abandoning the chase in disappointment, they instead saw the ferocious mob scaling up the wall after them like spiders, scuttling up its smooth stony surface with surprising ease. Even Cherophobe had begun the climb, cackling with his booming, wicked laugh as he smashed handholds into the side of the pit, the earth shaking with each strike.

"They are fine climbers indeed!" grunted Lazlo. "But worry not. Even Cherophobe cannot puncture the Lonie gate! If we can reach the top and seal the portal safely behind us, there is little to worry about." Franklin allowed himself a grin: while the Mites were indeed scrambling up the rock face with alarming speed, Lazlo was propelling them at least twice as fast and in no time the companions were shooting up in their elevator like a rocket.

CHAPTER TWENTY-ONE

THE SIEGE OF THE SANCTUARY

$\mathbf{F}$inally, after what seemed like an eternity, the gate came into view and the light of a setting sun along with it; they had made it back just in time. At once, the children and Hess began to wave their arms and holler at the sea of Lonie faces waiting before them. "Start closing the gate! Start closing the gate! We're being chased! Start closing the gate!"

Jamjar, who had abandoned his useless position at the elevator crank, nodded and hit a button. Slowly, creaking and moaning, the gate began to crawl down its rails. The Lonies gathered together and, after lassoing the basket, they heaved all together, drawing the makeshift elevator back toward the sanctuary, back to safety. Even Old Sacks had his hands on the rope, leading his people as they pulled. His long, frail arms bulged with taught muscles built up over decades of toil.

Delighted to be in a well-lit and dry place again, Franklin and his friends hopped down out of the basket, strongly resisting the urge to kiss the ground.

The Lonies held their breath in anticipation, watching as the gate slid further and further toward the ground, for now they could hear the lusty screeches and howls of the Mites climbing up towards them. At last, it seemed the day was won, for only a foot or so remained between the gate's bottom and the dirt below. The Lonies began to cheer, hooting and hurrahing, but went dead silent after only a moment of celebration.

A colossal blue hand, as wide as most of them were tall, snaked under the gate and barred its closing. They could hear **him** laughing on the other side, each cackle quaking the ground beneath their feet. Cherophobe had reached the top of the well and now, slowly, he slid another hand under the gate and began to lift it, the muscles in his immense wrists bulging under the strain. But he was not to be deterred.

Now, as he widened the space beneath the door, Mites began surging fourth out of it like a pot rapidly boiling over. One, two, three, ten, twenty, fifty- soon, hundreds of the beasts were swarming forth out from under the gate as their chief raised it higher and higher. Franklin's spirits began to plummet.

"Come!" Old Sacks declared suddenly. "To arms! This wickedness can still be undone so long as we draw breath! To arms! Let us push them back into the hell from whence they have crawled up out of."

Roaring with a ferocity to match even Cherophobe's mighty bellows, the Lonies unsheathed their various clubs, spears, axes, and machetes, and charged forward into the Mite horde, falling upon the beasts like an angry tidal wave does to a helpless sand castle. The Lonies would not let their home, which had stood stalwart for two centuries, be invaded quite so easily. Immediately, the Mite line wavered and broke. The monsters scattered as the Lonie charge thrust into their ranks.

Lazlo turned to the children and Hess, nodded grimly, and dove into the fray after his brethren. Despite their exhaustion, despite their fear, and despite their longing to simply take the thruster core and leave all of this nonsense behind, the children dove right in after their robotic companion, brandishing their clubs and bracing for a fight to be remembered.

At first, it seemed the Lonie initiative would succeed. Together with the council members and citizens, they formed a phalanx out of which so many menacing, sharp objects poked that it must have resembled a bristling metal porcupine lumbering towards the Mites. This formation overtook the monsters before they could scuttle too far into the room and pushed them back to the gate without mercy, stabbing and slicing left and right.

It seemed, Franklin noted as he hammered a Mite on the toe and then walloped it in the face while it was distracted, that the Lonie army was nearly invincible, at least in the front where the warriors had formed a sort of impenetrable wall of spears and pikes. The Mites fell upon this wall like shish kabobs and retreated howling away from it, much to the excitement of the Lonies

Now, the determined brigade plugged up the space under the gate, which was still getting larger as Cherophobe continued to lift, and staunched the flow of beasts entirely, smiting the monsters before they had a chance to pull themselves over the ledge and sending them tumbling and shrieking back into the pit.

Stingwhit, Nimrod, and Fluthers rushed forward, past the spear wall, and began to drive their long pikes into Cherophobe's great fingers in the hopes he would relent and release his grip on the gate. Though the giant's hand began to leak massive blobs of indigo blood that could have drowned a fully grown man, the colossal Mite would not release the gate. In fact, he began to laugh again, making the Lonies shudder in their boots.

"Demon! Demon! Demon King is he! Take your spears and follow suit, Lonies, plunge them into the flesh of yonder demon king!" yelled Old Sacks, leaping forward with the rest of them and hacking away at Cherophobe's tremendous claw, rapping the giant on his knuckles with his parking meter staff.

At his command, all the Lonies sprang toward the spot, those on the outside continuing to cut down Mites, and those on the inside helping to drive more and more spears into the giant's hand. In a matter of moments, Cherophobe's claw resembled a leaking pincushion.

Franklin and Joey, who had become separated from their companions in the confusion of battle, ducked and wove their way under prodding spears and slashing claws to the edge of the fray, where they could better survey the combat at hand.

They could see Lazlo and Ellie on the frontlines, clobbering any beast so bold as to climb up out of the Well. And there was Hess, whirling left and right as flames spewed from his wrists, an angry little cyclone of fire battering his way through the Mite ranks. The monsters fled in fear before him. It seemed to the children that the battle had been all but won, and they began to smile when Cherophobe, after Stingwhit had managed to drive a pike underneath his massive fingernail, roared in pain. Surely he would release the gate now.

Suddenly, a great red eye as big as Franklin's head appeared at the gap under the gate, smoldering and furious. It vanished and was quickly replaced with Cherophobe's deep, ravenous gullet, which was wide open and grinning maliciously with several rows of sword-sized teeth.

"Get out of the way! Retreat! Retreat!" cried Joey and Franklin over the commotion for they were among the few who had spotted the danger, but it was too late. A fireball came thundering out of the giant's throat and plowed into the Lonie formation, scattering them like bowling pins.

Even Stingwhit, Fluthers, and Nimrod, mighty warriors that they were, found themselves dazed and smarting on the ground as blue flame licked the air around them, singeing their jerkins and making all their manly arm hair sizzle away.

Franklin and Joey rushed to rejoin the disorganized fray, helping up each grounded Lonie they could reach, but many would not so much as budge. Some were too frightened to lift their heads and kept them buried against the ground instead. Some were dead.

With the sudden lapse in the impenetrable spear wall, the smaller Mites seized their chance and surged up and into the sanctuary out of the well, like a soda bottle shaken too suddenly, and rampaged into the chamber. Chaos seized the battlefield now as the monsters' overwhelming numbers obliterated the Lonie formation entirely and separated the desperate fighters into small, isolated groups left to fend for themselves. The Lonies had lost their only advantage. Where once they had countered the overwhelming Mite numbers by funneling the creatures into a more manageable bottleneck underneath the gate, they were now overrun entirely and stood little chance.

Franklin and Joey had managed to reach Hess, Lazlo, and Ellie just in time; for now the reunited companions fought side by side once again against the Mites, which swarmed in every direction conceivable.

Through the tumult, Franklin could see that Old Sacks had managed to rally a small battalion to him and was now carving his way through the center of the battle, back towards the gate where he likely hoped to reestablish the phalanx. But now, Franklin beheld not a gate still half shut, but one open completely, instead.

And there, out of the gateway, emerged the titan Cherophobe, drawing himself up to his full height and stomping his feet on the ground, sending tremors through the earth and nearly knocking the desperate army of men over. He waded through the combat as easily as one wanders through a flower of daisies, flinging aside Lonies and Mites alike and squashing any of those souls unlucky enough to stumble beneath into his destructive path.

"Ogre! Vermin! Demon!" cried Old Sacks as he rushed to confront the giant head on.

"Bhasma," growled Cherophobe in retort with a voice that sounded like an immense, ferocious dog barking through a loudspeaker.

Old Sacks leapt at the monstrosity, beating away at his feet and shins, crying "Be gone! Be gone!" But Cherophobe simply plucked up the elderly little Lonie in between two of his fingers and flicked the man across the room. Old Sacks sailed through the air, reeling and shouting, till he struck the sacred garden's dome and bounced to the ground, crumbling where he lay. Cherophobe cackled.

"We are overrun!" shrieked Stingwhit as he and Fluthers were engulfed by a mob of howling Mites and disappeared from view entirely. Cherophobe continued to laugh, making quick work of what remained of the Lonie forces.

"I've had enough of this meathead!" grunted Ellie, picking up a discarded machete from the ground. "I'll show him just what it means to really be ferocious!" Vaulting over the Mites, which surrounded them, she sprinted off in the direction of Cherophobe.

"Mistress Mars!" cried Lazlo in a panic. "Wait! Please! He's much too large!" At once, the robot sprang after her. Now Hess, Franklin, and Joey were left to sigh at their impulsive companions and sprint after them.

Ellie stopped, blocking Cherophobe's path, and scowled up at him. "Eat this, you dirty mammoth of an idiot!" She brought her arm back and sent the machete spinning through the air. It found its mark and the blade burrowed deep into Cherophobe's ribcage; only a bee sting to him but it looked painful nonetheless.

The giant roared in pain and, after reeling for a moment, stomped forward to retaliate. He brought his knee up and, with a wicked grin, sent his foot plummeting down towards the small girl. Franklin's heart stopped: Ellie was finished, there was no way even her fiery bravery could prevent her from being utterly squished now.

But Cherophobe's tremendous foot halted just before it reached its target. There was Lazlo, standing above the girl who had fallen to the ground in fright, pushing against the monster's foot with both his metal arms and all of his might. Cherophobe growled, surprised at the robot's strength, and began to push harder, intent on squashing the both of them.

Though sparks began to fly from his neck and shoulders,

and though the creaking of his metal joints was audible, Lazlo's resolve held.

"Franklin!" grunted the robot, his voice garbled and warped through the strain. "Take Miss Mars. Take her away from here! I leave her in your charge, now. Please! Do not fail me!"

Franklin nodded and dashed forward. He seized the dazed Ellie by the shoulders and quickly dragged her out of harm's way, out from under the shadow of Cherophobe's looming foot.

Now, the monstrosity roared and his calf began to shake as he exerted even more downward force. Lazlo's heels began to sink into the ground, the earth cracking beneath him. His limbs buckled. He turned his head towards Franklin and Ellie, who both looked on in horror. His emerald eyes sparkled for a moment. "Farewell," he whispered. Without warning, his arms snapped in two and Cherophobe's foot plowed into him like a boulder, driving the flailing robot into the ground below and covering him entirely.

"Lazlo!" Ellie shrieked. "Oh God no! Lazlo! Lazlo!"

Cherophobe, noticing the girl's screams, did not remove his foot. Instead, he smiled wickedly and began to twist it cruelly. They could hear metal being smashed and crunched beneath it.

She dashed forward to again confront the giant and save her friend, but Franklin restrained her.

"What are you doing?" she demanded, face wet with tears and blood.

"It's no use!" he cried out. "Don't let your anger get the better of you! We don't stand a chance against him!" Though she struggled and flailed, Franklin managed to drag her back to where Hess, Joey, Chunk, Suds, Mia, Zaki, Nimrod, and even Old Sacks (who had sprang up from his temporary defeat) were making a desperate last stand.

Ellie continued to shriek, "Lazlo! Lazlo!" But through the sea of Mites, they could not make out what had befallen their robotic companion.

Despite their valiant efforts, they could only contest the swarm for a few moments more. Quickly, the beasts fell on them from every direction, even seeming to leap out of the sky like rain drops. Franklin's club was knocked from his hand and soon he found his fingers entwined with Ellie's and Joey's. Even Hess had given up the battle and, hugging them all close to his metal breast, he hung his head and awaited doom.

Everything went black as the Mites swarmed over them, and soon they found themselves being pried away from each other and pulled off, deeper into the mob of beasts. Though they were ferociously kicked and beaten, none of them were killed yet, and they were quite surprised at this.

Several of the Mites who held his hands pinned to his back forced Franklin to his knees. A long, curved claw was slid around his throat where it hovered, probably waiting for some order of execution. Though his head was well restrained, Franklin cast his eyes about and saw his friends and many of the Lonies in the same predicament: forced to kneel and watch whatever horror was to come. Most of them had resigned themselves to their fates, letting their heads hang and weeping quietly. But not Old Sacks. No, the Lonie leader struggled against the Mites' grasp, barking and snarling like a chained up dog. The battle for the sanctuary had been lost, but Old Sacks refused to give up the fight.

Franklin himself found it difficult to struggle; his exhaustion had gotten the better of him and, completely drained of adrenaline, his limbs had gone limp and numb.

Now, the cackling and jeering of the Mites quieted a bit and they forced up their prisoners' heads. Cherophobe towered before them, picking his teeth and smirking triumphantly. Perhaps he would stomp them out, one by one, or cook them all into a stew and have Lonie leftovers for weeks, thought Franklin morosely. No matter what was to come, the boy dared not move a muscle; the Mite behind him had begun to smack its lips hungrily and drew its claw closer about his neck, pricking at him till a small line of blood ran down his throat.

Cherophobe strode back and forth before his prisoners, reveling in their sobs of despair, picking up the dead and discarded bodies of their Lonie comrades and flinging them carelessly away as if they were litter. Now, he turned and glared at Old Sacks.

"We will not be undone, demon!" shrieked the man, still struggling against his captors.

Cherophobe chuckled a deep and guttural laugh that sounded like gravel and turned his eye to the sacred garden dome. Two tremendous strides carried him to it and he stood over the little glass bubble with the lonely tree inside. The giant cast a malevolent grin over his shoulder at Old Sacks, raised his two fists over his immense head, clenched them together, and brought them thundering down onto the garden's top. The glass dome, which none of the Lonies had been able to open for two centuries, shattered like it was nothing and shards of glass sprayed the Mite mobs, who jeered and howled with devious joy.

Old Sacks became frantic now, foam leaking from his mouth and onto his beard below; his eyes wild and tortured. "No!" he shrieked, though his words were barely intelligible. "No! You mustn't! You cannot! You cannot!"

Cherophobe simply smiled, took a great breath in, and belched out a pillar of blue flame. The fire engulfed the garden and set the lonely tree alight.

The roar that escaped Old Sacks' lips now was the sound of ultimate suffering, a cry so filled with rage and anguish that it split through even the Mites' deafening racket. Franklin could see it in the old man's eyes: Old Sacks' heart was burning away in his chest as he watched his precious garden smolder.

Now, the frantic Lonie leader broke free of his captors and raced across the chamber, shouting and screaming. A group of Mites scuttled forth to reclaim their prisoner, but Cherophobe shook his head 'no' and allowed the Lonie his freedom.

Old Sacks shrieked, "Chaos! Chaos! There is nothing but chaos! Forfeit this world while you can! The storm thunders with too much strength; we are no match for it and live only to be blown away by the howling winds. Oh, cruel! Oh, cruel! To what end but to have our roots torn from beneath us by the storm and to be blown away? Chaos! Chaos! There is nothing but chaos!"

As his people watched in horror, the crazed Old Sacks dove head first into the flames that engulfed the garden and disappeared into the blazing, blue inferno. He was gone. Burned with his tree.

As the Mites began to jeer and laugh, Cherophobe joining them in their awful, victorious chorus, the Lonies started to wail, lamenting their miserable fates. Franklin could barely comprehend what was happening now, his eyes blinded with tears, muck, and dried blood.

Cherophobe raised his hand, about to give the order of execution. The claws tightened around the helpless humans' necks. Franklin gritted his teeth, preparing for death. At least having his throat slit would be better than being squashed to death by a mutant leech trapped under several feet of mud. He glanced to Joey, who had closed his eyes and blocked out the world, and then to Ellie, whose pupils burned with resentment and tears, gaze still fixated on the spot where Lazlo had been crushed. Even Hess had been restrained and lay trapped beneath a humongous heap of Mites. They wouldn't be able to slit his throat, but Cherophobe would have no trouble stomping on him like had done to Lazlo, Franklin was sure.

"Bhasma! Bhasma! Bhasma!" chanted the Mites in anticipation of the blood which was soon to be spilt. Surely, they'd lick it up and revel in their victory, prancing on their victims' corpses and singing praise to their colossal leader. Franklin scowled and spat in defiance.

Just as Cherophobe was about to bring his had down and seal all their doomed fates for good, Franklin caught something in the corner of his eye. Through the hole in the window where the thruster core had fallen into the sanctuary, nearly a hundred feet above them, he spied a black speck against the setting sun in the sky. It was travelling rapidly, like a missile launched from space, and grew larger and larger with each moment.

Suddenly, it smashed through the window above and slammed into the earth inside the sanctuary, making the ground shiver: a silver figure, like that of a man, but mostly featureless and nearly as tall as Cherophobe was.

"The Stalo!" breathed Franklin.

"Of course," whispered Hess. "I should've known. Mozi wasn't telling us to 'stay' in those mixed up transmissions! He was warning us that the Stalo had come to 3000 AD as well! It must have followed our trail all the way across the wasteland."

"Great," groaned Joey, opening one eye to stare at the silvery figure, "another monster who wants us dead!"

Franklin could not tear his eyes away from the Stalo; he had spied something the others had not. There, carved into the spot where the Stalo's face ought to have been were it a human, was the same symbol he had seen so many other places: the many pointed star, glowing red just as it had on Sachem's Head. It was the same star as the one on his cloak. The same star that had been passed down through Bess Spero's family for millennia. A grand conspiracy of some kind, noted the boy, but there was no time to think about it in such a pressing moment.

Now, Cherophobe turned and faced the Stalo, puzzled at its sudden appearance. The silver figure ignored him, however and lunged toward where Hess was restrained; intent on shooting its crimson lightning at him again, they were all sure. But the strange metallic giant stopped mid stride and turned its head towards where Franklin. Its rage seemed to calm and it strode across the chamber towards the helpless boy. The Mites and Cherophobe could do nothing but watch in silence; never had they seen such a puzzling creature.

The Stalo stopped and stood before Franklin quietly. The boy had been ready to have his throat slit, now he prepared instead to be incinerated by a bolt of crimson instead.

But the Stalo did not attack. It knelt so that its head peered down into Franklin's watering eyes. Slowly, it reached a long and silvery arm out and gently touched the base of the boy's neck. Franklin looked down to see its giant metal hand resting upon the brooch, upon the same sort of many-pointed star which the creature wore upon its own face.

The Stalo made a low, rumbling noise, and then its facial symbol stopped glowing red, fading instead to a dull, black color. It continued to peer at Franklin, as if wondering what the small boy was thinking. It nodded like it had read his thoughts, and drew its long arm away from the brooch. Now, it turned to face Cherophobe. With a screech, it launched itself at the Bhasmite giant and began to grapple with the massive demon.

"Out of the frying pan and into the fire!" hollered Hess and, while the Mites were distracted, watching their chieftain tussle with another colossus of equal size and strength, the armored began to beat his captors off of him. In an instant, the battle was begun again and the room flung into chaos. Franklin, Joey, and Ellie seized the moment of confusion and sprang toward one another, out of the Mites' grasp, snatching up weapons and cutting their way to Hess, who several other Lonies had rallied to.

The Mites, while still innumerable, had been thrown into a panic: the enormous feet of the wrestling titans crushed those unlucky enough to have been standing near Cherophobe when the Stalo arrived. Some of them had been driven back in fear, only to fall onto the weapons of Hess's small brigade or, worse, into the burning garden where they vanished in a puff of soot and singed hair.

The two giants exchanged blows, pounding away each other as hard as they could, but the Stalo was slowly overpowering Cherophobe, crimson lightning travelling through his silver hands and electrocuting his gargantuan opponent. "Stalo!" it screeched with that metallic groan.

"Bhasma!" retorted Cherophobe, unleashing a plume of blue flame into the Stalo's face, though it only seemed to bounce off the creature's metal skin.

Hess cried out to the children and the Lonies, ushering them behind a fallen hunk of wreckage. From their secret perch, they watched as the titans fought, their battle ranging all over the chamber as the Mites fled in panic before their stomping feet. Finally, the two giants threw each other to the ground and began to strike out at one another with terrible ferocity. With each blow, another window shattered above and the ground shook and rumbled beneath the children's feet.

In a last and desperate effort, Cherophobe seized the Stalo by its shoulders and lunged forward to bite into its neck. But the Stalo lunged also, and the two collided in the midair and were sent reeling, tumbling towards the open gate into which they stumbled, plummeting into the Well below. The children could hear the two titans wailing as they fell, their battle cries mixing together into one last ferocious scream. "BhasmaStaloBhasmaStaloBhasmaStalo!" they went on, till an enormous 'thud' sounded, the earth trembled, and everything went quiet.

Seizing the moment, Hess sprang up from their hiding spot, unleashed a passionate cry for "One more charge!" and led the Lonies (and the stumbling children) down into the chamber. The Mites fled before their clubs and spears, panicked and confused by the apparent and sudden death of their chieftain. Franklin battled several of the stragglers, thwacking them back with his club till he had chased them all the way back to the pit, which they scampered into to join their fallen leader.

Without missing a beat, Jamjar (who was covered in cuts and bruises, but still able to stand) rushed forward and pulled a lever. Again, the gate began to shut, and the remaining Lonies watched it intently, not daring to breathe till it had sealed firmly to the ground. At last, the portal was closed, the Mites driven away, the Stalo and Cherophobe vanquished by each other's hands, and the battle won. But a bloody fight it had been, and they had only come to a pyrrhic victory in the end.

A great quiet gripped the chamber as the din of combat and the ringing in their ears faded away. Heaps of bodies were piled about them, made up of dead Lonies and Mites alike, their corpses mingling as their living beings had never been able to do so in life.

Death, Franklin noted, ignored all prejudices and hatreds. It was simple, succinct, and absolute. In this way, he glumly supposed, perhaps it was less cruel than life; certainly less ambiguous. There was no gray area in death, really, simply a fine line that you'd either crossed already or you hadn't. And it didn't matter if you were a Lonie or a Mite, a saint or a sinner, a man or a beast; death had no favorites.

The Lonies turned and faced the wreckage which had only an hour before been their home, at a loss for words and actions, too. The companions were equally speechless. Though what seemed like thousands of Mites littered the floor, dead or dying, it was the several dozen Lonie corpses which disturbed them the most. For a tribe of peoples only a few hundred in number, the Lonies had just suffered a near fatal blow to their society.

Among the dead, Franklin could recognize several familiar faces, though the majority of the council still lived and stood now by his side, injured though they were. Stingwhit was missing an eye (Jamjar had leant him his eye patch), Chunk had broken an arm, Nimrod leaned heavily upon a staff, Mia and Zaki had two black eyes apiece, and even Suds was covered in cuts and bruises. But no one cried out or moaned in pain; the air was choked with grief and purposelessness.

Slowly, what remained of the meager Lonie population disbanded and they began to shuffle off to see to the wounded and bury their dead. There was no Old Sacks now to instruct them, to give them orders, to encourage them. Where once the air had rung with his barked orders, now there was only silence.

Ellie, snapping out of the dazed, post-battle trance that had befallen them all, raced out onto the smoldering battlefield, leaping over piles of corpses, till she came to the crater of a footprint Cherophobe had made when he brought his foot down on their companion. Franklin,

Joey, and Hess rushed to join her, sliding down into the hole to where she was. She was sitting, cradling what remained of Lazlo in her lap. The robot's limbs were strewn across the ground and most of them crushed beyond repair. His torso, bent, battered and broken as it was, was still intact and attached to his head, which had several dents in it. Ellie cradled the robot's head, wiping dirt gently away from his eyes, which only glowed very faintly now. The boys stood back, afraid to approach, not ready to see what they already knew to be true.

"Lazlo?" whispered Ellie softly, caressing the robot's face. No response. "Lazlo?" she repeated. "Oh, Lazlo." She buried her head into his chest. Now, his eyes flickered.

"Miss... Mars," he rasped. His voice processor had been damaged badly, for now his tone was low, broken, and uneven. She lifted her head, eyes shining with tears.

"Oh, Lazlo," she cried. "I'm so sorry! What a fool I've been! If I hadn't been so stupid and brazen, you would have never gotten so... Well, look at you! You're a wreck and it's all my fault! How can you ever forgive me?" She choked back another sob and a tear rolled down her soft cheek.

"Miss Mars," he managed to garble. "There is... nothing to forgive. Would that I could... reach up and wipe away those... tears. But, alas, my arms are no longer... attached to my shoulders. Please... Please do not cry... It grieves me sorely to see such an angelic face stained...with tears. Please, Miss Mars."

Now, Fluthers appeared at the edge of the crater and, at the sight of Lazlo's crippled form, grew infuriated. "Look what-ees have brought on us poor Lonies!" he shouted at the children. "Why did so many have to perish? Why did a kindly fellow like Lazlo here have to be mangled? For this?" He gestured at the thruster core clutched to Hess's chest. "The Lonies have been massacred for a hunk of metal? How can-ees explain all of this." They were silent. Franklin couldn't even meet the warrior's angry, tear streaked gaze. "Answer me! I have buried more friends today then ever I had even cared to count in their living days! For the treasure of-ee angels?" He spat on Hess's boots.

"Master... Fluthers," Lazlo croaked weakly, and the warrior's face softened. "These folks carry upon their backs a greater burden than any of us can imagine," explained the dying robot. "They seek to undo all the maelstrom and malevolence that has been so unjustly done to the world. They seek to break the iron shackles our time has been cruelly locked into... Though their treasure may seem but a hunk of metal, it represents something greater, a stepping stone across a river wider than you or I can possibly conceive. Besides... a hunk of metal need not be a meaningless one. Behold, a hunk of metal lies mangled in the center of this hole, yet he speaks to you now, Master Fluthers."

Fluthers hid his eyes from the robot, ashamed.

"Do not begrudge these children their quest, my friend; they do not make it for themselves," Lazlo went on. "They quest for the betterment and salvation of all of us, even you and I."

Fluthers nodded, wiped his eyes and, after bowing, plodded off.

"Lazlo, it's all my fault!" repeated Ellie again. "Your ruined body, your missing arms and legs-- all because of my stupidity! How can we even start to repair you?"

"Repair me?" Lazlo chuckled weakly. "My sweet child, I am too far gone for any such notion... Even now, the circuits in my core are shutting down... one by one."

"Oh Lazlo!" sobbed Ellie, holding his head close to her breast. "Please forgive me!"

"Miss... Mars, there is nothing... to be forgiven," insisted the robot. "It was you and your...friends who saw fit to help the helpless and repair my frozen body on that fateful day. I know, to you children, that it seems a negligible act, but from it stems all of my happiness. Even the smallest drop of kindness shines brightly in a dark... storm of uncertainty. I owe you my life, children. And Miss Mars, to you... I am especially... indebted. I believe my actions today have only begun to repay that debt, and the rest of it you will have to forgive me, for I am... not long for this place."

"You don't owe us anything!" cried out Franklin, unable to keep silent. "You're the kindest person I've ever met!"

"I owe you my allegiance," said Lazlo. "I owe you mu friendship. That is why... I was so willing to abandon these Lonies and set out with you all." His voice changed to static for a moment, then returned, but it spoke more slowly, now. "I... would have... followed you to the end of time itself, for that is where I expect you are going... I would have seen the children of the Noah safely... across the cosmos... But now... I cannot... Please, Miss Mars... Children... This friend of yours, our illustrious Mr. Hess, is in dire need of assistance, for his mission is grave and even he, brave lad that he is, cannot go it alone... Please, forgive me that I will not be able to help you all after this day... Forgive me... You must band together, now, for fate itself relies on... your courage...Please... For me... Forgive me... Miss Mars..."

His torso rattled and the sound of electronics short-circuiting issued out from inside of his head. He shuddered and managed to croak, "From the very beginning, we are set adrift, children. But we are not so lost as we think ourselves to be. Even now, as I fade away... I do not feel quite so lost... So long as you are near... Here, child... Be near me. Be... Near... Me." His voice trailed off.

There, in the ruinous pit with his mangled limbs strewn about him and Ellie clutching in her arms what remained of his shattered body, Lazlo's emerald eyes went dark and he faded away down that quiet path from whence even robots may not return.

CHAPTER TWENTY-TWO

APPLES FOR THE LONIES

That evening the companions helped to bury the dead and then retired to Lazlo's former apartment where they spent a wordless, sleepless night in the chill. Absent were the glowing eyes of their lost companion, the same eyes they had so often seen hovering peacefully in his dark corner.

Franklin's mind swirled with activity. There was, of course, a great deal of sadness, but a question plagued him, too. Why had the Stalo, the creature who had once hunted them, turned coat upon touching the brooch and fought on their side instead?

The next morning, after they had gathered up their belongings, they came back to the battlefield where the Lonies were still tending to the wreckage and burying the fallen, man and mite alike. Where the garden had been there was now ash and soil; the lonely birch tree had all but vanished, and Old Sacks along with it.

Stingwhit and Nimrod looked up from their morose work and then proceeded to where the grim faced children stood. Franklin hadn't gotten a wink of sleep; his mind was so racked with misery and guilt that he felt it would burst any moment.

"Well met, Strange-ees," growled Nimrod, whose arm was in a sling and hobbled weakly upon a crutch. "I take it-ees intend to depart us now?"

"Yes," admitted Hess. "We hate to leave you like this, but we've got pressing business back home."

"Think nothing of it." Nimrod waved a dismissive hand. "The Mites were sure to attack sooner or later, I suppose it's better that it were sooner and at least-ee got something out of it." He eyed the thruster core disapprovingly. "Besides, the Mite dead easily outnumber our own, ten-tah-one! Certainly we've put a dent in 'em for at least another decade, and I don't think they'll be bothering us much more without their fearsome ogre of a leader. That silver fellow saw to that. Speaking of which, we Lonies have been wondering- what in blazes was that thing?"

"We're not entirely sure ourselves," said Hess. "But he's been hunting us since we left home. We're not sure why it is he attacked Cherophobe, but we're glad he did."

Nimrod shrugged. "Makes no difference to me, so long as they're dead and gone, the both of 'em."

"I don't suppose there's been any word on Old Sacks?" asked Franklin.

"Not a trace of him, or our beloved garden," said Stingwhit. "All we've got left of the old man is this-" He held up Sacks' broad brimmed, pointy hat. It was scorched in several places. "It seems the fire gobbled him up completely. To see that tree burning drove him mad, I suppose. Madder than I can imagine. Ole' Bess rest him."

Franklin glanced to his left and noticed that Joey, while Hess and the others had been speaking, had slipped away. Now, he was hunched over, kneeling on the soil where the garden had been. Crowds of curious Lonie onlookers were watching him. Franklin and Ellie trudged over to see what all the fuss was about.

Joey was digging a small hole, only a few inches deep and wide, in a patch of clean, ash-less soil. Finished, he stood and dug his hands deep into his pockets, pockets overflowing with various odds and ends, bits of nature, mostly.

"Ah!" he exclaimed. "I thought this might come in handy. I was going to add it to my collection back home, but I think it'd be a lot more useful here." He drew out the tiny, apple tree sapling which he had collected all those days ago in Cankerwood. Miraculously, the little sprout was still green and healthy. It appeared that Joey had been nurturing it and keeping the little clump of dirt that clung to its miniscule roots well watered and taken care of deep inside his trousers. His pocket was like a little nursery. The Lonies gasped at the sight of it, unused to anything so green and vivacious in their midst.

"What is it?" called out Jamjar.

"It is an apple tree sprout," replied Joey and planted the sapling, patting down the soil around its base delicately.

"A tree?" echoed Suds. "You mean like..."

"Yes," answered Joey, "like your old birch tree. But this one will bear sweet and delicious fruit when it grows up."

"Oh my!" exclaimed Fluthers. "Then we've got to manufacture another glass dome to put around it right quick!"

"No!" snapped Joey, his typically serene features suddenly becoming stern. "No, this can't be like your old tree. You can't just look at it! You have to touch it, take care of it, and water it everyday! It's only very young, now, and it'll take some time to grow- so not all of you will get to taste its apples or sit under its branches. But I guess that's the beauty of a tree: we still plant baby saplings like this one even though we know we'll maybe never get to sit in the shade of their branches. But our grandchildren will, and so will theirs."

Joey finished patting down the soil around the baby tree and drew up to his full height. "In any case, you've really got to take care of it, if not for your sake, then for your descendants'. Who knows? Maybe it'll blossom and, after you've eaten up all the apples it gives you, the seeds will scatter to the winds and the planet will start to breathe again! Wouldn't that be nice? Imagine: a whole new Green Time. In every direction you look there will be seas of green bristling with treetops that rustle softly in the breeze. There will be apples for the Lonies."

Several onlookers had removed their hats and begun to weep as Joey spoke. Seeing a fresh little tree, something they had never beheld before, planted on the very spot where their old leader's ashes lay scattered, was at once both a sad sight and tremendously hopeful one. Though many of them had sworn they never would again after such a bloody day, the Lonies smiled through their tears, applauding the young boy. Joey was oblivious, of course, that he had had any sort of emotional affect on the people, but he returned their smiles nonetheless. Now, at the center of New Hollow, in the ruined Lonie sanctuary and set amidst heaps of smoking corpses, life was rekindled on Planet Earth, a speck of green in a sea of grey.

☆

The Lonies saw the companions out, a crowd of them going so far as to travel all the way through New Hollow and up the Lamentable Step to see them safely off. They heard nary a Mite as they passed through the ruined city; it seemed the monsters had indeed been subdued, at least for a while. Now, the children and Hess faced the Lonies on the lip of the shelf that surrounded New Hollow on all sides, gazing out across the destroyed, urban sprawl.

Jamjar was first to speak. "Oh-ee strangees! How I will miss-ees!" he blubbered, grabbing each of them in a bear hug in turn. "Now-ee must remember everything ole' Jamjar taught to-ee: how to open the gate and such. Ee never know when a gate's going to need quick opening- not to mention closing," he added sheepishly.

"Goodbye, Jamjar Brickbeard," said Ellie and kissed him on the ruddy cheek. He began to blubber even more at this, dabbing at his eyes with his dirty sleeve.

"Farewell, Jamjar," said Franklin and Joey in unison. "And don't worry, we'll remember: flick of the wrist!"

"Aye!" sobbed the emotional gatekeeper. "Flick of the wrist! Oh my! Oh my!" He sniffled. "I'll see that-er tree gets plenty o' sunlight, plenty o' water, and plenty o' love; Jamjar's got a lot of love to spare what with so many of his late friends dead and now his new friends leavin' before they hardly have had the chance to stay! But don't-ee get me wrong, we really are elated to have it—never before have we felt leaves in-between our fingers and, I must say, the sensation is 'eavenly, like nothing I've ever felt. I only wish poor Old Sacks had lived to see it. And Lazlo, too! He used to love the flowers and plants what he saw in the projections so, he'd yammer on about them all the time. He used to help Ole' Bess in the garden, he did!"

Ellie hung her head at the mention of the robot's name. "Now, now, chin up, little miss," cooed Jamjar, stroking her hair and patting her shoulder. "While Lazlo might have loved the tree, I ain't never in all my days seen him love a bunch of folks so much as he loved-ee lot. Never. He saw something in-ee all, and I do too, I must admit. But why do-ee all look so glum?"

Franklin sighed. "We feel terrible, Jamjar. We feel like we've brought all this destruction and death right to your doorstep, and you never asked for any of it! In fact, you helped us in our time of need; and how do we repay you? Like this? We feel rotten! How can you ever possibly forgive us?

Fluthers stepped forward out of the crowd and scratched the back of his head guiltily. "I feel that I might have caused-ee some unnecessary grief, strange-ees. I spoke with harsh words yesterday, much too harsh to fall on the ears of such a kindly bunch as-ee all. Please, pay me no heed."

"But you were right!" cried Ellie suddenly. "You were right about everything! Your people have been massacred and it's our fault! Lazlo, Old Sacks, and countless others, all dead because you **helped** us get what we were looking for, and now that we've got it, look what you ended up with: the shortest stick in the pile- except this stick is half burned and soaked with blood. That's a really twisted way of saying thanks, if you ask me. You should have never even let us into your home, we've only brought misery into it!"

"Enough!" grunted Nimrod, and silenced the girl. "To blame er-selves for what has befallen the Lonies this past day is a ridiculous notion. Did-ee slaughter our people? Did-ee burn our garden and force our leader to smolder along with it? Did-ee squash our friendly robot into the ground? Nay! Nay on all charges and counts! To blame anyone but the Mites is foolhardy indeed, for it is their malevolence and their malevolence alone which has proved our undoing."

"Aye!" Fluthers agreed. "If what Lazlo said was true, then-ee have given the Lonies who died a reason to do so, something none of us have ever truly had before. They have served as the casualties of a great mission, one that should prove to prevent all the terror that has befallen this, our wasted and ruined earth, and usher back the Green Time. Their deaths were not in vain if-er journey is so important as-ee claim it to be!"

"Aye! "echoed Chunk. "Add that to the fact that-ee brought Lazlo back so we'z could see him one last time. Why, if-ee strange-ees had never come along I think we would've never laid eyes on the old chap again. He was sorely missed indeed and-ee allowed him one last visit!"

"Aye!" Now Suds stepped forward. "And you have given us a tree to care for. Not a forbidden, sequestered shrub that we can do nothing but gaze lustily at, but a true tree, which someday our descendants might climb and look out at all the other trees that have spawned forth from it. 'All these magnificent forests were born from this tree, right here!' they shall sing happily as they flourish and prosper. 'And it's all thanks to those strange-ees who came along out of the blue. Our country was all dust and wasteland before they arrived, but now look at it: a landscape painted lovingly with green and blue, a real paradise!'" Suds' eyes glazed over as he imagined the loveliness that was to be.

"Can't-ee see?" pleaded Jamjar. "Can't-ee see what happiness-ee have wrought through all the blackness and blood? How happy we are with our new tree and the future it brings. I think we shall call the soil it's growing in the 'Strange-ee Garden' in-er honors, if'n ee don't mind!"

"That's fine," said Ellie, sniffling and dabbing at her eyes. "I only have one request: please let the tree be named after Lazlo."

"And Old Sacks," added Franklin meekly.

"A splendid notion!" Jamjar was half bubbling, half blubbering now. "Why, the Adam Sacks and Lazlo-Bot Memorial Tree it shall be known as, and exalted for all of time. So long as Jamjar Brickbeard lives, a Mite shall never lay its filthy claws on anything what's green and grows ever again! I swear it before-ee all here today, and with the Strange-ees as my witnesses, so-ee know I mean business." Ellie managed to smile, and giggled a bit through her tears as the weepy old man clapped the children into another hug.

"You're sure you all don't need any more help?" asked Hess, hefting his sack over his shoulder and checking to see that the thruster core was safely stowed therein.

"We'll handle things from here, methinks," replied Nimrod. "It's about time we took matters into our own hands and stopped waiting around for that garden to open up. Progress is what we've begun here, today; at least I think that's what they call it. In any case, the Lonies wish-ee well whither so ever-ee wander, be it back to the heavens or even deeper into the earth. I'm sure the ill trodden path is never so pleasant as we hope it to be, and that is certainly where-ee lot are headed, so may Ole; Bess and the spirits of Lazlo and Ole Sacks bless your path and keep it smooth."

Nimrod saluted and bowed low. In an instant, the rest of the Lonies joined him, bending their heads in reverence to the exciting figures who had only just flitted into their lives and now were bound out of them only moments after. The children returned the gesture and, after a few more tearful hugs with Jamjar, some manly chest thumps from Stingwhit and Fluthers, and a kiss on the cheek each from Mia and Zaki, the companions set out once again across the wasteland. Periodically, they glanced back over the shoulder to see the crowd growing smaller and smaller till it was only a speck in the distance. But, even from so far away, still they could make out the glittering smiles and waving hands of the Lonies. They stood out like stars in that empty, dusty wasteland.

The journey back to the Noah was a quiet, bleary-eyed affair, though it only took them a day's worth of travel this time- they had set out quite early in the morning. Even with the kind words of the Lonies still ringing in their ears, the children felt terribly about what had happened and could not rid themselves of their morose expressions. This, coupled with their sleeplessness the night before and their still aching muscles, made for a silent, meandering trip indeed.

But Hess, who managed to see through the dark, was in high spirits: the thruster core was intact and the mission could carry on. Burke had advised him there might be casualties along the dangerous road. 'But remember, boy,' the doctor had said to him, 'whatever suffering is brought about by this mission, it will be utterly eradicated if we are successful. You must keep this fact in the front of your mind at all times. Though it might make you appear detached and indifferent, every moment you must remember you are working in service of a greater good.'

All throughout their trials, Hess had done as his master had instructed him to, and the notion had kept him going.

CHAPTER TWENTY-THREE

A FLASH OF BLUE

The sun had nearly set by the time the Noah, a lonely little dot sitting far off on the horizon, came into view. But the companions did not hasten, for they no longer feared the Mites; the creatures had been driven back deep into the earth from whence they would not emerge, even when night came and the light faded. "Besides," as Joey had rather cheerily put it, "I'd like to walk under these stars one last time. We won't ever get a chance to see such a pretty night sky again, I guess; unless you're taking us all the way back to the Cambrian next, Hess." And so they did, wandering toward their long abandoned craft as shafts of starlight fell shimmering down from the heavens and pooled in silver puddles around their feet.

When they finally did climb wearily aboard their vessel, Mozi was positively elated to see them safe and sound. "Why, Mr. Hess! Children! Little brother! You're all back!" cried the computer in amazement.

"Yes, we're back, Mozi," Hess said, exhaling a great sigh of relief as he took in the familiar surroundings that formed the interior of the Noah. Though it was a cramped cockpit, it was home nonetheless. "And we've got the thruster core!" he added happily.

"Big Brother! Big Brother! How I've missed you!" squealed Mozi Box.

"I tried so many times to contact you, and when I heard nothing, I thought you dead for sure! The Stalo appeared suddenly, though I do not know how, and I tried to warn you several times! It rushed off across the wasteland in the same direction you had gone. But it seems the creature did not prove the end of all of you! I can only imagine what wild tales you have to tell me," said the AI. Now, his voice became alarmed. "Why, children! You're all so bloodied and bruised, and your clothes are caked in mud! What on earth has happened to you poor people? Mr. Freeman, my sensors are detecting a rather nasty gash in your chest underneath that marvelous new cloak of yours; before you regale me with the stories of your adventures, let's march you all into the medical bay and see that your wounds are well treated and all that mud washed away!"

Hardly even awake anymore, the children drowsily shuffled into Mozi's 'medical bay' (which was really just a particularly clean and white corner of the cockpit). They rubbed their eyes and yawned as two slender, robotic arms emerged from an apparatus built into the wall and prodded at them to apply bandages and antiseptics to their wounds.

Mozi chattered on. "I suppose you're all quite tired now, but we'll have plenty of time to debrief you on the journey to come. At this moment, I think it's best you gave those dirty clothes to me so I can properly clean them, wash off, then hurry to bed."

Franklin handed over his tattered clothing to Mozi, taking care to remind the computer not to wash Spero's cloak (he reckoned it was likely dry-clean only), and stumbled into the little head of the Noah where he was delighted to find a bathtub with a showerhead above it. It seemed mankind still hadn't forsaken the irreplaceable pleasure of a warm bath, even in 3,000 AD.

As the hot water sprayed down on him and mud began to pool around his feet, Franklin closed his eyes and let his thoughts wander. The water was paradise on his skin and all the tension that had been building in his muscles slowly drained away. Too many questions plagued his mind to relax fully, though, and he could hardly keep all of them organized in the exhausted state he had been trapped in for the last forty-eight hours. What was this mysterious symbol that continued to show up in the most unlikely of places? Who was the dream girl and why had she helped him? Was she real at all, or a kind of Jiminy Cricket construct who had taken up residence in the depths of his disturbed and roiling psyche? And what of the Stalo? How did the silver giant figure into all of this nonsense? Where had he come from and why did he want Hess dead so badly? Why had he betrayed his mission and turned on Cherophobe at the sight of the many-pointed star? And what about Bhasma? What on earth was the terrifying, apocalyptic storm cloud? Franklin nearly lost his balance; his head was spinning so severely. All these questions would have to wait till he had had a proper night's rest.

At last, he left the comfort of the shower's warmth and found a clean, white bathrobe waiting for him, lovingly folded in one of Mozi's machines. The soft material felt heavenly on his parched and dry skin as he pulled it snugly around his shoulders; he had spent so long drenched with muck and dry blood he had become accustomed to the feeling and nearly forgot just exactly what comfort felt like. Upon exiting the head, he nodded to Joey who was waiting for his turn outside.

"You're up, Joseph," he yawned. "Sorry I took so long."

"That's alright, Franny. I don't blame you. At least you don't look like the Creature from the Black Lagoon anymore. I wasn't going to say anything, but that look really didn't suit you at all."

Franklin chuckled and then paused reflectively. "That was a good thing you did back there, Joey, planting the tree and all. I think that's maybe the nicest thing anyone's ever done for them. It certainly seemed to lift their spirits given the massacre and all."

Joey shrugged. "I was only going to plant it in my backyard, anyway. I probably would've forgotten about it after a week and it would've died. At least it's gone to a good home."

"I **know** they won't forget about it. Not ever," said Franklin. Joey nodded, adjusted his glasses, and then disappeared into the foggy bathroom. Franklin strode through the cockpit toward the elevator; he was hoping to snuggle into bed as soon as possible. Hess was there, busy at work reattaching the thruster core to the ship's mainframe. "We ought to be up and running in no time!" he remarked as Franklin passed him by. Nodding, Franklin left Hess to his work and rode the elevator down to the cabin deck. Ellie was sitting on her bunk, wrapped in a white bathrobe of her own, running her wet and washed hair through her fingers absent-mindedly. As Franklin entered the room, she looked up and smiled weakly. "Hi, you."

"Hi," he replied, sitting down on the bunk next to her. "All cleaned up?"

"Yes, and thank goodness, too. It took forever to get all that dust out of my hair, not to mention that toxic sludge and all the dried up blood." She sighed. "It's been a helluva time, hasn't it?"

"Sure has."

"The worst part is, I don't think we've even seen the half it yet," she muttered.

"Or maybe that's the best part, depending on how you look at it," said Franklin, doing his best to offer the girl an encouraging smile.

"No, I don't think so Franklin. I don't mean to be a downer, but none of this is turning out how I thought it would. I can remember a time a few days ago when I was wiling, excited even to be along on this 'adventure'. But now, after everything we've been through in those horrible dark tunnels and with the battle and all... After Lazlo got crushed protecting **me**… For god sakes, we watched a man throw himself on a fire and burn to death because he had been driven mad with grief watching a twenty-foot tall monster scorch his only true love! This is no adventure! This is a trial, an ordeal, a nightmare! I've never seen such grisly acts before in my life, and now I've even committed a few myself; I know they were only a bunch of mindless, heartless monsters, but I still beat them with that club like there was no tomorrow. I'm sure I even killed a few of them. I'm positive, actually! We all did. And though they might have deserved it, killing even a Mite is a heavy burden to bear for the rest of our lives." She shook her head. "I just wish I was back in Maine. I wish none of this crazy stuff had ever happened.

"Ellie," whispered Franklin softly. He reached out and took her hand in his, but she turned her head away and retracted her hand almost instantly, recoiling from the embrace. "Did I… Did I do something wrong?" he asked.

"No, Franklin, of course not," she muttered. "It's just that… I can't do… **this** right now. I thought you and I might be able to- well- you know, even with this crazy trip and all. I thought it might've been nice. But I can't now. I can't. Every time I get even a little happy inside, I can't help but picture Lazlo's eyes going dark and his broken arms and legs all over the ground around him. I'm sorry, Franklin, but… This… this won't… Not anymore…. Not now."

Franklin looked down to see their hands resting on the bunk next to one another, pinkies frightfully close just as they had been on the balcony beneath the stars, but now the two hands seemed impossibly far away from one another, and impossibly lonely. "Ellie… I," he whispered at a total loss for words, but Mozi's voice blared out over the intercom and cut him off.

"Children, I know you were planning on drifting peacefully off to sleep, but I thought you might like to know that our industrious Mr. Hess has completed the necessary repairs to the Noah and we will begin the launch sequence shortly. I tell you this not only because I thought you might like to watch, but also because the launch would have woken you up anyway if you had already gone to sleep. Mozi out."

Ellie sprang to her feet, flustered and blushing. "Well, I think I'd like to see us take off, wouldn't you?" Without waiting for an answer, she hurried into the lift and shot up toward the command deck, leaving Franklin alone, his hand still outstretched on the bunk, grasping at the blankets absent mindedly.

'So that's that, huh?' he thought. It had certainly been short-lived, if it had been anything at all. 'But maybe it's for the best. Yes, I think she's right. We haven't got the time or energy to spend worrying about this sort of thing. We'll just put it on hold, or better yet never revisit it again and pretend it simply never occurred in the first place. Yes, I think that would save us both a lot of grief; after all, breakups are inevitable at this age. Whenever there is a meeting, a parting has to follow! It's not like I was going to marry her or anything...' Franklin shook his head and grimaced at how silly he sounded, even if it was only in his head. 'What are you saying you great, stupid buffoon? You're just going to bury your feelings! Why not? You've done it a million times before. But then again, if you keep up with that habit, you're sure to get an ulcer or a hernia or something sooner or later. And where does she get off, anyway? I think this is what they call being led on.' He wanted to kick himself now. 'Being led on? How could you be so callous and cold? She never intended for any of this mess to happen!' She was a guiltless as he was. Franklin resigned himself to the reasonable conclusion, though he could not completely deny the feelings that burned deep in his core; but for the time being, he resolved to shrug them off.

Soon, he joined the others on the command deck, strapping into a seat between Ellie and Joey (whose glasses were still foggy having just emerged from the shower) and directly behind Hess. The armored boy turned to them, proud the thruster core had been reinstalled so quickly. "I never thought all of this would take so long!" he chuckled. "It was only supposed to be a minor detour, really, a little ruffle in the plan.

Who could've known the device would've fallen into the depths of hell itself. But that didn't deter us, I suppose. You've all performed admirably these last couple of days, and I'll admit I've been glad to have the company. It would have been a lonely journey to New Hollow indeed without all of you, and I probably would've never met Lazlo to boot! But now we're through with all that madness and you all can catch up on your rest while I take care of the remainder of the mission. Don't worry about a thing, just relax aboard the Noah and I'll handle everything from here on out; you've earned it!"

"Relax aboard the Noah?" echoed Ellie, her voice ripe with sarcasm.

"Well, yes…" Hess was puzzled. "Aren't you tired?"

"Of course we are!" replied Franklin indignantly. "But so are you! We've come so far, we're not going to let you go the rest of the way by yourself!"

"But why bother?" protested Hess. "What about all that guff about it not being 'your future'?"

Franklin sighed. "It might not be **our** future, but it's someone's. It's like Joey said, we've got to think about what's going to happen down the road, even if we're no longer travelling along it ourselves. Seeing all of this mess, seeing what a wreck the world really becomes has given us a… new perspective on things. I might just be speaking for myself here, but I want to help you with your mission more than ever. I want to see this Bhasma Cloud, whatever the hell it is, defeated before it can cause any of this trouble."

Hess glanced at Joey and Ellie. "You both feel this way too?" They nodded. Hess shrugged. "Oh well. I'd try dissuading you, but that hasn't worked in the past; you're a very stubborn lot for a bunch of stupid, prehistoric kids. But you can come with me, I suppose, so long as you don't get in my way."

"The same goes for you," snarled Ellie.

Hess chuckled and extended his hand, palm down. "Then I guess we're officially the new crew of the Noah. If you're all with me, I'd like to get this tub into the air."

Ellie placed her hand on top of his. "I'm in."

Joey added his palm to the stack. "Me too."

Finally, Franklin joined his friends in the gesture. "Let's get going," he said, and smiled.

Hess didn't have to be asked twice. "Alright then, kiss 3,000 AD behind. We're travelling forwards- or rather backwards- to its great great grandfather year, 3,000 BC, six whole millennia away. Maybe we'll even find what we're looking for there. "

He seized the throttle in his hand and, like a feather taken by a sudden breeze, the Noah fluttered up into the air and began to cruise along the wasteland. In a flash of blue, the time machine disappeared into a wormhole and left the barren earth far behind.

End of Book I

ABOUT THE AUTHOR

Born in 1994 and raised in Branford, Connecticut, Evan DeCarlo grew up on a steady diet of fantasy novels, B Movies, and a whole lot of stage plays. Now, he's finally embraced his fondness for writing and published his first novel, *The Children of The Noah- Book I: The Barren Earth,* at the ripe young age of 19. Currently, he resides in Manhattan and studies screenwriting at the School of Visual Arts. For more information about his upcoming novels (including the other two books in the *Children of The Noah* trilogy) visit his website at www.evandecarlo.com

ABOUT THE ILLUSTRATOR

New York born, Jersey bred, Raisha Friedman has returned to NYC to study Illustration at the School of Visual Arts. She comes from a large, efficiently dysfunctional family of artists, astronomers and all other creative crazies, allowing her to stew in a myriad of artistic juices.

Friedman dreams of having her name on everything from Children's book covers, to Brooklyn Brewery beer labels.

http://graphicallydelicious.tumblr.com/